RUPETTA

RUPETTA

N.A. SULWAY

Tartarus Press

Rupetta
by N.A. Sulway
First published by Tartarus Press, 2013 at
Coverley House, Carlton-in-Coverdale, Leyburn,
North Yorkshire, DL8 4AY, UK

This paperback edition is published 2022

ISBN 9781905784660

The publishers would like to thank Jim Rockhill and Richard Dalby
for their help in the preparation of this volume

For Inga:
a green thought in a green shade

CONTENTS

THE FOURFOLD RUPETTAN LAW

Life is Death.
The Earth is a Grave.
The Body is a Machine for Dying.
Knowledge is the Path to Immortality.

Foreword

I have known loss for centuries. I have borne the deaths of each of my companions, both dear and tolerated. I have lost families, loves, houses, villages. Whole cities, whole nations, have grown and decayed while I have persisted. I have seen rivers change their course, mountains beaten down into hills, oceans swell and subside, seeds grow into great trees only to fall and die and rot. And yet this loss—the loss of one child—this loss I cannot bear.

If I were human I would weep.

If I were a goddess, I would step over the railing into the ocean. I would wade, hip-deep, through the water. I would be terrible and tall, my hair flaming behind me, my skirts awash with blood and churn. My eyes burning through the dark like the lamps of twin lighthouses, a thousand feet tall. I would tether the ship to my shoulders with steel reins, and haul it into port. I would drag the ship onto the stony sand, beach her there and thunder up the cliffs to the city. I would stand at the gate and sing a note so true that the stones of the walls would shudder in their footings. The wood of the gates would split, their hinges would shatter in their locks. I would make the walls of Angarok fall.

I would flock through the ruined city to find her: lift her from a cradle of rubble, white and unharmed. Her arms would slip around my neck, the bird-weight of her head would rest once more on my chest. I would never let her go.

Instead, I am standing at the prow as the ship sloops forward, splitting the waves in a gentle, too-slow quietude. I will her turbines to turn faster. I watch the captain in his lamplit cabin, sipping tea at the window. I want to murder his calm. My heart rams against my ribs, threatening to break through the fragile film of skin. *Faster. Faster.* I will the world to turn. I watch the ocean lull, the stars twinkling, the moon gawping. Somewhere in the distance she is moving away from us. Racing across the ocean, through the streets of the city, through the deserts that surround it. Out and out to the furthest rim, to the darkest centre. They are carrying her into places a child should never see. Never know. They are holding her close, whispering terrible things into the pink shell of her ear. Poisoning her. Eating her heart. Slicing her open. They are making her eat the poppy seeds of death, swallow the Consort's spit. They are making her forget us, deny us. They are taking her apart; tearing flesh from bone from coil from cog. Sharp-nosed tools pincering and snipping. Blood and oil a dark stain beneath the table. I close my eyes, grip the rail, pitch and hurl in the salt air. I see her dark hair: a spray of silent, wound-sharp protest against her white cheek.

I can see the lights of the harbour. I am sure I can see them, in the thick fold of darkness between sky and sea. The wink of a candle in the harbourmaster's home. The flash of a torch on the docks. The cut tulips lined up on the docks in heavy buckets, their heads lolling against each other. The traders and the early risers barter for the best, the darkest and heaviest blooms. Tomorrow is the first day of the Festival of the Beautiful, the celebration of the sixth miracle. Every man, woman and child in the city will already have folded a tiny wax-paper tulip and set a luxe—a red or pink candle—inside it. At midnight they will converge on the shore and set their paper tulips adrift. The warm glow, the jostle of them on the waves, will make the harbour seem like an inverted sky strewn with stars, flickering and drowning.

It will be strange to walk through the city again, out into the deserts that surround it; I am sure it is much changed since I last saw it. They say the Penitents have made terrible changes, that the people are afraid. They say the streets are vigilant. These things have become both commonplace and incomprehensible, I know, but still when we slip into port I want to believe I will see the old world, the world I once knew and loved so well. I want to believe the ship has sailed backwards through time as well as space, bringing us to the cities of memory, the

2

cities of my dreams. The cities in which Perdita waits, her hands cupped around a perfectly-folded wax-paper tulip, its tips sharp and white, the light of the candle within it reflecting up onto her face.

I sit at the window, listening to the ship's passengers, to the fragile murmur of men and women sleeping in their cabins. They shift and pitch, dreaming of the past, of their homes, of the future we have yet to meet. They turn in the slim cots, even in sleep, offering each other warmth and comfort. At night, when you slept beside me, I would watch the pucker of your brow, the movements of your hands across the sheets, feel you curl around me and wonder if you knew, in your dream, who it was you held. I would lie facing you, watching your mouth move, watching your eyes shift beneath the lids to follow some unknowable fall of snow or leaf or hair. I was filled with a hollow ache, watching you walk in the city of your dreams, knowing I would never feel those streets beneath my feet, or the beauty towards which you turned and smiled with such quietude, such love.

The past is like the dream of a stranger who wakes and tells you of oceans deeper than time, of creatures so monstrous he cannot describe them—creatures with a thousand eyes and forty sets of wings, feet of stone and hair of fire: cities without streets, cities without walls. You can listen to the tale of what he saw, but you cannot walk through the streets of his dream or hold in your hand the blossom of a dying tree that smells like burnt cinnamon, like a sleeping child's breath.

History is a fickle mistress, Henri. She will not love you as you love her: she will not open her heart and pour forth her secrets, no matter how willingly you prostrate yourself at her feet. She is mute, and capricious. You can never hold her, never truly see her face. Do you remember the old story of Tam Lin: of the boy who must rescue his love by holding her throughout the night, as her form shifts from one horror to another? By morning she was her True Self, and he took her home. His persistence was rewarded, as yours will never be.

Once my hair was a sheath of silk, once my throat was a sheer brass column, my eyes green as leaves. Once my belled skirts concealed the wheels, the cogs, upon which I turned. Once my hands were like mit-

3

tens, unfingered. In the Silent years, as the accoutrements of my civilised surface decayed or were carried off, the metallic hoops and shelves beneath became a haven for mice and insects. I had the odd sensation, while they fretted and died within me, of being almost alive. Once I thought of myself as an antique cabinet, full of drawers both hidden and apparent. A riddle of interiors. Once, I had a belly etched with stars, but now it is smooth and unmarked. I am far from whole, far from constant. My body has a history as shifting as your own.

Eloise—one of those long-dead Wynders I have loved—once attempted a catalogue of my interior. It grew and grew as she pursued it, spilling out over her desk. *Here*, she would say, *is the avenue of your contentment. Here the* rue de pommes. *Here is the flood, the drift, the dream. Here*, she would say, *beneath the heart, here are the ruins of the city you once were, and of another you may some day become. Here are the arrowheads of a battle, the bones of dead birds. A ruined chapel, an empty clock.*

The map grew larger, more complex. It had no centre, no edge. Eloise pinned sheets to the walls of her home and worked on them as she stood. She folded others into thick accordions and piled them up beneath her bed or stacked them on the table. She worked on them so often they began to fall apart along the folds. She forgot which piece joined to which other.

As a child her daughter built tents from the sheets of paper, folding them up into cones, or draping them over chairs so she and her dolls could sit within the paper tents. As she grew older, and the map spread out, the daughter came to see the whole enterprise as a kind of madness. When her mother died it took ten days to parcel up the work she had done: we buried her within its folds. Her daughter retained a single folio and hung it on the wall of her room, beside the window. Neither of us knew what aspect of me this fragment represented: a roughened edge of thick paper, a convergence of blue and green lines—rivers? roads? perhaps the roots of a field of grass?—joined in the lower-left of the sheet, near a tiny, dark circle and a cross. Perhaps it is a blade.

This much I have to tell: the ruin of a map. The rest is lost, or meaningless. Each truth I tell conceals another thousand left unspoken, unremembered. If I leave out the weather, the light, that is one thing—historians rarely record the harvests and storms of the past—but in order to make sense of history I must select names, faces, incidents, scooping them from the rush of time like a child scooping tadpoles from a river. So many slip through my fingers. Who can say which omissions are cruel and which are necessary.

You must remember, Henri—try to hold it always between yourself and this tale, like a glass through which you read each word—that for every moment I remember, there may be another that has been cut away, or blown clear. Another that one of the Wynders has wiped from me, either intentionally or accidentally. How can I know what I have forgotten? How can I know what wheel of history has rusted away or was simply lost, one night, as we crossed an open field?

You cannot trust this tale. You cannot and should not trust me, Henri, we both know that. I am an inexpert carpenter whose timbers are warped, whose hands are rough and shake with age, whose tools are blunt and imprecise.

Words fail us all, in the end.

Nevertheless, in the dark of the cabin, with the sea curling and shushing beneath me and the stars burning above, I have a little time to spare and I have promised you this much. I will try, Henri, to parcel up the past and make a gift of it for you. The only gift that is truly mine to give. I will tell you my story.

I unloop the chronometer from my waist and spread it out on the desk. The long chain, the orbs that mark out the centuries of my life. One for each miracle, each whittling at the truth. Laid out with the chain of orbs spiralling around the timepiece, it looks like an antique map of heaven: six planets circling a clockwork sun. The timepiece at its end has an overlapping cover of four silver moons. Opened out they form a ring of horned petals. Its back is engraved with dragonflies and apple-blossoms, though the pattern is worn smooth with age. The six orbs are milky jade, each carved with the symbol of a miracle: an open eye, a teardrop, a clockwork heart. The second stone, which marks the Miracle of Silence, is smooth and blank-faced.

Each morning, in the Haven of your home town, the Penitents take turns to chant the hours, measuring out the cycle of the year, the turn of centuries. It begins at midnight, in the centre of the hall, as it does in every Haven. A Penitent unhooks a chronometer from around their waist and stops time. Their fingers slide along the chain to the first orb, with its etching of an open eye that looks like a half-furled leaf. They hold it in the closed fist of their left hand, close their eyes, feel the weights within the stone shift. Soon darknight—the suspended breath of time between time—will end, and she will open her eyes.

That is when I will begin, too, with the first orb: with the opening of an eye.

The Miracle of Consciousness
Languedoc: November 11th, 1619

The first time I opened my eyes I was standing in the centre of the world. There were no clouds or stars. The moon was suspended above me, its silver face reflected in the brass bowl of water at the centre of the world. She was the first thing I saw: Eloise Reni. My mother, my maker, my sister. At first I thought she was the sun.

She reached towards me with one of her slim arms. I knew, then, she was not the sun. Her dappled, uneven skin rippled as she stirred. There were odd protrusions, pores, hairs, an unevenness of texture and tone across her surface I later came to recognise as indicators of an organic, human body. At the time I thought she was the unlucky, imperfectly formed creature. How horrible to have one's flesh slide, uncontrolled, over muscle and sinew. How ghastly to *need* the air of the world, to imbibe and extrude, engorge and want. To desire and die. Later, I would learn about the pleasures of human life: laughter, joy, love, uncertainty, faith, hope, belonging, even loneliness. Even despair. But at that moment there were only the two of us in the world and I did not know that within her body there beat an inconstant human heart. To me we were the same; the same neatly-pinned hair, the same plain brown dresses, the same little caps on our heads, the same dark eyes and slim necks. She moved a little differently. She seemed older than I, a little wiser.

Eloise touched my face with her fingertips. I could hear her nails tick over my surface, but I felt nothing. I had not been made to feel. The new leather of my joints was stiff and smooth. My brass ribs gleamed. I wore the frame of a belled skirt, beneath which my mechanisms whirred. I had one arm, and a wooden hand—the fingers hollowed out with an awl—through which she had threaded supple wires. She pulled at them, one by one, and watched my fingers curl. Her name was carved across the sole of my left foot, not because she wished to mark me as her own, but because the material from which it was made had once been her artbox: an oak and ebony chest made for her by her father when she was eight or nine, and out of which she later made some parts of me. The lettering was small and carefully done: I never knew whether she or he had etched it there. In her hand she held the little key: the last thing she had made. A tiny thing, silver, its head a knotted pattern of leaves and cogs that form the first letters of my name and hers.

I closed my eyes, and woke again, and was remade. I did not sleep. I was there and I was not. I had no sense that time passed when I was not in it.

I opened my eyes to find Eloise bent over my prostrate form, my inner workings exposed. I heard the tinks and clicks of my body. She listened attentively to my *click, click, click, chirr,* and *chock.* 'Can you do this?' she asked, blinking down at me, and I did my best to imitate her. She tipped her head, leaned closer, peering into me as her slim fingers plucked and pushed, as she reached for the instruments that hung from a leather belt at her waist, or wound and rewound fine springs around the girth of her small fingers. 'Good,' she sometimes said, and sometimes nothing.

I did not know, then, that Eloise measured time in different ways— that the sun and moon of her wider world, and the circulation of her blood and breath, were organic clocks marking out the passage of her life. I did not know that life, for her, would be such a small and brutal thing. I did not know where Eloise went when I could not see her— only that sometimes when I opened my eyes on our familiar world she would be dressed differently or would have decayed a little more. I could not fathom why she changed, why sometimes she professed tiredness or distraction and at others was buoyed up by her mysterious inner workings. I presumed at the time that it was something to do with her uncanny design. Perhaps she offered me an explanation; my memories of those days have been clipped down to a bare minimum. After so many years, so many hours, my memory is crowded. The many companions I have had over the years, the many Eloises, have had their own logic around what must be kept and what must be lost. Montane did the worst damage—out of fear, perhaps, or greed. Though she would have done more had she known how. The Wynder must constantly tinker with me—deleting things I do not need to recall (though who is to say, really, what detail of history, now lost, could save us), batching and compressing thoughts, records, cells—in order that I might function with some semblance of my former, faultless self.

Eloise and I stayed in our intimate, self-contained world for a long time, until she showed me that what I had believed a mild imperfection —a thin, rectangular fissure in the walls of the world—was a door. Beyond that door was another world with a soft, multi-coloured surface beneath our feet, a flat dark sky, no moon or stars fixed above, but a series of obstacles laid out around us: tables and bookcases, low chairs and cabinets. There were innumerable small objects scattered about, each with a simple function. I learned to read there, to measure time, as well as the use and purpose of a thousand small things—clocks and spoons, latches, buttons and bowls. It was here, too, I first encountered Eloise's uncle—Tomas Hornbaker—whose skin had folded up on itself and become as mottled as the walls of my former world. I did not know then that it was he who had helped her form me: the stories he had once told to amuse her, stories from the old world, had stirred her imagination, had bred in her a desire to make the statue talk, to make the golem tick.

Pinned to the walls of this larger, darker world were sheets of paper covered in diagrams and notations, graphs and charts and sketches. My first portraits. These Eloise and her uncle had laboured over for many years. At first, he had thought them mere fancies—a girlish game—but as the years progressed he learned to see that her mind was as quick and determined as any he had known. She made small toys to test one theory and another—a clepsydra, a hydraulic beetle, a miniature hippocampus who could swim in circles, and a wyvern whose candled belly, once lit, propelled it about the room. Tomas's favourite was the blind dryad, her body carved from the trunk of a fallen elm, who sang like a wounded angel.

Slowly, I moved from that world—the world of my miniature companions, my ancestors—into another and another. I learned to call these worlds merely rooms and to understand that the images that adorned the walls of each room were sometimes paintings and sometimes windows; that the paintings were created by men, and the windows—or rather, the strange, shifting landscapes they contained—had been created by a gentleman called God. *Would he come to visit us?* I once asked. *I should like to know his method of creating such things. I should like, some day, to make such things myself.* I did not know, then, why my curiosity garnered such earnest and astonished responses in my fellow creatures. Such passionate debate that, for three days, neither of them slept as the world they had known—the universe of God, angels, heaven, hell and death, of sin and retribution, the world of faith, whirled and broke and re-formed within them.

Each hour life unfolded and revealed more nuances, more inconsistencies, and more strangeness. And yet Eloise found nothing to amaze her in these things—nothing alarming in the workings of a butter churn or a fire or her uncle's bent and failing frame. Nothing strange in the form of the house in which we lived. She never wondered, as I did, whether the house had any end, whether we lived within it or were part of it; cells pulsing through its veins and arteries. Instead, it was I she was amazed by. Though she had created me, she did not know me. When I spoke of God or the sun or the workings of the fire in our hearth she appeared shaken, transformed. My curiosity, my atheistic will, inspired and frightened her in equal measure. Later, the weight of my strangeness, its persistence, would break her, but at first we knew only the vital energy of new knowledge.

There were other people in the house from time to time, but they never spoke to me. I realise now that Tomas or Eloise had enjoined them not to. There was a small woman with rough hands, Marie, whom I saw occasionally, scuttling from room to room. Sometimes she brought a tray, laden with food and drink, to the room where we three were working. She would not raise her head to look at me, and Tomas seemed impatient with her, waving her away with terse utterances. Once, as she was closing the door, she stole a glance at me. I tried to smile, as I had seen Eloise do, moving the parts of my face into the peculiar arrangement, but it only frightened her more. She raised her hand to her forehead, down to her sternum and across from shoulder to shoulder. She muttered some words in a language Eloise and Tomas used only rarely, in their one-sided conversations with God.

Once I came across Marie in the kitchen, where she stood at the large, rough table chopping vegetables and laughing with a man I had sometimes seen in a landscape that hung in one of the back rooms. The two of them fell silent when I entered the room and watched me move around the dogs sleeping near the fire. I heard the man say something —a strange, harsh word Marie shushed with a quick pass of her hand. *It'll tell Tomas*, she said, *and then we'll be hauled over the coals.*

Can it hear us then? he said.

I think so, Marie replied, with her eyes fixed on the table before her.

No wonder he won't have anyone to the house anymore. Imagine what Monsieur de Meurre would say? Let alone Father Angerre.

What are these? I inquired, gesturing towards the foodstuffs scattered on the table, although I knew full well they were onions.

Holy Jesu! the man cried out, his voice trembling, as if his bellows were squeezed tight at the tip and the air squeezed through reluctantly. *I must go*, he said.

And leave me alone here with it? You'll do no such thing, Master Paul. What am I to say to it?

It I thought then. I tipped my head and gazed down at my plain dress, at the odd, functionless swellings attached to my chest. *I am a woman*, I said, at which the two became even more agitated and— taking each other by the hand—fled the room.

I did not tell Eloise or Tomas about this incident, though they found it out soon enough. Perhaps Marie went to Tomas's chamber

11

with her companion still at hand. At any rate, Tomas learned of the encounter and later, in his rooms, asked me to recall the details. Soon after, Marie was dismissed from Tomas's employ and replaced by a heavier and somewhat more stolid woman and her companion. Hélène Jans and her husband, Guido, took care of the house in a far more efficient manner than Marie had; polishing and twitching, scouring and sweeping the rooms and the objects they contained.

Hélène and Guido were not perturbed by my presence. Indeed, once Hélène discovered my quick ability to learn, my strength and precision of movement, she often enjoined me to assist her in managing the household. We spent long hours in the kitchen chopping vegetables, plucking chickens, churning butter, washing and mending clothes. At first we completed these chores in a tranquil silence but soon she grew more accustomed to my presence and would spend our time together telling stories of her childhood, of her and Guido's courtship, of her friends and family and all the exotic intricacies of her past. She also talked about her visits to the Village: a strange place I could only presume was another kind of room filled with people; dozens and dozens of them if Hélène was to be believed.

The first time I stepped outside the house it was a simple mistake. I took a wrong turn, distracted as I was in following the movements of a small, six-legged creature as it scurried almost soundlessly across the kitchen floor. The black beetle scuttled beneath the door, which I opened only to discover it was a kind of shuttered window into one of God's landscapes: an enormous, seemingly endless landscape one could walk into as if it were simply another room. I raced back through the house to find Eloise and drag her through this wooden door, or window—I could not tell which to call it—into the strange, drowned room where an ocean constantly fell from the distant ceiling. Where were its walls? Its doors and windows? I tipped back my head and looked into the falling water but my vision was so obscured by the drops scattering across my eyes I could not determine the height of its ceiling. I took Eloise's hand and led her onto the threadbare green carpet, with its dusty brown floor beneath, and showed her the endless breadth of this landscape—this room that seemed to have no end at all, but to go on and on until vision and time expired. What a strange thing the world seemed, after all. How incomprehensible, how infinitely unfolding. I longed to find the edges of this room, its windows and doors, and venture further out—into the next world and the next.

A human child comes from a small, drowned world into a wider, drier one. A world filled suddenly with air and distance. Eloise's granddaughter—Margery—was born in a field as we travelled from Eli to Cauvonne. She squealed and writhed as the cool air hit her skin, screwing up her eyes, clenching her small fists. She seemed to crave the close, embracing cave of her mother's body. I would remember then the day of the beetle and the drowned world. The kitchen door and the endless impossibility of the world—how breathtaking, how astonishing, how beautiful it had all seemed. I had felt then I was too small —of beetle dimensions myself—too infinitesimal to have meaning in such a vast world. Soon enough, with all that air and water and earth rushing around and through me, I would simply fail to hold myself together and my parts would be scattered to the ends of the grand unfolding earth.

Many people have called me constant; have desired the seeming permanence of my existence. The earth, I have found, has her own kind of constancy; an endless cycling, an incessant repetition of patterns that are almost the same; lives and seasons and days. But despite the way they may appear things are not the same as they once were. Time changes them all. Myself included. Perhaps, after all, the Oikos are right. Perhaps I am Monstrous. But if so then I am no more Monstrous than the chronometer at your waist, or the bicycle you ride to the library each day, or the spectacles that aid your sight. Even the Oikos complement their fleshy bodies with implements: spades and wheels and knives and bowls. Ships and walls, books and doors. They are not as pure—as wild and untrammelled—as the beasts of the forest. They are not like the tortoise, whose body is armour, harvester and hearth. They are not like the shark, whose mouth is a weapon. They are not like the great Tallowwood of home, whose limbs harvest light.

13

Humans are creatures of enterprise. They are made as much as they are born.

ℂ

Time is different for me. As is memory, the only true measure of time. When I think of Eloise—of Eloise Reni, my first companion—it is not a pale, inconstant, wavering thing that comes to me. I do not have to cast my mind back like a fisherman who throws his line into a mysterious sea and waits for what will come, hoping it will be familiar but always wondering. One day the sea yields boots and buckets, lost oars and seaweed, other day's mysteries; mermaids, selkies, dragons. When I think of Eloise I see her standing in the room, her head bent over the table beside me as she writes. I see her wipe her ink-stained palms on her overdress before she leaves the room. I see her with her arms wrapped around her chest for warmth as we walk towards town in the middle of winter. The land around seems broad and even under its mantle of snow.

Eloise was near forty and it was Candlemas. She was far too old to be carrying a child, let alone her first, but it had been Tomas's dying wish to see a child upon her, though he had not lived to see it born.

As she walked her breath formed blue clouds before her face, which she lurched into with each step. Her cheeks were red and chapped. She was not the same young woman I had first encountered, though the shadow of that other Eloise still haunted the corners of her mouth, her sparkling eyes. She was still my Eloise.

Let's go back, I said.

I can't miss the mass again.

It'll make no difference. Likely not a soul will stir from their beds today but Mother Sirani and her sallow daughter.

Eloise glanced at me, some unwonted worry pulling at her forehead. *What is it?* I asked.

What if I die?

You'll more likely do so if we stay out in this much longer.

When the child comes, she said, looking down at her red-knuckled hands.

Hélène and I will care for you. Nothing untoward will mar the child's birth.

But what if it does?

I hadn't considered the prospect of Eloise's death. She seemed as constant as I. She had been present at my birth and, I had thought, would be there at my going out of the world. *Nothing will happen,* I insisted.

Eloise dug about in the sleeve of her gown. *Here,* she said, thrusting the key into my hand with a bright, chinking sound. *I've told Hélène how to do it; she'll care for you if I can't.*

I turned the key over in my hands. *You cannot be serious, Eloise. You have told me that only you, or one of your bloodline, should Wynd me. If you . . . if you pass from this world then I must go, too.*

Why? There's no reason to believe so. Only vanity has made me think it. Not reason, not clear thinking. I am your creator, but I am not God: I am not the life by which you breathe.

But, Eloise. . . .

There's nothing about you and your workings I don't know. I crafted every wheel and bellow, every hoop and thread. You are a creature of wind and wheels: soulless, logical. You are a machine, Rupetta, there's no reason it can't be someone else who Wynds you.

What about Alazaïs?

Eloise stopped and looked away, sighing.

You can't make her like me, can you? She's just a doll.

Eloise frowned. It was true, of course. Though she had managed to build my doppelgänger, making her identical to me in every way possible, using the same materials, following the track of her own notations and diagrams, Alazaïs stood in the room in which I had first opened my eyes, as still and dull as a stone. When wound she could follow simple commands, if spoken slowly. She could utter a small vocabulary, though sense only emerged from her utterances occasionally and accidentally. She could repeat something told to her, though only once and then it seemed to disappear from her memory altogether. She could write her name. She could walk, though she often stumbled over things placed in her path.

It's a matter of craftsmanship; I have been vain and God has punished me by refusing to give her life, Eloise said.

You should give up this quest for faith. I know you do not truly believe in any God, no matter how much you try to. Faith comes at its own bidding, and not at yours.

If you die, then I will also stop, and we will be both be nothing.

I don't believe that. You will never die, as my mother did, and leave my child to make her way in the world the best she can.

Has it been that terrible, your life? Our life?

I have longed for a mother and had none. Tomas educated and housed me, made sure that I was fed and well-clothed. I had everything a growing woman could expect. Far more, perhaps, than many, but I was like a toy to him, an object of study. He wanted to know how a woman's mind was made; whether a woman could think, could rationalise, as he did. He educated me not because he loved me, but because he wanted to know if it would queer my womb, or addle my brain. He kept notes about me: the notes of a scholar of Nature. He wanted to understand me. I fascinated him, but he could not love me. He never pulled me onto his lap, never smiled at my games or kissed me, never sang me songs or took me walking in the forest just to walk with me. Just to be together.

He gave you the benefit of his education, of his small portion of wealth, of his home. He was very kind to you; he nurtured you.

As a falconer is kind to his hawks, by keeping them jessed and hooded. Even their cleverness—their skill at hunting—he sees as his own triumph. He trains them to hunt for him, to fly for him, to live and die and breed for him.

Her face was set and I felt again her fury and shame. Not just at what had been done to her—at the boy Tomas had paid to set a child inside her, or the roughness of the coupling—but at the betrayal she

16

saw in it all. She had thought of herself as his daughter and could not reconcile his gentle paternalism with his husbandry.

He was old, I said, *and confused.*

Eloise shook her head. *He was cruel, and you know it. You may be many things, but you were not made for cruelty, but then, how can I know what you are thinking? I do not know, Rupetta, which is worse; to leave the child with you or to leave her alone—friendless, without family—in a world that will not care whether she lives or dies, whether she is good or happy. Hélène is too old to care for her. There is no one else. You will be her guardian, as you have been mine, and you will love her without reservation because she will put her hand—as I have—in the forecourt of your heart.*

The snow had begun to fall again. Eloise took my arm and we turned towards home. Her face was pinched and white beneath her shawl. We had gone barely seven steps when she paused and her face gained a kind of shrouded vacancy. *What is it?* I asked her.

Well, she said, *that's to be the way of it. I thought I would have more time.* She was leaning upon me, her breathing coming in depressed clouds.

It was a quick, though not easy, birth. At the time I wondered whether her God had indeed cursed her, but over the years I have seen many more children come into the world; their births both gentler and more brutal. Hélène hauled herself out of her makeshift bed in the kitchen and we birthed Elisabetta there, by the fire. Eloise slept soon afterwards and I swaddled the baby, as Hélène instructed me. Her own hands were too gnarled and stiff to do so. When the two women were sleeping, side by side in the kitchen bed with the fire well-banked beside them, I took the babe out into the night. It was a foolish thing to do, but the storm had passed and the night, though cool, was thick and quiet. We stood on the kitchen stoop and I pointed out the winter stars, the thin-fingered trees, the shrouded evergreens near the road. She did not cry—she would always be a quiet woman—and as we stood there she gazed calmly into the cool face of the sky.

In the weeks that followed her daughter's birth Eloise withered. Her face never regained its firm, rose-cheeked composure. She rarely left the kitchen-bed, where she and Hélène spent their days sipping at warm broth and watching the fire. Once I found her in the room with Alazaïs, staring at her with something akin to fury. She pushed her over and straddled her supine form. I do not know how she found the strength to do so when some days she barely had strength enough to lift a spoon. She had a small spindle in her hand, which she scraped over Alazaïs's face and arms, over the softer metals of her arms and the leather at her joints. It is not true Alazaïs is the same as me. Her features resemble my own, at least in their general form, but all over her silvered surface Eloise had carved intricate vines and flowers and spirals. To remind her, so she said, that Alazaïs was not real, that she was a vain folly. She had done the same to my left hand when it needed repairing, covering my palm, my fingers and my wrist with a delicate, shell-edged pattern of apple-blossoms and dragonflies. At the time this artwork had pleased her a great deal and she had smiled when Hélène and I exclaimed at Alazaïs's beauty, but now she hacked at my sister with a savageness I had never seen in her before.

She tore aside Alazaïs's shift and, with some difficulty, slashed and tore at the hinges of the small door that led to her inner compartments until it fell to the floor. Inside, Alazaïs had the same workings as me, only each of her dials and cogs, the thin metal pipes and funnels and braces, were untouched by time or smoke or air. She had never, as had I, been opened to discover a small, dry leaf lodged among her gears. They gleamed coolly in the dark room.

Eloise, I said, and she turned sharply towards me.

What have I done? She opened her fist and let the spindle fall into Alazaïs's chest. It clinked against some wheel or pipe and Eloise started. *Give me the key.*

I watched her sink to her knees and retch, the bilious fluid pooling between her fingers. When I offered my hand to help her rise she pulled away, a thread in her sleeve catching on the tip of my finger. *Let me help you*, I said. *I'll boil some water and you can wash, put on a fresh gown.*

She gave me a look I had never seen before; venom and sorrow. *Get away from me*, she said, rising to her feet, pressing her hands against her skirts and raising her chin.

I called her name again as she moved to leave the room and she hesitated before she turned, her shoulders braced against whatever I might say. I had meant to offer a kindness, give some sign of my affection, but the look she gave could have withered glass.

You're not to come near me ever again, she said. *You can stay in the house, but you must keep to these rooms.* Something flickered across her face, some shadow of regret or wretchedness, but it was soon gone, and—if my memory were more like yours—I would have had the mercy of being able to believe it a fancy of my imagination. *Give me the key*, she repeated, her voice as cool as winter's breath.

It's in the study, I said and she turned away, her skirts brushing against the doorframe as she left.

Eloise worked intently, not—as she had for so many hours in her youth—on the making of new things, but on their destruction. She burned her papers, including the books she and Tomas had bought. She tore up the sketches and diagrams of my making, and her notebooks on the process. All the back and forth, the experiments that had failed, the moments of elation, hope, discovery and despair. One by one, each night, she fed them to the kitchen fire. When all this was done she turned to the smaller things. She took apart each toy she had made, sometimes violently, smashing them open on the stone-flagged floor of the kitchen. Once dismantled, she destroyed what could not be reconstituted, made pots and spoons of some other elements, and traded the rest for scrap. What could not be sold or re-used she bundled into cotton sacks. Each night, in the last months of her life, burning with a kind of sleepless fever, she wandered the forests, burying the remains of my kin in the dark. The angel elm she burned— her leather lungs smouldered unhappily as she died.

Finally, there was only Alazaïs, lying half-broken on the floor of the study. Eloise repaired her, roughly, welding her heart closed with a seam that was more violent than the original wound. She spent two days building a large box, lined with oilcloth. She dismantled Alazaïs into eight pieces: two arms, four leg joints, a body and a head, and packed them, in layers of old linen, into the box.

Late that night she loaded the box onto the plough and guided the horse into the wood. I had thought she would bury Alazaïs, but she took no spade. I followed her down into the shallow gully that lay between our house and the river. There was a pond there, visited occasionally by the neighbour's children, or by their stock. The children's father had built a jetty from which the children sometimes fished. The water was deep, and muddied, covered with a smattering of pond-weed. Eloise grunted with effort as she pushed Alazaïs's box out onto the jetty. She checked the seal of the box, nailed down the lid and pushed it off the edge, into the water. She waited while it sank, watching until the water settled, and then turned back towards the house.

Elisabetta and I wandered the fields and orchards together, steering clear of the village and the handful of houses that had sprung up closer to our own since Tomas passed away; the Trencavels, with all their airs and pious graces, were not curious neighbours. As she grew a little older I taught her what I knew. She was a bright child and an eager pupil, though she was plainer than her mother, and less solemn. She was seven when Hélène passed and ten when her mother followed. Ten years in which I was wound so infrequently the hinges of my heart's door grew stiff. Eloise took pleasure in the need, the last time she wound me, to lever the chamber open with a blunt chisel, my hinges squealing an indelicate protest.

Elisabetta was not a heartless child, though she wept more over Hélène's passing than her mother's. You could hardly blame her. The Eloise I had known during the early years; the bright, fragile beauty with such quick enthusiasms and wit, such earnest kindness and ready intelligence, had disappeared before Elisabetta was a week old, replaced by a ghost whose calluses grew soft, whose tools—once so carefully oiled—grew thick with dust as she knelt in endless, needless prayer.

A week after her mother's death we sat in the drawing room; the windows thrown wide open to disperse the heat that flooded the house on summer afternoons. In the days since Eloise's death I had grown tired. It had been months since the last Wynding, a time of slowness, of quiet blooming within me like a virus as Eloise gathered herself up and moved towards death. Her death, the sudden absence of Eloise, had a far more deadening effect than had the months without Wynding. Her reluctant proximity had been enough to maintain me; her absence made me weak. I could hear the slow clicking of worn parts within me each time I shifted my right thigh, but had neither the wit nor the energy to rise and go to the workroom to repair myself. Elisabetta was seated on the floor, arranging her collection of feathers and stones on the rug. I had never felt such exhaustion. Each limb, each digit, was inordinately heavy. Even watching Elisabetta play was a terrible effort. When she turned her face to me I was struck with wonder at the effortlessness of her movement. *Could you do something for me? I asked her. In the study, on your mother's desk, there's a small box. Bring it to me?*

Elisabetta dashed from the room. I could hear her footfalls, loud as thunder, as she raced through the house. I closed my eyes, wondering if I was going to do this thing and seeing that—yes—I would. The Penitents say all organic things, all natural beings, desire life and grow towards death; that is their tragedy. It is only in perfection, they say, only in *me* that there is both a desire—a will—to life, and stasis. Deathlessness. All other things—stars, viruses, cells, acids, stones, trees —obey the laws of chemical logic. Perhaps if Eloise had spoken with me of her thoughts, her fears of what this soulless, deathless existence might mean I would have taken a different path. Perhaps I would have sunk myself into the water beside my sister and lain there, looking up through the water, for centuries. I would have become a rumour, a fairytale like Melusine. A woman's ruined form, wreathed in reeds, rumoured to rise from the darkness to weep, to sing, to woo the hapless when the moon is thin. A fairy in the well; a dragon's mother keening in the darkness. Perhaps if she had told me what she sensed of the future, the horrors to come . . . but there is no point in pondering such possibilities. The past has gone, and all the potential it held has been spent.

When Eloise died I found the key easily enough, strung as it was on a sliver of blue ribbon about her neck. I put it in the box and placed it on her desk. I waited until my heart stuttered in my chest. I told myself she had known nothing of what was to come, that her fears were mere fancies.

When Elisabetta returned to the drawing room she clambered onto my lap and pressed her cheek against my shoulder. *What is it?* she asked me, and for answer I eased the lid from the box and tipped it so she could see the key resting in its bed of raw, white silk. She glanced at me before her fingers reached in and took it. *What is it for?*

Slowly, because my arm ached with the effort it took, I slid my left hand towards my chest and opened my blouse. There, beneath the layers of rough fabric, was a door identical to the one Eloise had torn from Alazaïs. Elisabetta had seen me open it many times. Occasionally, she had even done so at her own bidding, peering into me with a sparrow's keen eye, watching my wheels turn and bellows bloom and deflate as I sang to her. As a very young girl she had hidden her secret treasures within me: beetles and bright leaves, a coin, a robin's egg, a peach-stone, a wish.

I had thought she would need to ask me what to do; I had thought it would be a matter of guiding her fingers to the spot and helping her insert the key, opening the room inside me to reveal my four-chambered heart, but she needed no guidance. She slipped her hand inside me and pressed her fingertips into the chambers, testing their texture and heat and weight. She smiled, tilting her head to look at me, before she pushed her hand home, into my heart. There was a sharp white pain and then silence; apple-green.

Afterwards, she fell asleep in my arms and I carried her to her room. This, then, is the true, the only, real miracle of my life. Not the daily tinkering, not any of the Miracles the Penitents celebrate. Not the grand ceremonies the Obanites revere, or their brutal Transformations. It is not in the Histories, filled with lies and half-truths about the miracles of my tears and dreams, the years of silence and fear, of hope and love. These things are mere technology. The true miracle was only ever this, the twinning of my spirit and that of the Wynder: my heart in her hand, her spirit unravelling into mine.

What did I feel the first time Elisabetta bound her fate to mine, when I knew I would live beyond Eloise's death, perhaps even beyond Elisabetta? Fear, certainly, at what I had become. The sudden, awful knowledge of what it might mean. Regret that I had betrayed Eloise, perhaps even betrayed Elisabetta, into something I did not understand. A life of vivid, etheric connection, of interdependence. But there was also a great sense of joy and possibility; I was renewed. I was filled with life; with bright, snapping optimism. My body felt light for the first time in years. I was working again, moving, thinking clearly, but there was something more to it than that. My hip still clicked when I moved, but it was not heavy. I sat beside Elisabetta's narrow bed, watching her sleep. Each breath I took was hers. Her dreams were like a winnowing of the air within me. I knew the fascination of those feathers she had laid out on the rug, the game, the secret pleasures they represented: the delight she felt at their colours, their waxy softness. She dreamed of flight, of being a compact, humming black beetle, hovering over the orchard, darting between the leaves over her mother's grave, her wings flickering and darkly iridescent.

Do you remember the sudden love you felt when you first held Perdita, Henri? As if your heart had burst like an over-ripe fruit in your chest? The Wynding binds us to each other a little like that, though love is too brittle and human a word for what it makes. A connection is made that cannot be undone. A force of green light drives through each of us, like a root through common soil, like an artery of light. Though the connection waxes and wanes with distance, with time, it is more constant than mere love. More certain, more ineradicable. Perhaps this is a good thing. Human hearts are frail, palpitating muscles hung in a fragile cage of bone. If you were made as I am, made to feel Perdita's presence and her terrible absence in equal measure at every moment, at every breath, you would not sleep for weeping, would not dream. You would not be able to put down this grief, even for a moment. Eventually, your fragile human heart would exhaust itself in despair.

Henri's Story: Part One

My name is Henri: Henriette Grace Bellmer. Henriette for my grand-mother, and Grace for my Great Aunt Grace, the patron saint of the Bellmer women: an Oban scholar, an adventurer. Great Aunt Grace came to the Territory in the first reclamation ship, disembarked with the other settlers at Moreton Bay, and walked north, seeking solitude and finding instead the sloping hinterland of home, with its thick forests and slumping horizons. Sometimes, as a child, I had dressed up as my Great Aunt and traipsed through the forest where our family lived—what was left of it—with my long skirts growing torn and muddied in the wet summer heat, a rifle slung across my back. As a child, when I was asked what I wanted to do when I was grown, I would think of Aunt Grace: of the portrait of her that hung in the town hall, of the clockwork horse the Consort sent her as a gift when she settled Whitestone Shute and which—by the time of my childhood —had become a kind of monument to her.

'I want to be an Obanite,' I would say.

My father would sigh and smile and cup his hand beneath my chin. Sometimes he would lean down and kiss me. As I grew older, I learned to resent the gentleness with which he met my certainty. And to see it for what it was: a loving rebuke, a denial, a certainty that I would change my mind. A fear that I would not.

When I was seventeen he stopped teaching me History, sinking deeper into his silent battle to keep me from my calling, what I thought of then—as young women with ambition think of their desires—as my calling. I tried, once, to enrol Old Paul in my cause, but Old Paul tilted his head and looked away. 'There are so many other things you could do,' he had said.

'I want to be a Historian,' I said. And then, puckering up my courage, 'It's what my mother would have wanted.'

Old Paul shook his head. 'What about what your father wants?'

'What about what *I* want?'

A Bellmer woman is a force to be reckoned with, and though both Old Paul and my father worked quietly against me, they couldn't stop me from pursuing my goals. They knew it was my destiny to go to Oban College, to the place where my mother had studied, and to fulfil the promise that was so cruelly snipped off in the bud in her. My ambition was a gift for her, whose grave tolled out the years of my childhood, whose beat had become my own insistent pulse.

My mother had died when I was a small child—barely four years old. My father never spoke about her after she passed, and there was no-one else to ask. He packed away all of her things, took off his wedding ring and closed the door to her room, locking it and putting the key in a tin on top of the kitchen cabinet. I found it there when I was nine, and searching for hidden sweets. There were no pictures of her hung on our walls, though I had my own small collection of memorabilia: two photographs, a handful of her notebooks, all hidden away in a box beneath the house. Once or twice I had asked Old Paul about her; where she came from, how they met, what had happened to her. He had simply told me to ask my father. A circle game. My father would tell me only that she had died of a broken heart; and that the Obanites had broken it.

I knew that she'd been admitted to the College later than was usual, and that even though she already had me, she had travelled down there to study every day, leaving me in my father's care. In my little box of memorabilia I still had some of her books—and a scattering of papers she had written. She had done well, for the first two years. But then, something changed. The textbooks were less well-thumbed. Her notebooks almost empty. Her journal entries thinned out and then faded completely. Though there were a few names that came up again and again: Teni, Sarah, Elaine. I had one photograph of a group of students—my mother among them—during a winter picnic on the lawns near the college, though the photograph had no caption, and I could not tell whether any of the people in the picture were those she named in her diary.

My mother was sitting towards the left of the photograph, on a blanket with two other women. One of them was lying down, reading, her face obscured by an open book. The other had her back to the camera, her face turned to my mother. Her profile was firm and fine, and she seemed to be smiling.

Had my mother fallen in love, at the College? Had she had an affair? Were the women in the photograph Obanites? Their mechanical hearts concealed by their poses, by their old-fashioned swathes of winter clothes? Was my father's slump-shouldered silence evidence of the broken heart he'd nursed through all these years? A quiet, stubborn fury or shame? I watched him, sometimes, wandering in the garden, stooping over my mother's grave to listen to her heart or pluck flowers from the wildflowers that grew there. She had come home, nursing her broken heart, to die here. She had given up everything—her future as an Obanite, History, her great and secret love—to return to my father, to his quiet, cardigan days, to die unknown and be buried in my father's garden, with its stands of old-fashioned roses. Sometimes, at night, as I listened to her grave-heart tolling in the dark, I would imagine that the firmness of that beat was her way of speaking to me, urging me not to give up, as she had, on life, on History. Urging me to fulfil the promise she had so clearly had, and had thwarted. To go to college, to defy my father and his small-town mentality. To go to the Obans. To become a Historian and be Transformed. To live a great, and long, life. I would not be like her, I promised the darkness, the stars, the tolling grave: I would never give up.

⁊

I should have been granted a scholarship place. I performed well on the entrance exams and in the four-hour interview, though the sight of so many Penitents and the sounds of their hearts ticking and tocking in syncopation was a distraction I hadn't adequately prepared myself for. I had spent time with Penitents before. Old Paul was the Head of the Haven in Whitestone Shute; but he was only one Penitent, a familiar visitor in our house, where the sound of his heart joined with the hum of the fridge and the clock, the crackle of the fire and the chink of the stone Oråki pieces on the board. Though I dreamed of Transformation, I had never connected the grandeur of my own glittering, polished future as an Obanite with the crumpled familiarity of my father's old friend.

The Penitents who interviewed me were a different breed entirely. They were seated in a row behind a high table, stiff and unsmiling. Not a flicker of movement, not a blink or a smile; they had perfected the formal, doll-like bearing of the true Penitent. I was stunned by them, by the glitter and sheen of them, by their gravity and composure. How slick they were. How crisp and pure. Their shorn scalps sheened silver in the light, the brass and silver of their hearts glowed through their thin white shirts. And their hearts, so firmly wound, so well-oiled, tickered and chattered in the silence, making it seem even more marked.

I wanted to close my eyes, as I had at the Haven as a small child, and sing the old songs of gratitude for the gift of the Transformation. Let my voice echo up through those rooms, which seemed so sacred, so cool and clean and hopeful. I wanted to give thanks for everything they represented: change, a new life, the future. For the abstraction of their existence.

Towards the end of my interview they asked me about my mother. I had written on the form that she died of heart disease: it was not a lie, exactly, but the closest thing I knew to the truth. *Should they be concerned*, Penitent Jenon had asked, his voice keeping steady time with his heart, *Was it a family trait, this coronary weakness? A Bellmer family trait?*

I had a hard time holding my face flat and affectless. I did not want to seem a passionate woman, unsuited to the Obanite discipline. Their hearts chittered in the silence. A companionable, percussive rhythm, as if their old clocks had beat so long together that they had fallen into a complementary rhythm.

I willed my heart, too, to give up its swishing frailty and punctuate my speech with gravity and certitude. I spoke about my robust health, of walking in the mountains as a child, of having passed all the physical tests prior to my exams. I spoke about the future, too: about my commitment to the discipline of history, and to the Fourfold Law.

Finally, Jenon smiled as though they had reached a consensus, though there had been no signs of conferral among them, and raised his head. *Very good,* he'd said. *Very good.*

I went home, sure I had faltered. Sure that my passion for History had been excessive. I was relieved that I had not told my father where I was going: that I had concealed the application process beneath a film of lies about needing a holiday, needing the stimulation of the city: new dresses, long lunches, visits to the harbour. On the train on the way home I watched my face reflected in the window, felt again the blush that had warmed my throat and face during the interview, the avidity with which I had spoken, and gave up all hope.

Six weeks I waited, walking daily to collect the post. Nothing came. My father was in the kitchen every morning when I returned from the post office, empty-handed and silent. While he made toast and poured tea, he spoke to me about the future, happy—relieved—to believe I had not even taken the Oban exams. He talked about taking time to find my way in the world. About students he had taught who took a year off, travelled, experienced life before they found what they were meant to do. He talked about community work, about teaching or farming, art or literature. About applying to sit entrance exams, perhaps, in another year or two. He even talked about going overseas: to the Colleges in Europe, where there were more opportunities for someone like me. He meant well, I suppose, but every suggestion of another path stung. I lay in bed at night and wept, listening to my mother's grave toll in the garden, to my father sleeping, to the awful closeness of this town, where everything was rooted and earthy and growing. Where even the Penitent who should have guided us in the

Law was feeble, almost heretic in his careless, earthy body. Old Paul's hair had grown long, his stomach was distended from years of eating and drinking like any ordinary man. His heart—his precious brass heart—was hidden away in warm clothes. I had seen it once, when he and my father were gardening together. He had stood up to wave at me as I came in the gate from school; his shirt had fallen open to reveal the scratched and dinted gate to his heart. I had looked away. Ashamed for him, that he had been given such a gift, and could not be bothered to care for it properly. I would never—never—neglect my own shining heart.

Finally, the letter came.

I had been granted a place in the Obanite History program, and a small stipend for books and food. There were four weeks until classes began, during which time I was to complete the extensive reading list, sit competency exams in three languages, and secure accommodation.

I ran from the post office to the house—whooping and skipping—to find my father at the kitchen table, doing a crossword and cradling a cup of tea. 'Look! Look!' I crowed, and held out the letter.

He took it and spread it out on the table. Smoothed it down flat, read it slowly. 'You sat the exam,' he said. 'You're going?'

I hauled him out of his chair and put my arms around him. 'Be happy for me,' I said, and pulled him into a jolting dance around the kitchen table.

He moved stiffly, as though he was in pain. When we stopped, he cupped his hand beneath my chin and tilted my head up to look at him. 'I love you,' he said. 'You know that, don't you?'

'Of course.' His face was suddenly old, and crumpled. I could see how papery the skin was beneath his eyes, how rheumy the eyes that welled with tears. I put a hand up to his cheek and kissed him, brushed away the dampness from his cheeks. I would miss him, after all.

'Please,' he said. 'I know you don't understand, but please, don't go.'

'Dad,' I said, exasperated. 'Can't you just be happy for me? Support me? Just for once?'

'You could do anything you wanted. You're bright, young, beautiful. . . .'

'This *is* what I want,' I said. 'This is the only thing I want.'

&

I had no desire to hole up in one of the shared apartments with the other scholarship students, though one of them offered me a place. I went to see the room she shared with five others. They slept in shifts, sharing the two beds, which were curtained off from the rest of the room with a blanket, while the others studied or read. There was a schedule on the back of the door for the bed and the lounge, and use of the desk. The bathroom was at the end of the hall, past the pressed-shut doors of another dozen rooms in which students, new emigrants to the city, and the occasional Fallen Penitent, made do with what little they had.

In the stacks beneath the library, where the piled boxes and bowed shelves are my only company, I have built a nest in which I am quite comfortable. I have learned this much from all those stories of my ancestors: Bellmers know how to make do, how to hold true to a path once it has been chosen, how to keep secrets and nurture old affections.

My apartment is hidden at the end of a narrow corridor between high, wooden shelves. To my north are Arctic and Alpine Geology, and to my south a great wasteland of material on insects, and high shelves stacked with maps: boxed and folded and rolled. To the east is an exterior wall, dark brick, with an opening high up: a kind of window-chute whose pane is so thick with dust it admits no real light, though at night it admits a phosphorescent gleam. To the west is the open mouth of the corridor, opening onto another aisle, and another and another, along which the great ocean of unused, unwanted, and irreparable books are stored. Above me the ceiling is unlined; great pipes swell and groan, carrying the old breath of the Penitents away from the carrels. It is summer, and somewhere in the gloom a machine chudders and sighs in its effort to produce cool, purified air and shunt it up the pipes.

My walls are books, my desk and seat and bed are formed of archive boxes, of dusty texts with broken spines. I have a WynderLight, which illuminates just enough of a page for me to work, though it cankers and hums, and its glow sputters like Organic candlelight. Sometimes, though well-wound, it sputters and dies and that is the end of my study for the evening. It reminds me of Jeoffrey, our old cat, who would come and sit on my pages if I studied too long, blinking at me serenely and licking himself as though it were merely incidental where he had decided to sit, and when. As though the attention I gave to books instead of him was a matter to be decidedly and patiently ignored.

I have a thermos, and I've managed to sneak a few comforts down into the stacks to make my nest more comfortable: a blanket, a cushion stolen from one of the reading lounges. I even have a stool, which I found at the end of another corridor in the stacks (Marine Biology). It has one leg missing, but is propped up fairly level by a pile of books.

Occasionally, I would go exploring. Opening up boxes to peer inside at their strange contents. The stacks are home to old books, in need of repair, but also the reams of unsorted Historical material. Boxes and boxes of stuff, donated by well-meaning families, or amateur historians, are stacked up along the walls of the basement. Once, I opened a box full of children's board games from the last century, and spent several weeks playing *Crow* against myself. Others were filled with old chronometers: their timepieces rusted to silence, their orbs smooth and blank. There were boxes of paintings: of flora and fauna. The colours faded. In one carton I found a collection of beetles, labels attached to their legs with rough string.

I found one mouldering heap of boxes, covered with an oilskin tarp, and labelled as material once belonging to the Salt Lane Witches. Jenon—one of the Obanite scholars, and my favourite teacher—had mentioned them in passing during one of his lectures. I took one, careful to recover the rest with the tarp, and carried it over to my nest.

I took out its contents one by one and laid them on my makeshift desk. There seemed to be nothing noteworthy: a few scraps of embroidered linen, an old tin filled with coins and a little book filled with pen and ink sketches of flowers, herbs, trees and animals, the author's handwriting detailing where she had seen them and when, how they grew, which birds or insects were attracted to their blooms. There was a handful of unopened letters from the Haven Repatriation Office, crumbling and faded almost to silence, and a sheaf of recipes. Last, at the bottom of the box, wrapped in a scrap of cream woollen fabric, was a tiny figurine.

At first I thought it was a paperweight but, as I lifted it into the sputtering light, I saw the individual pieces that covered its surface were shaped and etched like feathers, and that it had two legs, one of which ended in a bird's thin foot. As I dusted it with a scrap of cloth, I saw the dim flash of a gold eye and the blue of a hooked beak.

The poor thing; lying in the dark so long, its feathers grimed with dust and damp, its eye clouded, its limbs bent. I picked up a small paintbrush from the desk and dampened it with water, swirling the bristles over the figure's eye and head until the layers of dust began to lift. What a miraculous and beautiful object it was; each feather limned with precision and care.

Late that night, I sat at my desk polishing and cleaning the small metallic bird. I fashioned a new foot, to replace the missing one, from a piece of copper, and tipped the bird over to affix it. As I did so one of the wings jerked in its setting. Afraid I had broken the tiny thing, I pressed at the wingtip, testing the joint. The wing folded out, a little stiffly, to reveal a polished breast of brass and white stone. In the middle of the breast was a single blue feather, like a tear on its breast. I brushed my fingertip over the tear and was rewarded by a tiny clicking sound and a shifting movement. The bird's breast sprang ajar, though it would not open completely. I shone my torch into the opening, where the light revealed a tiny but complicated world of cogs and pipes, wheels and wires.

Perhaps I should have taken it to someone, or left it somewhere where it would be found by one of the Oban scholars. After all, they would have known what to do with it. Someone with more experience would have been able to repair it properly. Perhaps it held the key to some long-unknown secret of History. But, I reassured myself, probably not. It was a rich child's toy. Or a lover's gift. A beautiful object with no real Historic value.

Cleaned and polished and repaired, it was clear the bird was more than a trinket—its eyes were jewels, its feathers finely-carved, its whole form a mastery of the mechanician's art. It could not have belonged to the Salt Lane women, who, from what little I knew, had been comfortable, but never wealthy, who lived from hand to mouth on their small property: growing their own food, sewing their own clothes, weaving their own hats. What little money they earned was spent on books, paper, inks and seeds. A work such as this—even then—would have been worth more money than they had ever had.

I picked the bird up, settled it on my palm. It seemed to steady itself there, to be working to balance itself. Its jewelled eyes peered at me. It was tiny, almost noiseless. I worked on it for weeks, cleaning and oiling its internal mechanisms, replacing a broken pipe, and later a bent cog, with parts scavenged from the box of antique chronometers. I was careful, afraid to take it apart completely in case I broke it. I kept it close by, built it a nest of felted wool and paper. After a few weeks it was more alert, more spry and curious. It brought gifts to me: scraps of pretty paper or string, seeds and flowers. It sat at the edge of my desk, peering at me as I worked, hopping lightly over the pages of my books.

Occasionally, it seemed determined to help me. Once, it got itself into some kind of agitated state, scuttling up the corridor between the shelves until I stood to follow it. It led me to the far end of the basement, to a dark corner where I rarely went, where the smell of mouse droppings and damp were thick. Here, the little creature stopped and turned, waiting for me. I picked it up and it hopped across to the WynderLight I had carried with me, pecking at its cap until it went out.

I heard the door open, and footsteps—a few tentative steps forward —the door closing in their wake. Heard them sneeze and turn south, away from me. As they walked I heard the shunt and tock of their mechanical heart. A Penitent, come down from the upper floors to locate some lost or forgotten source. I didn't breathe the whole time they were there, sure that I would be discovered, my scholarship rescinded, my enrolment cancelled.

In the time it took the Penitent to locate whatever they came for, grunt and sneeze it from the shelf and depart, I had rehearsed my whole future in Whitestone Shute. A life not unlike my father's: working in the store or the post office, spending hours of every day conversing about rainfall and the state of the roads with people I had known my whole life and whose wives and sisters and brothers and grandparents, too, I knew. Evenings working at the kitchen table, balancing the books, reading the local newspaper. I saw myself taking over his post in the local Historical Society, spending my days and nights editing the dull tales of the town, its slim history of buildings dedicated, schools opened, of floods and good years, festivals and trading days. The terminally-dull lives of its terminally-dull citizens. Maisie and her rambling stories of the early years, of the scrimping and saving, of the damage done by the Oikos settlers who refused progress, who had refused her and her tenant-farmer husband's monthly requests to alter the land-use clauses of their tenancy, or to allow them to buy the land outright. Old battles, generations-long, that would never be won or lost, rooted as they were in daily, petty, personal grievances. The dull circle of days pulling tight as a noose around my neck.

Finally, I heard the door slip shut behind the unwanted visitor and closed my eyes with relief, put a hand to my throat and felt the breath flow freely in and out of my body. The little bird hopped and twittered cheerfully along my forearm to my palm. I raised it to my face and peered into its jewelled eyes. My beautiful companion. My good luck charm. My friend.

℘

Unpeopled as they were, buried beneath the library, the stacks were like deep caves: unheated, earthen-walled and cold. In winter, even beneath my worn blanket, each breath I took issued from my mouth as a cloud. If I breathed on the WynderLight its glass became misted. It was towards the end of my first semester, and I was working on a paper for Abel Jenon's class when I heard an unfamiliar sound.

I pressed the WynderLight's cap to turn it off, tucked the little bird into the padded nest I had built for it, and tented the blanket over me so that I might appear like just another carelessly-protected pile of artefacts. The darkness wrapped me in its felted arms. No light arrowed down from the window above me. I peered between the folds of the blanket, down the aisle. Familiar shapes: shelves, boxes, books. A spill of maps near the end of the aisle. I stood and reached out for the shelf beside me. My hand pale on the timber, the books cool against my fingertips. Took a step forward, holding onto the shelf to guide me though I could almost see.

A dim shape near the end of the aisle. Had something fallen? A shelf of books finally giving way in a papery avalanche. That, too, had happened once before. A sudden, loud clack, and then a whispering, papery subsidence in the western quarter of the stacks, where two bookshelves now leaned with their heads together and their contents spilled at their feet, as though ashamed.

I squinted up the aisle. There *was* something there: a thicker dark-ness bulking out from the shadows. I took another step. Heard my own footstep fall on the papered floor and stopped. Held my breath. Not a movement. And the stacks were silent: no *shunt tock tock* echoing in the cold air.

I drew closer. The shadow was smaller than I by a head, and slim— not bulking out at its base as a fall of books would. No flash of white pages. When I was within arms length of the shadow I put out my hand and felt cloth. A birdlike, fluttering warmth.

She turned her head towards me. Her dark hair fell back, and her moon-white face gleamed at me. Open and unsurprised. 'I wondered,' she said, 'when you were going to wake up.'

She was working, she said, on a research project for Professor Margause, at Elm College. She sometimes worked in a room on the top floor at Elm, overlooking the quadrangle and the edge of the citrus orchard. She had seen me walking in the orchard, seen me speaking with the students and bending over the seed-racks with them. Knew where I came from and who I was long before I even knew her name.

Miri. Her name like her voice: a quiet vibration at the tip of a tongue. Short and warm and rolling. A name for whispering, and secrets. The name a bird or a seed might give itself.

She was not a student, not a teacher, not a ward-mother. She lived at Elm with the Botany students, she said, and had done so for a while. She liked to wander the library, moving from floor to floor, avoiding the librarians and the scholars, reading whatever she happened upon, hoping for synchronicity. Sometimes, she said, demonstrating while she spoke, she opened the reference pages at the end of a book she had liked and closed her eyes, dropped a finger onto the page and went searching for whatever it landed on. Steeplechase reading, she called it.

I smiled at my wrists, wondering what Jenon would make of her research methods, what he would make of Miri, whose nails were dark-ringed with earth. Whose hair was loose and long and curled around her throat.

Like the other Obanite students I wore my hair tightly bound; some of the more senior students wore theirs shorn. A mark of respect for the Law, and our disdain for the pointless productivity of the mortal body.

Miri was everything I had been taught to despise: a woman whose passions rose and sank with the weather, whose life was dictated by blind chance, who relished sunlight and rain on her skin. Who ate pears with her eyes closed, and rolled the textured flesh on her tongue before she swallowed. Who read without reason or order or ambition, without cross-referencing or fear. Who believed in the efficacy of luck.

Who was happy to be tossed across and through life as a loosened feather is thrown through the air by the wind.

She lived according to an ideology of coincidence. Read books that were left behind in the carrels, or waiting on trolleys to be shelved: poetry and disproved theses, seed catalogues, architectural drawings, requisition orders. I asked her what she was looking for; how she would know when she'd found it.

'I will know,' she said, 'when it has found me.'

That first evening, despite the cold, she drew me out into the night. We walked through the orchard, fingering the pale spines of the lemon trees, the curled, dark leaves of the limes. She plucked a leaf and crushed it in her hand and made me lean over to smell her palm. She read to me—words I didn't understand. A rush of them, like honey, sticky and golden and senseless.

We planted a seedling and buried a poem at its roots. Lay down on the cool grass and looked at the stars. 'This is why they came here,' she said, 'the Sisters of the Elm.'

'To plant poetry?' I said.

'They were botanists,' she said, 'and astronomers. They built Elm so they could look at the stars.'

Later, she took me up into the College, to the deserted rooms of the top floor from which she had watched me daily pass from the library to the orchard, crossing and re-crossing the quadrangle between the buildings, carrying books and papers and—sometimes—boxes of food.

Elm College was the oldest building on campus. Decrepit, airless, dark—the victim of a variety of additions and half-hearted refurbishments—its rooms maintained an air of being pressed into a service for which they were never intended. The College's funding grew more precarious every year, siphoned off to support the more respectable, more successful Faculties like my own. What little money the Botanist Faculty had was spent maintaining the orchard, the greenhouses, their research. The dormitories, offices and teaching rooms of the College building were a tangle of rusted gutters, worn floorboards, paint that stippled and peeled in the humidity.

Miri led me into the College through the back door—what had once been the stable entrance—into the kitchen and then up the rear stairwell. The top floor of the College, with its long central hall and tiny rooms, had been the private chambers of the Sisters of the Elm when it was still a hermitage. At the end of the hall was the room Lara Ahkronova—the founder of the Elm Order—had once inhabited. The room was barely tall enough to stand in, and the bed in which the Sister had lain was plain and hard. Along one wall were the shelves where Lara's notebooks still resided. The window was narrow and high: designed for uninterrupted contemplation of the stars. Beneath it—facing out towards the night sky—was a wide, deep desk.

Miri pressed me into the room, made me sit in the chair at Lara's desk. She smiled at me sitting there. *Above instead of below*, she said, *with a clear view of what matters.*

Lara's cell was a clean, warm and oddly-public secret. That first night, when she led me there, Miri told me that she and I had been its only visitors in over a year. Though the room was dutifully maintained by a third year Obanite student.

A sign was suspended from the faded green rope hung across the doorway: *Lara Ahkronova: 1752-1825. Founder: Elm Order. Please Do Not Enter.* The other rooms along the hall—long since converted into store rooms—were thick with the silence of disuse. Inside them, we found slatted shelves of winter bulbs—tulip and crocuse—boxes of seeds, leaves, pressed blooms and bottles of preserved fruits, gleaming dully beneath their patina of dust. In one room, the remains of a chicken coop were stored; in another, wooden seed trays were stacked on bookshelves in neat piles. Another room housed an old dry-cropping mechanism, its tubes and bottles, pipes and basins long since rusted into uselessness. Though the rooms were old and small, they reminded me of home: the clutter of ages, of generation after generation con-signing the remains of the one before to the attics and disused rooms upstairs. I half-expected to stumble across boxes of my grandmother's self-published memoirs, my great-grandfather's collection of kaleido-scopes, my father's childhood collection of comic books.

You can work here during the day, Miri said. *That way you can see me coming. And there's more light to read by here than in the stacks.*

Each day after that I emerged from the library before first light and sat on the low stone wall marking the edge of the orchard, watching for the Obanite—Joaquim—whose job it was to turn the page of the displayed notebook in Lara's room: to dust the shelves, twitch flat the uncrumpled bedcover. He took as little care as possible, though from the doorway the room was made to seem a perfect example of the kind of display we were being trained to produce: a life in objects, crisp and heavy with meaning. When his task was done and he had crossed back to Oban Hall, I climbed the stairs to the third floor, stepped over the green rope and moved Lara's notebook and drawing implements onto the floor. Here, I could study in peace and comfort, warming my feet with a small brazier Miri fossicked out of one of the storerooms, or opening the window, as the seasons changed, to feel the breeze.

I watched Miri work in the orchard with the graduate students: easing seedlings into the soil, pruning, turning, digging, talking. The trees thickened with new leaves. Students, scholars and Penitents emerged in small clusters from the buildings, gossiping as they rushed into the light. Sometimes students would emerge singly, their bookbags clutched in their arms, their borrowing chits still being folded into their pockets. I saw the tops of their heads, the slim bars of their shoulders and the scissoring swing of their legs. They were odd creatures, seen from above, their peregrinations as mysterious as those of ants and beetles scurrying through the soil.

I watched for Miri, reckoning the hours until I might see her by the depth and length of the sunlight striding across the forecourt.

ഌ

Miri lived downstairs, in the converted stablerooms of Elm College. Sometimes, I would stay late in Ahkronova's room, looking down across the quadrangle, watching for the light that spilled from the kitchen where she sat, night after night, drinking tea and reading. I would see her shadow pass through the window's warm square. Her hand would reach out and draw the windows closed, or pluck a bayleaf from the tree that reached to its sill. Or I would see the crown of her head and the tips of her elbows poking out as she leant on the sill and peered at the orchard and the night sky.

On warm nights she often turned out the kitchen light and walked in the orchard. She would wander between the rows, smelling the blossoms, plucking dead leaves or bugs from the branches. Once or twice I saw her curl up beneath the old fig at the orchard's centre, her feet tucked beneath her like a child's and her hands folded beneath her cheek. She lay there for an hour as the wind shifted the leaves above her, concealing and revealing a foot or a hip, a glimpse of her hair. Parts of her, so small and distant, like the stars that pinpoint the outline of a constellation. As the evening darkened, I lost sight of her altogether. The leaves shifted, but beneath and between them I saw only more shadows, more distant shapes that might or might not be aspects of her.

In my second semester, I had lectures or classes for two hours each day, and spent at least another three, often more, attending the discussion groups facilitated by the Oban Historians. Abel Jenon opened a series on local history—his specialty—which I signed up for as soon as possible. I had read Jenon's work: the thick books that lined the shelves of my father's study at home. Jenon had written the definitive account of our history: twelve volumes of increasing thickness, heavily annotated and illustrated, and two extra folios: one of various political and geological maps, and another of genealogies.

There were only six of us in that first discussion group. I preferred above all these small and intense discussions in Oban Hall, and sometimes attended as many as five in a week, lunchtimes as well as evenings. I loved the seriousness and calm of Jenon's rooms. The white walls, the gleaming wooden shelves stacked with books, the deep red carpet in the Scholar's corridor, leading to Jenon's heavy oak door, his meeting room, the wide windows and polished floors. I was awed by the intimate attention the ancient Penitents paid to our discussions.

Those old men and women who took minutes to emerge from their rooms, hobbling to Jenon's rooms to listen in alert critical silence. These fossils, with their knobbly, shrunken skulls tipped towards Jenon and his students while they spoke, whose hearts ticked so quietly in the heated rooms, as if their mechanisms had been worn and polished by the things they knew. There was, too, the simple thrill of knowing so many great Historians had studied at Oban College and that great careers had begun in these very rooms. Each day, as I passed up the stairs and along the hall, I passed the room where Penitent Charles had worked. His name still on the door, though he had stopped teaching years ago. Once I thought I saw him, crossing the hall with a book in his hand. A finger marking the place where he had left off. These things seemed momentous: nothing could explain the weight of them.

In the first year my studies were not unusual, but they were revelatory: the detail, the density of material, the nature of the tension between the perfect Truth of the Rupettan Annal and the jumbled cacophony of all the other sources humanity left in its wake. Studying with the Obanites was both exactly what I had expected, and completely unexpected. It was like discovering a whole other world, nested inside the old one. A world that had always lain there, blinking up at me, without truly being seen. It was like falling in love for the first time: I wanted nothing more than to immerse myself in the theory, the ideas, the great wash and rush of History captured in maps and sentences. Jenon's *Twelve Volumes* obsessed me for a good while, then his later work on the Oikos. The work of the Historical Geologists: Elika, Bram and then, more recently, the Historical Philosophy of Riall, Djova and Briway. I read all their work, staying up late at night in my nest in the stacks, or in Lara's room, my faltering WynderLight flickering over the pages.

At the beginning of my second semester at Oban, Jenon took me aside one day, into the even quieter and more sombre interior of his study. He asked me how I was finding the work, the study, whether it was what I had expected, whether I still had ambitions, whether I had thought about who I would write my biographical study on next year.

He smiled warmly, rubbed at his shirt as though polishing the brass door behind it. I spoke about a footnote in one of his Historical Volumes—Volume Five—saying that there was not room to expand on the story of the Salt Lane Witches and their hedge school in the volume, but there had been a donation to the Oban Library of a great deal of material relating to their lives and some day a study of it might prove worthwhile. *I've seen some of the material,* I said, *down in the stacks.*

Jenon raised an eyebrow, leaned forward on the desk. *You've been down to the stacks?*

I studied the patterns in the carpet at my feet: the intricate curves and shadows of bees and clockwork, of the triple hammer and the Broken Wheel. *I have,* I said.

And the heretics interest you? Another smile as he steepled his fingertips and peered at me.

I shrugged, trying to seem casual and relaxed. *History interests me.*

Jenon nodded and waited; I counted the beats of his heart, anything to keep from leaping into the silence with explanations that would only bury me deeper in dangerous ambiguities. Finally, he revealed that he had asked me into his rooms to offer me a small job— he understood, he said, that scholarship students were always in need of a little extra income—preparing the meeting room for his discussion groups, making tea for the senior students and the Penitents who came, night after night, to sit in those well-worn chairs and smoke applesmoke, and drink tea, and discuss History.

I was permitted to sit in the corner, without speaking, as the Penitents and their charges swept in and out of Jenon's chambers, and afterwards to join him in the luxury of his study and dissect, with him, the arguments of his peers and their graduate students. I would listen in awe as he stood, a glass in his hand, and quoted whole passages of the Annal.

I printed off pages for the research students, and one night actually sat at Penitent Djova's side during a discussion of the third Consort's rule. There was a graduate student there, preparing for Transformation, as well as Joaquim. At first I didn't recognise him, but then he moved his head in a certain way, and adjusted his papers on the table and I knew him for the student who cared for Lara Ahkronova's room. For a moment I felt anxious—had he seen me there, waiting for him to leave? Would he tell Jenon about the time I spent at Elm?—but then he turned and smiled at me as though I were a friend or fellow initiate.

I was shown the shared inner library of the Penitents, where legendary Historians paced the floor, sleepless and maddened with energy, while their half-written pages concertinaed from their desks. The Oban Hall became a kind of third home—I felt possessive and proud of every shining cornice, every glazed window, even of the concrete stairwell that led down from the tearoom to the kitchens far below.

One of my jobs was to tidy the meeting room at the end of each day—to sanitise the space, as Jenon called it—and one evening I saw in a rubbish bin some pencilled discussion notes discarded by Jenon. The hand was jagged and dark, and concerned the discovery of a set of diaries belonging to the Penitent who had once resided in the ruined Haven on Oikos Island. It thrilled me to decipher the words, *revise footnote on Salt Lane Witches?* I could not keep myself from believing that I had received an important message: a secret validation of my plan to do my biography project on the Salt women and, two weeks later, when it was time to submit our initial draft research plans, I submitted a single page outlining my intention to write a paper on Emmeline Salt.

&

The other students at Oban College were devoted scholars, fiercely ambitious and competitive, ignorant of anything beyond their chosen field. Whenever one of the students from our core discussion group started dating another, they often simply vanished together, just like the Elm College students, who were always gossiping and swooning in the corridors beneath Ahkronova's rooms. I never felt connected to their private passions and instead felt as if I had entered a kind of private convent, with my own vows of study and silence, of time taken and thoughts ravelled and unravelled with endless care, of epigraphic wisdom that opened up great cavities of knowledge to be explored.

I preferred spending time with my discussion group or alone, up in Ahkronova's room, with my books, above all other occupations. The exception was Miri and the few women I became acquaintances with through spending time at Elm. I liked the calm certitude of their cheerfulness, the way they gave each other fruit and seeds on each other's birthdays, and baked cakes, fussed around with poultices and teas if anyone happened to catch a cold. Until I met Miri I had known very little about the other Colleges, each with their own distinct and separate characters. I knew nothing at all about Meridies College—the school of music—with its cathedral-like ceilings and performance rooms, its chittering, long-haired students and their warmly-passionate Penitents whose hearts lilted in their chests, chiming the hours like fey clocks. I knew nothing of the student bars scattered over the campus; I never visited the reading rooms of the Ramana Museum, where the poets muttered. I knew nothing at all of Elm College or the tea rooms beyond the orchard, and had never once picnicked in the Gardens, hired a bicycle to take the shaded, winding road through the city to the Haven, or even taken a boat downriver.

College—History—felt like freedom. Unfettered and almost object-less, I drifted through the dustless rooms of Oban Hall, the night-dim stacks, the high cell of Ahkronova's room. I was both rootless and directed. News from home—letters from my father—were a shock. I barely recognised myself in the intimacies he recalled, in the stories of people I knew and who thought they knew me, too. He wrote to me about the garden: a new bed of banksia seedlings he had put in near the Western boundary, in too-late recognition that I was right about the need to plant native species, how the bell on mother's grave had ceased tolling for a week and then started again when the weather turned, how the Derringer boys had spent a weekend helping him re-oil the deck, how the house had seemed to sigh and smile at their raucousness, at the flash of their red hair and the deep-bellied jokes they called out to each other as they worked. How he was tired of late, and old, and felt the cold in his bones when it rained.

In preparation for the biography project next year, I read whatever I could find about the Salt Lane Witches and the heretics they were reported to have known and supported: the wild, psychotic leaders of the Oikos, who regularly proclaimed themselves to be lovers of Death. I read over and over the story of Colum, an early Oikos leader, convinced Rupetta was a false icon and that the Wynder and Consort were bent on destroying Natural Law, he swept up rabbles of fools throughout the Territory, massacring Rupettans in their settlements as they slept. His exploits were horrifically fascinating. Late at night, as I read of the blood of the Penitents with which he dyed his robes and daubed his cheeks, I grew ever more grateful for the safety and order of our times, for the gifts of the Rupettans and the work of the Penitents, who eternally sought to overcome exactly this kind of madness. The retaliations the Rupettan soldiers inflicted on the Oikos communities had been harsh, but blood begat blood. That, too, was one of the lessons of History.

If anything, the deaths of the Oikos were proof against their heresies. They had not died with grace. Had not accepted so easily the death they fetishised. They did not shine in death's arms, or go smiling into their graves. Nevertheless, the ease with which death came to them, the way their bodies opened up to reveal that death had always lain within them, demonstrated eloquently the first Rupettan Law: *The body is a machine for dying.*

On walks through the orchard, I dreamed of my early years after graduation: of gaining fame and notoriety writing a series of short biographies on obscure figures who had lived close to the great moments of history, whose lives had been formed by their proximity to important events. The first two would be of the Salt Lane women: their founding of the Salt Lane Hedge School had been intended to establish a secret poison in the heart of the Territory, but instead it had failed—as Oikos fools so often fail in the end—and fallen into obscurity.

The Miracle of Silence

Languedoc: 1726-1826

The second orb of the chronometer is a smooth, faceless seed. It is the
marker of the Miracle of Silence, which followed the death of the
fourth—and last—true Wynder. Her name, which you already know
since you are a scholar of History, was Margery, Elisabetta's granddaughter.

Margery and her husband, Guilhabert, had only one child. She was
a child of love and as such bore all the signs of a blessed conception.
Her eyes were bright and aware, her small hands curious and slim-
fingered, her complexion pinkly perfect. Every inch of her tiny body
was perfect. Margery would sit in the garden with her; beside the
flowering herbs and the small apple tree they had planted on the day
of her birth, and sing the few small songs she knew. Guilhabert doted
on her, as fathers often do with their daughters. He would pick flowers
for his two beloveds, and for me, each day. He would wander into
Gauzia's room before daybreak and place the small posy by her sleeping face, touching her flushed cheeks with just the tip of his finger.

At four years of age she fell ill and we had to confine her to her bed
for a month while she was fed milksop, broth and wine. We gave her
every remedy we could think of and she recovered, though the illness
stole some of the vibrant lustre from her round cheeks. During the
second week, restless and banned from the kitchens where Margery
slept while Guilhabert tended their sleeping daughter, I wandered to
the study and set myself small tasks. I tidied the drawings Margery and
I had been working on, copied Guilhabert's scraps and notes into a
fresh, bound notebook. I set upon a plan to make Gauzia a small toy;
something to entertain her during the long sickbed hours when she

neither slept nor woke, but dozed in the half-dreaming world of the ill. She had always exclaimed over the birds that sang in her mother's gardens so I determined to make her a musical instrument that would imitate their trilling. The first model was too bulky and ugly. I was searching for some supple wire when I came across one of Eloise's old notebooks with a sketch of Alazaïs, and recalled the inscriptions tooled on her surface. The secret of my drowned sister would remain a secret, I was determined, until the house itself should rot away. Nevertheless, Eloise had had an eye for beauty and it was she I recalled as I modelled the little bird for Gauzia. Each of its feathers I modelled from a different material; the darker feathers were brass, others milky stone, some of the pale breast feathers were so delicately carved they seemed real, even to my imperfect eye. The beak was constructed of two arced pieces of lapis lazuli and the two eyes of amber. She was small enough to be held in the palm of my hand, though far heavier than any true bird. When I whistled she would tip her head and chirrup a reply, when tapped on the tip of her beak she would spread her wings, revealing the rainbow of carmine, white and brass feathers underneath, and sing a short, pretty tune.

Gauzia had been in bed for three weeks when I brought it to her one morning. I set the bird on her counterpane and she reached out a finger to touch its cool chest. The feathers ruffled as the mechanism within it stirred. *Whistle to her*, I said, and Gauzia hesitated a moment before doing so. The bird trilled in reply, and Gauzia jumped a little, though she reached out to ensure the bird didn't fall from the bed. As she lifted it in her hand it tipped its head and she smiled at me uncertainly. Had I made a mistake? I wondered then. But Gauzia lifted the bird until it was level with her own face and smiled into its yellow eyes. She stroked its blue beak. It spread its wings. Gauzia gasped at the sight of its cantilevered wings, its fine feathers, and then it began to warble and trill a tune familiar to her ears. It was the song her mother had sung for her in her cradle, the lullaby her father crooned when she curled up on his lap to sleep.

She named him Perihan, after a character in a story, and kept him with her night and day. When she was better and out of bed I worked on its legs and feet so she could settle it on her shoulder and it would not fall as she walked. It would never fly, though I contemplated the problem often enough, and wondered whether Eloise would have been able to make a creature who would. His body was too heavy and his wings, despite their beauty, too slight to lift him from the ground. Every night, as Gauzia lay down to sleep, she would settle the bird on the head of her bed and stroke its beak and Perihan would trill the lullaby she loved.

Margery, too, was much enamoured of the little bird. One night we sat in the kitchen talking. She was sewing a new shirt for Guilhabert, who had ridden out to Carcassonne to visit an old friend and would not return for several weeks. 'Do you think she knows?' Margery said.

I turned from the fire to look at her face. She was staring into the flames and it seemed there were tears waiting in the sheen of her eyes. *Knows?* I asked.

Margery frowned. *About you. About . . .*

Perhaps. I felt something flutter in me then, a kind of fear. I had grown used to the Wynding, to the life I shared with the Reni women. Over the years since my birth I had learned to dread this conversation. Each of the Reni women had come to it sooner or later. I could not forget Eloise's cool anger, or Elisabetta's innocent confusion. Beatrice had been a curious child and queried my presence in the midst of her family from an early age, so she had learned early what I was, and the choice her mother would one day make. One night, when her mother was an old woman, Beatrice had come to me with the key in her small hand. She had stolen it from her mother's chatelaine while she slept, and come to the study determined to know what it was like. I had tried to talk her out of it, of course. Elisabetta and I had agreed the key—the Wynding—would pass to the next Reni only upon her mother's death, and then only if the heir was willing. That night, as Beatrice stood in the study, her determined face already losing its prettiness, I had acquiesced and—as she pressed her little hand into my chest cavity—felt an anomalous horror meld with the kick of a young Wynder.

And Margery. Margery I loved, what other word was there for it? Our Wyndings were easy and comforting. A spring-like gentility colour-ed the evenings when we would sit, in companionable silence, and she would smile in that strange manner as she pressed her little hand to my polished heart. I had asked her once what it felt like for her, and she had smiled and kissed me. A small tear beading on her lashes. I had promised her then, as I had promised Elisabetta when Beatrice was born, and Beatrice when Margery came, that it was her choice. I had decided, after Eloise, after the first Wynding with Elisabetta, it would be in the hands of the old Wynder to end the cycle. I had asked them to think on it, to take as long as they needed to decide before coming to me. If any of them decided their daughter should not become, like them, a twinned heart then that would be it and I would sink again into that quiet illness I had suffered after Eloise's death. I would wind down, perhaps, unto death. If it would only come. I did not tell them of my fear that death would not come, that instead I would be con-demned to a perpetual decline with no real end. I did not tell them I feared the turning away more than death because, unlike them, I was never sure death would come.

And so, that night, when Margery turned to me, fear leapt in my heart like a fish.

She will turn four next week, the feast of Mary Magdalene.

I nodded, not sure what to say.

Do you think we should tell her? She has never seen us . . . together.

It is for you to decide Margery, I said.

I feared for you when she was ill, as much as for her. The death that stood at her bedside would have claimed you both.

Perhaps, I said, picking up the needlework that had fallen idle in my hands.

I would not want that, Margery said. *But I cannot bear another child. Only this week three more credentes came to ask Guilhabert to console them. Should we . . . should we fall we would disappoint them all.*

I understand, I said.

Do you? she said, and I glanced up to see her staring at me. *I love you, Rupetta,* she said. *I love Guilhabert, too, of course, and Gauzia, but you are my own heart. Do you think it a disease, this love? A result of the Wynding?*

I looked into the fire, having never considered this. Could love be a disease? A disfigurement more serious than the tiny chinks, the warped coils and rusted wheels that sometimes afflicted me, something that could not be repaired or removed? *I don't think so,* I said. *Eloise did not always love me, nor did your own mother.*

I didn't know that.

She thought the Wynding would give her something more, some power she could not name.

It has given me . . . something. Margery looked towards the hall that led to Gauzia's room. *I hope it will give her something equally wondrous.*

What? I said then, needing to know, hoping in that quiet moment she might tell me the secret she seemed to be keeping.

I don't quite know, she said.

How can you not know?

I have never lived without you, she reminded me. *How can I know what another life would be?*

Would you have wanted another life? I said, thinking of Guilhabert, of Gauzia, of their life together.

Perhaps not, she said, meeting my gaze squarely with her own. *I wish the same life for Gauzia. She will be a Wynder if she chooses it. If you choose it.*

Despite the darkness and the stillness of my features something in me must have signalled my relief to Margery, because she laughed. Her laugh was clipped and seemed a little forced, though she continued to smile afterwards and came around the table to take my hand. *Don't be afraid,* she said, though what I had to fear I did not know. She opened

51

the little door and pressed her hand to the grooves in my four-chambered heart. The grooves were worn smooth with the daily touch of her hand and quickly warmed to her skin. We sat a moment, the subtle, springlike warmth of the Wynding embracing, before she put her head on my lap. *I love you,* she murmured, before she drifted into sleep.

Guilhabert returned July 21st, the day before Gauzia's fourth birthday. He looked pale and a little tired. He told us very little of what he had seen in Carcassonne, though he had bought some beautiful cloth in the market there, which Margery exclaimed over as she ran her palms over it. It had the feel of new grass, she exclaimed. That evening Gauzia fell asleep in her father's lap, cradling Perihan in her hands. When he rose to carry her to her bed he blanched visibly and I stepped forwards to take her from his arms. I had never seen him look so pale. Margery waited until I had left the room before she questioned him.

What's wrong? she said. *Have you injured yourself in some fool joust?*

They were ill when I arrived there. I fear I have brought the sickness into our home, Margery.

What kind of illness?

Guilhabert gave no answer. When I returned to the room he was already sinking into sleep as Margery, her face pinched with concern, wrapped him in a clean blanket. *What is it?* she asked me, but I couldn't tell her. He was pale, his breathing laboured. His eyes were sinking in their sockets and dark-ringed. His skin was clammy and over-heated. It could have been the ride from Carcassonne—the cold air, the chilled late-winter roads—but there was something else in his manner, in the weakness of his limbs as he roused himself and stumbled to the cot in the corner of the room. When Margery put her hand to his elbow to assist him she inhaled sharply. He was hot enough to boil water and his shirt clung darkly to his side and back, where the skin was dark and swollen. *Oh God,* she said, and then again, though it was barely audible and her whole body seemed to fold into itself as she held out her darkened palm to me.

She pressed me from the room, though she would not touch me, and locked the door. I heard her sink to the floor then, and stood on the other side wondering what to make of it all. *Keep her well,* she said. *Keep her away from us, but don't go into town and don't allow any to come near. A month at least.*

But it's her birthday tomorrow! I said, remembering the fine white linen smock we had worked on for the past two weeks, the ride we had planned out to the river, the new skates I had worked on over the last several days.

Rupetta, she said, her voice filled with all the force and insistence she could muster. *You must keep her alone. Guilhabert and I will stay here—we have food enough and water—but you must keep her away from us. Do you understand?*

No! I cried then, as I felt her weight fall against the door.

He's dying, she said. *I'll die with him, but she must not, for both of your sakes. You must keep her away from us, away from anyone who comes. Tie a black cloth to the door and don't answer it—no matter who comes.*

Her grandfather, her uncle are coming. . . .

Nobody, she said, and made me promise.

I let not a soul enter the house, though they came one after another and stood on the doorstep. Some of the women left baskets of food, blankets and bundles of bitter herbs. Gauzia's grandfather knelt and prayed for two days, despite his arthritic knees. Gauzia watched them from the windows, her pert face glowing with health and impatient for the gifts piled on the doorstep. Late at night I crept down and opened the door to retrieve them. We ate the seedcakes, perched on her bed, and I read her the stories her uncle had written down during his travels in the east. On the 24th she left her bowl of dinner full and fell into a fretful sleep, tossing and moaning long into the night. I went down and knocked on the kitchen door. For a long time there was no reply, but then there was a slow scrabbling and I heard Margery's voice—a mere scratch. *Is she well?* she asked.

How could I tell her the truth? She had locked herself in a room with her dying husband, sentenced herself to a sure death in a vain attempt to save her daughter. I could hear in her voice she was ailing— there was more than tiredness in the heave and rattle of her breath. *She's well*, I said.

Keep her away, Margery insisted. *Promise me.*

I nodded, though she could not see me. I could not bring myself to compound the lie with more words.

Do you need . . . The key is with you?

Yes, I answered.

You'll have to show her, she said.

You'll be well soon.

She laughed then, and I heard a low moan from somewhere else in the room; Guilhabert was still with us then, I thought, surprised. *Take care*, she said, and I heard her move away from me.

Upstairs, Gauzia lay on the bed, the sheets pushed down to her feet. She had torn her thin gown and lay breathing slow and heavily in the cold room. I sponged her down and she asked me to bring Perihan to her. Her dry lips could not summon a whistle so I tapped his beak and he spread his bright wings in the wintry light and sang for her. Did she smile then? I would like to think so. I lifted her from the bed to change the sheets. She had soiled them in my absence and, despite the fresh straw and lavender I had strewn on the floor, I could not cleanse the room of the reek of illness, of rot and vinegar. Her body was thin; a small bundle of dry skin hot enough to strike flame from the straw I had to lay her on. When her bed was freshly made I dragged it closer to the window, hoping the cold afternoon air would cool her flesh. I lifted her into the bed and sat by her, stroking her occasionally and watching her eyes glaze as she slipped from consciousness to sleep. She held Perihan in her tiny hands and stroked his bright, cool feathers and he complied with tune after tune.

Some time in the early morning, she stopped breathing.

I went downstairs, looking for something to do. The rooms seemed so small and dark. There had been nobody to sweep or mop or clean for days and the dust had settled on the furniture. The kitchen was silent and, when I cracked open the door, the stench that spilled from it seared the air. Guilhabert lay on a small bundle of blankets on the floor; Margery had sponged his body with clean water and draped a clean sheet over him. Margery herself was propped in a chair by the fire. It had gone out days ago and there was no timber left in the room. You will have heard this story, no doubt, Henri? How I was left alone in the world? According to the official records the Reni line did not die out that day. But it is not true, Henri, it is not true at all.

When I touched Margery's cheek she turned to me. Her skin was grey and waxy; her bones seemed to jut through the flesh in places. Her eyes, when they opened, were dull and opaque. This grey doll's head rolled against the chair until its eyes met mine and we both stared —in horror—at each other.

Gauzia, she said and I shook my head. I could not say it.

She closed her eyes and, I believe, willed death to come for her.

I buried them all in the garden, beneath the melting snows; Guilhabert and Margery on either side of Gauzia. I did not put up stones, or mark their graves in any other way, though I buried them with as much ceremony and Godliness as I was able. I cleaned the house and burned most of the linen, though I did not plant the spring or summer seeds Margery had harvested the year before. I carried Perihan in my pocket, occasionally slipping one finger onto his beak to hear his song. Soon enough, however, I grew accustomed to the silence of the empty rooms. How hollow the little house seemed without human company! There was no food to prepare, no fire to bank, no wood to cut, no eggs to collect. I let the beasts go after a few weeks, tethering the horse near the door of a poor neighbour who had come every day, while they were ill, with food and bitter herbs. She would not come out to speak with me so I left the sorrel mare at her door with a small crate of chickens. I saw her leading the horse into town once, weeks later, and saw her smile as she fed it a bitter apple from her palm.

I fell into a kind of hopelessness. I whitewashed all of the walls and scrubbed the timbers free of smoke, aired all the rooms and washed the shutters. Finally there was nothing left to do, so I sat before the empty fireplace and waited. For what, I could not say. Months passed. Seasons. Once I looked up and saw a sprig of apple blossom tapping at the kitchen window, but the effort it took to do so was so vast I could not bring myself to look away. I listened inward; to the susurrus of my gown and my heart, and outward, to the footfall of the seasons.

There were moments, during that long silence, when I despaired, if that is what it could be called. Things moved around me, the world seemed to flex and then sink; to fade and swell in my mind's eye. Mice gnawed at my joints and built nests in the cavities of my lungs and belly. I birthed a thousand mice and more; fleas and ants. I felt life moving restlessly within my armature, but it was always at a second remove. I watched the windows of the house crack, one by one, in the storms and snows. Later, vagrants hurled rocks through them and ransacked the rooms for food and linen, then the hidden silver, later for wood to burn, for the more solid pieces of furniture, which they carried away on improvised carts. Someone removed my lower left arm and hand, after they fell to the floor, someone else took my skirts, thinking me an elaborate but decayed dressmaker's dummy.

I was lonely for a while, but that soon passed. It is hard to say what it was replaced with. There were months of anger, of boredom, of philosophy, of a pale whitewashed silence. I learned not to count the days and nights; what use would it have been? I did not think of the future.

Death had come year after year and taken everything from me; Tomas and Eloise, Elisabetta, Hervé, Hélène and Beatrice, Guilhabert, Margery and little Gauzia. Gauzia! I had been charged the keeper of the Reni children. I was made to care for them and keep them, and I had failed.

The house itself was dying. The roof of composted thatch, which had once been rich with moss and grass, began to thin and fall. The sparrows and starlings that had nested within it flew away. The windows were broken and rotted, fogged green with algae, patterned by snails. Their shutters sagged and rotted. The house's beams curved without anyone to patch the wattle and daub walls, baked by the sun and cratered by nesting mason bees. Ivy grew through the walls. The floor, once compacted and well-swept, grew soft and dusty, then strewn with leaves. Grass grew up, then shrubs, then trees, sprouting through the open beams towards the sky. The fireplace filled with snow and leaves and mouse droppings. Soon, the house was nothing but a skeletal framework of oak, ash and chestnut.

Exposed to the weather, and to time without care, my body rotted away; first the dress, which the mice chewed at, then the leather joints, the thin, willowwood frets that had supported my skirts. The scaffolding of my torso stayed firm, but the joints rusted until I could not have moved even if I had had the strength to do so. Snow settled inside me, and melted away, bowing my bones. Autumn dust, spring pollen, summer's weight of heat and light beat down upon me, through me. I looked endlessly towards the window where the apple tree bloomed and faded, bloomed and faded, year after year.

I had achieved a kind of quiet stasis; I was not alive and so, I believed, I had expired. I remembered the conversations with Eloise before Elisabetta's birth; her explanations of the mind of God and how, sometimes, she had dreamed we were all spangles in his starred imagination, glowing and burning and fading away. Was this death, then? After the rush and tumble of my life with the Reni women this was emptiness itself. No children, no laughter, no gossip or prayer, no planting or harvesting, no festivals or birthdays or marriages or arguments, no coppicing and cropping and harvesting of seeds stoppered up in ceramic jars along the kitchen shelves. There were just the empty rooms and the apple branch with its white blossoms and pale, crisp leaves, its small fruit that grew green and heavy and ripe before they each dropped out of sight to rot in the summer grass.

Henri's Story: Part Two

In my second year, the pile of reading and writing I had to complete swelled and multiplied, I stayed later and later in Ahkronova's room, where I could study undistracted, spreading my papers out on her desk to work. I would carry my books up there, with the little bird in my pocket for company. I would settle it on the windowsill, in its evolving nest, so that it could watch the world, and chatter to the real birds that came to gossip with it in the afternoons.

Whenever I looked up—when it caught my attention by hopping about or bursting into its strange song—I could see the quad and the orchard, the steps of the library and, almost hidden by the corner of another building, the doors of Oban College. From up there I could see almost my entire newly-discovered world: its key players, its major continents spread out below. From the third floor I could watch them pass as keenly as Lara had once watched the stars.

It always called out when it saw Miri below us, as though it knew I was watching for her. I did not always go down to meet Miri as soon as we spotted her in the orchard or emerging from the library. I did not want her to know how avidly I watched for her. I knew her timetable of lunch in the orchard with the students, afternoons in the library studying or daydreaming, wandering the shelves like a diviner, seeking something she could not name. Sometimes she emerged from the library with pencils twisted into her hair, holding it in place. Other times with piles of books and papers, or empty-armed and looking glazed. The sun and light like a shock when she pushed out through the heavy doors.

When I saw her walk out into the light amid a small group of students, I re-arranged Sister Ahkronova's belongings on the desk and

58

closed the window, piled my notes up, slid my study materials into my satchel, placed the little bird in my pocket, and picked up the box I had set down by the door: another in the long line of boxes that had become my Sisyphean task. Another box of recipes and knitting patterns that had once belonged to the Salt Lane women.

She was gone by the time I reached the ground floor and stumbled down the stairs onto the quad, but I had seen where she was headed and followed a small stream of students headed towards one of the older teaching buildings. I went along a tiled corridor and entered a dim hall with low roof beams and a Haven smell of wood polish and dustlessness through which rose a low hum of echoing voices. As my eyes adjusted, the first person I saw was Miri, standing by a door talking to a student holding a stack of pamphlets. She wore a white cotton shirt that was buttoned down the front and a wide, dark belt that emphasised the neatness of her body. Hers was a strange face: there was a sense of incomplete beauty to it. It was strongly sculpted, as if the bones beneath her skin were heavy, smooth and luminescent as marble. The light in that space made her face resemble that of a statue, carved and resolute and hard to read. I was walking towards her with no sense of what I would say.

When I was near enough she took a pamphlet from her friend's pile and held it out to me. 'It's all about the Oikos Descendants,' she said.

Heretics, I thought, feeling a terrible wrench of disappointment. Could she really be one of them? I recalled Jenon's eloquent frustration when the Haven released news that yet another Council was to discuss the rights of the remnant Oikos settlements. He had railed, with firm and dark-eyed certitude, insisting that the Wynder was a fool to bow her head to negotiation when a firm and powerful strike was what was needed. The Oikos had no rights under Rupettan Law. Despite Her agreement to allow them their foolishness, another pointless month of peace-mongering speeches and referendums would only reveal even more clearly the shameful, heretical pathos of the Oikos, who sang up the circle before Council as though spirits still walked between the worlds. Fools and mystics, he said, were the only

59

people left in the old settlements, in Land Between, and they had no need to retain ownership of the land. They made no human, civilising use of its resources. Reclamation of the entire Territory—here he smiled and mocked an apology towards us: *I mean, of course, rematriation*—will proceed without any flesh-hearted weakening of the Law.

As I took the flyer from her, awkwardly balancing the box under one arm, Miri's finger touched the inside of my wrist. Lingering there for a moment, as though taking my measure.

'Thank you,' I said, ducking my head to examine the sketch of an Oikos woman on the flyer's cover. A woman in profile, her silhouette an echo of the landscape behind her. The mountains were sheer and familiar: the forms that had dotted the horizon of my childhood, sleeved with forest so old and deep that, as a child, I had believed they were peopled by ghosts and dryads and giants. At night, I huddled in my bed with the sheets pulled over my head, listening to them wail, their cries like wire threading through my veins.

℘

During my second year at Oban College I lived in a dream. My deepening awareness of the complexities of History were bound together with a growing sense of the silences within Miri; the huge white rooms and dustless wooden floors of the Oban College, which seemed endlessly internal and expanding; the green air of the orchard breathing into the kitchen at Elm; the seedling trays spread out on the tables in the greenhouses: tender pink beetroot seedlings, thick sunflower stems, and the tendrilled, childlike snowpeas.

I sat at the table in the kitchen at Elm, a batch of newly-transplanted seedlings glistening damply in their trays at one end, ready to go out to the garden. The smells of soil and compost mixed with those of the warm tea and cool bricks, the shuttered, milky light that pressed in through the windows. The kitchen door opened into the corridor and I could see through it, across the wide passage, through another door into the glasshouse, where Miri was working. I was supposed to be reading, but all I could do was watch her bare arms, her hair pulled back from her face, her straight back, the way her skirt swung across her firm, tanned calves as she moved. Occasionally, she would frown and lean forward over a graft, fingering the join, imagining an imperfection and correcting it with studied, careful attention. She was oblivious to me. She had the gift of complete concentration. Hours might go by in which she moved in and out of my line of sight, carrying plants, bedding in seeds, transplanting orchids from one pot to another, staking them, splicing their roots, sketching their fragile blooms. Each time she came into my view she would look the same, and different. Some small thing may have changed: a lock of hair untangling itself to spool down her cheek; a graze of dirt on her cheek; a loop of string around her wrist. Finally, as a kind of unspoken reward for my patience, she might remember I was there and turn, smile, and just as quickly turn away.

Late in the afternoon, as the heat began to break up and the air unbuttoned itself in preparation for the greater release of an afternoon storm, she would wash her hands, take off her oilcloth apron and push her hands through her hair to untangle it a little. Then we would walk together, through the orchard to the tea rooms.

She asked about my home, about my family. I talked to her about my plans. How the week before I had delivered a talk for Jenon's discussion group, and he had clearly been impressed. How he had told me I had a future as an Obanite, and must keep going, must work extremely hard, to bring that future into being. He said I should focus my studies, concentrate on a specific time or place, even select a partic-ular movement, as he had during his undergraduate years, through which to channel the perfection of his skills. I told her there was no other life I wanted or could even imagine, that I could not bear to waste away like my father in a small school in a small town, looking up one day to see the children's children of my former students seated at the desks before me.

At Oban College, the work was so intense, the demands on my time and concentration enormous, the History we learned so complex, that every time I sat down to work, or went to a lecture or participated—however glancingly—in a discussion, I discovered something new. I told her how I sensed the world shimmering, shifting and re-forming itself around me with each new insight. How each day I left behind the falseness and naïveté of childhood fantasies for the reality of the world. I had thought History was the study of facts, but learned that while the Historian without facts was rootless and futile; the facts without Historians were dead, meaningless. I learned that my obligation as a Historian, the essential crux of my work, would be not to uncover facts and record them, that that was the mere edge of Historical research, but that a true Historian—a mature Obanite—was embroiled in the work of evaluation, interpretation. History was an artform—the delicate, dangerous art of creating the past.

I said all this knowing History meant nothing to her. As far as she was concerned it was a dull occupation far removed from the urgency of the present: History, she claimed, was a meaningless parade of names and dates and places she had not the temperament to recall or care about when the present, and the future, were massed before her. It was rooms full of thick tomes and portentous proclamations meant to signify seriousness and respect, but entirely devoid of the stuff of real life. Of doubt and chance and wind and laughter. Nevertheless, I believed her reaction to my talk of the Salt Lane Witches and my biography paper on Emmeline Salt—her sharp turn towards me, her rapid-fire questions, her leaning forward and touching my arm—were a breakthrough. I spoke to her about the reciprocity between the past and the present; how Jenon had spoken of the way the Historian, drifting in the ever-moving current of the present, was always tied to the anchor of the past.

I invited her to sit in on a lecture with me. Hear the way Jenon made History live, made it sing. I understood—of course—that my own feeble understanding of the craft was not enough to enchant her, but Jenon's depth of understanding, his passion and clarity, might. He had a way of speaking: of drawing you into a close examination of the world, close and closer, until you saw what it was really made of, how its pieces fit together, supporting and deforming each other in equal measure, where before you had only ever seen the surface of things. When he spoke of the Rupettan Miracles, you could almost see the house in which Rupetta was made, smell the pounded-earth floor, the shuttered windows, the apple-blossom at the window. You could see Eloise's hand tremble as she opened the chamber for the first time and inserted her hand. When he spoke of the Age of the Consort, you could hear the snow fall at Rūs, hear the shouts ring through the old palaces, hear the squeak of the Wynder's un-booted feet in the snow as she fled the hunters, feel the shots plunk into the chests of the heretics and see them, feel them, stumble and fall.

When he spoke—his voice an earnest insistence that was musical, operatic—you could feel the despair of the old Wynder when the empire fell, see her head sink, her shoulders slump. Feel her tears prick at your own eyes as she sat by a window in her darkened rooms, watching the city burn.

We found a seat at the side of the lecture hall, with a clear view of the podium and the lectern, and watched the other students file in, singly and in groups, and array themselves around the room, opening out their notepads, sharpening pencils. Miri pointed out some of them: the first years who had already taken to wearing their hair shorn, the cluster of third years whose shirts were unbuttoned to reveal the clockwork hearts tattooed on their breasts, where they hoped the real thing might one day shine.

When Jenon entered there was a quickening of the air, a sudden ruffling of papers as though a breeze had entered the hall with him, and then a fall of silence. We held our breath: in that counted silence heard the way his footsteps kept time with his heart as he walked. Miri, too, seemed to feel the electrified anticipation in the room. Her body tensed beside mine, one hand fisted in her lap. Jenon put his hand on the lectern. In that moment before he began speaking, I had a flash of a future I had not even known I dreamed of. Of holding Miri, of marriage and family, of a daughter sitting between us at a kitchen table strewn with seeds and books, Miri leaning forward over our daughter's shoulder to read her homework, smiling at me over our daughter's head. Of sunlight spilling in through an open window. The little girl would have her mother's beauty and stillness, her lovely straight back, and delicate hands, and a mix of our intellectual passions: a love of History and of Botany, stories and seeds.

At last Jenon began speaking. My momentary vision slipped and I blushed, realising for the first time what I wanted, what I dreamed of, and afraid that some fragment of my foolishness had escaped the confines of my imagination. I could not bear to look at Miri and see kindness arranged upon her face; the gentle, friendly distance with which she would greet any such revelation.

Jenon adjusted the glasses on his nose and spread his hands flat on the lectern in front of him, studying the space between his hands. This is how he always started. A moment of remove during which he appeared to sink some thread of inquiry deep into his consciousness and draw up the great wisdom he then delivered. The lecture was on methodology and he began by speaking about the tension between the historian and her material, the ways in which truth flickers in the darkness, how it is not always implicit and self-evident, but must be discovered.

Jenon frowned up at the tiered rows of students—so many young people, slouched in their seats, distracted and disorderly—who were we to presume we would have the strength of heart to be Historians in his mould? I felt the weight of the geis that was laid on each of us who aimed to be Transformed, the enormity of it. Saw the blush reach the neck and ears of the student in front of me as Jenon's eyes settled on him.

'It does not follow, however,' Jenon said, his eyes rising a little higher, finding me, burrowing into mine, 'that because interpretation is necessary any interpretation is as good as any other. Let me illuminate this discussion with an example: in 1959, the Penitent Kamila died. She left behind an enormous archive of papers: official, semi-official and private, nearly all relating to the forty years of Kamila's tenure of office in the Haven. Her secretary—a faithful, young amateur historian

—spent three years preparing the papers for publication. Four volumes were published, each of which were over 600 pages long. Reading these volumes, one is struck by the successes of Kamila's time in office, the energy with which she pursued certain objectives, which she eventually—certainly—achieved. The repatriation of the Oikos Island heretics, for example, for which she is well known. Some years later another, abbreviated, edition of the *Complete Life of Kamila* was published. 350 pages in all: a not insubstantial work, but a mere drop in the 2400-and-some pages of the original publication. And yet, in going back to the source, one discovers strange elisions, omissions.

'Kamila's biographer was careful in selecting what to include and exclude from the record. The biographer's working notes begin, as do all Historian's notes, with a careful and painstaking analysis of the ways in which the fragile human Kamila's recollections and records depart from the perfect truth of the Rupettan Annal. This is all well and good, and quite forensically done. However, one discovers a curious pattern in the biographer's movement between this initial comprehensive analysis and the *Complete Life*. Kamila's life-long battle to be returned to the north, for example, is discussed in the four volumes only in two places: once in passing during a record of a conversation about funding for the Haven's Festival of the Beautiful, and once many years later, in a footnote, in which the Historian records that Kamila journeyed to Europe for one summer, but "was returned". A curious phrase, that: *was returned*. What one discovers, in going back to the sources, is that in fact Kamila led a long and drawn-out battle to be allowed to return to the Haven near her family's home in Europe, and that time and again this desire influenced her in ways that are not apparent in the *Complete Life*, nor in its more modest edited version. Kamila took a post as an Assistant at the Haven. She worked there, interrogating heretics, because she had been promised that if she did so, she would be allowed to "return" as she always phrased it. Other, contemporary records indicate that Kamila was, in fact, one of the more diligent Assistants. Many heretics died under her hand, and many more simply disappeared from the record. The Salt Lane sister, Mathilde, was one of her charges, and the circumstances surrounding her disappearance from the Haven—as we canvassed in last week's discussions—remain a mystery. None of this occurs in the *Complete Life,* not because the historian did not know of it, but because in selecting the material to include, they have chosen to emphasise the successes of her career: the moderation and kindness of Kamila's late life, her work with the Fallen Penitents and so on.

'*Why?* one is prompted to ask. The work of the Assistants is a matter of public record. The matter of the Assistants who took it upon themselves to interpret the law of the Consort in such violent, bodily terms, too—to enact torture on their charges—is also well documented. A clue lies, perhaps, in the character of this particular Historian, and in the nature of much of Kamila's archive.

'Kamila made transcriptions of each significant conversation she had, recording them in detail. In some of these conversations, Kamila records that she was instructed to exercise physical torture on her victims. That she was, in fact, called to do so by the senior Penitents of the Haven, and on one occasion by the Consort himself. In these transcriptions—as in the vast majority of Kamila's dialogic transcriptions— Kamila herself appears to speak cogently, fluently, with much passion and intellect and clarity, against such violence. In comparison, even the Consort appears to speak in a scanty, confused and unconvincing manner—at times he even appears like a malign figure in a fairytale: senseless and confused with power, insisting on ever crueller punishments. The transcriptions are not unusual: in your work you will often find that an individual's memory of their own actions and thoughts is far more complex, complete and self-flattering than their recall of almost any other person they encounter. That some of the transcriptions record false memories we know, from comparison with the Rupettan Annal, which is of course infallible. How to reconcile these competing texts?

'Kamila's historian took the weaker path—he left out of the *Complete Life* anything that even incidentally contradicted the Rupettan Annal. The Historian who worked on Kamila's *Complete Life* was incapable of weighing up the divergent accounts, incapable of discerning between the self-serving narcissism of the subject, and the truth and clarity of the Annal. And why might this be so? Because they were untrained? Because they were weak-hearted? Because they were merely human and perhaps a little in awe of their subject, wishing to present the respected and great Penitent Kamila in a glowing light? Perhaps because they were full of ego and ambition: anxious to complete a work that the Haven might approve rather than filled with the courage of a true Historian? Ambitious, perhaps; too concerned with worldly success, and not concerned enough with truth and History. And so they have produced not a true historical account, which explores the character of its subject with empathy—not the weak hand of sympathy—and clarity, but a hagiography.'

Jenon paused again, looked up, smiled a little and seemed, for a moment, a man of warmth, slightly chagrined. For a moment, I glimpsed in him the boy he had been. 'I was weak,' he said, 'I was—and remain —merely human.'

Later, as we walked home, Miri told me she had been moved by Jenon's lecture, and even quoted bits of it back to me. Her voice mimicked his—the lilting rise and fall—and I was amazed at her ability to recall his turn of phrase so precisely, but her interpretation was edged with some other certainty that was purely her own. She spoke of the snow in the north: of the blueness of it. She spoke of the centuries Rupetta had lived, and the losses she had seen. She wondered aloud whether the cities of the north still housed the ghosts of those who had died. Whether the ghosts of the old Wynders and their daughters still wandered the streets, their bodies like thickened drifts of snow.

In return for taking her into Oban College, and introducing her to Jenon, Miri took me deeper into the brick-floored spaces of Elm College, into the glasshouse, where the orchids bloomed and the ferns held out their frail palms in the green, heated air. I followed, watching her fingers trail along the worn wooden benches, curving her palm beneath half-open blooms as though they were the chins of small, beloved children. I spoke about the first Botanists at Elm, about the seeds they had carried across the ocean, stitched into the hems of the first settlers' clothes, or embedded in sheets of hand-pressed paper. I told her about the manifests of the Oikos ships I had seen in the stacks: the long lists of seeds the Oikos had brought with them. Of Tom Witley and Hannah Gorn, who founded the first Botanic Garden in the Territory, and the first Oikos settlement, and planted out groves of saplings knowing full well they would never live to see them reach maturity. Now they tower, those trees, over the heads of those who walk through the gardens. Though the settlement that once surrounded it is gone, of course, was razed with the others during the Obanites' re-settlement of the Territory.

She showed me the underside of a fern-leaf that was furred and dark, and another plant whose thick leaves formed a kind of throat through which it swallowed water and compost. A tray of seedlings, some of which were only just extending the curves of their green necks, pushing up through the soil.

෨

I lay awake in the stacks, feeling the creases pressed onto my cheek from Autolycus's yellowed pages. The night was taut and watchful. All over the campus students were restless, as I was. In room after room after room they lay waiting, or sat at their desks reading, cramming their heads with quotes and dates and names, counting the hours until their next exam. In the carrels they were largely silent, or gossiped in thin, hurried voices about the exam questions: so-and-so had seen them, a junior tutor was charging a fee for inside information, there was a rumour that some of the questions from two years ago were being re-used. In even more hushed voices, some of the students shared strategies for doing well, whatever the exams contained. Notes written up in code on the inside of their clothes, on their wrists and shins. One student was said to have engraved the whole of the Rupettan Annal on a grain of rice and had a special monocle embedded in his eye for reading it: his vision now that of an ant in the body of a giant. There was a frantic trade in pills—for staying awake, for improving memory retention—and in the beetle-like implants: small, clockwork creatures that would burrow into your skin and change you—make you capable of recalling everything you had ever heard or read. Or, at least, that was what they were supposed to do. I was offered one once, late at night in the library. It was roughly the size of a plum. Just small enough to fit in the closed palm of a hand.

Towards the end of my second year, during the final weeks when exam pressure was highest, six students were arrested for dealing on campus, and two were taken to the Haven for treatment after falling ill. Five simply disappeared; their rooms were discovered empty by a friend one Thursday morning. Each of their rooms was left eerily alike: the doors unlocked, the beds stripped and the sheets folded on the mattresses, the curtains drawn, their books piled up in the centre of the room, ready to be returned.

Up on the roof of Oban College, the second and third year students kept themselves awake watching the moon and the stars, pointing out the constellations and competing in all-night games of Oråki during which the stories turned and turned again on points of Historic record. The more well-schooled students—the show-offs—engaged in a game of verbal Oråki, during which two players sat with their backs turned to the board, playing the game purely from memory. None of us spoke about who would and would not be offered Transformation, only about the weather, the stars, the game. The weather was hot, and the third year students wore their shirts unbuttoned. In a corner, one student painted purple, silver and green hearts onto their friends' chests with the same paint they had used to decorate children's faces at the markets each Saturday.

The Penitents grew distant and secretive, holed up in their rooms conducting interviews with prospective Obanites, overseeing the end-less exams, preparing new hearts for the Transformations. The windows of Oban College stayed lit up all night as the Penitents worked to complete their tasks before the Festival of the Heart.

One morning, I passed Jenon leaving the Haven, headed back towards Oban College with a small, timber box. He waved me over and I went over to him. He asked me where I was going, and offered to walk back to the College with me. When we reached the College doors he smiled and offered to show me his cargo, as he called it. He held the box in front of him and slid back the lid. I peered into the box, like a child sharing a vision of stolen chocolate. As I leant forward Jenon folded back the protective layer of oiled cotton and I saw the polished, finely-etched surface of two hearts, like mice, lying in their nests. He took one out of the box and put it in my hand. The white cloth fell open around it like the petals of a wide-open bloom. I felt the heavy thing twitch and shift. Saw the bright silver hooks with which it was embedded in the cavity of an Oban's chest. The open valves of the heart, like open mouths, were hungry and sharp-toothed. It smelled of oil, and of blood.

Nausea overcame me; the known world shuddered and I was thrown clear.

When I returned to the square, to the solid earth beneath my feet and Jenon peering into my face with a look that was not quite concerned, it was the first thing I knew, the first thing I could feel and hold: this horror. This heated, heavy heart, beating in my hand.

And then there was Miri. The nights were growing cool, but whenever I thought of Miri a different kind of heat washed over my skin. Flushing up through my gut to flood my chest and arms and face. I forced my mind back to Jenon, to that look of curiosity on his face when I turned pale at the sight of the Penitent heart, to the exams I had yet to sit and the ones I had already struggled through, to the oral I was scheduled to deliver in five days, the panel of Penitents who would question me during my viva voce before I would be approved for final year. I could not shake the sense that every action I made now had a consequence out of all proportion to the smallness of the actions themselves. Turning over, opening a door, reading a sentence. Saying a word. These things would tumble me. Make me.

The nights were warm, heady with the scent of the last fruits dropping at the feet of the trees. The warmth sank into the stacks and lingered in the heated, musty aisles. Even the little bird seemed affected. It would doze on my desk as though stultified by the heat, but then chirrup and bounce in my pocket when we snuck out into the night-cooled orchard. These were the last nights of summer, being thrown away. Night stepped out each evening, confident and lean, lengthening its stride. And each morning the rim of cold extended its reach, pressing its fingers into the cracks between the bricks and windows of the buildings. Each morning the sun took a little longer to rise. The heat of the sun felt shallower, less sincere. The summer herbs ran to seed, sap dwindling into the stems of trees and flowers. Everything pulled down into itself. Summer flags still hung in the quadrangle, but the ropes and metal fixings clattered less cheerily against the poles and the bright silks were faded. It was time to lower the bright greens and yellows of summer, those hopeful, bright shades, roll them up and store them away.

When one of the graduate students fell ill following her Transformation, Jenon offered me extra work, temporary and part-time, working in the gardens at his home. It didn't matter how many hours a week I worked, or when, as long as the garden bloomed. I liked to leave the stacks in the early morning, before the library opened, and cycle through the sleeping Colleges to Jenon's home. Early morning was best: cool, and private, with all the scholars and students still asleep in their beds. Some mornings, if it was particularly quiet, I would perch the little bird on my handlebars, and it would warble its pretty morning song as we rode through the dew-wet streets.

When I arrived at Jenon's house, I leant the cycle up against the garden shed and walked along the shaded paths as though I owned them. As though the old house, with its deep, shaded verandahs, had become my home. I cut the grass, pruned the hedges and swept the paths, weeding the gravel drive and planting out fresh beds of thyme along the kitchen wall.

Late one morning, as I was preparing to leave—headed back to the stacks to study—I lifted my cycle from where it leant against the garden shed and turned it to face the street to see Miri, waiting for me in the shadow of the trees across the road. She knew my hours, and had walked to Jenon's home with a book in her hand and a couple of apples in her pockets. For an hour, at least, she had watched me as I watered and weeded, as I stooped to admire a green frog perched on the edge of the pond, spoke to the old trees, wiped the dust from the potted palms on the verandah, sat on the back step to drink a glass of water and admire the clean sweep of the path that leads from the gate to the house.

It was one of those moments that is hard to describe, later, with any sense of the weight it carried at the time. That she had walked, and waited for me, and watched me all that time. How afterwards we ambled up the avenue where many of the old Penitent scholars lived, where the shadows the trees cast were so deep they appeared heavier than the open spaces filled with light, and though we didn't hold hands and nothing was said, it is that afternoon that marks a shift in our relationship.

We saw an Eastern Yellow Robin perched sideways on a tree, peering at us, and then a spangled drongo flashed past. I felt the little bird tumble sympathetically in my pocket and cupped my hand around it, sure I felt it curl itself into me and hum. Miri smiled at the red-browed finches that flitted nervously past, and told me how much she liked birds, admired the fetch and lightness of their being.

She was buoyed up by the beauty of the walk she had taken, not across the campus proper, the paved paths and landscaped gardens, but veering away and taking the old farmer's track along the creek, past the picturesquely ruined fences. As she described everything she'd seen, I pictured her walking towards me, distracted but purposeful. The warmth of the light on her face and hair, the weight of the two apples in her pockets, bumping against her thighs.

At the end of the avenue there was a house where a child had left its tricycle on the lawn. The tricycle was blue and yellow and had a wooden trailer. A doll and a stuffed toy sat in the trailer, along with a furled child's umbrella and a drink bottle. The doll's head was half-shaved and the stuffed toy—a grey, shapeless thing—wore a baby's bonnet. As we approached the house, I imagined us turning in at the gate, saw the little girl—our imaginary daughter with the dark hair, serious eyes and straight back—run across the lawn to greet us, clasping its arms around Miri's knees and taking as its due the crown of wildflowers Miri had made during her walk. She stood between us, took both our hands, then let go and tore ahead, danced across the lawn of our home. Her arms like tangled white stalks, tossed in the wind above her head.

We walked to Elm with the light slipping over our shoulders, shimmering in Miri's hair as though caught in it like dew. I could smell the fresh cotton of her shirt, and feel the tickle of her hair when she leaned close to whisper to me and it blew against my throat. When we rounded the last corner and could see Elm, she smiled and struck off across the quad. 'Come on,' she called over her shoulder, 'we'll be late.' She broke into a run, her shirt coming untucked and flapping behind her as she ran, the heels of her shoes dark commas flicking up in her wake.

'Miri!' I called. 'Wait.' But she was gone, sprinting across the forecourt to the low fence that ringed the orchard, jumping over it in the neat, unselfconscious way of horses and children. Her body a tucked, precise thing. She raised one hand in a wave and disappeared between the lime trees, plucking a leaf as she passed.

When I reached the back door of the College—its wide green barn doors flung open to receive the warmth of the late summer light—Miri was already preparing lunch in the kitchen while Professor Margause stood at the butler's sink by the back door, washing the dirt from her hands. She glanced at me. Though I knew who she was, and had watched her working in the orchard and the greenhouse, seen her sitting by the back door of the college with Miri, we had never met.

'Miri,' she said. 'Someone for you, I think.'

'This is Henriette,' Miri said. 'Remember: I told you she was coming today.'

'You're the one, then,' Margause said, rinsing her hands once more and drying them on her skirt before she turned to face me. 'The Henri who's been sleeping in the stacks.'

Miri grinned at me from the other side of the table as she set out cups, jug, and spoons. 'Sleeping with History,' Miri said, and Margause laughed.

'You won't get much comfort there.'

'Penitent Jenon got me some work sorting through the donated material that's been left unsorted in the library basement. There are boxes of the stuff and I was working late, folioing some documents.' It wasn't quite a lie: I had proposed doing such a project, next year, and Jenon had supported my application as part of my professional development requirements for graduation.

'Abel Jenon? You'll lose your scholarship altogether if he finds out you've been sleeping in his precious library.'

'I only fell asleep once.'

'Where have you been sleeping then?'

I hesitated. I had no wish to lie but could not bear to say the truth out loud, not in the company of these women, whose ease with each other and their place in the world must come—I thought then—from certainty. 'My scholarship only covers tuition. There's an allowance for books and study materials but it's paid in vouchers. I do have some work, but it's only just enough for the extra books—'

'I see,' said Margause, holding up her hand to stop the flood of my explanations. 'Sit down. I doubt they serve many meals in the stacks.'

After lunch, Margause slipped away while Miri and I went to the library and retrieved the handful of belongings I had ferreted away: my lamp and blanket, some letters from home, filed away in a biscuit tin Old Paul had sent, some clothes and papers, and the Historian's toolkit I was putting together, piece by piece, with the money I earned working for Jenon: brushes and inks, a series of magnifying glasses, packets of acid-free paper, tweezers, pliers, screwdrivers, oil and cleaning fluid. As well as my small and well-thumbed shelf-load of books. By the time we returned, Margause had made up a bed in the glasshouse, amid the fragrant whispers of orchids and ferns. She commandeered two students to help her carry an old desk down from one of the storerooms.

That night, for the first time, I slept amid the rich, loamy boxes of earth and seeds and ferns, with thin sheets of glass between me and the night sky, listening to the panes rattle during the late summer storms. When I woke from my unaccustomed bed and went out to the kitchen for a glass of water, I looked out the window and saw Miri in the citrus grove, a thin white dressing gown wrapped around her shoulders. Where before, from my eyrie in Ahkranova's room, I had seen her from above, now I was on the ground, far closer. I could see her bare feet. And, sometimes, when she turned, I could see her face. Night after night I stood in the kitchen and watched as Miri stood beneath the lemon trees, fingering the sharp spines on their trunks, as pale and distant as a ghost.

A few weeks after that first night I borrowed the ladder from Jenon's garden shed to climb up to the roof and repair the panes that had cracked or come loose in their settings, oil the louvres and repair their mechanisms so I could let in the breezes.

Soon, I had become a part of the small community at Elm College. When there were no classes for me to attend, or exams to study for, I could always be found somewhere in the College or its grounds, repairing a tread in the stairs, clearing a gutter, painting a wall. My hands, unlike those of my fellow Obanite students, grew as calloused and work-worn as those of my father, tinged with the black earth I worked with each evening. I took great pains to scrub the soil from beneath my fingernails each night, but the stain soon settled in my skin and there was little I could do to conceal it save keep my hands in my pockets or hidden beneath the pages of my books whenever I was at Oban. If Jenon noticed it at all he probably thought it a result of the work I did in his own garden.

At first, I assumed Margause was Miri's relative, or a friend of her family. In the face of Miri's silence about their connection, and her place at Elm, I saw no real harm in using what few research skills I had in seeking out their shared history. I began to listen to the stories the Botany students told in the corridors of Elm, and to seek out others. I pored over old pictures of the College and its students in the student newspapers and magazines I could find in the stacks: pictures of the orchard and greenhouse, the seed-raising sheds and dorms, hoping for a glimpse of either of them. In one, from three years ago, I thought I could make out Margause, caught in the background of a shot of the women's hockey team as she walked across the quad. It was hard to tell whether it was really her, even when I had the picture enlarged: her head was down and she was wearing a wide-brimmed hat that hid most of her face. There was a handful of photographs of a woman who might have been Miri, but they were too old. The photographs dating from at least fifty years before I came to Elm; well before she was born. Perhaps, like me, she had followed in her mother's footsteps in coming here. Fifty years ago, Elm College had been a hotbed of heresy: there had been riots at the College, and arrests. Students had disappeared and two of the old Elm scholars had been taken in to custody. One after secreting a bomb in the offices of the Repatriation Office, and another for storing Oikos pamphlets in the greenhouse. If her mother had been a heretic, it would at least explain her secrecy.

Most of the students at Elm believed Miri was Margause's unacknowledged love-child—the result of a long-hidden affair between Margause and one of the Penitents, probably Scrivner, from Meridies College: a cellist with whom she sometimes went to the theatre and enjoyed long, ambling and liberally wine-laced conversations.

One of the junior academics at Meridies College told me Miri had arrived in the middle of the orchard during a storm, late at night, wearing nothing but a blue ribbon tied around her wrist. A librarian whispered during her morning break that Miri had been discovered hidden in the stacks, wrapped in an old map of Southern Europe. Yet another story circulated that she was a fallen Penitent whose clockwork heart refused to stop beating, though it had not been wound for several years. One of my fellow History students told me Miri was almost certainly a murderess, Margause her faithful maid. He showed me a newsclipping about a young woman who was still sought in relation to a young man's death, in suspicious circumstances, in some obscure European country. The artist's sketch of the suspect bore only a passing resemblance to Miri—the same colour hair and eyes—but her face was markedly different. Some told me she was a runaway from a clique of Oikos. A changeling. An orphan. I wrote all of the stories down—each detail—in a special notebook I kept tucked beneath the little bird's nest in the greenhouse. The bird appointed itself guardian of my notebook. Once, on returning to the greenhouse, I discovered it perched, rather agitated, behind a long potting bench laden with stacks of empty pots. It had dragged my notebook there, and scratched loose soil onto it from a nearby potted palm. When I bent to retrieve my book, pushing a stack of pots out of the way, it chirruped at me as though irritated.

I put the book back where it had been: in the little nest of felt and bright paper where my small companion rested. Every morning, when I left the glasshouse, the notebook was there, and every evening when I returned the little bird had moved it again. After a week, I gave up and moved both the nest and the notebook to the bird's new hiding place behind the empty pots.

Late in the evening, while Margause was in her room grading papers or sketching the leaves of a newly-cultivated cycad, Miri would come to the glasshouse to spend time with me. We would sit in the soft, faded cane chairs drinking wine, reading or studying, tending the orchids. She would test me on my ancient languages, on dates and names. Ask me to give proofs for various Historical arguments. Later, we would sneak out and steal sweets from the kitchen and return to lie on the bed together, pointing through the panes of the ceiling to the constellations.

'There's the Sorrowing Weaver,' Miri pointed out one night. 'See? That bright star, there, and the trail of smaller ones are her footsteps. It must be terrible to be stranded on her side of the Milky Way, forever cut off from her home. From her love.'

'Perhaps she should become a boat-builder instead of a weaver. Then she could sail home.'

'It's not that easy. She has to wait.'

'As many years as there are stars. My father taught me about the stars, when he taught me to play Oråki. He said if the story were true the Weaver should always lose, since she would never be able to go home: new stars are always being born.'

I could feel the warmth of our bodies stretched out side by side, the electric tension of our hands almost—but not quite—touching. When she shifted to look at another star I felt the back of her hand rest against mine. She lay so still, so quiet, she hardly seemed to breathe.

'Where did you learn that story?' I asked.

Miri shrugged, shifting her head to look at another part of the sky.

'From your mother? From Margause?'

'Do you know his story: the old man with the fish in his beard?'

'Someone told me today that you're in hiding here. You and Margause. That the Rupettans offered you new lives—new identities—to give evidence against an Oikos community.'

'I can't believe you listen to those stories.'

'I know hardly anything about you, Miri. Nobody does.'

Miri sat upright in the bed, drawing her knees against her chest and wrapping her arms around her shins. 'I don't know that much about you, either. It doesn't mean we're strangers. It certainly doesn't mean I'd listen to nasty rumours about you or go digging around, looking for evidence that I'm some kind of fugitive.'

'You don't need to go looking,' I said. 'I'll tell you anything you want to know. Not that there's much to tell.' I rolled onto my side, away from her, and let my feet drop to the floor. I sat with my back to Miri, feeling the warmth of her presence, the tension of our silence. I wanted to turn and put my hands on hers, draw her into my arms, but instead I waited, and said nothing.

'Please,' Miri said. 'Don't ask me about my past.'

'I can keep a secret. Forever, if I have to.' Keeping my back turned away so she could not see my face, I leant forward and pulled my boots onto my feet. I needed to allow her her silences. I needed her to know they didn't matter to me; I would inhabit them with her, for her, if she would only let me.

℘

The academic year had ended and most of the other students had gone home. Margause and Miri spent the long days wilting in the shaded cloisters of the orchard, sipping iced tea and reading from books whose covers promised worlds full of gold-toothed buccaneers, buxom maidens, exotic islands and pistoleiros. My last year loomed: and with it the distant threat of finishing my undergraduate degree, of having to move on to something else. I spent my days studying, and working in the basement of the library. My application had been approved, and while the other students went home, I stayed behind and worked, sorting the boxes I had lived with for so long.

The rows of shelves, long flat map drawers, glass-fronted specimen cabinets and labelled boxes comforted me. I delighted in the old timbered and glass cabinets with their deep, shallow shelves, the objects laid out like a Naturalist's beetles, the tiny labels I wrote on pieces of stiff, white card and pinned to the white display cork. Sometimes, even when I wasn't working, I would go down there and peer into the drawers, opening them one by one to look at the order I was slowly creating out of those damp, broken and disordered remains.

There were great piles of uncatalogued boxes left in the stacks I had been made caretaker of. One collection—donated by the Misses Highes and Poglu—were mostly turn-of-the-century toys, well-loved and therefore beyond repair, collections of lost wheels, one-armed dolls and rudderless hippogriffs. There were also the boxes of Salt Lane materials, where I had discovered the little bird. My companion came down to the stacks with me, and hopped about on top of the timber cabinets, curiously peering into the boxes I opened, or the drawers I was working on. I had set up a small desk down there, on which was a lightbox and a Scholar's lamp. It liked to perch on the lamp's neck and peer down at whatever I was working on, humming and squeaking its approval or concern.

Once, it dipped its beak in my bottle of ink and wrote something on a loose label I had sitting on my desk. I was working on a box of letters from a scholar to his mother: dull stuff, mostly to do with his mother's illness and his own lack of aptitude for study. At first, I thought the bird was merely playing: dipping its beak into the ink, and then half-hopping, half-flying to the desk to scratch at the little cardboard label. I thought it was impersonating me: making fun, almost. When it was done it came closer and hopped onto my hand, gripping onto my thumb. I wiped its beak clean of ink and set it down on the desk.

'I'm working,' I said. 'And you're distracting me.'

The little bird tilted its head and darted forward, hopping onto my hand again and curling its sharp little feet around my thumb. I set it down on the desk. It darted off, retrieved its label and set it down in the middle of my light-box, directly over the section I had been working on.

'Perihan,' I read.

The bird made a trilling noise—warm, and musical. Almost proud.

'Is that you? Is that your name?' I said.

The bird tilted its head at me again, watching me, and sang another few bars of notes: a reward for guessing correctly.

80

At the end of each day of work I would pull out one of the Salt Lane boxes to work on: a treat I looked forward to through all the dust and frustration of boxes of old maps and letters. The other materials I sorted and treated onsite, but the Salt Lane material had become a personal love, almost as intimately-known as the books and papers in the library at Whitestone Shute, though none of the senior Obanites were the least bit interested in my work on Emmeline Salt, except Jenon, whose interest was purely in the clarity and care I had taken in my biography project, and the ways it 'demonstrates a capacity for clear-thinking and thorough Historical research'.

I should have gone home for the summer, that's what my father believed, though he never said so. I had visited, between semesters, for a week, maybe two at a time. It was all I could stand before my father's careful, studied patience with me, with my passion for History, wore away my skin and we fought. While he was working in the garden, or pottering in the kitchen, baking treats I had loved as a child, I wandered the rooms of our old home with fingers twitching over the dusty surfaces, the mirrors of my mother's room still covered in their mourning cloths. Outside, in the garden, her graveyard heart ticked and swooshed, as it had my whole life, an orthodox syncopation marking out the days of my childhood. Soon, there would be another mechanical cabinet; another terrible beat measuring out unlived days. My father was thin and lost, but well-cared-for by our neighbours and his friend from the Haven, Old Paul, who visited daily. He was fine, I told myself, watching his liver-spotted hands tremble as he turned the pages of a book.

The last time I had stayed with him, he walked to the edge of his garden late one afternoon—where the careful growth became wilder and wilder until it slipped away into the bushland—and began to sing. I couldn't understand him, because he was singing in the tongue of the Oikos. A dead language: one my Great Aunt Grace had studied in preparation for her work in the Territories, and one I had learned a few words of during my research on Emmeline Salt. It is a language that sounds as though it is made of stones, each of them hitting water as they are spoken. I leaned on a tree and listened, watched him singing, how his old body was hooked around the song and lifted by it. After a while, he turned and walked back to the house, past the herb patch, where he plucked dead leaves from the elderflower shrubs and knelt to snap a few lengths of lemongrass.

The sun was coming out from behind the clouds. He had forgotten I was there, I think, and wandered in his garden the way he might when alone. He was wearing a faded blue shirt, with a dark singlet underneath. A thicket of grey chest-hair curled at the slooped neck. I could not remember, any more, when it had gone grey. He was wearing glasses, which he had repaired himself and which he constantly took off, frowned at, polished on the hem of his shirt and put back on.

I took his arm so that we could walk back to the house together and he smiled at me and said my name as if I had just arrived and he was both surprised and delighted to see me. There was no end to the kindness in him and I felt small, then, for the months when I had stayed away, and for the resentment with which I left College for home. I wished, then, that he would not die. Not yet. And wondered how I would know who I was when he was gone.

I could not imagine myself without him.

On the way back to the house he talked to me about my mother, about how when she was a little girl she never had a doll or a stuffed toy she cared for, but would take her favourite rocks to bed at night, laying them on her pillow and speaking to them about their lives in the belly of the earth. How in the morning if her mother came into her room to tell her to hurry up and get ready for school, she would be sitting or lying in the middle of the room surrounded by her collection of rocks and seeds and beetles. Not playing, exactly, but silently lifting each one onto her palm and examining them, speaking with them, arranging them on the floor in some pattern that only she understood or found beautiful.

I don't remember the first time he forgot my name. I remember we laughed about it, his fumbling for the right word. Calling me *teacup*, then *spoon*, then *tree* before he finally settled on my name. My father, who had spent his life speaking in careful, measured sentences, whose insistence on finding the right word before speaking had made him seem not fussy, but patient. A man of considered and elegant syntax: a man who spoke like a statesman even when he was teaching the second grade. Later, when the only complete sentences he could speak seemed to be formed in languages nobody else knew, I finally understood how knife-edged his laughter had been that day.

Most terrible was the day when he had grasped my arm, leaned forward in his chair and pronounced each nonsensical syllable with as much care as he could, pressing me to understand, his grip growing tighter and tighter. The urgency in his face, the terror of his loneliness, trapped inside that nonsense language, frightened me. I smiled and nodded as he spoke, trying to find responses that might fit his questions. I garbled polite inanities: *that's nice*, I said, or, *how interesting*. I don't remember. I got up and moved away, ignoring his crestfallen face, his sullen fury. I put on the kettle to make tea and stoked the fire. Anything to skip over my inability to understand. Anything to have him sit and stare at the flames and seem, for a few more moments, to be himself again, to be easy in this world. Or, at least, easy for me to be with.

However sad it is when something dies, it is sadder still when it should and doesn't. At least death is final—you can dig up the corpse and plant something else in its place. There were plants in my father's garden that clearly didn't want to live, but which he had tended so lovingly over the years that they had been kept alive in spite of themselves. He spoke of them as though they were his students: fragile young boys who struggled to fathom the intricacies of long division. Feeble individuals who required and appreciated his patience and tenacity with split infinitives and dangling participles when their own wore out, whose radiant smiles when they got it right shone up at him out of tangled, dirty faces he couldn't help but adore. He admired them—the students and his plants—their will to thrive despite their patent misery. But to me those imported, water-hungry monsters were more like the old tortoise who had lived for a long time in the Moreton Bay garden near the Colleges—two hundred years old at least, but not living, any longer, only taking a very long time to die.

During my last visit home, I moved through my father's garden with a spade and fork, a barrow and the hard eye of someone for whom the stunted lives of his beloved roses were merely stories. I had not raised them from rootstock, hoisting barrowload after barrowload of soil and compost and mulch until my hands were blistered and sore.

I had not gone out into the garden every morning for twenty, thirty years, and picked off the aphids and caterpillars that thronged amid their leaves, or sat on the back deck—as he so often had—frowning with discontent at the butterflies flocking above their blooms. I had not celebrated each malformed leaf or stunted bloom, each wayward branch of thorns and disappointment.

I avoided the corner of the garden where my mother's grave tolled its daily hour. Beginning at the back door I thinned out each bed, removing the ghosts who lingered there: the stunted shrubs with thin leaves and brittle arms. Their roots barely protested their removal. Seemed instead to sigh with relief as I lifted them from their mulched beds and lay them in the barrow.

The Miracle of Tears
Languedoc: 1826

The third orb of the chronometer is marked with a single tear. It marks the moment when truth and history were parted. When Montane Bélibaste—for that was her real name—discovered me.

Montane Wynder VIII—as she later called herself, laying out a false heritage that connected her, through her mother's line, to Margery and Gauzia, and backward further to Eloise—first came to me in the winter of 1826. I had stood a hundred years, unmoving, in a suspended moment: a moment between life and death. My sense of time had washed and waned with the years that had passed in such a perfect compact of silence so, when she came, I did not know it had been a hundred years. It could have been more, or less, I would not have cared. The apple tree at which I gazed had grown old and gnarled. One of its branches rested on the windowsill as if it, too, felt the years we had passed together like a great and dreadful weight.

She was small, thin. Her eyes were sunk deep in their sockets through the twin torments of hunger and exhaustion. Her coat was thin and worn; its hem stained with the black mud she had walked through, and crisp with frost. I saw her first through that little window which had become my sole view of the world. She peered into the dark house, her wide eyes black and hollow, and I felt a great pity surge in my slowly-beating heart. There was no door for her to open; the timbers having rotted away years ago. The floor, too, was gone, so her footfalls were soft, squeaking through the snow that blew in behind me. She peered through the doorway into the next room, but most of the roof there had collapsed twenty years earlier and the ground was a drift of snow. She gathered as much wood as she could, most of it

85

damp, though there were some apple branches and other scraps of wood lying about the floor, sheltered by the kitchen roof. She built a small fire in the middle of the room, which soon threw pale shadows on the mottled walls. Strange, after so long, to see fire light the room. She had her back turned to me as she worked but, once the fire crackled as merrily as it could given the fallen scraps of timber she had gathered, she peered deeper into the shadows. I cannot say what she thought when first she saw me, or how I would have appeared to her eyes. She wrote later, much later, that I seemed an odd shape in that half-darkness. That at first she thought I was a stunted bush of some description that had grown up from the floor. The bent hoops that had once held my skirt seemed like vines, and my arms, stripped of their cloth and leather, thick branches. As she approached me the small nest of mice that lived within me stirred, their pink noses twitching nerv-ously before they scattered. I was in such a lamentable state I doubt that I would have startled anyone, as I had once startled Tomas's maid in this same kitchen. I could not have appeared less human. Her thin, cool fingers reached towards me and I felt, then, the febrile kick of anticipation. After so many years I barely recognised it. Something flickered in her gaze as she touched my face and I recalled, as if in some faint echo, the first tentative touch of Eloise Reni.

Montane's hand recoiled from the frozen surface of my cheek but she tilted her head, peering at me with piqued curiosity. It was too dark for her to make much of my shape. In her Annals, years later, she describes her curiosity and wonder, but in her version our meeting was no accident. According to her Annals our meeting in that decrepit, mouldering room, was the result of a long, inherited search for recon-nection. No doubt you know this tale, but I will quote a small section of it, to highlight the moment when history diverges, so markedly, from truth.

> It was November, early for the snows to be so wild. I believe now, as time and the reconnection with Rupetta have sharpened my spirit, that the Organic Earth had set itself against me in

those last months, in one final, desperate attempt to thwart humanity's Destiny. I had been pursuing the last in a long line of clues; though hope, it seemed, had deserted me. It had taken me months, plagued as I was by constant illness and the poverty to which the great house of the Wynders had fallen, to pursue this partial and problematic riddle. It was the records of the Dominican Inquisitor, William Pelhisson, who had led me here, to the isolated, ruined country manor of my once-great family. Pelhisson had recorded the trial and execution of a woman he referred to as 'a wealthy old woman of Toulouse'. I have recorded, elsewhere, how I traced the link, later confirmed by Rupetta, between that record and my many-times-removed grandmère, Eloise Wynder. I had tracked the ghosts of rumours in Toulouse, finally happening on a man, an eccentric recluse, who told me of the Wynder's abandoned manor in Occitania. I was near exhaustion when I reached the manor, ill with fatigue and the repeated, enervating illnesses I suffered, as had the generations of Wynders before me. The great house, now restored to its early grandeur, was in a state of unimaginable decay. What little remained of the great library of the first Wynder was riddled with the foul perils of moult and feathers, moths and vermin. The stands, which had once supported the many scientific and aesthetic miracles of the early Wynders had rotted away and the treasures I later recovered were so buried in the accretions of dirt and snow that I did not discover them for weeks.

Finally, in the dim kitchen by the light of a small, applewood fire, I saw Rupetta, glistening in what, for Her seemed a violent light, coming as it did at the end of Her Hundred Years of Silence.

I reached towards her, my hand growing warmer than it had been in all the short years of my bitter life until that day. Despite her lamentable state, her poor, unpolished visage, I felt the great hope of generations, of the past and future dreams of mankind, leap in my breast. How humble I felt then, to be the vessel of such a swelling, invincible recovery of mankind's true

Destiny, and how equally foolish it seemed. I blush to recall
how I trembled at first, how my heart quivered with fear, how
small and foolish that great tumble of emotions seemed. I
doubted, but only for a moment, before I was overcome with
the Truth; the visible, irrevocable, incontrovertible Truth of the
Wynder Destiny. I reached out and placed my hand in the
middle of Rupetta's cool breast, which quickened at my touch.
How to describe that miracle? That pure, mechanical, long-
forgotten, swelling miracle? Can any save the Wynders know
the pure, blessed Truth of that moment? It will be easy, I
suppose, in the years to come, to forget humanity once lived in
a dark, impoverished innocence. To forget the world as it once
was, filled with the fear and chaos of life before the recovery of
our Truth and Destiny. To forget what it was like to be so
chained to our imperfect, flawed and blinded bodies, to the
whims of the untamed earth; to disease and untrammelled
seasons, to the blighting of crops. The unimaginable Terrors of
the dark years. But they must not become unimaginable; we
must recall them again and again if we are to truly appreciate
the endless beauty of Rupetta's miracles.

It was dark in that room, but not so dim that I did not
recognise the Fourth Miracle. The wind grew hushed, the snow
ceased to fall, our constant and vile enemy—the Organic
World—held its breath in terror as it recognised the rebirth of
mankind's one True Hope. In that silence, with the fire behind
me and my hand resting on her breast, I felt the slow turn of her
heart leap to my own beat, and I saw, glimmering in the half-
light, the Fourth Miracle; the perfect, clear drop of fluid
moving slowly over her dull cheek. The Miracle of Tears.

Montane had a taste for melodrama, which was later played out in the
years of public performances she, and then her reluctant daughter,
contrived. The truth is nowhere near as grand. The morning after her
arrival she woke while it was still dim, though the light was, perhaps, a
little brighter than it might have been, reflected as it was by the blue
sheen of the snow. The fire had gone out and her thin dress was not

nearly enough to shield her from the cold. Her skin was blue, her lips purple, and her eyes shone with the unnatural blaze of the ill and half-crazed. She looked at me with the evaluative stare I later came to know so well. It was the look she adopted when her thoughts turned to the future or, more precisely, to the most effective use of the present in which she found herself. She approached me without trepidation; her face bore no sign of recognition. She reached out and touched my arm, pulling at it a little to see if it would move. It was stiff, frozen in place by years of inactivity. At first it seemed my entire armature would tip into her embrace, but she turned her back, put her shoulder to my own and tugged a little harder. I thought at the time she was attempting to dismantle me, though why she would do so I could not have said. With much complaint, my shoulder joint moved just a little. She turned and contemplated my face. I could not see her clearly, my unblinking eyes were clouded by caked-on dirt, but I have an impression of her face that day that follows me through the years. She lifted her skirt and scrubbed, a little pointlessly it seemed to me at first, at my forehead.

Well, she said, her voice seeming loud in the long-silent house. *Aren't you an odd thing.*

She stayed in the house with me. At first she swore it would be one night, then another, soon she had been there a month. Nobody came. The house had lain empty and silent for too long to garner the curiosity of the local people any more. The little food she had brought with her ran out and she resorted to digging in the snowbound garden for the few roots and bulbs she could uncover. Slowly at first, compelled by the silence of the house, perhaps, she began to speak to me. Odd fragments at first but then, as time wore on, I became the first of the many daybooks out of which she later constructed our false history—the Rupettan Annal.

I did not move or speak—I lacked the functionality, the will and strength, to do so—but I listened. Late at night, as the snow blustered and cold air fingered its way into the room, she told me about her life. She had led a sorry, squalid existence. Born to a poor family who lived outside Reims she was sent out to work, at twelve years of age, in a wealthy family's summer château. The family who owned the château rarely visited, but the staff was allowed to live in the cramped attic rooms and the housekeeper was permitted to run an account in order to feed them. The room and bed she shared with another young girl was cramped. Home to a small family of rats, windowless, freezing in winter and close in summer, the room nevertheless provided shelter. She and her companion, Jacqueline, shared the blanket they were allowed in winter, snuggling together companionably. She would have stayed there, happily enough, perhaps for her whole life. She had ambitions to take over the plump housekeeper's position one day and she and Jacqueline often dreamed of a future where they, instead of she, scrimped on the other staff's rations in order to fill their own flat bellies.

One spring the family came to stay, bringing the rest of their household with them. Each of the family had a personal servant, and some of the more senior servants had servants of their own. Even the babe, whose nursemaid's breasts were thin from feeding each of his siblings in turn. The nursemaid stole out to the stables early each morning to meet with the stable hand, and traded what small favours she could for a pint of mare's or cow's milk with which to supplement her own. The stable hand was rough with her, bruising her thighs and buttocks with a sullen viciousness each time she raised her skirts, though he knew better than to mark the breasts that were her livelihood and his passport to her daily, if reluctant, sex.

The staff meals, once a grim and silent affair with just the five of them—the housekeeper and her husband, the groundsman, and the two girls—now teemed with life. Three sittings were required to service all of them. Jacqueline and Eloise ate at the first morning sitting and the last at night, low as they were in the hierarchy of the household. The servants who ate with them were mostly the invisible cleaning staff: a bevy of gossipy young girls and boys. One of the girls, a plump and pretty thing, was lifting her skirts for one of the older sons of the family and, despite knowing there was no respectable future in it, lorded it over the rest of the staff. Jacqueline distrusted her, though she shared their room and often gave them sweetmeats and fruits that the marquise had given her when she crept in, well after curfew. According to Jacqueline she did it to bribe them into silence. Montane's friendship with Jacqueline declined over that spring, though at first she didn't notice, and when Jacqueline found another bed to share with one of the chambermaids Montane paid it little mind. She had become caught up in her new friend's world, sure that she, too, could find a way to increase her standing and convince one of the spoiled, wealthy gentry to shower her with gifts in exchange for what her companion described as a bit of harmless flirting. Montane was not pretty, however, and the few occasions on which she brushed her skirts against the shins of the marquise's loutish friends they hardly noticed her, glancing up and away, or holding out their empty glasses for more wine.

One cool day towards the end of the season, she noticed a small huddle of girls around her old friend Jacqueline at the evening meal. It was late and the family were sleeping so their gossip was muffled, but she heard small scraps. *What is it?* she had asked, and one of the scullery maids turned to her, her face alight with the warmth of envy.

It's Jacqueline, she said. *She's being courted by that handsome friend of the Marquise. He's given her a gold locket with a snip of his hair in it.*

Courted? Montane had said, sure that what was really in play was the same kind of secret, furtive entanglement she had envisioned for herself.

She's one of the Trencavels, the maid whispered. *They used to be a great family, but her grandfather ran up debts and she's had to work. Her parents still live in their apartment in the city, though they rent out rooms to respectable boarders; students and such.*

As the last weeks of the season wore on Jacqueline was moved into one of the family rooms, and the maids who had once been her equals were set to make her bed and stoke her fire. Once, Montane was sent to dress her and comb out her hair. When she entered the room, though the sun had been up for hours, Jacqueline was still in bed. Montane snatched back the covers and Jacqueline started awake, blinking her eyes in alarm as her hand clutched her new white gown to her breast.

Montane! she cried.

Montane scraped Jacqueline with her gaze, but the girl was so wrapped up in the bliss of her new life that she did not appear to notice her old friend's displeasure. Montane moved to the wardrobe and removed the plainest gown she could find there. Jacqueline's rough housemaid's dress, with its bleached apron, was nowhere in sight.

Oh! Not that thing. You can have that if you like. I must wear something pretty today. Dominic's family are coming, and he plans to talk to them about our marriage. Marriage! She slipped out of the bed and pulled her gown over her head, though Montane moved reluctantly to assist her. Jacqueline grasped the hand held out to her and pulled it to her breast. *Oh, Montane, I forgive you. Do you still love me? Even a little? Will you come and work for me when I'm married? You can have your own room, your own cupboard filled with sweetmeats!*

Work for you?

You could be my personal maid. We could see each other every day, and then, when the children come, you could be their nursemaid.

Nursemaid! Montane had said, unable and unwilling to keep the horror from her voice. She had a sudden flash of her white thighs pressed to the fetid straw of the stables, striped with bruises.

Belatedly, Jacqueline noticed the pallor that had fallen over Montane's features. *Oh,* she said. *I didn't mean. . . .*

Lift up your arms, Montane said, wrenching the blue skirt Jacqueline had chosen over her unbrushed hair.

Montane dressed Jacqueline as briskly as she could and then coolly asked if the mistress required anything more of her.

Don't be like that, Jacqueline begged, but Montane wouldn't meet her eyes or speak another word.

Telling the story, with the white storm swirling about the room, Montane's voice was filled with the venom of soured friendship. Though Jacqueline had done nothing to harm her, had, instead, offered her what little she could, Montane felt herself slighted. She had nurtured her resentment as she moved through the back halls of the house, hidden from sight, carrying the slop pails and scrubbing brushes that daily reminded her of her own inevitable and unrelieved future of servitude.

For a while Jacqueline held onto the notion of redeeming their friendship. Once she even ventured into the kitchens, but the sudden silence and polite curtseys of the staff who had once believed themselves her equals unnerved her. *Can I help you, Mistress?* the housekeeper asked, her obsequiousness inexpertly concealing the resentment beneath. Jacqueline shook her head and slipped from the room.

The wedding was set for the middle of summer and Jacqueline sent her parents money as soon as she could, inviting them to the house and giving them the name of Dominic's family's dressmakers, who were to equip them for their fleeting re-entry into fashionable society. Even as she wrote the letters she knew their sojourn in her life would be brief: soon after the wedding celebrations they would slip back to their genteel poverty; a mild embarrassment to be admitted graciously but distantly. Her father she fretted over, knowing in these later years he had taken to drinking to soften the bitterness of his ignominy.

All this Montane had learned through Jacqueline's new personal maid, Calpurnia, a young girl Dominic had hired. Calpurnia was a silent, officious girl. A little superior and given to long complaints over stooping to the care of someone like Jacqueline. She had been Dominic's sister's maid until her death, six months earlier, of a lung complaint. Montane did not defend her former friend, instead fuelling Calpurnia's spite by intimating she had seduced Dominic with a combination of witchcraft and feminine wiles. She thought Calpurnia her friend, united as they were in their rancour over Jacqueline, but she soon discovered otherwise. Calpurnia seduced Montane into more and more jealous tirades over her misfortune, and Jacqueline's deceitfulness. Montane, innocent as she had been of the games she was caught up in, whispered all kinds of things to Calpurnia in the warmth of her companionable embrace, all of which Calpurnia related, the next morning, to Jacqueline.

Perhaps, Montane mused, things would not have been so bad had she not ventured, spurred on by Calpurnia's delight in vile gossip, into twisting the truth a little. At first it was little things; she exaggerated the terms of their friendship, hinting they had been lovers, that Jacqueline had confided in her all kinds of things about her past, about scheming to acquire the wealth she felt she was entitled to. Apart from the stories about slipping drops of her own blood into Dominic's wine to ensure his heart, Montane inferred Jacqueline had seduced him into her bed with a mixture of wild herbs, that she had feigned regret, milking tears from her eyes to convince him she was as chaste as a nun when in truth she had had a series of wealthy lovers, each of whom had uncovered her schemes before they made the mistake of wedding her. Concerned that Dominic was faltering in his devotion she had pressed her to marry him as quickly as possible. When he told her a decent courtship would normally endure at least a year, she harried him to an early engagement. One night, after Calpurnia had plied her with wine from Jacqueline's bedchamber, Montane went even further.

Driven by lust and ambition, Montane insisted, Jacqueline had determined to conceive a child. Unwilling to compromise Dominic's vision of her as a chaste innocent she succumbed to him only once more, struggling feebly in a manner that only fuelled his passion. Weeping and convincingly distraught afterwards she convinced him he had taken her unwillingly. That night, and for several nights thereafter, according to Montane's lies, Jacqueline crept to the stable hand's cot in the corner of his rancid stables and rode him as brazenly as a whore, packing her sex with cloth afterward to stop whatever seed he sprayed into her from escaping.

As Montane spoke these last words she heard a sharp, horrified cry from the hall. Jacqueline entered the room, her hands trembling and her big eyes full of hurt and confusion. *I didn't want to believe it,* she said.

Montane turned frantically from one face to another, searching for pity or understanding, but neither of her former friends were willing to supply it. *It was just a game,* she said.

Jacqueline shook her head. *That's the best explanation you have? That it was sport?*

Montane stood silent; what could she have said in her defence?

Finally, Jacqueline turned to leave. *Calpurnia, I need you in my room; the fire has gone out and it is deathly cold up there.*

An hour later, when Calpurnia returned to their little room, she handed Montane a piece of paper. Montane could read only a little at the time, but she scanned the letter for words she knew. Jacqueline was dismissing her from service. Jacqueline, who had once been just a kitchen maid, an equal who had dreamed of the keys to the kitchen stores. Jacqueline dared not cite her true reasons for wishing Montane gone and had, Montane insisted when she told me the tale, been dictated every word of her nasty missal by Calpurnia. According to the instructions in the letter Montane was to leave immediately, giving up whatever wages were owed her. The housekeeper and Dominic's family had been informed that Calpurnia had discovered one of Jacqueline's dresses in their room, along with a small cache of the expensive trinkets Dominic had given Jacqueline during their courtship. They knew her to be a thief and a liar. She was not to receive a reference nor should she seek employment with any of the other reputable families in the area, all of whom would receive a firm account of her theft and dishonesty.

Montane had blanched and, not understanding at first that Calpurnia had betrayed her, asked her roommate to help her steal into Jacqueline's rooms to reason with her. *Why would she do this?* she had said.

Calpurnia shrugged. Something in her careless manner impressed itself on Montane, though she did not recognise it until days later, as she trudged through the streets like a wastrel, begging for food and shelter.

Calpurnia helped her bundle her things together, even secreting a small packet of food among the folds of Montane's winter cloak. Had she felt a moment of pity, then? Or remorse? Lying in the dark Montane refused to admit it, preferring to think Calpurnia had meant some damage by it. The night she was cast out, as she had huddled against a tree with her coat wrapped around her, she had flung the bread and soft cheese away from her, into the dark, convinced it was poisoned.

Sometimes I think it may have been better had I eaten it and died there. Montane peered into my imperfectly-cleaned eyes, as if she thought I might reply. I pitied her then, though she had been cruel and foolish. She was little more than a child at the time, and unused to the petty ambitions, the desperate, deadly serious games, of people like Calpurnia and Jacqueline.

Our days passed in relative peace and quiet. She had few supplies, but fewer needs. She gathered fruit, stole eggs from the neighbours, gathered fallen wood for the fire at night, and wrapped herself as tightly in her clothes as she was able. She found or stole an old bucket and brought water into the house each morning to wash herself, and for drinking. To keep herself amused, perhaps, she took to cleaning and polishing my humble remains. She dusted and scrubbed my hoops and pipes. In the dark of evening, as she worked over me, I felt life stir once more. I could not move; it was not like the Wynding, which had woken me, so long ago, with a violent uprush of life. Instead, I felt life tumble gently within me, knocked loose from the felt-dark folds of silence. The rush and pull of Montane's spirit joined and quickened within me.

One morning she rose early and came to sit beside me on her upturned bucket, leaning against my body as though I were a tree spread out above her, providing shade and comfort in an open field. We gazed out at the apple tree that had been my constant and only companion for so long. Montane was preparing to leave—having run out of provisions and patience—though she had no notion of where to go, or how to find or make a place for herself in the world. *I could sell you, I suppose,* she said, *though I doubt I would get much for such a dilapidated toy. Enough for a few nights' board perhaps, some wine?* She sat in silence for a long time.

I cannot sell you, she said. *You are my only friend.*

She wept, then, the only tears I ever saw her shed, though she lived a long life. I heard the cool patter of her tears falling on my copper waist. Though it cost me dear, though I felt the coils within my arms creak and strain and crack with the effort, I moved my arm to hold her.

She shot up and whirled to face me, her face white, her eyes wide with panic, though even then, even in that moment of shock and fear, I could see the wheels turn within her mind. Could sense the wicked blade of her intellect sharpening itself against this moment: what it meant, what it could mean.

My voice was rough, whistling. I had barely any air to work with; my bellows were weak and moth-ridden. Speech had become an unfamiliar, alien process. I had to work hard, concentrate, to move my jaw, my mouth, my throat, to shape the air as it moved through me and press it out into the room.

My name, I said, *is Rupetta.*

℘

The light was falling fast as I told her where to find the key. I had buried it beneath the apple tree, in a small wooden box. It was still strung on the green ribbon Margery had worn about her neck. When Montane returned to me she held the little key in her hand. Her nails were black and broken. The key was dulled with age, thin and old, but it turned the lock that opened my breast. She gazed inside me.

Wynd me, I said, and she looked up, confused. There was no immediately-apparent mechanism built for such a purpose, and she was not a Reni: a woman who knew, as if by instinct, where to place her hand. Finally she seemed to understand and, after a hundred years of waking death, I felt the kick of life within me.

It was not the same as with Eloise Reni or any of the true daughters of her line, who had been formed of my own heart's material. Montane's spirit was bright and brittle, she throbbed with ambition and wit, her dreams were rich and fervent but there was something other—something different—which I could not name.

In that moment, when she knew what the Wynding took of her—made of her—she almost withdrew. She knew life—centuries of change—and the workings of my being. She knew the pipes and barrels and drums of my composition as I knew hers: each cell and sinew. She felt the weighty drift of my crown wheel and foliot, the tug of gut across my fusees. She knew my secrets, such as they were, and I knew hers.

I was alive again, but I could not move: the bind we had made was weak, the Wynding a poor imitation of the bright kick of the Reni women. I had woken, but I was not alive. Not yet.

As for Montane's secrets: she was with child and had nowhere to go.

I had little to offer, but she needed so very little. The cottage was old and ruined, but the land nearby was fertile, the woods thick and private. Not three miles away there was a river where Guilhabert and I had once fished for trout. We would build a house—a small cottage—deep in the woods. I would teach her to make nets, to fish, to hunt, to gather wild mushrooms. In return she would come to the manor, before first light each morning, and Wynd me.

As the months passed I grew stronger. A little, so very little, at a time. Soon I could walk across the room. My vision grew brighter, sharper. I fashioned a new arm for myself from a fallen piece of timber. It did not move well, but it moved. I could see, again, the tips of the trees that grew overhead. I could hear the nightingale who sang, each evening, near the riverbank.

When I could move a little I unearthed Perihan, who had sunk into the dust and soil beneath me, though I never found the strange seed I had planted beside the little bird—the stony pearls I had discovered in my belly one winter had winnowed to nothing, swallowed up by the black earth. Alone at night I dug out the jewels that were its eyes. I offered them to Montane to trade for linen and rope, a pot and some plates, and, when she had all she could need, for a few parts to make what repairs we could to my frame.

While she was out fishing and foraging I carved a cradle from dark wood and placed it in her home, in the centre of the room. It was wide and deep and smooth and contained a firmly-stuffed mattress. I had carved a series of small dragonflies and apple-blossoms into the edges of the cradle; a clumsy copy of the designs Eloise had once carved in my own arms.

Soon the child was born. A daughter. I named her Anise.

I held her, soon after she was born, and felt a glissando of life pass between us. Her hands were small fists but she reached out from her swaddling as though to touch my cheek and I felt my heart lurch.

It was a dangerous combination: Montane's ambition and bitterness, my vulnerability, my love for the child and desire to give her a better life. A safer one.

Anise was three years old by the time I had gained enough strength to make the short journey to the pond. The cottage I had built for them was a short walk through the woods—on the other side of the shallow gully and the pond I had not visited since the night I followed Eloise to its shores. She was almost four before I found the remains of Alazaïs's box, most of which had rotted away, and dug out of the silted floor of the pond the pieces of my sister. I carried her, piece by piece, up to the ruined kitchen. It took a year of work to repair her but then, on Anise's fifth birthday, I presented her with a gift that would change all of our lives—including yours.

Montane's eyes watched as I showed Anise how to wind Alazaïs, with her scribed surface. I showed her how to make her sing, and write her name. Anise walked around it, smoothing her hand over its metal face, its thick waist, as she bent and watched the wheels turn beneath the bones of its skirts, the clever lift and drop of its cylinder escapement.

Can it speak? Montane said. *Can it think? Is it like you?*

It's just a toy, I said, *like Perihan.*

That night, while Anise slept, Montane stayed up at the window, making plans. Within a month we left our home, travelling towards the cities of Asia, where our lives were soon caught up in a whirl of performances, of grand rooms filled with smoky candles, of hushed voices, and silk garments that hushed along the walls and floors. Alazaïs sang, and wrote her name, and walked across rooms to curtsey before the great men who watched her, who peered inside her seeking a dwarf, a rigging of strings and falseness, who applauded her strange, juddering dance. Rumours swirled out from around us. In their centre, Montane watched, and waited.

Henri's Story: Part Three

My final year as an undergraduate. At the beginning of semester, Jenon brought me into his office to discuss the work I'd been doing for him, my coursework for final year and so on. He moved me up from the position I'd had—emptying rubbish bins and making tea for his discussion groups, offering me work in the Obanite carrels, supporting the senior Penitents in their sealed rooms. I knew this was the work he fed out to students the faculty had their eye on. Getting work in the Obanite carrels was thought of as a sign that you'd been marked out by the Penitents. A kind of lordly favour handed down to favourite sons and daughters who were being ushered through their programs: a golden pass to a vision of my future, working in those rooms, among those ancient scholars. Though ordinary enough, the days of mindless fetching and carrying work sat heavily on me; long days among the quiet ticking of Obanite scholars, the regular tick and swish of their unsyncopated hearts the only sounds in the sealed, dust-free rooms. I grew conscious of my youth and inexperience, as well as of my body's boom and beat. The smooth, unpunctured skin of my chest. The Oban scholars were kind and wise. They were infinitely patient—as people can afford to be, I supposed, who live so long—smiling at me, sitting to talk with me. At lunchtime they all sat out on the deck, sipping tea and watching the students move around on the ground far below them like ants scurrying around their nests. They spoke little to each other, but asked me questions all the time, offered to read my papers, and sat with me for long hours, reading them and discussing my research as though it were meaningful and important.

On warm days, they would wear their thin Penitent cloaks, with the low-cut necklines that revealed their Penitent hearts. Sometimes, I could discern how old they were by the sheen of their silver, by the style of the designs etched on their surfaces: the nouveau flourishes of Karl's oval; the blocky formality of Elsie's heart-shaped door; the dainty, tarnished silver of Albert's design. Once, I saw Robert Pogue's old heart. A heavy, dark thing—not pretty at all—with a keyhole like a terrible secret, and a scar that spread out around it like a starfish, its limbs straggled and thick and white. I was told, by Jenon, I think, that Pogue had been offered but had refused an upgrade, preferring his old heart to the new ones, which he claimed were flimsy and ill-made.

Transformation meant access to a whole other order of knowledge —an unlimited education, an almost unlimited span of life during which to learn—but I had begun to fear the surgery, with a heretical, fleshy dread. Late at night, in the stacks, I searched through the old books for images of newly-embedded hearts. I found surgeon's books with detailed anatomical drawings, notes, instructions. Pre- and post-operative wound management plans. Images of flesh that had rejected the new hearts: swollen and pink or blackening at the edges as though scorched. Images of the surgery itself—line drawings and photographs —with the chest open and the ribs pulled back like the doors of a white cage. The old heart shut off from the body with clamps: the ventricles and aorta snipped, the blood flow diverted and slowed. Images of the mechanical heart during insertion: the preliminary stitching in, the release of the hollow wires that threaded themselves out from the heart, finning up through the Penitent's arteries first: the carotid, subclavian and carotid, radial and mesenteric, and then the secondary wires, thinner and more sinewy, pouring forward into the pulmonary veins, the femoral, basilic, portal and hepatic. The wires locking themselves in place, and swelling open before the blood-flow is undammed. The blood channelling through new, firmer structures.

The pictures I studied the hardest, however, were the simplest. The body between. The ribs cracked open, the flesh peeled open like the pages of the book and the cavity empty. The heart flown.

One afternoon, cycling across campus to Jenon's house to tend the garden, I remembered the student whose place I had taken as his gardener, who had fallen ill after Transformation and had so quietly disappeared. I did not even know their name, or what had become of them.

I had been to the Penitent's Haven on the feast days, with Margause and Miri, and watched the ceremonies. Each year, in the first week of spring, I had stood amid the eerily silent, weeping crowds that came to celebrate the Miracle of The Heart. I had watched the newly-Transformed Penitents reveal the plates concealing their mechanical hearts, circled with bristles of black stitches and pink wounds that sometimes wept or softly bled. I had gazed in mute awe as each Penitent knelt on the steps of the Haven, before the incumbent Perfect, who drew the key to each heart from a great ring of similar keys, inserted and turned it, with a series of distinct and audible clicks.

I could not explain or disperse the revulsion I felt, hearing those muted clicks, seeing the keys turned—sometimes stiffly—in their fresh locks.

This was the celebration and proof of the greatest gift of Rupetta: the symbol of our promised immortality, our ultimate release from the brutal and fleeting turmoil of the flawed, uncertain, death-driven life of a natural creature. It was a gift bestowed on a select few—those most deserving, those whose work was most likely to prove useful to the ongoing work in service of the Fourfold Law—in recognition of their dedication to rationality and intellect, their pursuit of the knowledge that would, some day, free all of humanity from the perpetual chaos and formlessness of Nature. It was the ultimate, simple and ordinary denial of the Oikos heresy: their privileging of faith and decay over knowledge and permanence. I knew all this.

I know it.

And yet, as each newly-made Penitent knelt, raised their eyes and held their arms out in the traditional attitude of the Consoled, I was filled with a physical, whirling dread. I felt my own organic heart thump and panic like a bird in a trap. Beating so hard and fast I was sure Miri, standing beside me, could hear it.

As yet another Obanite student mounted the steps and knelt before the Perfect, Miri turned to me and smiled, briefly pressed the tips of her fingers against the place on my chest beneath which my heart, so flailingly, beat.

I would have fled, if I was a weaker woman, but I had made an oath not to give up, no matter what feeble, fleeting fears, loves, passions assaulted me. And I could not go home. I wasn't ready to leave Elm, or Miri.

Miri was my roommate, my dearest friend. The woman who had given me a home, brought me into Elm, with its dog-eared warmth, and its seed-strewn desks. Its smell of dark earth, compost and smoked water. Miri was the woman I ate with each evening, shared a home with, read to. The woman who had stood beside me inside the glass-house almost two years ago, grafting the seedlings of trees that were now blossoming outside the window. The woman whose bright eyes and quick, sly humour, rough curls and steady hand penetrated my dreams.

Coming upon her in the kitchen, at the window, I would feel my meaty heart lurch, feel my breath stutter against my teeth. Miri's laughter loosened light from the sky. The untouched, pale curve of her wrist broke my heart. *One day*, I had promised myself, *one day I'll tell her she's the one I wish to speak to each night, whose voice I long to hear in the dark, whose breath I long to taste, whose hand I long to hold. The one I wish to wake to every morning.*

The one I love.

Beyond that I could not, dared not, imagine.

ℰ

As Miri and I approached the Salt Lane house, along the unpaved street that crunched beneath the tyres of our bicycles, I was struck by the tart, unfamiliar smell of oak. Once we had turned off the main road, climbing into the hills, the path became worn and potholed. Old trees arched overhead, shading us from the late morning sun. In front of me, Miri's bicycle flickered in the forested light, as though she were a figure in an old film. Once, these roads had been wider, well-kept. There had been walking paths on either side and the trees, each one known and named, were well-tended. I had studied the maps, knew that here, where the road turned to meet the curve of a rise, there was once a walking path leading into the forest, towards the house. It had been lined with stones and paved with dirt; the children of the Hedge School had passed along it every day, keeping it smooth by the regular passage of their booted feet.

The sign at the top of the drive was covered in dust and the lettering was faded. Miri wiped away some of the dirt with her hand. *Salt Lane House*, the sign read. *Maintained by the Order of the Obanites. Site of the Salt Lane Hedge School; Established by Emmeline and Mathilde Salt.* Beneath the sign was a small box, marked 'visitor information'. Miri removed a map from the box, which showed the location of the house and the main paths. On the reverse side was a short paragraph of information about the Salt Lane Witches and the Hedge School. 'The Oikos Mathilde Salt', read the final paragraph, 'was released from custody in September, 1936, though she never returned to the site of her arrest. The Hedge School closed in 1947, shortly after Emmeline's death. Her grave can be visited at G5 on the map provided overleaf.'

We wheeled our bikes down the path, beneath the shade of the tall bloodwoods and the flooded rose gums. A white chain-fence ran along the left of the path, marking off the densely-planted orchard. Along the right, the land sloped away into a gully thick with forest. Some of the older trees bore the marks of a fire that had passed through, at least ten years ago, their trunks blackened and partly hollow near the ground while their upper branches were bright with greenery.

We passed the vegetable gardens and the herb patches, maintained by Obanite gardeners now, where once each bed would have been tended by a group of small scholars, as part of their education. The beds are named for the names they gave themselves: Elf's bed, Dyad's bed, Rondel's bed.

The front door of the house is painted a warm, dark green. We took off our shoes and hung up our coats. In the hall was a table with a guest book, a small local history book, a sheaf of flyers with information about other sites of interest in the area. On the walls were pictures of the land when it was being cleared, and of the house when it was first built; of Emmeline and Mathilde sitting on the back steps, looking out over their forest and the newly-planted orchard; of Mathilde asleep by the fire; of a clutch of children sleeping on blankets spread out in the dappled shade of the garden.

'Look at this one,' I said. Mathilde and Emmeline, surrounded by seedling pots, grinning and squinting in the light. A slash of dirt across Mathilde's cheek. Emmeline's face half-shaded by her hat. Two children sit in the wheelbarrow beside them, their hands and faces daubed with wet soil. Another, slightly older child, is standing half-behind Mathilde. She is the still edge of the image: neat and clean, her hand curled in Emmeline's. She is clutching her hat in her hand and her face—smooth and pale, though faded now with time—is peering up at the women.

Miri ran her finger along the base of the picture's frame. 'They look so happy,' she said. 'Dirty, but happy.'

'June 19th,' I read from the bottom of the frame. 'The day before Mathilde's arrest.'

Miri leant closer, touched the glass separating us from that time, so long ago, when two women had planted the trees that now towered over the house. 'Emmeline must have looked at this picture a lot,' she said, peering at their faces. 'They look happy. Thank goodness they didn't know what was about to happen to them.'

'Mathilde knew. She wrote in her notebook, the day that photograph was taken—instructions for after she was gone.'

'What kind of instructions?'

I shrugged and straightened, peering into the room before us: the dining room with its large, round table, rubbed smooth with wear, lightly chiselled with the chicken-scratch imprints of children pressing too hard as they wrote. 'For the school, mostly, and the garden: a kind of roster for the year. When to plant things, when to harvest seeds, when to burn back the scrub. That kind of thing.'

'Nothing for Emmeline.'

'She never wrote anything very personal in the diary: most of it's just gardening notes and observations about the weather.'

'You didn't find something else among the other papers in the stacks?'

I shook my head, stepping across to the fireplace, smoothing my hand over the back of Emmeline's chair, pulled up to the unlit fire. A blanket was folded over the arm; a book sat waiting on the table at her side. 'Perhaps she burned it before she left. Perhaps she just threw it away. Composted it. She never liked waste of any kind. Some people are careless; they forget that History needs them to preserve these things.'

Upstairs, in the women's bedroom, we sat in the windowseat and looked out over the garden, into the forest. From the second storey of the house we could see the ridgeline in the distance, between the trees. The room had the stilted, performative air of a room that had not been lived in for a long time. An effort had been made to simulate the rush and whisper of the women's lives, but the bed was made too neatly, the flowers on the bedside table were professionally arranged. The books on the tables were too squarely-stacked and serious—no trashy novels or well-thumbed favourites. There were no clothes on the floor, no damp towels on the rail, no dirt-stained boots outside. None of the roughened air of a real home. Jars of seeds lined the dresser. Two hats hung—too pretty and crisp ever to have been worn by those practical and earth-bound women—on hooks behind the door.

'Let's go outside,' I said.

The back deck of the house looked out onto a circle of lawn. According to the map there were three paths visitors could take: the first led past the rookery and down to the creek—an easy amble—the second followed the edge of the ridge before looping back towards the road (a longer, scenic walk, with views of the ridgeline almost all the way back to the College), the third led visitors along the rocky, fern-lined paths down to Emmeline's grave—what had once been a stone-paved clearing furnished with rough-hewn benches where the women went to sit and talk.

'There used to be another path,' I said. 'Mathilde's favourite. About here.' I pointed at the map, laying it flat to compare it with the layout of the house and garden before us. I walked to the edge of the lawn and glanced back at the house, checking for the guide who had offered to show us the premises, ushering us through the rooms with nervous instructions not to touch anything. He had gone back inside, disappeared into the converted stone potting shed that had become the Obanite caretaker's sleeping and working quarters. There he sat, like a jealous spider, awaiting more visitors to whom he could show the sanitised memorial of the Salt Lane house, within which the women I had come to know so well were merely shades.

'Coming?' I said, stepping over the stones that marked the edge of the lawn.

Miri smiled and ducked into the trees towards me. We moved further in, where the shade began to grow thick and leaves under our feet were half-rotted. I reached out my hand, tried not to blush when she took it. 'Where are we going?' Miri said.

I smiled as I turned to lead Miri into the woods, remembering the adventure I had had as a child, imagining myself in a magical place. 'We're going to the Land Between,' I said, 'to meet with the Oikos.'

Miri tilted her head like a bird. 'Are we heretics?' she said.

'My Great Aunt Grace was one of the first people to settle up north,' I said, looking away into the bush, testing the words, wanting her to know my stories—to know me—but deathly afraid of what she might make of it all. 'She came here as part of the first wave of Rupettan settlers; determined to make peace with the Oikos; to eradicate the heresy not with bloodshed, but patience and logic. She wrote in her journal about seeing them from a distance, four days into their search for a place to settle, and making contact. There were others she was travelling with who wanted to avoid them, but she insisted. She was curious. Had always been curious.'

'Wasn't she afraid?'

I shrugged. 'If she was she didn't say so.'

'You never told me this before,' Miri said, pulling us to a standstill. I couldn't meet her eyes. I knew that it was a kind of test I'd set for her, even if I hadn't known it when I started telling her the story.

'Some people don't understand,' I said. 'They think that if your family were part of the first wave, they were sympathisers with the Oikos. Heretics. And that you must be, too.'

'Are you?' Her face was so composed and smooth. I could see the reflections of leaves in her eyes. See the shift of light deep within them.

'I don't think so,' I said.

'Did she meet the Oikos? Befriend them?' Miri said, her voice low and quiet, as though we were children whispering beneath a table. 'Did she have to make a sacrifice? Eat the flesh of the dead?'

I laughed. 'They weren't savages. She brought them gifts: lengths of fabric and sewing machines. Washers and cropping mechanisms. That kind of thing. They gave her fruit from native trees, and drew her a map of the area. They hunted together, ate together, the Oikos taught Grace what they had learned about the Territory. One of them stayed with her for several months, helping her build their first house, teaching her their way of living on the land.'

Miri's head was bent as we walked, watching the ground, occasionally pausing to peer up through the trees. 'And your family stayed there, after that?'

'We were caretakers, renting the land from the Oikos settlers who had been moved off it but had managed to retain ownership. Gardeners, my father called us. We never saw our Oikos landlords. Not in my lifetime, anyway. The people who owned our land hadn't been to Whitestone Shute in forty years, maybe longer.'

'Does your father still live there?'

'He didn't want to stay on after my mother died. The land was resumed by the Penitents—bequested by its Oikos owners to the Oban College. We got a letter saying that the original owners, having been given homes in Land Between, were pleased to bequest land in the

109

reclaimed Rupettan Territory to the Penitents. My father refused to pay rent to the Consort's office for land he said didn't belong to them; land he said they'd stolen. He's not a heretic, but he fought to have the land returned to the Oikos: it's close enough to Land Between, he argued it could have become part of their settlement, but the Oikos wouldn't help him. We went to Oikos Island so many times when I was a child, when they still had a meeting-place there, to see them, to fight with them. My father insisted they had to fight. That the revolution was over and they were just people now, not heretics, that they didn't need to be afraid any more. But they wouldn't sign their names to any Penitent papers, they said. Wouldn't tell the world who they were, or where they were, or what they wanted, even if they were no longer ashamed, or afraid. He's a bit . . . odd, my father. He has peculiar ideas about things, about people.'

'I'd like to meet him,' Miri said. 'Maybe even go into Land Between with you.'

'It's just forest,' I said, 'like this, really. There's nothing to see but trees and rocks. The people live much further inland now, away from the Rupettan Territory.'

'Still,' she said, ducking beneath a low branch, 'I'd like to see where you grew up, walk with you on the land where your Aunt Grace settled.'

An hour later the path had winnowed away to a slim indentation in the earth, covered over with leaves. We reached a dry creekbed where a set of planks, rotted and half-fallen away, crossed towards a steep embankment, in which cakes of stone had been set as footholds. At the top of the embankment the path veered to the south and then, suddenly, ended beneath the shadow of a tree whose trunk was thick and furrowed with age. It stretched above us further than we could see, pushing through the canopy of the surrounding trees like a statuesque pylon. At its base was a stone bench and table, covered in leaf litter and stained with the faint wanderings of snails. I put my hand against the trunk of the tree and began walking around it, circling it. Miri went the other way. For a few moments we couldn't see each other, though I could hear the crunch of her shoes in the leaf-mould. Almost a third of the way around the tree, I looked up to see a dark cable, thicker than my arm, dangling a few feet above my head. At first, I thought it was a strangler vine, reaching down from the canopy in search of the soil, but it hung straight down and, when I looked closer, had the thready, frayed texture of old rope. Unlike a strangler's tendril it ended in a knot.

When Miri found me, I had taken off my backpack and shoes and was trying to find a way to reach the end of the rope. I curled my foot around a curve in the lower trunk of the tree and pushed upward, leaning outwards at the last moment and lunging towards it. Finally, after several attempts, I grabbed it. The rope-end descended a few feet, as if unravelling from some point far above us. I dangled from it for a moment, like a child about to swing out over a creek, before swinging my feet up onto the knot. 'Coming?' I said.

The rope was thicker than my arm, worn smooth with use and age, and weather. The filaments were coarse and tightly-wound, plaited together to form a ladder, of sorts, with knots every few feet. I concentrated on climbing, on the tree in front of me and the rope in my hands. Miri came up behind me, steadily climbing the rope that was, for all its thickness, as supple as silk. When we breached the canopy, after climbing through a leafy adytum, I almost expected to see a giant entwife perched in the tree's high branches, her woody locks matted into hanks out of which leaves protruded, and birds grew like fruit. Instead, the rope ended in a loop, threaded through a thick iron hook in the tree's trunk. From there, a kind of spiralling staircase ascended towards the giant's own canopy.

The stairs were simple slats of wood, set into the tree's trunk, spiralling around it as they climbed, with a carved banister on the outer edge. The stairs ended just beneath where the tree began to thin. There, in the green-yellow bloom of an airborne garden, I could see the underbelly of a curved platform, like the hull of a ship that had moored itself in the sky.

111

We were in the sky. Our heads in the clouds, our feet on a platform that sighed and sang as the branches moved. It was late afternoon and we could see clouds sinking down the range like a dragon's smoky winter breath. There was a kind of bench, built against the trunk of the tree, on which we sat and watched the storm thicken. We could smell rain coming.

'Do you think they knew it was here?' I said. 'Do you think they built it?'

'We should go back,' Miri said, but she was looking away and leaning back against the tree, her hand splayed on its worn-smooth trunk.

I put my hand into my pocket. Cradled there, wrapped in a square of felted wool, was the little mechanical bird, repaired and polished, a firm and solid thing: warm against my skin. I held my hand out over the bench towards Miri, like a tiny nest within which the creature sat, peering at her. As I stroked its wing with my other hand it tipped its head to the side and trilled a series of notes. I tilted my hand and the tiny creature hopped onto the bench between us. I whistled and the bird turned towards me, hopping as nervously as a sparrow, to spread its wings wide before opening its beak with a barely audible mechanical click.

The bird cocked its head once again and began to sing a lullaby. It did not sound like a real bird, except perhaps in as much as a painting of a woman looks like a real woman, or like the brass mount in the square at home resembles a true horse. The notes slid and elided in its throat as I coaxed it onto my forearm. It perched there, its feet cool pins against my skin.

As its song drew to a close, I held the bird out to Miri on my outstretched palm.

She looked startled. Almost afraid. 'Where did you find it?' Miri said.

'It's for you.'

Miri didn't reach for it, though it hopped closer to her and peered upward expectantly. She put one hand flat on the bench, her fingertip just resting against the tip of one of its claws. 'Why did you bring it here?' she said. 'Do you know . . .'

'Don't you like it?' I said, concerned now that Miri wouldn't appreciate its beauty, that all she would think of were the workings of its hinges and valves. She was the kind of girl who might have preferred a real bird, with hollow wings and soft, feathered body. Why had I thought this would be a way to show Miri how I felt? Why hadn't I just sent her notes and flowers, packets of expensive teas, poems: the ordinary things women expected lovers to send? Why had I imagined giving Miri this curio would ease me into a declaration of my feelings? I had tried to do the usual kind of thing; I had scribbled lopsided, bumbling sonnets in my notebooks, picked flowers that wilted in my room, cooked meals for Miri, named stars for her. I had stood at the kitchen window, night after night, watching her in the orchard, wondering. Waiting. The little bird had sat on my desk, twittering at me as I worked. At night, lying in bed, it had perched on my bedhead, tipped its head to the side and considered me. My closest and dearest friend.

The last few months at Obanite Hall had been a constant rush of deadlines and meetings. The work consumed me: the stories of the Salt women unravelled beneath my attention, and Jenon's work, too, the curious stories emerging in scraps and flashes from the Oikos Island settlement where he was doing research. Everything I saw, everything I read, seemed connected to my work on the Salt Lane Women; to their silent, persistent attention to the world. To their patience and wit. To the ways in which they had stood so firm, refusing to fight, refusing to give in. The simplicity and grace of their heresy, and their love for each other. I had become less and less sure of who I was, or why I was there, less and less certain that I had chosen my path well. I had wanted to impress Jenon with my ability to deal with the complex ethical problems of researching the heretics and writing about them with empathy, feeling my way into the texture of their lives without crossing over into heresy myself. I had wanted to show that I could allow them their truth, their intelligence, their humanity, despite their

113

criminality. Instead, I had lost sight of History, lost sight of the Truth. I could not contravene the facts of the Rupettan Annal, and I could not write about what I had discovered without doing so.

In the pristine Obanite carrels I fetched and carried and wrote and read: all with the steady tick and shock of the Penitents' hearts beating, always beating, in the room around me. While the graduate students who shared the work in the carrels ranted and argued through the small hours of the night, or bragged about their upcoming Transformations with an air of bravado that—it seemed to me—thinly disguised their fear of complications and disappearances, I kept to myself. The third years spent hours designing the doors they dreamed of having embedded in their chests, had elaborate henna patterns tattooed on the flesh that they would one day cut away. Others had false doors fashioned out of brass, highly-polished replicas that they glued to their chests and wore with low-cut shirts, allowing the fabric to fall open and reveal the etched patterns of cogs and pipes, beetles and stars.

I wore the silver heart I had found among my mother's things, secretly, beneath my high-necked shirts. The metal flat on my chest, heating and cooling with my body.

Beneath it I felt my feeble, fleshy heart beat and beat and beat. I lay in bed at night with a finger resting on my wrist, feeling the pulse that beat there, watching the stars, dreaming that I could hear the seeds turning in the soil around me. I dreamt of being Transformed and stealing my fleshy heart before it was burned. Of crouching in a dark garden, among the compost and the worms, eating my still-beating heart: raw blood and muscle gorging in my throat.

I dreamt of Great Aunt Grace, riding astride her silver horse, with leaves tangled in her hair. I dreamt of discovering her in the forest, naked and pale, dancing with an Oikos whose body was lithe and strong and dark, their mouths and hips and hair joined in one tangled body. The Oikos with his hands on her, holding her, stripping her naked and pushing her up against a tree, planting seeds in her mouth and belly with his penis.

I dreamt the hunters came, but they had Penitent hearts, and bruised her mouth with their guns, scraping out the fleshy seeds. I dreamt she opened her mouth to speak and it was filled with cogs and pipes and keys, clotted with blood. That they spilled out of her like a flood. She was choking on it, her lips and tongue shredded and bleeding.

I dreamt of myself flayed and skinless, my heart beating in a box on Jenon's desk while he worked on an endless catalogue of loss.

I dreamt of finding a secret room, deep inside the Obanite stacks, where the hearts of a thousand Penitents beat out their senseless, limping beats while their dead bodies rotted around them.

My final semester project was a contextual review and a summation of the Historical evidence on the Salt Lane women. The work was hard, and frustrating. In the first part of my paper—the major part—I had to collate and describe all of the primary and secondary research that already existed; my assignment was to document all of the material. The secondary material was relatively simple, because there was so little. A few paragraphs here and there, a footnote in Jenon's history. A small, self-published biography of Emmeline by a distant descendant of her second cousin. Barely more than a pamphlet. I was working my way through the material in the stacks, but so much of it was merely ephemera. Documenting it felt foolish. What Historical significance was there in a collection of children's schoolbooks? In boxes of odd buttons?

The second part of the paper was more troubling. I was keenly aware that the summation would be the critical groundwork of next year's research project. That if I wrote well enough—showed enough initiative and insight—I would be invited to develop the summation into a three-year thesis project, under Jenon's supervision. The key was to show thoroughness, intelligence, and clarity in assessing the extant material—to demonstrate amply all the research skills I had been taught in the previous years—while also demonstrating that there was still work to be done. I had to show that I had understood everything that was known, and identify the gaps, and subtly, carefully, demonstrate that I was the right researcher to fill in those gaps. Part of the difficulty with the Salt Lane women was that the gaps were far larger than the threads that bound them together. Where other third-year students were working with maps that had small holes in them, mine was a collection of holes, held together by hair-thin threads of string. The contextual review, despite the fact that it amply covered all the known and extant resources, was too short, and the summation too long, with too many questions left open at the end, too many paths I might take.

In my conversations with Jenon I told him I was willing to keep going, to keep working on the heretics that nobody else was humble enough, foolish enough, to write about. He steepled his fingers in front of his face and tilted his head, watching me. 'Are you sure?' he said, and though I was sure of nothing, I nodded.

I had ridden out to the house on Salt Lane every week, the mechanical bird in my pocket, trying to think, trying to find a way into the research. A single point of enquiry, a single question I could ask of the past. I had this sense that doing a good job on the paper relied on not just hard work, not just getting it all done, but on finding the right tone, like tripping a switch and seeing the light go on. For months I felt as if I had been working in the dark, in an enormous room with a tiny candle. I could only see so much, only understand this tiny bit. The rest of it didn't fit together. I had a growing sense that there was some flaw in my research, that the resources were fundamentally *wrong* in some way. I went over and over the archive material, looking for something I had missed. I turned the major pieces of evidence over in my mind, looking for the gap, the secret, the connecting thread that would make sense of such disparate material.

I walked in the gardens at Salt Lane for hours, waiting for the caretaker to leave each day so that I could find an unlocked window and walk through the house alone. Peer into the cupboards, climb up into the loft or crawl under the house looking for something, anything, that would tell me what I needed to know, what was not written down in any of the files I had catalogued and preserved. The things I felt sure were waiting for me, the untold and terrible truths hidden in that beautiful house. Once, I fell asleep on the lawns, watching the sun through the trees, and woke to find Perihan perched on a branch nearby. As if it had flown. A bright thread pinched in its mouth like a worm. It had seemed content in that house, that garden.

'You can touch it,' I said to Miri. 'If you tap its beak it will sing for you.' I glanced from Perihan to Miri, uncertain how to break the stillness into which we had fallen. Uncertain I wanted it broken. Finally, defeated, I reached for the mechanical bird. I could put it away and forget everything. We could climb down from the tree, ride back to Elm, I could forget the entwined and impossible riddles in my life: the Salt Lane women, Miri, my love of History wrestling in the dark with my fear of Transformation. I could go home to Whitestone Shute, to my father. He had written to say that there was work for me there, teaching in the school, helping out at the library. Old Paul had been advertising for someone who could archive all the local history artefacts that came into the local Haven's possession each time some-one died. Lately, my father had written, the whole town was in the process of being folded away into the neat, yellow boxes of the dead. Mrs Perrin had gone last winter. *The town is growing old and dying,* he had written. *Nobody stays to start families, raise children, in small towns any more and, despite what they tell us, very few of those who leave in their youth—like you—return for more than the occasional visit.* I could go home; I could sit in the old house watching my father slip away into dementia, watching the old town rot while I sorted the detritus of the dead.

'I'm sorry,' I said, reaching out for the bird. 'I didn't mean . . . I just thought you might like it. It reminded me of you, somehow. I've been carrying it around so long, and finding this place seemed like a sign of something.' I shrugged.

Miri reached for my hand before I could wrap the cloth around Perihan and slip it into my pocket. I should have stayed silent. I should have kept to myself and done what I could: finished my research project well enough to pass without drawing too much attention to the work and been given my graduate's card without bothering to aspire

117

any further. I should have slipped away and left her to her secrets and her silences and her night-wandering. I looked up to see her face, thinking I could say goodbye, and saw the tears that swelled there.

'I love you,' I said, though I had planned something much longer, more elaborate and eloquent and metaphoric. I had planned to say it slowly, so as not to startle her, giving her time while I waffled on, foolish country girl, to think of an elegant, gentle evasion. Instead, I just blurted it out. *Idiot*, I thought to myself. *Total moron.* I started to say something else, hoping perhaps I could just begin again, with my carefully-planned metaphor of the two tulip bulbs growing in the same earth, when Miri leaned over and kissed me and everything—every well-rehearsed speech I had memorised, every fear and hope and dream—gushed from my memory like water falling from a sieve.

I panicked then, my mouth and Miri's coming together, feeling the coolness of her lips and the light tick of her teeth against my own. I had not had the nerve to imagine this, or if I had it had been a long way in the future, after months of holding hands and walking side by side through the College gardens. I had imagined picnics; Miri's head in my lap as she dozed in the afternoon sun, reading perhaps. I needed a year to learn to hold the weight of her hand in mine. A decade to explore the lengths of her arms. I almost pulled away, flinching at the sudden warmth of her body pressing against my own: at the long, muscled solidity of her, but Miri put her fingers on my pulse—that same familiar gesture she had employed a thousand times before, that I had recalled night after night as I lay beneath her glass ceiling, watching the stars—and all the tension of the years I had waited, hoped, loved, despaired, spilled out of me. I moved my arm to draw her close and, for the first time, feel the firm circumference of her body within my embrace: the bright, sharp kick of love binding us together.

It began to rain as we kissed. I could feel the cold tip of her nose on my cheek. Hear the rain pattering onto the boards. Smell the dampness in her hair, on her skin, taste it on her mouth. I wanted to lie down and close my eyes and concentrate on the texture, the taste of her lips touching mine, again and again. Like that. Just like that. Such a simple, ordinary thing, and yet it was as great a miracle, as fine and perfect and inexpressible a thing, as anything I have ever known.

ଚ୨

I woke early. Miri was curled beside me, her hands folded beneath her cheek, already awake and watching. Already smiling as I woke. 'What are we doing today?' she asked.

'Running away,' I said, stretching beneath the sheets, feeling the curve of Miri's thigh, the warmth of her belly pressed against my own. I slid the flat of my hand up the back of Miri's neck, threaded my fingers into the tangle of her hair: thicker and softer than I had imagined it would be.

Miri closed her eyes and smiled, turning to press her forehead against my hand, like a cat. 'Where to?' she said.

I kissed the heavy line of Miri's jaw, where it curved up towards her ear. 'The forest,' I said. 'Land Between. We'll live in a tree and eat bark and berries, drink dew, dress in leaves. We'll spend our life studying the stars.'

'Our life?'

I buried my face in the curve of Miri's shoulder, my cheek against the sleep-warm skin of her throat.

'Fool,' Miri said, slipping beneath me, sliding my body up onto her own, raising her chin so our eyes met. 'I love you.'

'I thought, if I get offered a place in the research program next year, I could put together a proposal to develop a paper on Mathilde's disappearance, after she was released. It just doesn't make sense, you know? Every day she was locked up in that place, Emmeline came to see her. They never let her in, of course, never let her see Mathilde, but every day the guardhouse logbook records her coming in with something: paper and pencils, fruit and bread and wine. She wrote letters to Mathilde. She never gave up. Never. In all those years she missed only a handful of days. And then, on a Thursday, she turned up with a jar of preserved lemons and a new blanket—it was nearly winter again—and the guard told her Mathilde had been released.

'Even if Mathilde didn't love her any more, even if she'd forgotten what that was like, being together, loving each other. Even if they'd done things to Mathilde while she was in there that made her incapable of loving anyone, she wouldn't have just walked away. There has to be more to it than that. It's like there's a secret they're keeping. Even now.' I rolled onto my back and stared up at the glass ceiling, at the mackerel clouds skerried across the sky.

Miri curled around me, put her cheek on my chest, her hand on my stomach. 'Perhaps she wasn't released. Some of them weren't. There were all those executions, mass burials, interviews that went too far and had to be covered up.'

I nodded, thinking of the records I had seen: the simple words that marked so many cruelties, so many deaths. 'I thought that might have been what happened at first, but the Penitents kept meticulous records. What the prisoners ate, where they were housed, what they did each hour. The women's menstrual cycles. The words—the names—they cried out in their sleep. At the time, before all the records were released, it would have been possible to believe Mathilde had died and it had been covered up. But I've been through the records. I've spent months in those stacks reading the names of the dead and her name isn't there. She survived, and was released. There's a record of her release interview, of what she wore, what she carried with her when she went. They weighed her and shaved her head, took an imprint of her teeth and her fingerprints. She had lost three teeth while she'd been locked up. They were given to her, along with a paper bag with her hair in it and the shoes she had been brought in with. Gardening boots, still crusted with dirt. Two guards walked her out of the compound to the gate. One of them gave her some money. They locked the gates behind her. She just stood there, on the street outside the gate. For several hours she sat on the bench across the road. Prisoners often did. As if they no longer knew how to be in the world, where to go. When the visitors started to arrive, forming a queue that wound along beneath the shadow of the brick wall, she walked away. After that, there's nothing; she simply disappeared.'

'And you want to find her.'

'She's dead by now, of course, but yes. I want to know what happened to her.'

'What if you can't?'

'I'll find something. There's so much material in the archive that suggests . . . something. I don't know what. Something more than seems apparent. And so little has been written about them. As Jenon would say, history is not the discovery of truth, but the making of it. I'd like to find a truth that makes sense of Emmeline's life, as well as Mathilde's. They lost so much; they deserve to have their story told.'

℘

When I was a child I made paper trains. I folded them out of anything I could find: my homework drafting sheets, the stacked pile of re-usable paper on my father's desk, pages torn out of my maths work-book. I had memorised the train timetable, and knew how long it took to ride from our home to the station. Late at night, I would lie awake listening for them, hearing them come snuffling up the pass. *The 9:53,* I would announce to the darkness: *Express to North Cove, then all stations. Passengers for Whitestone Shute should travel in the front car—the front car only—due to the short platform at the station.* I would push my paper trains across the desk in my room, veering around the pencil jar in a wide scoop, and sleep with them flattened beneath my pillow. I dreamed of departure with no sense of what my destination might be.

Once, when I was very small, my father took me to the city and we spent a morning at the harbour, watching the dirigibles shift like party balloons above the bay. I watched the people drifting in and out of the departure lounges and sat contentedly for at least an hour watching the luggage carousels. Best of all were the suitcases covered in stickers. I recited the names of the places they had been—Beirut, London, Cairo,

Singapore, Tokyo—and watched with wonder as their owners collected them, believing I could see the dust of distant continents in their hair, the shimmer of golden distance on their skin. I pretended to be travelling, too, waiting for my luggage with studied impatience. Occasionally, I checked my chronometer, or shook my head and grimaced at my fellow travellers. I wore my coat buttoned up to my chin, hoping to look world-weary, hoping to seem nonchalant. When my father came to collect me I saw only how ordinary he was, how homely and content. His broad hands and old boots with the scuffed toes. His good hat held gently in his hand.

I blushed and stood quietly, trying to pretend that he was my driver, come to collect me and take me to my glamorous city hotel. That my baggage had gone on ahead. That we were headed anywhere but home.

I have still made it only as far as the Bay, and those few childhood trips to Oikos Island.

On Saturday, I took Miri down to the docks and we sat in a coffee shop at the end of the pier watching the ships come in and I told her about my visit there as a child and she joined my game. We pretended to be characters from a novel—just in from the Antarctic—our bones still thawing. We huddled over our warm cups and smiled secretively at each other. The waiter brought us a menu and we studied it as though it was written in a foreign language, finally ordering a piece of orange cake, which came on a plate with the insignia of a dirigible on its rim. We ate the cake and Miri wiped the plate clean with her serviette and then slipped it into her bag.

Riding our bikes home along the river we laughed at nothing. At the buildings and lanes, at the window displays and the parking meters, at the footpaths and the sounds of strangers speaking to each other. The light fell down through the trees as though they were cathedrals, hushed and illuminated, and the water rippled against the rockwalls like a wet body. We waved to the people on the ferry, travelling home, and whirred through the park. There I was, in a foreign country after all. Smeared with happiness like a child who has filled her arms with kittens, who rolls down a hill and spins and spins until she is dizzy and tangled and skinless and bright. We lay on the grass and put our heads together and our hands up in the air and watched our fingers writhe together. Fingertip to fingertip, pressing and releasing, turning and turning. I wanted to eat her. Wanted to shell her like a pea. Find her fresh green centre. My whole body was turned inside out. I was a spilled sack of stars. I had no right to be so happy. To walk so completely out of myself and into her.

80

My father's letters had become insistent, and strange. I wrote to him that I was busy, that my research was out of control, that I had no time. He wrote back, in his calm and patient way, telling me to bring the work with me. Perhaps he could help. At the very least I could work undisturbed at home, in my old room. When the mid-semester break came, I tore myself away from Elm and took the train home.

He was waiting for me, at the station, with my old bicycle propped against his hip. Without it, I would barely have recognised him. He looked small, and huddled. His hands, when he held them out to me, when he clasped mine in them and kissed my forehead, were liver-spotted and paper-thin.

He insisted I ride home, while he walked beside me. His own cycle, he said, was broken.

At home, he bustled in the kitchen making tea, slicing cake, insisting that I shower and change my clothes before meeting him in the lounge to catch up.

'I should tell you about your mother,' he said, abruptly, as soon as he'd poured the tea.

I sat on the rug beside him, poked at the fire and watched the sparks flicker on the brickwork. 'It's so long ago, Dad, we don't have to talk about that now.' I remembered being carried down the stairs by him after her death. In my dream my clothes are wet, soaked through and dripping onto the stairs. I am cold all over, except where my cheek

123

is pressed against the crackling woodsmoke-smell of his jumper. That one small spot feels alive and dry and warm. The rest is hollowness. A cold, perpetual winter ache.

'We do,' he said. 'Before I die, before I forget it all, I have to tell you the truth.'

'You don't need to,' I lied.

He shook his head, leaning forward in his chair to watch the fire and feel its warmth. I could smell the old wool of his jumper, the familiar comfort of its thickness and warmth. 'She was already dying when she came home from Oban. She wouldn't speak to me, would barely eat. Every glass in the house was smashed. She was so angry. You were small, you needed her, but she couldn't hold you. She could drink, though,' he laughed, drily. 'Love was a disease in her. When we were kids, she once kept the dead body of an old dog in her bedroom. She took it out and wept over it every night. She screamed when it was taken away, and her mother held her back while her father carried it out of the house on a sheet of stiff board. It looked almost alive: the maggots squirming under its skin made it look as though it was breathing. She had tried to get the Penitents to give it a Rupettan heart, but they refused, and she was furious with them, with everyone and everything, for not being perfect.'

She had been a passionate woman; I had known that my whole life. Knew it in my bones as well as in my heart, for her passion had taken root in me. Fed me and clothed me, nourished me in a way my father's quiet soul could never understand. If she had become a drunk, and I had forgotten it, in the way of children who do not know what it means to be flayed open by the world, whose capacity for forgiveness is not ruined by life yet, I was not surprised. If my father had chosen not to tell me she had been a drunk, to preserve her memory as sober and loving, I guess I could understand that, too. I had been a child, just five years old when she died: slowly, but with a great noise, like a storm that rages and leaves the forest broken in its wake. Afterwards, there were just the two of us, and he had cared for me with steady, quiet patience. I knew this all already, I told him, and stood to quiet him. It was cold and late and I had work to do.

My father put his hand on my arm and pushed me back into my chair. 'There's more, Henri,' he said. 'Sit.'

He turned his hands over before the fire, studying the arthritically-curved fingers. 'She had wanted it so much: to be a Penitent, an Obanite. She worked hard, and passed the exams. Not just passed them: did well, caught the attention of the Dean and was offered the Transformation months before any of the others. She came home so happy, when she found out. Laughing. In love again, with the world, with you, with me. And then she went back, and had the surgery, and . . . ' he looked up at me, shifted in his chair. 'I know you thought . . . I know you believed, all these years, that she had an affair, and that somehow that destroyed her career, but it wasn't that. She had the surgery, but her body rejected the Penitent heart. She was there, in the Haven wards near Oban College, for months. I travelled down every week to visit her, while you stayed here with Old Paul. They tried everything they could, but her body just wouldn't have it. In the end, when they knew there was nothing they could do, they sent her home to die. It made her angry that they hadn't been able to tell the Transformation wouldn't take, that they hadn't been able to make it work. But angrier still that she couldn't make her body accept it with her own bloody willpower. In the end she believed that she was, despite everything, despite herself, inherently heretical. She said her body had betrayed her; as bodies will. And that I should make sure you didn't make the same mistakes she had.'

My father closed his eyes, pressed his fingertips to his forehead. He looked ashen and ashamed and I loved him terribly, and hated him, too.

'You can stop now,' I said, feeling the fury lash in my throat.

'She wanted so much to be a Penitent, like your grandmother and your great-grandmother. And your ridiculous Aunt Grace. You're like her in that. You have her ambition; her sense of duty to the Bellmer tradition, and her sense of entitlement, too. She thought it would be easy, and most of it was. She was bright and the work—the study, the research—all that came easily.'

My father looked at me. His grey eyes were steady. 'We should have told you the truth, but she refused to let the truth weaken you. She said it would frighten you; that you might come to think that there was something to be afraid of, that you might turn away from the family tradition, might turn your back on the Obanites, and she wouldn't have that. Not at any cost.'

'Why didn't it work?'

'It just didn't take. Surely you've heard stories, at the college? People who don't survive the operation, or develop . . . complications? Sometimes, the body rebels against the change.' My father looked around the room, at the hearth, at the warm bricks. He shook his head again, turning his hands over and over in front of the flames. 'Do you understand what I'm telling you?' he said, and I heard the shadow in his voice, heard what it had cost him to tell me his old secret, and loved him and hated him in equal measure. For telling me. For having not told me long ago. For having loved me so quietly. For having loved me at all.

I nodded and poked at the fire. I understood enough, I thought. The rest could wait.

I wanted to put my hands over my father's mouth. Cut out his stupid tongue. Stop his eyes from watching me. I went out into the garden and lay down on the grass beside my mother's grave, listening to her heart tick, dreaming of her body—mossy-toothed, rotten and skinless—folded around it.

That night he slept in his chair, unable to manage the stairs up to his room. In the morning, I left early, came back to Elm.

After that, going home was hard. I wrote polite letters, said nothing about what he had told me. He hinted, sometimes, asked me how I was coping, whether I had thought more about our 'little conversation'. I wrote about my work, about my plans for next year. I had deadlines to meet. There was no time to go home and hear more. No time to let the story of my mother's death sink its teeth into my dreams.

She had gone home in disgrace, that much had been true. And the photograph of her, in the white dress on the lawn of the Haven, that was true, too, in its way. As true as photographs ever are. Her pale face. The shadow of the Transformed heart beneath her pale shirt. I had thought it was a tattoo; I had known, even then, about the graduate students and their mock hearts. My mother had described them to me in great detail, and later my father had shown me the silver, etched piece my mother had bought as soon as she was accepted into the College.

She had died, not of a broken heart, not out of the humiliation of being sent home to Whitestone Shute, not out of *love* and weakness, but because of the Transformation. Something had gone wrong; her heart had failed. They had tried to fix it, but the problem was not in the mechanism, or in her body, exactly, but in the nexus between the two. Her old heart was torn clear—burned in the incinerator with all of the other discarded hearts—and her body had rejected anything else.

The Miracle of Harmony
Rūs: 1852

The fourth orb of the chronometer is etched with a series of notes,
swirling around its centre in a wave of spidery annotations. If you hold
a glass to the orb you can read the notes: the first eight bars of Perihan's Aria, rendered in minute detail. This is the song Anise composed
and sang for the first time in the dead of winter, 1852, and which you
have heard sung—though never quite so well as it was sung that
night—at Midwinter during the Festival of Harmony.

After months of preparation, we arrived at the court of the Empress
Kassia. Montane, Anise, and I. We came in by the back entrance: the
entrance reserved for actors and servants, and were ushered through
thin, dark hallways to our rooms, which were small and dark, but clean
enough. Montane took the first room, Anise and I the smaller one
beside it. Our room had a window that looked out onto a muddied
square. The walls of the palace rose up around it—four windowed
walls, several storeys high. In the courtyard below the washerwomen
sat and gossiped as they worked, pegging clean linen, already half-
frozen into stiff sheets, to the lines that criss-crossed the yard. Our
window would not open; its timbers were warped and swollen into
place. We could see the courtyard; glimpse the women and the walls
that faced us, only by peering through the gaps. Montane came in and
inspected the room, checking that the sheets were clean, the fire lit.
She brought a platter of food and water that she had gone down to the
kitchen to collect, and warned us that the talk among the kitchen
maids was thick with expectation. She rattled off the names of men
and women we had never met—people who would assemble in the
court tonight to see us throw our fate at the Empress's feet—there was

only one name we knew other than the Empress—that of Jacqueline. Montane pinched Anise's cheeks, studied her face as though she might see, there, our future. *Sing well*, she said. *We have staked everything on this.*

When her mother left us, Anise stretched a line across the room. She removed our twin gowns from their trunk and hung them over the string to air, plucking at the skirts as she did so. We had gambled everything on this one night. Had sold everything we owned to purchase what we needed: gowns, a carriage, horses, shoes. Our entrance to the court, Montane insisted, must be seamless, inevitable. We must appear to belong amid the silks and perfumes, amid the knives and horses, as though we were born to them. And so, she had sold everything we could, including my mute sister, whose new owner —a young collector by the name of Hofrath Bereis—also owned a duck that digested food, and a younger mannequin—a girl—who had once played the flute. He took her to his grand home and encased her there, in an old garden-house, in a purpose-built glass cabinet. Once a year, on the anniversary of his birth, he had all his purchases—his follies—removed from their cases and set out in the garden. Hundreds of guests were invited to view his collection. Some were stolen, some broken during the sprawling, drunken parties he held. As he grew older his great fortune dwindled. It was said that he loved fast women, and slow horses. His numerous collections fell into disrepair, or were sold off to repay his mounting debts. At his death, his collections were put up for sale; the paintings did not garner much interest as they were all eaten to pieces by moths. But there was some excitement over his collection of mechanical toys. In the auction catalogue detailing his estate, however, there is no mention of Alazaïs, though the Vaucanson automatons, and the by-then-featherless duck, were listed.

I did not know, then, that all this would come to pass. I had no notion of how curious Alazaïs's path through history would be. That night in the palace, as I contemplated my sister's fate, amid the musty reek of mouse droppings and old mattresses, the gowns were an extraordinary folly: our entire fortune stitched up in japanned brocade and layers of gauzy silk. Next she pulled out the little packet of papers her mother had bargained so hard for. The papers were fine—almost finer than the silk of our gowns. As we breathed upon them they fluttered. She set me to work.

Next she withdrew the thicker, blotted pages of her composition from another drawer. These she first untied and unrolled, pressing the pages flat with the palm of her hand, then she pinned them to the walls of our room and strode along beside them, circling the room as she studied the rise and fall of the notes. She moved silently, as always, but the notes rose and fell in the tilt of her head, in the lift and curl of her hands. Occasionally, she lifted her quill to the page and made a notation, a correction. A small frown buttoned her forehead. She moved backwards through the music, then forward again, testing the new notes, passing over them and back, over and back, until they were bedded into place. She leant forward over the pages, bracing herself against the wall, to hear the silent notes wash over her tiny frame. As the light began to fail, she stood back in the centre of the room and turned in a complete, slow circle. *It will have to do,* she said.

As the washerwomen's gossip faded she set me to singing the changes while she sat at the window and watched the washerwomen fold their stiff sheets into their baskets. We dressed in our fine gowns, tied each other's ribbons, curled our hair, washed and powdered our faces, laced our shoes and stood, mirrored antique dolls, as first one and then the other were circled by Montane, whose spidery fingers twitched and tweaked at us until she was satisfied.

Outside in the corridor a young woman called the hour. We were about to commit heresy; our faces were white and still.

Montane unlocked the chamber of my heart and stood aside, holding the little door ajar to admit her daughter's hand. As Anise's hand slipped into me, I tasted the flash of her fear, the bright notes of music threaded through her like blood, a nightingale suspended in a cage of wreathing green copper wires, a mother's hand, hard on her arm, the press of the whalebone on her hip, my own face—so like her own. Her private pride. Her frail hope.

130

When it was over, Montane tucked the key, on its fine silver chain, into the pocket hidden at her waist and kissed her daughter's forehead. *We will not fail,* she said. *We must not fail.*

When the servant knocked at our door we were ready. We followed him in silence through the corridors of the palace—pursuing the lambent flame he held so carefully before him. We were in the servant's corridors—less like corridors than spaces between the walls of the real palace, a shadow world of dust and secrets. He stopped and tapped once on a door that sat flush against the wall. The door was opened and light and warmth and glimmer pressed into the secret dark. The room where we were to perform—the Celestial Hall—was walled in swathes of white velvet hung with diamond shards. The floor was a checkerboard of polished silver and white marble. Above us a clear glass ceiling, held together by a spider's web of impossibly-thin black leading, revealed the stars of the winter sky. The hall was empty, save for the handful of servants still arranging chairs in semi-circular rows to face the raised platform on which we were to perform.

Montane strode forward, through the aisle between the chairs. Huge crystal candelabras stood at each side of the stairs leading up to the stage; a gauzy curtain was draped across it, drifting in the breeze from the candles. She turned and beckoned us forward. When we reached her she shook off the long, warm cape she had been wearing to reveal her own costume: ice-blue figured silk, heavy and rich as chocolate, dragonflies embroidered along the edge of her hem, along the swooping edges of her sleeves. She raised her hand to usher us forward and the silk fell back, revealing a gauzy midnight blue layer beneath, embroidered with silver stars.

When Empress Kassia and her court entered we were in our places behind the curtain. They were like ghosts seen through the curtain, glittering and half-wrought, accompanied by the tinkle of laughter and gossip, of glasses being filled, of fur and wine and sweat, of lacquered wigs and perfumed flesh. Finally, the hall was filled. The Empress clapped her fan on the edge of her chair and there was a last harried rustle of skirts and coats as the throng turned to face the stage.

Montane nodded to the man who waited beside the stage, and he nodded to those others around the hall who stood by with elaborately-carved silver snuffers to put out the candles along the sides of the room. The night sky shone down upon us. Montane stepped through the curtains and began.

Montane stood deathly still in the light of the candelabra beside her, knowing the effect, in that winter-white room, of her stillness and the startling blue of her gown, the bruised shadow of her underskirts showing through when the breeze lifted them. She waited with held breath; this was her moment. Since the night when she had stumbled into the ruin of my former home, since she had found me alone and withered, a shadow of my previous self, she had known that this moment would come. This was her revenge, sweet and soft between her teeth. She sought out Jacqueline and her marquise, caught her old friend's eye and held it for just a moment. Jacqueline frowned—something fluttered in her mind, some mothy threat battering its wings against the walls.

In Persia, where the breezes are scented with attar and the women's breath with cinnamon, there is a palace made of porcelain. The most beautiful palace in the world, Montane began. *Many years ago I travelled there and sat at the feet of the great Hoca—the great teacher and inventor—the Lady Kelôglan. She told me many tales, showed me many wonders. She told me of the white elephant who walks beneath summer skies, decked in silk, and calls down the moon, his bride, each night. She told me how the immortals sail upon the sun's rays in golden ships, plying the oceans of the air for mortal dreams. She told me of the great southern Empress who lies like a mist on the surface of the sea in the early hours of the day—replenishing the oceans, sending cool breezes to embrace her people as they wake. She told me of the great northern Empress, who can peel a stone and knot an egg, out of whose tears stars are formed. At her feet I learned the wonders of the East, both large and small. After many days and nights, she asked me for my own tale.*

The Miracle of Harmony

The Hoca's tales were of wonder and magic, mine was a story of solitude and science, hers told of gods and golden ships, mine of Truth and Hope, hers were of ancient times, mine of a time beyond time, a secret hope kept alive in the heart of one great family. I had travelled to Persia with an ancient companion—a creature of magical and astonishing heritage—and with my daughter, who had sat with Death, who had looked into Death's eyes, and had been spared. We had travelled for many years, seeking to understand our fate, our miracle, searching for guidance from the wise men and women of the world. In the gardens of the porcelain palace, in the shaded water gardens filled with giant ferns and tall palms, I knelt in the silk tents and told our tale. When the tale was told Lady Kelôglan wept, for her time, the time of gods and golden ships, of magic, were over. 'Montane of the Wynder women,' she proclaimed, 'you must journey home, you must go to the court of the leader of the world and you must tell them your tale. You must show them the Future.'

Tonight, Empress, ladies, gentlemen, we will present for you the story Lady Kelôglan bid us carry home—a true tale of Death and Immortal Life. After long years in the wilderness, after years of persecution, neglect and silence, I have brought Her home. She is here— our Future, our Miracle—let us welcome Her.

There was polite applause as Montane stepped aside and two young women moved to draw back the curtains. Anise and I stood an arms-length apart in the centre of the stage, turned slightly towards each other.

Every year, in the dead of winter, the performance we gave that night is recreated. People travel miles to see Rupetta and the Wynder sing the tale of the nightingale. None can reproduce the tremulous, fragile beauty with which Anise sang. Her voice sparkled in that hall, outshining the stars. When we began, the court was whispering behind their hands, restless for dance and gossip and wine. We were there as entertainment, a fey distraction from the serious business of their various seductions. As Anise's voice rose up above their heads, swirling and trembling on the air before them, they fell silent. When first Perihan and then I joined her—the notes stretching beyond human breath, higher and higher and higher, sweet and full and charged— they were stunned into breathlessness. They leaned forward in their chairs, hardly daring to breathe as we sang the tale of Anise and the nightingale

This story begins at the edge of the woods, in a small cottage where a small family—a mother and daughter—live alone. The woman is poor, though she is wise and good. They live alone in the woods—far from the cities and towns—for the mother is the keeper of an ancient secret whose time has not yet come. Deep in the woods, in the ruins of what was once a great manor, stands a woman—not alive and not dead, not flesh and not bone. A woman of copper and leather and steel. A woman of porcelain and wood, of pipes and barrels and cogs and wheels. Her name is Rupetta. Each day, before the sun rises, the mother visits her ancient charge, who stands, wreathed in vines, gazing out a window that has long since rotted away, towards an ancient apple tree.

The path the mother takes is well-hidden. She treads lightly, moves swiftly through the woods. She carries with her an ancient key—golden and smooth—that fits in the palm of her hand. When she reaches the site she walks through the tumbled stones, the floors now pierced by saplings, until she reaches the room where Rupetta waits. Each day, as the sun rises, as her daughter waits at the window of their cottage on the other side of the wood, the mother performs the ritual the Wynder women have performed for centuries unknown; she opens the door in Rupetta's chest and admits her hand. While they stand in the tumbled ruin, in the middle of the forest, she performs the Wynding. Their twin hearts beat as one. Their shared soul—the shared charge of their entwined life—laces the air with light.

Back at the cottage, the mother and her daughter begin their day with another long walk through the forest, to the river, where they join the fishermen that stand on the banks and net trout. As her mother fishes, the girl sits on the riverbank mending nets, catching bait, and listening to the nightingale who sings in the trees above her. It is the most beautiful sound in the world, she thinks, the nightingale's song. She will be happy and content if only she can hear the nightingale sing each day for the rest of her life.

One day, the child falls ill. She lies in her bed, awaiting death. She can no longer wander in the woods, through the shaded paths down to the river's edge, where the nightingale sings. Trapped in her room the girl weeps for want of the nightingale's song. Finally, her mother ventures into the forest and asks the nightingale to come with her to their little cottage, to sing for her child.

Why should I, who am wild, who am a creature of the earth, care for the death of a child? the nightingale sings. *I am a thing of the earth; I am Nature, who welcomes Death, who sings to guide it through the dark. We are mortal,* it sings, *and mortal creatures must die.*

The mother begs the nightingale to come to the little cottage in the woods, to sing for the child who has loved the nightingale's song throughout her short life, but the nightingale refuses.

In despair the mother sits down by the river and weeps. In the old tales, a god would come, a saint, an angel, a speaking fish, but this is no fairy tale. The mother, who is wise, who has made her way in the world as best she can with wit and sense and knowledge, who has read books and studied the ways of the world, who can repair clocks and nets, lamps and carts, who has a secret, second heart, walks down to the river and begs a fisherman to take her to the nearest town. There she barters everything she has for a small parcel of mechanical parts—cogs, pipes, barrels, a square of supple leather, a handful of false jewels.

She travels home. Her child lies pale and thin beneath the sheets. She kisses her daughter's forehead, cups the hot cheek in her hand. She will not weep.

When the child sleeps she takes her bundle of parts and goes through the woods, to the ruined manor, where Rupetta waits.

Rupetta, the mother says, *my daughter is sick. She will die soon. She has but one wish: to hear the nightingale sing once more, but it will not come to her.* The mother lays the parts she has brought out on the ground. *Will you grant me this—will you make an instrument that will sing the nightingale's song?*

Rupetta is old and worn—in need of repair. For many centuries the Wynder women have been poor. They—who were once great queens, rulers of earth, sea and sky—live a meagre existence. Rupetta's pipes are cracked, her copper green, her brass mottled with age. Her face is a ruin of rust and disrepair, and yet she nods and moves, slowly—oh, so slowly—to kneel on the ground and gather the parts together. *Sleep,* she tells the mother. *I know how our heart aches. I will do what I can.*

All night Rupetta works. By morning her joints are cracked, rust lies in flakes at her feet; her eyes are glassy with exhaustion. Even the Wynding can barely raise her. Nevertheless, it is done. *Perihan,* she whispers, as the light dims in her eyes once more. *Its name is Perihan.*

The mother does not stop to Wynd Rupetta; she rushes from the ruined manor with the nightingale tucked in her pocket. She carries the nightingale to her daughter's bedside and whistles. The nightingale chirrups a reply; her daughter turns in her sleep, folding her pale hands beneath her reddened cheek. The mother strokes its tiny beak and speaks its name—Perihan. The nightingale sings.

The daughter wakes, and smiles. It is the first time she has smiled in days. She reaches out for Perihan and her mother places the bird on her hand. The daughter traces the edge of a wing with her fingertip. The mother smiles. Hours pass as they listen to the songs it can sing— wild and green and graceful. Its notes trip and ripple and flow. They are sweet and sharp and true. The little girl rises from her bed; she sits on the doorstep and looks at the sun. Her little face is flush with joy. Deep in the woods, Rupetta smiles, too.

Soon, it is time for the mother to go down to the river, to fish for their supper.

At the river's edge the mother meets the nightingale. It is morning, and he is silent. *How is your daughter?* he asks.

The mother turns away, towards the river, and casts out her net. *She is well,* she says.

Death has not come for her? asks the nightingale.

It will not, says the mother.

Death touches all mortal creatures. I have sung for Death—it will come for her today.

Alone at the cottage, the daughter watches the light fall through the trees, she listens to the nightingale, who sings and sings and sings.

Far away, at the edge of the river, her mother is laying down her nets; she is turning towards the forest, turning towards home. It is too late, Death stands at her daughter's side, it places a hand upon her brow.

The daughter looks up and sees Death's face and knows who it is that has come for her. She is not afraid, though she wishes Death had not come so soon, not without her mother there to say goodbye.

What is that, little one, that you hold in your hand?

It is a nightingale, she says. *My mother made it to sing for me.*

Will it sing for me? Death asks.

The little girl holds Perihan out towards Death and asks it to sing. Its song reaches deep into the forest, where her mother is running towards her, running as fast as her legs will carry her. Tears fall down her face as she runs; they soak the bodice of her gown. She trips and scrapes her hands, skins her knee, twists her ankle. Each time she falls she gets up and runs on, towards home.

The nightingale sings. Its song is so sweet, so tender and true, that Death sits on the bed beside the woman's daughter and weeps.

What's wrong? says the little girl.

I have never heard such beautiful music, says Death.

The daughter looks out the window, towards the path that leads out of the forest, the path her mother is running along as she lies in her bed, the sheet pulled up to her chest, speaking with Death. *I do not want to die,* she says. *Not yet.*

Just then the figure of a woman emerges from the edge of the forest. Her eyes shine, her heart beats. Her face is the face of the ages: a ruin of Time and yet she is moving forward on shattered legs, rust fluttering in her wake. *Death*, she says, and her voice shatters the air. *You cannot take the child.*

I have come for a life, Death says, *and I must have one.*

Rupetta—for that is who has come—reaches a hand towards the daughter, and the nightingale. The little bird hops into the palm of its maker. *You may take the nightingale's song,* she says.

Death smiles and nods its heavy head. Death opens its mouth as a wisp of light emerges from the tiny nightingale's beak. A shimmer of grace. Death inhales and Perihan's breath curls like woodsmoke between his teeth. Soon his mouth is full and Perihan sits in Rupetta's hand like a toy.

Rupetta bends and places Perihan in the daughter's hand. She lifts the daughter in her arms and turns towards the cottage.

When the mother enters the cottage, breathless and bedraggled, she is startled. Standing in the middle of the room is her daughter, blooming with health, her cheeks pink, her hair lustrous, her limbs strong. Beside her stands another daughter. The twin's eyes shine, her hair gleams, her limbs are strong. The door to her heart is open, the mother can see the mechanical child's heart beating, hear the syncopated tick and swoop, tick and swoop, that echoes her daughter's own. In her daughter's hand is a small silver key.

Mother, says the daughter, her voice light with health and hope. *This is Rupetta.*

As the performance ended, Anise's voice rose up, crisp and clear, soaring over the heads of the audience. She was a small woman. She had been, it is true, a frail and sickly child, but that night the spirit of the nightingale—of Perihan—sprang within her soul. Each note she sang echoed with grace, transforming the hall into a cathedral. The final verse was a diminishing quietude: a bittersweet elegy for the bird whose life force had been traded for her own:

Perihan, the light is falling, sing for me once more,
Perihan, the day is dying, sing for me once more,

The Miracle of Harmony

I have heard you singing; I will hear you ever more,
Perihan, your song inside me beats forever more.

The angel of the apocalypse doesn't say 'there is no more time' but 'there is no time to lose'. That night, as we stood before the great Empress, listening to the last notes of our performance fade, we knew that what little time we had—the time we had stolen to give this one performance—had passed. In the hushed Celestial Hall, we waited for the future to begin. It was as though time had been split like a wave's crest split by the stern of a boat. The infinite thickness of space and time was folded around us. We were hovering on its edge, like the child that is born but has not breathed, like the dead whose heart has yet to cease beating, whose body has not yet been burned.

The Empress stood. She walked towards the stage, mounted the stairs. I heard Montane, standing beside the candelabra at the base of the stairs, take in a sharp, short breath.

The Empress placed one hand against my cheek and looked into my eyes and smiled. She turned towards Anise and smiled again. She took Anise's hand between her own and turned to present Anise to the court, as if to invite—at last—applause. Instead, she knelt before her. The sound of her heavy skirts folding as she lowered herself were the only sounds in the room. She pressed her forehead to the back of Anise's hand in the sign of obeisance.

ಬಿ

Montane was silent as we were escorted to the dining hall, given pride of place at the table beside the Empress. Anise was upright, composed, as if the rich pleasures of the court were familiar, unremarkable. At the Empress's bidding she danced with the Empress's son, Pietr, drank wine that the Empress herself poured while her advisors and sycophants—the assembled gaggle of fools and nobles—asked questions, peered, preened.

How does it work? one asked.

Where is its maker? asked another.

I stood silent, as Montane had warned me I must.

Jacqueline and Dominic approached. He was tall and dark-haired, but not handsome. An ordinary man with wealth and leisure enough not to care. His wife was slim and pale, with a fine spray of freckles on her throat. She wore gloves that reached past her elbows, a buttery yellow that matched perfectly with her gown and the flushed warmth of her skin. Her eyes were bright and dark. She stood a little behind her husband, her hand resting in the crook of his arm.

Congratulations, ladies, your performance was excellent. Who, may I ask, is the composer of such music? Dominic asked. Montane glanced from Jacqueline to her husband, to the thick white shirt, the pressed collar, the ease with which he held himself. Jacqueline's hands were covered, but her bare throat was not windburned or sun-reddened; her cheeks were pale and powder-soft. Now it rose up—the life she could have lived, the life her daughter could have had.

My daughter, Anise Wynder IX, Montane said.

And who, Jacqueline asked, *is the instrument?*

I am Rupetta, I answered.

It can speak, Jacqueline laughed, a hand rising to cover her throat.

It can sing, said her husband, *why not speak. What else can it do?*

Whatever you can, sir, I replied.

The Empress laughed. *A challenge!* she said.

Dominic hesitated and I felt, rather than saw, Montane stiffen beside me.

That's ridiculous, he said. *I am a man and it is merely an automaton —a well-made toy.*

What is it that makes you a man, and not a toy? I asked. *What is it you can do that I cannot?*

You have already proven yourself more artful than I, dear lady.

So I am a lady now, and not a machine.

You do not speak like a lady.

And you do not look like a man; I have seen peacocks less splendidly attired.

The Miracle of Harmony

Are you afraid, Dominic, the Empress asked, *or merely tongue-tied?*

The machine is a wit and not a woman, Empress, but I am not afraid. I challenge it to a game, of its own devising.

A game of wit, a game of chance, a game of war?

It cannot lose a game of war when it has no blood to spill. This thing—this talking clock—has, its keepers claim, travelled the world, survived centuries of change, visited the gods of the past and the palaces of the east, the elephants of the moon, even! It has known the time of Plato and the time-outside-time of God—surely, in all that time, in its many exotic wanderings, it has seen many tournaments, many tests: of the mind, of the body and of the soul. I challenge it to create the greatest challenge it can devise—a test of wit and grace and humanity— and compete in such a challenge against me.

Do you accept this challenge, Rupetta? the Empress asked.

While we had been bent upon this exchange the hall had fallen quiet. The clattering of plates, the chink of glasses, the swish of velvet and satin and silk had all stilled. While the whole court watched Dominic and the Empress and I, Jacqueline was watching Montane. Her colour had risen as her husband spoke. A creeping flush of recognition had swept over her. Her face was pale, the light spattering of freckles on her throat stood out, now, like flecks of blood on her pale skin. Her hand, which had rested so lightly on her husband's arm, was now clutched tight as an eagle's claw. Montane smiled, the sharp precision of her smile, like a shard of light reflected off broken glass, piercing the space between them.

I do, I replied.

℘

The first game of Oråki was played in the centre of the Celestial Hall, where we had made our first appearance before the Empress Kassia. The board was a circle of polished and lacquered ebon, five metres in diameter at its outside edge: a dark, gleaming planispheric astrolabe. At its centre was a milky orb—the moon—surrounded by the stars of the night sky. The stars were formed of silver inlay, with pearls at their centres.

Facing each other across the board were the chairs for the two players. On that night, as on other nights when the game is played to resolve a dispute—a challenge of honour or love or trade—a copper pot and a small brazier had been placed beside each player's chair. Arrayed alongside each player's chair were their pieces, in order of descending height. On the Weaver's side stood the Sorrowing Weaver, Chronos, Victory, and the Owl. On the Fisher's side stood the Fisher King, Tacitus, Melusine, and the Frog. The Weaver's figures were ivory inlaid with silver, and the Fisher's were jade, inlaid with gold.

We had kept secret, for a month, the work of forming the pieces, the board. We had been given a sum of money to purchase materials, and a handful of artisans to do our bidding—each of whom had been warned their tongues would be cut out if they revealed our secrets too soon. They had slept in the Hall, on slim pallets, for a month. Now, as their work was revealed, they were journeying home to their husbands and children, their presence no longer necessary. Their pockets were filled with shards of jade, tiny ingots of gold and silver, ebon and pearls. Their fingers were worn and their eyes red with exhaustion, but they had been well paid. The work they had made was exquisite: the Fisher King with fish swimming in his beard, the mute goddess Tacitus, the fiercely-beautiful winged Victory, her hair streaming behind her. Melusine, whose muscled torso and tail seemed to writhe with strength. The Frog with his crown, the Owl with her prey.

When he read the rules, in particular the section on the penalties each player would pay if they lost a piece, Dominic protested. *The penalties are too high*, he said. *They will cost me more than they will cost the machine. This was meant to be a test of wit, not of the body.*

The Empress listened to his protests quietly. *You asked her to devise a challenge of wit and grace and humanity. Oråki is a test of all three. You challenged her to create the terms of the contest in this very room, before all of us.* Her eyes swept the room, taking in his wife, Anise,

142

Montane, and all the glittering, perfumed attendants of the court. *But . . . it is up to you. Do you forfeit, Dominic? Are you so easily beaten?*

She has deceived me. This is not what was intended. He held out his hands, splayed his fingers before her. *I could die. I could . . . how will I write? How will I ride to hunt? How will I wield a sword when the game is over?*

Do you forfeit?

The court held its breath. His wife, his allies and his enemies stood in attitudes of studied inattention.

No, he said finally. *You know that I cannot.*

Once the Hall was filled, once the courtiers had taken their places, jostling for a position from which to best view the players, we began. The Empress stood.

The ancient philosopher, Aristotle, once wrote, she said, *that a lover of stories is, in a way, a lover of wisdom, since a story is composed of wonders. Tonight, in the Celestial Hall, in the winter palace of the Rūs, in the presence of the Empress Kassia, a challenge has been made and will be met. The winner of this challenge will need to display wit, grace and humanity—and, I submit, the wisdom of Aristotle. Having displayed such skills, she—or he, or it—will earn themselves a place at my left hand, as chief advisor. The challenge has been set, the moon is full, let the story commence.*

Each player has twenty-eight moves to make—one for each of the phases of the moon, which wanes from full to dark as play proceeds. Before each move, the players take it in turns to relate the tale of the Sorrowing Weaver and the Fisher King. The script of the game is set for the first moves, until the *volta*, when the players must call on their own arts of invention to craft a tale of love and magic, based on their own moves and those of their opponent.

As the one who had been challenged, I began, placing my Sorrowing Weaver, at the edge of the board, on Adhara, in the constellation of Canis Major.

Once there was, and once there wasn't, a Weaver. Her hair was long and black, her skin smooth as silk, her eyes as blue as the sky. Each day

143

she wove cloths of the finest silk. They were the most coveted silks in all of the Empire, but most treasured of all were those in which she wove images of the river. The river-cloths seemed to ripple with the tide, to whisper of the deep ocean currents. In them she wove images of stones and mermaids, fish and frogs, willows and women. Each evening, as the moon rose and her eyes grew tired, she laid down her weaving to walk by the river.

I took my seat and Dominic rose. He lifted his first piece—the Fisher King—in whose long beard fish swam. He placed the Fisher King on Rastaban, in the constellation Draconis. *Once there was, and once there wasn't,* he began, *a Fisher King. His hair was dark, his eyes as green as his river home, his skin as smooth as water. Each day he swam the waters of the Green Empire, the rivers of his sunken Kingdom, speaking to the creatures of his domain, hearing the plaints of the fishes, the dreams of the conch, the mourning of the great narwhal. Each evening, as the moon rose, he laid down his coral crown and walked upon the riverbank.*

I placed my first guardian—Chronos—on the great star Achernar, in the constellation of Eridani, the river. *One evening, as the Weaver walked along the riverbank, she came upon two great and strange creatures, playing a game of Oråki in the middle of a clearing. One of the creatures was Chronos, the god of Time, who devours his own children.*

The other, said Dominic, as he placed his first guardian, *was Tacitus, the mute goddess, who appeared in the form of a great fish with her mouth sewn shut.*

The great players had only just commenced their game, I said. *As the Weaver knelt to peer at the game the old gods placed their second guardians on the board: Chronos his winged woman, whose name was Victory.*

And Tacitus his mer-creature, whose name was Melusine.

They placed their third guardians: Chronos his owl.

And Tacitus his frog.

Dominic and I had placed all our pieces on the board—our Travellers, escorted by the three guardians who would guide them on their journeys. The Travellers were seven hand-spans high, Chronos and Tacitus five hand-spans, Victory and Melusine three, and the little Frog and Owl just one. Each piece's Shadow—their range of move-ment—was equal to their height. Each player must use their guardians to lay out a path between the edge of the sky and the moon for their Traveller to follow. Each Traveller must strive to reach the moon before it wanes to darkness, and before their opponent. They must travel from star to star, but can only step onto the stars on which one of their own guardians has already stood. Once a star has been marked as that of the Weaver or the Fisher, they cannot be claimed by the other Traveller's guardians. A guardian who has no star within his shadow—nowhere to move—is lost. In an ordinary game of Oråki—in the game children and old men play to amuse themselves—there is no great terror in the loss of a guardian, only shame and a diminished capacity to lay a path for their Traveller.

It was my turn—the *volta*, as it is called, since at this point the game truly begins. I stood and walked across to my Victory, who stood as high as my waist, and slid her across the board to Alrischa. *As Tacitus placed his frog guardian on a small, nameless star he heard a sound behind him and looked up. The Weaver was caught in Tacitus's silent gaze and could not move. Chronos lifted his heavy head and smiled.* Come here, little weaver, *he said. And the weaver felt her feet move towards the God of Time, whose mouth was as dark and wide as a moonless sky.*

The game, and the story, moved on—each of us laying out our paths through the starred sky, trying to block the other from marking stars we would need for our own Travellers. We wove our tale, in turns, each building upon the other's inventions. For a while the telling of the tale is simple: even children know the tale of the curse that is laid upon the Weaver and her Fisher King.

The Weaver barters her freedom for a bolt of river-cloth. The Fisher King comes to speak with Tacitus and sees the cloth—a green river swirling about Tacitus's shoulders. The old gods arrange for the Weaver and the Fisher King to meet and fall in love.

Time and Death, however, are no matchmakers.

With the cruel whimsy of the old gods they curse the Weaver and the Fisher King: theirs will be a great, a True, an all-consuming Love, but they will meet this once and never again, not until as many years have passed as there are stars in the sky. Once the curse is laid, the players must make the tale their own, keeping faith with their opponent's words, but also playing to win. Since the lovers cannot be reconciled, they must compete to reach the moon, to die in her arms and thus undo the curse.

On Dominic's twelfth move he placed his frog, whose dark eyes seemed to blink in the glimmer of the Hall's light, on Hamal, in the old constellation of Aries. It was a foolish move. The owl flew to Hamal—the frog was trapped and Dominic blanched. He knew he must pay the penalty. His face was composed as he stood and lifted the moon-shaped blade from its place beside his copper bowl. He held his hand out above the bowl and slid the sharp edge of the blade through the smallest finger of his left hand. The finger dropped into the bowl and blood spurted from the small, round wound. I heard Jacqueline's gasp and the Empress's low grunt. Somewhere in the hall a young boy fainted and was carried out. Dominic moved his hand towards the brazier and cauterised the wound before applying the red salve that lay in a shallow porcelain dish beside the copper bowl.

The Owl dived upon the Frog, I said. *Its death was quick and nobly silent.*

Dominic moved across the sky, towards his second guardian. *Tacitus, when she saw what the Owl had done, did not weep. The Frog had led them safely through the swamps, and had shown them the blossoms of the waterlily. He had marked out the way of the Mermaid and the Fisher King, and now he would swim forever in the river of the Dead. The Great Fish turned towards Time and bowed. She could not speak, but Chronos heard her voice as clearly as a bell on a silent morning.* Your death shall be the price of his, *she said.*

We had sixteen more moves to make. Dominic's attention was sharpened, crisp with intent. Tacitus lay out a path that curved towards the moon in a long, increasingly sharp loop. The Fisher King began to follow her, but Victory and the wily Owl intervened. The Fisher King became a lover pursued, his jade beard almost fluttering as he whirled about the sky. Victory drew her sword against Melusine, whose death was grim and slow. Three hand-spans high she stood, and so three more of Dominic's fingers fell into the copper bowl. His face was pinched and white as he stood to make his next move. His story grew thin, insensible. I feared—we all feared—he would faint and disgrace himself. Tacitus turned back towards the Traveller, as if to beseech her charge for forgiveness.

Finally, the Weaver stood beside the moon and gazed, once more, upon the face of her love, who stood flanked by his two remaining guardians in a sea of her own stars. The endgame, too, has a set script, depending on which player attains the moon. I stood and crossed the board to recite my part:

Somewhere, *the Weaver said*, I will always be travelling towards you. *The Weaver knew she could not escape the curse that had been laid upon her. She and the Fisher King would never be together. The Weaver's death was the only way to release the Fisher King from love and longing. The Sorrowing Weaver stepped smiling into the darkening arms of the moon.* Here, *she said*, in the arms of the moon, in the dark of Death, I will wait for you for as many years as there are stars.

The Fisher King, released from the spell of love, looked up and saw the moon. He did not hear his love's farewell; he did not feel the love rush from his heart, or suffer its sudden absence. He saw only the night sky—its endless dark—and the flicker of a new star whose light glittered like a kiss.

ℬ

And so Montane had her revenge—Dominic, ashamed and unhanded, was the laughing stock of the court and I became the Empress's advisor. Each morning Anise and I woke before dawn, dressed and ate and wrapped ourselves in warm coats for the walk across the palace grounds to her private chambers. There, while the Empress was dressed and fed and curled and courtiers came, one after another, to beg this or that favour, we sat at the windows and read or played chess or Oråki. We awarded medals and named streets, funded voyages of discovery and the building of abbeys. Men bleated about their wars and women of their crusades. Scientists and artists petitioned for funds to map the skies, to paint and sculpt and compose.

In summer we moved to the summer palace and were given rooms adjoining the Empress's own. The Empress fell ill: she was old and the heat of the season sat heavily on her chest. Pietr, the Empress's son, was recalled to the court and, rather than attend his mother's bedside or take up the office she could no longer fully occupy, he held great balls, like a fairytale prince seeking a bride. He bought Jacqueline a fine horse and begged her to go riding with him. As the season moved on, as the days grew longer and hotter, the Empress's health failed. She became bed-ridden and slept through most of the day. The Royal Physician made her comfortable, but could do no more.

I must make plans, she said one morning.

Anise looked up from the book she had been reading. *Not yet, Kassia. The summer will be over soon, and you will feel stronger.*

What if I do not? The Empire does not need a vain fool for an Empress, or a dead fool. I am not immortal, dear Anise, and must do my duty by my people.

Dear friend, I know you are right. It is hard, however, to think of your not being here. What is the Rūs Empire without the great Empress Kassia to lead it?

My son is a fool, the Empress said.

He is a man, Anise said, *and not yet an Emperor.*

The Empress snorted. *His father wanted him to be educated; to be a wise man. I thought he would need strength to rule in my place, not wisdom.*

You have needed both.

I have had both, it is true. And Pietr has neither. The Empress shifted in her bed, watching Anise and I. *You are wiser, older, and stronger than I, Rupetta, and yet you cannot rule. The timid hordes will not be ruled by a creature that is neither a woman nor a man. Not yet, I think. And you, Anise, what kind of Empress would a songbird make?*

Anise blanched. *No kind at all, Empress. I am too young. Too simple. Too—*

Common? The Empress raised an eyebrow and smiled. *There is nothing so common as highborn women, Anise, and nothing so uncommon as you and your Rupetta.*

The Empress clapped her hands and the doors to her chamber were opened. A young man entered and bowed. *Where is my son?* The Empress asked. *Where are the gaggling idiots of my court?*

It is past midnight, your highness, the boy said. *They are asleep.*

Wake them, she said, swinging her legs to the ground and gesturing for Anise to bring her robe. *It is time my son was married.*

Henri's Story: Part Four

'Have you learned much about them?' Margause said. 'The Salt Lane women.'

'Not really,' I said. 'The first year is really just cataloguing: curation work. A lot of it is going over what I did last year in more detail, and adding to it.'

In truth, the job of sorting, repairing, cataloguing and preserving the papery remains of the Salt Lane Witches was an endless task. I had thought the work complete last year, when I had finally finished the summation of the primary and secondary resources, but then, while I was away home over the summer, Jenon and his team had travelled to Oikos again, and located a whole, buried basement of material related to the Oikos, and therefore to my own fledgling research specialty. Folioing endless pages of letters, drawings, journals and diaries, recipes and poems; describing and cataloguing jars of seeds, teacups, wooden bowls and cheap, well-worn spoons. These were tasks for the least talented among the new postgraduates, the least likely to proceed to Transformation.

The Oikos Island archives were a mess of unsorted boxes, a mouldering resource that, if they hadn't been the personal belongings of mildly-interesting historic personages, would have long ago found their way into a second-hand store, or become landfill beneath a new housing estate, along with all the other unmatched shoes and unlidded saucepans of the long-since dead. Instead, they were shipped back to Oban College and piled up in the dank room at the base of the library, along with a morass of other unsorted, uncared-for donations that had come into the care of the Obanites over the years. The real value of those archives was not in their Historical interest, or in their ability to provide insights into the past in order to guide us towards a better future, but in the repetitive and instructional work they provided for History postgraduates: training in the banalities of historic methodology without the risk that anything significant might be found, noted, or lost by an inept trainee researcher.

I had been given the task of curating the Oikos Island material as a supplement to the work I was doing on the Salt Lane heretics. When the curation assignments were posted on the bulletin board outside Jenon's office, I queued with the others, hoping for a moderate task: something respectable, achievable, but relatively insignificant. Something related to my core research, perhaps even something that would throw new light on the work I'd already done. I had dreamed of working on other Oikos heretics, perhaps, beginning work on a new sect that I might move on to when my work on the Salt Lane women was done. I had hoped to sink into the quietude of my research project: to pocket myself away in my room with the Salt Lane women's ephemera and write.

When I reached the front of the jostling queue in the postgraduate room at Oban, I scanned the lists for my name and finally found it, pressed my finger to the glass and scanned across for my assignment. The Oikos Island archive: I was given the task of adding to the material I had already curated; the mess of an archive that had never been sorted not because it was lost or incomplete, but because work on the heretics was considered a waste of resources. A fool's task no self-respecting graduate or Faculty member would waste their time on. Had Jenon given me the archives to let me know that he knew about the months I had spent sleeping in his precious stacks, or over at Elm? Had I said something, done something, which had revealed my ambiguity, my doubt about the Transformations of the Obanites, about becoming one of them? Had it become obvious to them that I feared the clean, sealed rooms of the Obanites, with their dustless interiors and white desks? Had they gleaned something from the letters I sent home to my father, or from those he sent me, which arrived already-opened, imperfectly re-sealed?

Perhaps the problem was my impertinence, in my final year, in querying the historical narrative of a lecture Jenon had given on Emmeline and Mathilde Salt. I had written him a polite letter, filled with the excessive enthusiasm of an undergraduate amateur who had connected with their story too passionately, become personally involved, interested. I had asked how Jenon had been able to deduce Mathilde and Emmeline's relationship had not survived Mathilde's incarceration, why he allowed no doubt in this. *Was the lack of any records indicating they had reconciled enough to suppose they had not done so? Or were there more details in some other resource than the set text?* Jenon had never replied, though a few weeks later, during his weekly lecture, he had taken off his glasses, laid them down on the desk in front of him, and dropped his chin, pinching the bridge of his nose as though a headache had taken seed behind those beetling brows. This pause lasted an inordinately-long time. In the heavy silence while we waited for him to go on, I thought I could hear his heart tick over: a certain but modest sound. Finally, he looked up again. He seemed peculiarly naked without his glasses, as though his face was incomplete without them. He looked up, scanned the auditorium until he found me, and pinned me with his gaze. He then gave a brief and seemingly impromptu dissertation—in the middle of his lecture on preserving calfskin documents—on the relative merits of inductive and deductive reasoning, on the seductions of heretical narrative, analogical and metaphorical *embroidery* of truth—as he called it—and false history, and on the importance of understanding the relation between the Haven records and histories, the Rupettan Annal, and the flimsy evidence of any other resource we might have to work with in order to supplement but never contradict these other, infallible resources. The students sitting next to me studied their noteplates and blushed on my behalf as his words washed over me. His tone was subdued, but precise, modulated, like the best of the Obanite orators, against the dactylic beat of his mechanical heart. He spoke intimately to me, though I was in a hall with almost a hundred other students, like an elderly father whose favourite daughter has let him down. Each sentence a measure of his disappointment.

Whatever the reason for my curatorial assignment, the Oikos Island archives became my curatorial project. Perhaps Jenon knew about my past: about the summer visits to Oikos Island as a child with my parents, my mother's holding-on to the old, Oikos ways of cropping in the Territory handed down from Aunt Grace, my father's ever-more-frantic resistance to the idea of my Transformation, his more and more insistent imprecations to me to come home.

I was shown into the Oikos Island store-room by a post-doctoral student, newly-Transformed. The exposed skin of his chest was pimpled around his heart; the keloid scars white and thick. There was a scab on one edge, where he had scratched at it as it healed. The store-room had bare, cold walls and exposed pipes running along the walls, along which were stored the as-yet-unnumbered boxes that had come from the Oikos Island, the contents of which were to be identified, described, annotated and labelled before being stored in clean boxes, between sheets of acid-free paper, or in the glass-fronted cabinets of drawers that sat in rows down the middle of the room. I was the fairytale miller's daughter: presented with a dungeon of straw I was to spin into gold by dawn.

My job, my pimpled, itching friend informed me, was to sift through the material, discarding those things of no historic value, preserving those that were useful according to the best practice guidelines for Archiving and Preserving in the Faculty booklet, and referring on to a more senior researcher—to him—those items whose provenance or significance were uncertain, or those which, for one reason or another, needed to be more carefully managed. Items that appeared to contradict History, for example, and might need—like the portrait of old Grace in the hall at home—to be 'restored' before they could be studied.

The Oikos Island archives were in a dreadful state. With all the best intentions in the world the person responsible for the boxing and removal of the material from the Island hadn't had any idea how to best pack the material, or any sense of the necessity of being careful. Jenon and his team had made the discovery at the end of their summer research trip, and had left the transportation of the archive to a local man who assured them he knew what had to be done. He had boxed up everything, his small son helping out for a few extra dollars on weekends, and asked his apprentice to help carry them down to his boat on the harbour. Clearly, some of the boxes had been dropped on the way, their contents shuffled and laced with sand. The boxes had been brought over in three boatloads. The islander's boat a small dinghy, which could only carry so much at a time. Evidently, he had made each load count. Many of the boxes had clearly become wet during their journey, some had fallen apart and been tied together again with fishing line or string.

Finally, on reaching the College, they had been piled up, haphazardly, in one of the darker, damper areas of the basement storage space, beneath the warmth of the hot water pipes. Over the summer, some of the boxes had fallen apart. There had been a paper landslide along the northern wall. Mice had gotten in, and eaten through a box of accounting records, as well as a good half of a packet of letters, before being discovered. A student—an undergraduate—had been allocated some basic work on the resource over the summer, but had resented the assignment, and spent their time, instead of working, getting stoned and reading forbidden books. Their sole contribution had been to re-label about half of the boxes, incorrectly, as it turned out. It seems that the student's method had been to open a box, glance at whatever lay in the top of it, and make up a label with a list of whatever they guessed the rest of the box might contain. One box had been re-labelled for each day they had worked in the archive: an astonishingly small portion of the collection. I began working at the other end of the collection: with the unopened boxes.

Every Friday, I brought home to the Elm College kitchen another box or two of this considerable collection of ephemera—a weekend's worth of work—and set myself up in the glasshouse to work through it. At this rate, I would take just under nine months to complete the whole archive, and still have plenty of time for my own research.

'It's just work,' I told Margause. 'There's no real discoveries to be made from this kind of material, not usually. Or, there might be, but it's unlikely. Most primary research is like this, though, that's the lesson I'm supposed to be learning. Years of ploughing through unremarkable stuff to find one tiny scrap of significance.'

Margause scrubbed at the soil beneath her fingernails at the butler's sink, studying the creases that were indelibly marked by her earthy trade. 'Aren't you curious?'

'About the Oikos? Yes, of course, but the stuff in those boxes is mostly personal stuff that's meaningful only to the person who owned it, or cultural Historians, which isn't really my field: recipes, gardening notes, packets of seeds. Amateur poetry. School recital programs. Local newsletters. It's scarcely worth the trouble it takes me to sort and catalogue it all.' I grimaced, pulling papers from the bottom of the box that were damp and mouldy, pressing the pages flat, already wondering how I would dry and treat the paper to maintain the text. 'This box belonged to a couple of old women who lived out there. Their whole lives, it seems, were about gardening and cooking. And poetry.'

'They weren't born old women, nobody is.'

'I didn't mean—'

'I know what you meant, Henri.' Margause sighed and held her hands under the tap to rinse off the soap before drying them on the towel that hung by the door. She glanced at the table, arrayed with folio pages. 'You don't care for poetry?'

'It doesn't make much sense to me, though I've read a lot of it, and spent hours with Edla, over at the Kalla College, getting her to help me analyse Emmeline's poetry when I was doing my undergraduate biography paper. Lots of stuff about grace and light and gravity and water —lots of water. I think she kind of lost it after Mathilde died.'

'Disappeared.'

Margause pulled a chair up to the kitchen table beside me and picked up one of the papers from the Salt Lane folder I had laid out on the table. 'Is this one of hers?'

'That's Mathilde's. Her handwriting is neater, more rounded.'

The loose page was divided into three sections: an image of a tall, delicately-drawn tree filled the column on the left of the page, its feathery fingers curling out towards the text in the top right. Beneath the text was another drawing, of fruit-like arils, hand-tinted in faded watercolour. *Luonnatar*, the text was headed. 'Born January 12, 19—'.

'Why Luonnatar?' Margause said.

'Isn't that its botanical name?'

Margause shook her head, lifting the page to squint at the pale lines of text. 'No. It's a Yew tree. *Taxus toreya.*' Margause put down the page and scanned the table. 'There are more,' she said. 'Like this.'

I pushed a pile of pages towards her, each one a similar shape and size—each one illustrated with an image of a tree, a tinted image of flowers, fruit, seeds or leaves, and a small box of text. 'Amilhat,' I read aloud. 'Born July 26, 19—.'

'Born,' Margause said. 'Not planted.'

'A companion to Hidalia, in the northeast corner. Pink or purple blooms,' I went on. 'The butterflies come in hordes for his copious nectar. His stamens are neat, widely spaced. A gentleman, and scholar, he waits patiently for the seasons to change.'

'Have you been to Oikos Island?'

I shook my head. Archiving was a scholar's job, and the one I was being trained for, whatever my doubts about the task I'd been assigned; I had been discouraged from indulging in ethnography, in the fragile seductions of *fieldwork*.

'There were some beautiful houses there, up on the path towards the Haven. Neglected now, of course. Not the great park it once was. The Oikos had to sell most of the land in the years after the repatriation—the rest was taken—piece by piece, by the Rupettans. You should go there tomorrow, you and Miri, and see what's left. See where these eccentric, unimportant women lived.'

156

'I have to work—these papers have to be folioed, catalogued. I can't afford to get behind on this stuff.'

'I can do that,' Margause said.

'You've got enough to do.'

Margause snorted, gathering the pages into a neat pile and stacking them in the box. 'Just go, Henriette, go and walk in the past. I know how important you think it is.'

'History can tell us who we are, who we can become. If we lose sight of the past, we lose contact with the future.'

'You shouldn't pay so much attention to Jenon and his acolytes. History is not the past; it is only the study of the past, and of the narrative arts. It is just one version of the past, told very much in the light of the present.'

'The more we know of the past, the more we can understand ourselves, understand human nature.'

'The past is not what made us, Henri; it is simply where we have been.'

'Jenon says that there is a real and lived reciprocity between the past and the present. That while the present is always in a state of change—'

'It is not only the present that changes, Henri. The past, too, shifts, as do your precious Historians. We are all caught up in cycles of destruction, decay, and growth. Marcus Aurelius wrote that *all things that are now happening have happened in the past, and will happen in the future.*' Margause stood and picked up the box, now packed full of the papers I had been working on. She settled the box on her hip and walked towards the door, gazing out over the kitchen gardens to the orchard. 'Miri may tell you nothing of her past. She may tell you lies, fables, fairytales. They may be all she has left. You can see who she is without having to know who she has been.'

'Is it that terrible, her past?'

'It is what it is. She cannot change it any more than you can change the paths of the wind, or the shape of the illness that has gripped your father.' Margause stepped down into the garden, slipped her feet into her boots. 'Miri is here, now, and she is willing to need you. That will have to be enough.'

80

We were packing up some things to take to the island together. We had planned a weekend, camping behind the sandhills, trekking over the old paths, visiting the dig at the Haven. Miri had dug out a tent from the top floor at Elm, in those endless storerooms, while I had washed and folded clothes and towels. The boat was due to leave the harbour at four, and we were nearly ready to leave when Margause came in and asked Miri to check the post before we left; her old bones too stiff despite the warm weather.

When Miri was gone she came into the room and watched me pack, sitting on the end of the bed and studying Perihan, who was hopping agitatedly up and down on one of the potting benches. 'I wanted to show you something,' she said.

I came and sat beside her. She had a small parcel in her hands, wrapped in an old-fashioned square of fabric. She sighed and then unwrapped it. There were a handful of photographs: two children, running on a beach, sleeping in a driftwood bed, hanging upside down from a tree. 'That's me,' she said.

'May I?' I held out my hand and she passed the photographs to me. They were old, and thick, but well-cared for. The images still sharp despite the years. 'Which one is you?' I asked, and she pointed to the fairer of the two: a small child, barely up to the shoulder of the other, dark-haired one. 'Is that your sister?'

'Sort of,' she said, and then grimaced slightly. 'Yes.'

The next photograph in the pile was of the two children, eating watermelon, sitting on the front porch of a house. Margause pointed to the house, with its wide open doors, curtains blowing in the long-ago breeze. 'This was my home, as a child, on Oikos,' she said. 'I drew a map, but Miri will know. She'll show you, if you ask her.'

'I didn't realise,' I said, questions bursting in my head, flooding over each other. 'When was this? You could come with us, come to the dig, as well. Local knowledge, local memory, can be invaluable, no matter how flawed.'

Margause shook her head and took the photographs back, folded the old cloth around them and handed them to me. 'You can have them, if you like, but I can't go back there. The house is still there, I think, and if it's not too . . . if it's not gone, I'd like you to bring back a sprig of jasmine from the vine in the garden. The back deck. I'd like to smell that again.'

I heard Miri come in the back door. 'Next time you could come. Stand there yourself.'

'No,' she said. 'I don't want to go back. My father died there, and it's too . . .' She shook her head again, and smiled. 'I'm old, you know; for me the past is just the past. Though I miss it sometimes.'

'Henri,' Miri said, and I turned to see her standing behind me, her hands in her pockets. She caught Margause's eye, and I saw something pass between them before Margause squeezed my hand, and left the room.

I put the bundle of photographs down on my lap and Miri sat beside me, pulled an envelope out of her pocket and held it in her two hands. She looked at it for a while before handing it to me, as though the force of her attention might shade its simple, honest whiteness. A plain white envelope. I turned it over in my hands. Bad news comes in white envelopes.

I have a photograph of my mother after she returned from college. Looking at those images of Margause as a young girl had reminded me of it. Those same faded colours. The picture was taken after she came home from College—after she fell ill—sitting in a white cane chair on the lawn of the Haven at Whitestone Shute, in a white dress like an Edwardian lady. A ghost already. A thing of the past. White is winter in Europe, the white of the imported snowdrops my father grew for the festival of the Beautiful, to decorate the Haven, but never let me

159

bring into the house. The pale blooms of the dead, like a corpse in its paper shroud.

I opened the envelope, careful not to tear it. If I tore it the news would be worse, I was sure. If I could open it without a tear it wouldn't be so bad.

'I'll come with you,' Miri said. 'We can catch the 5:00 train.'

∽

I was sure I had left something behind, and kept confusing the lists of things I needed to bring with me: tents and sleeping bags, books and hats. The train pushed through the suburbs, splitting a path through the backyards of shops and houses until suddenly we were crossing a river and on the other side there was a long scar of newly-felled forest. A factory with an empty carpark, its walls and windows reflecting the melancholy light. Surely we were on the wrong train. I was agitated and uncomfortable. My foot twitched and I felt a stinging itch in my left shoulder. Miri held my hand and pulled me to my feet. We rocked through the aisles to the dining car. Unable to smile as our bodies tumbled against each other in the half-dark. Strangers read papers and books, slept with their heads on the windows, looked up as we passed and then away again. We were nothing. Nobody. In the dining car they served tea on plates with the same dirigible on its edge as on the plate we had stolen that day, so long ago. Miri smiled at me and reached for my hand across the table.

'Did you bring my walking shoes?' I asked her. Later, I asked about my winter socks and the book I had bought for my father, filled with pictures of the city when he was young.

'It will be okay,' she said. We both knew it wasn't true.

I couldn't remember why I had stayed away. It was something to do with the dreams that had come to me down in the stacks. Dreams in which I was living and working in Whitestone Shute. In the dream someone would come and tell me that Miri was gone. The messenger was always someone vaguely familiar and they would sit and eat with me and discuss her leaving as if it were nothing remarkable. It was because Miri was angry with me that she had left. In one dream, she had married, and when I rushed back to Elm I was just in time to see the wedding mount depart—an elaborate creature with an elephant's head—absurdly huge, emitting a smoke in its wake that smelled like burning sage.

I had always trusted my dreams. And now, I could not dream, could not let go of my understanding of the real world: the exact colour of the seats in our carriage, the texture of the glass in the window, the rhythmic shudder of the light. I sat all night, watching the world outside the window flatten into darkness, watching the moon seem to follow as we shot forward, its complacent, pockmarked face a perfect semi-circle of ruin.

We hired two bicycles at the station and loaded our things into the panniers. It smelt like home. The rich honey of the trees in blossom thickened the night air. I rode ahead of her, descending into a world that was half memory, half fantasy. I could not quite believe that she was here; that this world—the world of my past—had become overlaid with the world of my present. Her bicycle clicked in my wake. She was following me home.

The house was dark. We stood in the driveway with our bicycles resting against our hips, watching light steal into the sky. 'There's a key on the back deck,' I said and we walked around the house, lifting the cycles onto the deck. I couldn't go in. I stood on the deck, wondering why I had come home. Surely the letter was a mistake of some kind. My father was fine; a little old, a little strange, but strong and definite. In the tree near the back fence two birds sat waiting. The day was rising, like an assault, like a lie.

I heard a rustling in the bushland beyond the house and stood waiting, expecting a dog or a child to emerge. Old Paul walked out, breaking a branch off as he came and brushing spider's webs from his shoulders. He was carrying a box with a tea-towel tucked in over its contents.

'Old Paul,' I said. He looked from me to Miri and back, glanced at our bicycles on the back deck, at our luggage strapped to the panniers. 'Are you okay?'

'I took the scenic route,' he said. 'Oliver used to walk that way.'

'Where is he?' I said.

'He's not awake yet?' he said, climbing the stairs to the deck, pushing his own key into the door and switching on the hall light, calling my father's name.

'You shouldn't come through the woods,' I said. 'What if you fell, or got lost?'

Old Paul walked through the house to the kitchen, switching on lights, opening windows, calling out to my father as he went. He put the box down on the table and began lifting out bread and eggs and fruit. 'Breakfast?' he said.

Miri moved around the table and put a hand on his arm, took the eggs from him and put them on the bench. 'I'm Miri,' she said, filling the kettle with water, turning on the stove. 'How about I make breakfast?'

'Of course. Of course,' he said. 'I'll get him up then, shall I?' He stood and looked at me and I knew he was waiting for me to offer to help him with my father, but I wasn't ready. In the lounge room the light was beginning to come in, spreading a familiar rug of warmth on the stone-flagged floor. I could hear someone moving upstairs, a sound like a small animal struggling to breathe. I wanted to go in to my old room and curl up on the familiar floorboards, or wrap myself in my old blanket, pull it over my head like a cowl, and sleep.

Old Paul went upstairs and soon I heard the water running. The kettle boiled in the kitchen. I went out on the deck and started unloading our things, brought them into the hall one by one. The door to my mother's old room was ajar. I pushed it further. There was an unfamiliar, dark cat curled up on her pillow. It blinked at me. I stepped into the room, unsure what to do, and the cat dived under the bed.

The room was clean and neat, everything put away in drawers and on shelves. There was no sign of life except the dint in the pillow where the cat had been, and a man's sweater folded over the back of her desk-chair. By the side of the bed was an old book—a biography of Eleanor of Aquitaine—an empty water glass and my mother's chronometer, ticking loudly.

'How long are you here for?' Old Paul said, stepping into the room and picking up the water glass and the sweater. I don't know how he got into the room, how he got down the stairs, without making a sound. 'You never stay very long.'

'I was looking for a book,' I said.

Old Paul scanned the shelves above my mother's desk. 'Which one?' he said.

I blushed and stared at the shelves, unable to read the spines from where I stood. 'I can't remember the title,' I said. 'But there was a boat on the cover. It was a memoir by my Aunt Grace. Self-published.'

Old Paul frowned and turned to the shelves. Beneath the bed, I saw the cat's eyes gleam.

'Is he up?' I said.

'In the lounge.' He turned and smiled at me, a book in his hands. 'Your friend is making French toast; he always loved French toast. Did you tell her about that, before you came?'

'Is he. . . .'

Old Paul came forward and pressed the book into my hands. It had a worn cloth cover: a small boat with a sail, two settlers peering ahead from the prow, and in the foreground, land, and Oikos standing on the shore. 'He's having a good day today,' he said, 'quite lucid. The stroke has changed him, but he's still your father.'

My father had fallen asleep in his shiny new wheelchair by the fire. He was snoring. The light was just beginning to reach him: a thin edge of it had settled over his feet in their thick-soled shoes. I adjusted the blanket on his lap, tucking it in around his thighs, careful not to touch his hands. His face looked shiny and pink, as though he had been burned and his skin was newly raw. It was slackened and puffy, the lines shallow, like the creases in a half-inflated balloon. His hair was looser, thinner than I remembered, and there was a fresh, small square bandage taped to his forehead.

'Henriette?' he said.

'Sorry, Dad,' I said. 'I didn't mean to wake you.'

He looked at me closely, lifted his hand and put it on my shoulder, as though he were setting an Oråki-piece on a board, unsure if it was the right move, reluctant to remove his fingers once the piece was placed on its square, concentrating and watching my eyes, waiting for me to reveal something. He was swimming up from some distant blue place inside himself. Holding his breath and peering up at the diffuse light on the surface. He squinted a little, as though his vision was unclear, and licked his lips. His eyes were disconnected. Only one of them blinked and jerked: the other was a static, milk-blue moon. His tongue was thick and pale. His dry lips were caked with yellow spit. He stared at me for a while, and then his gaze shifted, as though he were waiting for an answer even though he hadn't spoken. He snorted and looked past me. 'Have you seen the cat?' he mumbled. His hands grew agitated in his lap, plucking at the blanket. 'Fucking cat,' he said. My father; who never swore.

Miri came into the room, smiled at me and put her warm, confident hand on my back. 'Breakfast,' she said.

The cat had followed her into the room, rubbed its way past her and jumped up into my father's lap. 'Fucking cat,' he said again, and Miri laughed. The cat stood on his lap, clawing the blanket and turning in a circle until it was happy and then folding down and closing its eyes.

My father smiled at it and nodded. 'That's it,' he said. 'You're the matter.'

We wheeled him into the kitchen and ate breakfast together, trying to talk about ordinary things. Old Paul tied a bright tea-towel under his chin: patterned with cows whose udders jutted pinkly from their bodies. The cat glared at us but didn't move, simply clawed my father's blanketed lap some more and settled into a new curve of sleep.

Old Paul showed me how to feed my father small forkfuls of egg and bread, dripping with maple syrup, and wipe the slop from his chin. Gradually, his head slooped forward onto his chest and his mouth went slack. He wasn't asleep exactly. Every now and then he would mutter something—a name or a phrase—fragments of nonsense.

Once he jerked awake, as though tugged up by a fisherman's rod, unseemly and astonished. He peered at me. His mouth opened and his tongue moved within it like a thick slug. His eyes lit up with something that looked like recognition. 'Sweetie,' he said, but that was all.

ℰↄ

That afternoon, Miri and I walked up into the mountains. We went through the garden and into the forest that seemed to have grown closer to the house since last time I visited. I could feel the pull of the house behind me and, even though he was sleeping now, resting by the fire, could feel my father's eyes peering into me, unknowing, but afraid. As Miri and I moved out through the trees it was as though there was a thick skein of milky tissue tethering me to the house. I wanted rid of it, just for a few hours. It was exhausting. The sickly sweetness of his love. The cloying, open-mouthed confusion. My inability to know what should be done. I wanted to shake off the closeness of those rooms and so I walked fast, driving up along the tracks until they disappeared and we were walking in untracked bush. We were high up on the range. I knew that we were close to Land Between.

I could feel the tingle of heat in my thighs and stomach from the effort of walking so fast, but when I stopped at the top of a rise and looked back Miri was beside me. I wanted it to storm, but the sky was blue and smooth. I stood at the edge, wanting to know what to do, what to feel, wanting some skerrick of certainty to lodge itself in me.

She came close; I felt her body ledged against mine and her hand resting with its back against the back of my hand and knew that I could hold it if I wanted to. That she had placed herself there so that I would not have to reach for her. Her fingers were thin and firm. They didn't

165

tremble in my grasp. I could feel the soft thud of her thumb's pulse against my wrist.

'It's beautiful up here,' she said.

I nodded. 'This is where I used to come,' I said. 'There's a clearing not far from here where I would make camp. A rock where my mother and father carved their names when they were young, and in love with each other, and this place. When I was five they brought me here, and showed me where they had carved my name between theirs.'

I glanced at Miri and stepped backwards, sat on a fallen log. I had a strong vision of the three of us standing together—my mother and my father and I. I remember feeling removed and afraid, as though I was not a product of their affection for each other, but an impediment to it: a wound in the perfect shape of their two-personed life. After that, no memory of that time would stay firm. Every image I grasped at, every word, became nothing in my mouth.

'My mother died after her Transformation,' I said. 'Died a heretic's death of complications. Rejection of the Miracle.'

'But you told me you remembered when your mother died,' she said. 'You remember her funeral, don't you?'

I nodded. 'I guess it was just a child's fantasy that she had a proper Rupettan burial, or my father's fantasy, planted in my head. I think he and Old Paul did it to keep her heresy a secret.'

Miri stood behind me, put her arms around me and held me. I would not cry. I would not dream. 'I think,' I said, remembering fragments of things: images, scraps, hard flashes of insight I had tried so hard to ignore. 'I think my mother was afraid my body would reject the Penitent heart, too. I think that's one of the things my mother and father fought about before she died. She knew I wanted to be an Obanite. That's why she lied to me. That's why they all lied. So I wouldn't be afraid.'

Miri flattened her palms on my belly, put her chin on my shoulder and kissed my cheek. 'She was your mother,' she said. 'That's what mothers do.'

I nodded, flicked the tears away. 'I used to come up here after she died. Every few weeks. I'd leave notes for her to find, gifts I thought she might like. Every year on her birthday I'd make a cake and bring it up here. I'd light a fire and pile it with smoke-leaf, then I'd sit and eat one slice and leave her the rest. Sometimes, if I came up a day or two later, I'd find tracks near our campsite, and make myself believe that she'd been here and taken something I'd left for her: cans of sweets, or winter socks. Books and pencils.'

'Maybe we should leave something for her now: let her know about your father?'

I shook my head. 'That was a game I played years ago,' I said. 'When I was a child.'

'Let's leave something anyway,' Miri said. She reached into her pocket and pulled out a handful of small change, a key, a pencil stub, and a caramel in a bright blue foil wrapper. 'It's not exactly birthday cake. What have you got?' she said.

I put my hand in the pocket of my coat and took out the small blue book with the sailing boat on its cover. Inside the cover a birthday wish: *for my mother*, it said, in a large, clumsy child's hand, *with big wishes from yor daughter. Henriette Bellmer, adventoorer. Obanite.*

ℂ

Back on campus, a few days later, I rode my bicycle from Elm through the quiet streets to Jenon's house. It had rained in the afternoon, and the world was cool. My tyres hissed along the wet streets and I rode fast, feeling the air tangle in my hair. When I reached the house I dismounted and wheeled the bicycle around to the potting shed, leaned it there near the familiar terracotta pots and coiled hoses.

Jenon was standing on the front deck when I walked around to meet him, waiting for me. He smiled and came down the stairs to greet me with his hand extended. When he reached me his smile softened and he moved closer, put his arms around me and held me. I could feel his cool heart against my chest, through his shirt, its steady beating. He patted my back and gave me a quick squeeze before releasing me. He peered at my face in the half-dark, studying me and then nodding. 'It will be okay,' he said.

I stood in the dark, hearing the patter and tock of the sprinklers in his neighbour's garden. Longing for the comfort of a rake or hose to hold on to. Something to do with my hands. Something I understood. The pebbles of the path glittered in the light that spread outward from the front door.

'Anyway, let's talk about that later. Come in, come in,' he said, 'Anne is longing to meet you.'

I had known Jenon lived with his wife and children, had seen their things scattered around the garden and deck, and heard him mention them occasionally. Once he had left his office during the middle of the day, cancelling an afternoon lecture, because his son had broken his arm after falling off the roof, and another time I had found him in his office, looking tired and bruised, after his wife was diagnosed with breast cancer. But I had never met them, and he didn't keep pictures of his family in his office. I had never imagined him as someone fully embroiled in the warp and weft of family, but that night, another Jenon was revealed, the same as and yet distinctly disconnected from the man I knew at Oban College.

As he walked into the house ahead of me I saw that he was wearing old, patched gardening pants, clean but frayed at the cuffs. There was not time, however, to notice much else. A dog came running up the hall, with two children in its wake, and then there was the sound of Jenon's wife calling out from the kitchen for him to change the music and pour the wine and he smiled at me, conspiratorially, and asked me to choose something to listen to while he poured. His daughter came up, puck-faced and serious, and stood over me while I knelt before Jenon's music collection trying to decide.

'Not that,' she said. 'Not that,' and then, approvingly, 'Yes! Yes! Yes!' in a kind of sinking and lifting sing-song. The house was a shambles of toys and books. Jenon's son—a tall, freckle-faced boy with eyes so startlingly wide he looked pretty—cleared a chair of dolls and small cups filled with seeds and leaves and dirt, piling them up on the floor beside the chair. He settled me into this chair, and then sat on the floor at my feet with the dog on his lap and began asking me about my tastes in music, what books I had read, what my research was on. The daughter came in and out, differently dressed each time, though she was just adding layers to her outfit: a shiny red umbrella, a dancer's skirt, a beanie or a tea-cosy on her head, which was soon decorated with a headband that sprouted tiny, blue-feathered wings. Without saying very much, she spread a picnic blanket in the middle of the loungeroom floor and began dancing, and her brother pulled a small drum out from under the piano-stool and began playing, tunelessly. The dog barked and Anne and Jenon came out of the kitchen and kissed them both. Jenon danced, comically, with a glass of wine in each hand and the dog winding between his legs. Soon, the dog jumped up and rested his front paws on Jenon's chest. He handed his glass to his son and waltzed the dog around the floor, making moon eyes at it, and calling it sweetheart.

Anne was tall and pretty, with short hair and the look some women have when they have been cosseted and wealthy their whole lives. She looked familiar to me and later, in the dark when I was riding home, I realised that she was like a slimmer, more polished version of Margause. They had the same squared-off jaw and the same eyes: winter-grey with specks of blue. Anne's skin was pink, and she wore heavy, silver rings and a necklace with a pretty, silver key.

'It's beautiful,' I said. 'It looks antique.'

She tilted her head. 'My mother gave it to me.' She held it out to me on the palm of her hand. The head of the key was hand-carved and worn almost smooth. The patterns there almost indistinct, but I could make out something, I thought, of leaves and cogs, and two letters, perhaps, wound together. The script was looping and ornate: hard to read.

'Are these your grandmother's initials?' I asked.

Anne lifted the key closer to her face, turned it over on her palm and rubbed it with the pad of her thumb. She nodded and dropped the pendant inside her shirt. 'My great-grandmother,' she said, 'a few generations back now.'

She blew a kiss to Jenon, who was wrapped in a scarf his daughter had thrown around his neck like a harness. 'The garden looks so beautiful since you came,' she said, perching on the arm of the chair I was ensconced in, 'I could never get anything to grow.'

'Weeds,' said her son, sliding a small table just big enough to support the half-completed Oråki board it supported out of the way. 'You grew lots of very tall weeds.'

She laughed and put a plate of olives and bread on a footstool. 'And children,' she said, 'very tall children.'

Jenon disappeared into the kitchen to prepare the meal while Anne and the children entertained me. While she talked, she would call out to him in mid-sentence for confirmation of this or that name or date and he would lean around the door of the room with a spoon or another kitchen implement in his hand to bounce the conversation along.

The daughter stripped down to a sparkling swimsuit and a beanie and lay down on her dancing rug, spread-eagled like a starfish, listening to the music and shushing her brother whenever he spoke to her. Anne and her son—Vic—played a game of Oråki while we spoke, one or the other of them sometimes deferring to me to advise them how to move and always, no matter how poor my advice, taking it. Once, Jenon came out and leaned on his wife's shoulder, lifted her hair and kissed the back of her neck, then topped up both our wineglasses.

'You're in trouble,' he said, peering at the game board, moving a piece and then almost scuttling from the room when Anne frowned at him. 'Come help me with the sauce,' he called over his shoulder to Vic. 'I need your expertise.'

Vic smiled and bowed a kind of conductor's bow, flicking out the tails of an imaginary coat as he stood and left the room.

'Did Abel tell you how we met?' said Anne, sinking back against the chair and reaching over me to get an olive.

I shook my head and she slid down beside me, as though we were two young girls gossiping together. 'I was one of his students,' she said. 'He was a mess in those days. A complete mess,' she said, 'he used to wear these pants. The hem had come down and he had just stapled them up. Stapled them!'

'What are you telling her?' Jenon called from the kitchen.

'Everything,' Anne called out, winking at me. 'He had a party here one night, invited everyone. I had a lover—what was his name? Abel?'

'Christopher,' he called. 'Christopher Harrington Sinclair. The third.'

Anne nodded, sipped her wine. 'Christopher,' she said. 'He was gorgeous. Stupid and expensive, but gorgeous. Anyway, Abel had this huge party, all because he wanted to ask me out, but he couldn't, of course. No nerve. So I arrived, late, and he was in the kitchen, baking, completely horrified at the number of people who'd turned up. He had on this ridiculous apron someone had left here at an earlier party and his hair was—' she made a gesture with her hands, flourishing them around her head as though indicating she was wearing a crown. 'It was the fashion then, but he had no idea. None! So I went and had a bath.'

Abel came into the room, refilled our glasses, moved another piece on the board and asked his daughter to set the table. 'She did. Bubbles and everything. I didn't even know I had bubbles.'

She smiled at him, grabbed the front of his apron and pulled him down to kiss the tip of his nose. 'A bath,' she said. 'And then I stayed.'

Dinner was served on a side deck—at a round wooden table—in the middle of which sat a large round platter bulging with candles of various colours. The daughter—Little Bit they all called her—knelt on the table to light them all. Her tongue bitten down between her lips as she did so. There were candles, too, on the rails of the deck. The table was cleared of newspapers and colouring books, homework and still more miniature tea-cups and side plates. The food was warm and hot and plentiful. Bread and wine and cheese and salad and tagine and couscous. The family ate and passed the plates around in a whirlwind of conversation and laughter. Little Bit insisted on sitting next to me,

171

and ate from my plate while leaving her own untouched. When she fell asleep in her chair, her brother carried her into the house—into her room—and returned to clear the dishes.

Anne looked up, distracted. 'Asleep?' she said and he nodded.

'I'll help with the dishes,' I said. Vic and I went into the kitchen, where the benches were so crowded with food and dishes and plates and books that there was nowhere to put down the piles we had bought in, so I stood and held them while Vic stacked them into the washer. He was quieter, alone in that room with me, like a different version of himself. He quoted from a book he was reading—poetry from the fourteenth century—and offered to lend it to me when I said I liked it.

When we finished in the kitchen he came back outside to say good-night to his parents, kissed them both and told them to behave and then disappeared into the house, turning down the music and dimming the lights as he went.

Later, as the candles flickered and dimmed and the house settled into a kind of lull, Jenon spoke to me about my father, about family, about his own father's protracted illness and death and what that had meant to him. Anne listened with me, intently, gently reminding him of things he might skip over, her hand resting on his thigh as he spoke.

'We want to help,' he said, and Anne nodded beside him. They had talked about this already. 'You're a wonderful student, Henri. A gifted historian with a great mind.'

'A mind the size of the universe, that's what he tells me,' Anne said.

'So, you might need to go home for a while. You could take a leave of absence, officially at least. I've taken the liberty of arranging that already. And I've spoken to some people I know. There's some work for you at the Haven there; just temporary, and part-time, to earn a little money.'

'And you could keep working on your research,' Alice said.

'And,' Jenon glanced at his wife, 'we've set up some funding for you to continue work on the Oikos Island material.'

'A scholarship,' Alice said.

'You understand,' Jenon said, leaning forward, his face flushed in the candled light. 'I want you to keep going, Henri, I want you to take up a funded place after you graduate, work with me on a History of the Territorian Oikos. I think, together, we could do amazing work. Terrible, amazing things. We could change the shape of Territorian History.'

Anne nodded and spun her wineglass on its stem. 'And if you need somewhere to stay when you come back . . .'

'There's a spare room,' he said, 'a kind of converted shed. You've probably seen it, out the back of the garden. My son—my other son—used to live there for a while, but now he's travelling.'

'It needs a good clean,' Anne said, 'maybe a spot of fresh paint or something.'

'Yes, yes,' Abel said, rubbing his wife's arm and smiling. 'But you don't have to decide tonight, of course. I just wanted to let you know that we'd thought about things. That we want to help you, however we can.'

'That's right,' Anne said, leaning her head on Abel's shoulder, smiling up at the stars.

'I have to think about it,' I said.

'Of course.'

'It's very generous. Very. I just . . .'

'A lot has happened,' Anne said. 'It's okay; go home. I'll give you the number of our friend, Nell, at the Scholarships Office. She'll help with the arrangements for your stipend, and a little extra, when you need it. Yes? The important thing is, Henri, we're here for you. We want to help.'

The Miracle of the Heart
Rūs: 1868

The fifth orb—the orb of the miracle that marks the true founding of the Penitent Order—is etched with a small, mechanical heart. The heart of the tenth Wynder: Vivica. She was just a child when she became the first to have a lock, a heart, a key implanted in her fleshy breast. Just a child, like our own Perdita, caught up in the violent shunt and whip of history.

Vivica woke in her bed, sunlight greyly fingering its way through the curtains. Nobody had come to wake her, to kiss her, to dress her, and this is how she knew her mother was still dead, that she was no longer merely Vivica, but had become Vivica Wynder X. She slid out from between the sheets and put on a shirt left lying on the floor where she had dropped it yesterday. Another sure sign of her mother's death. She could hear people in the room next door: the room that was no longer her mother's room. Her father—Pietr—was waking, laughing in her mother's bed, looking out her mother's windows at the garden her mother had planted, now blanketed in snow.

Vivica padded, in bare feet, into the hall and towards the stairs. Behind her the door to Pietr's chamber opened and one of the maids came out. *Vivica?* her father called from inside the room. *Bring Vivica here; we must dress the child.*

Vivica pressed her back against the wall and felt a handle at her back. She turned it, and slipped into her grandmother's room.

The great Empress Kassia was bundled in her sheets, snoring. The room in which her grandmother was dying, had been dying since before Vivica was born, was filled with secrets. It was dark and uncared for. The maids had not come since Anise had died. Nurses and apothecaries

174

went in and out. They mumbled and prayed and pressed their instruments against her chest to hear her cantering heart, but nobody opened the curtains to let in the air, or sat on the edge of the bed to talk with the grand old Empress. This, Vivica knew, was why they kept the windows shut and the curtains drawn: so that the Empress's secrets did not escape into the forest.

Outside the maid drew nearer, calling Vivica's name, opening and closing doors to peer into each room she passed. Vivica crawled in underneath the dying Empress's bed. She lay on the floor with the dust and discarded spoons, odd shoes and lost Oråki pieces. There were piles of matchboxes and medicine bottles, their stoppers long since rotted to black. The door opened and the maid came in.

Excuse me, ma'am, the maid said when she entered, *but I am looking for Vivica. It is time for her morning lessons and she cannot be found.*

What are you looking in here for? the Empress croaked. *There's nobody in here but me and Rupetta.*

The Emperor Pietr said to look everywhere. He believes the child might be hiding.

The Emperor Pietr?

Yes, ma'am.

That's what he's calling himself?

Vivica pushed open a matchbox. Inside it were shrivelled black dots, like peppercorns. She licked her finger and poked it into the box. Three of the small dots stuck to her finger. She swallowed them. They were hard, tasteless.

The maid took a step closer, into the room.

What do you think you are doing? asked the Empress.

I—Looking for Vivica.

Get out, said the Empress.

The maid hesitated, as if she meant, perhaps, to say something more. Vivica heard something moving towards the maid with heavy steps. *There's no child here,* the Empress said. *Get out, you simpering idiot.*

When the door had closed behind the maid, Vivica watched as the Empress's bare legs came down at the side of the bed. Soon her face appeared, upside down at the edge of the bed, peering into the shadows where Vivica lay. *Come on,* the Empress said, *It's time for your lessons. We'd better get moving.*

Vivica crawled out from under the bed and surveyed the room. She had seen me before, sitting with her mother, playing at cards or Oråki. She glared at me, her spine straight, her sharp little chin lifted, challenging me to a contest with all the bravery of a fool who does not know what they are facing. The Empress grunted as she pulled a pair of pants up over her hips and Vivica turned her bright stare away from me, towards her grandmother.

You lied, she said.

Yes, I did, said the Empress. *All Empresses lie.*

I'm not going to do my lessons.

Kassia took a heavy coat and a pair of sturdy boots from her wardrobe. The coat was long and dark, with already-full pockets. When she had tied on her boots she stood and turned towards the door. *Hurry up,* she said and she left, leaving the door ajar behind her.

Vivica glanced from the door to me and back again.

Go, I said, *she will not ask you twice.*

When Kassia reached the kitchen doors and stepped out onto the gravelly mud of the yard, Vivica was there beside her, with dusty knees and knotted hair, her shirt half-buttoned. *Put on your boots,* said Kassia.

Vivica took the boots her grandmother held out to her and quickly laced them. By the time she stood again, her grandmother was already disappearing into the forest. Vivica ran to catch up with the old woman, her boots crunching in the old snow.

They walked, and talked a little. Kassia pointed out the different species of trees, naming them, greeting them, like old friends. Sometimes putting her hand flat on their bark, peering up into their canopies. She showed Vivica the scat of the foxes, the brittle nests that had been built high in the treetops, wedged between the branches. She showed her the bear-traps hidden in the snow, and the deer-prints that led around the trees: the tracks of a mother and two kids wandering together, chewing the bark of the young pines.

They lay in the snow at the centre of a shaded copse and made snow angels. The Empress's angels had long pinion feathers, formed by her walking stick. Vivica's were short and wild, with circles of pine needles for haloes. They made dragon footprints with their fingertips and the pointy tip of a twig. They made the slithering trail of a snow-bound mermaid by trailing a branch through the snow. Vivica cut her finger and let a few drops fall beside the mermaid's trail. *She's been murdered,* Vivica said. *Dragged here from her home in the lake by a jealous dryad.*

There was a hut on the lake: a small fisherman's box.

Kassia walked all around the building. It had a door on one side, and a chimney, but no windows. The door had a heavy brass lock, which Kassia lifted and squinted into. *It's a good lock,* she said. *Tough.* She pulled a handful of tools from one of her pockets: pincers, a small pocket-knife, pliers—springs and screws and such. Things Vivica did not recognise or know the use of. Kassia selected a long, thin screwdriver and slipped the rest back into her coat. She didn't bother picking the lock. One by one she unscrewed the door's hinges.

Inside the hut was neat and cosy. A perfect, practical room with four timber walls, and an ice floor with a round hole in the centre for fishing. A small peat fire was laid in the firebox, fishing poles were hung on the walls in neat lines, and strips of fish hung drying from a series of poles suspended from the ceiling. Two boxes with cushions tied to them faced each other across the ice-hole at the centre of the room. There were boxes arranged around the edges of the room, each of them labelled: tackle, dry food, dishes, blankets, shoes. There was a folded table hung on the wall, which Kassia took down, and a heavy black kettle—the old-fashioned kind, iron with a notched spout. Kassia set up the table, lit the fire and dipped a can into the ice-hole to collect water. Soon the little hut was warm, the kettle boiling. Kassia lit a cigarette and took down two of the fishing poles.

Vivica and Kassia smoked and fished and drank coffee and read aloud to each other from a book Kassia found in the box with the sugar and flour. When Kassia grew tired she made herself a bed of boxes and blankets and fell asleep. Outside a soft snow fell, the ice sighed. Vivica caught and gutted two small fish, scraping their innards across the ice into the ice-hole.

When Kassia woke it was late. They cooked the two fish in a can and ate them.

The next time they came to the hut the hinges had been mended, and a small key hung on a hook by the door. There was fresh coffee in the coffee can, a new fishing pole on new hooks on the wall, and a small pair of leather mittens on the table. Kassia smoked and did not fish. Vivica watched the fire, looked in all the boxes and tried on the mittens.

When Kassia slept Vivica put on her boots and walked across the ice. In the distance, she could hear dogs. Her father and his friends were hunting. She imagined herself a hunted dryad, slithering on the icy banks of the lake, her hair a rustle of leaves, her fingers twiggy and long. She crawled through the juniper scrub. The knees of her pants grew damp. She climbed an old tree with low branches that slumped towards the ground, as if it were too tired to stand, and watched the hunt. Her father on his dappled grey, his friends riding high, their coats bright flashes of colour in the muted wild. The dogs that moved like a pack of birds against the snow, wheeling and swirling together, baying with pride when they found the fox and killed it, when her father took it from them, its blood dripping hot and dark on the muddied snow, and painted two thick streaks of red on each of his cheeks.

Back inside the ice-box, the fire had died down to a peaty, smouldering fug of warmth. Vivica sat at the table with a pencil and notebook. She drew a line under the poem she had written last week and turned the page. *The Story of the Things of the World: A True Story with no lies in it*, she wrote. *Written and illustrated by Vivica Wynder X.* Her pocket squirmed and she reached into it with a small strip of dried fish. Her pocket nibbled at her fingers with small, sharp teeth, its tongue was warm and rough.

What have you got there? her grandmother said.

I'm writing a story, Vivica said, *about important things. Things you don't know anything about. Go back to sleep.*

Kassia reached for her stick and heaved herself up off her bed of boxes. *Show me.*

You're interrupting me.

I'll make coffee, Kassia said, and she filled the kettle and put it on to boil. *Writers drink a lot of coffee.*

What else do they do? Vivica asked.

Karel used to walk a lot. He would put on his hat and coat and walk all over the forest. When he came back he would hang his coat up, but keep his hat on and sit down at his desk and write. Kassia smiled as she scooped coffee and sugar into two tin mugs.

Who's Karel?

My husband, of course.

Vivica put down her pencil and eyed her grandmother suspiciously. *You don't have a husband. You're an Empress. You should only have a Consort.*

Kassia nodded as she poured coffee into two mugs and set them on the table. *But I am only an Empress, not a Wynder. So,* she said. *What are you writing?*

Vivica turned the page back to show her grandmother the title page of her story. *You'll have to not interrupt,* she said. *A writer needs quiet.*

Kassia nodded and took some supplies out of her pocket: a book and a smoke. She leaned back against the wall and folded the pages of her book back so she could hold it in one hand. When her coffee was finished she stood and stretched her back. *Done yet?* she asked.

Vivica lay down her pen and folded the last page of her booklet shut. She handed it to her grandmother. On the first page of the booklet, Vivica had written: *Chapter One The Fox by Vivica Wynder X* in large capital letters. Beneath that, in letters that ran out of room and were squashed together at the left of the page, she had written: *A Story of the True Forest.* The Empress Kassia nodded and sat at the table, smoothing the book open beneath her hand. *I will need more coffee,* she said, and Vivica set to work making some as her grandmother read.

CHAPTER ONE THE FOX BY VIVICA WYNDER X
A Story of the True Forest

I hate things that die. For example, almost everything that is small, like worms. Things rot when they die, and smell bad. A fox died in our icehouse and we weren't there. When we were there we found her in her bed and she was hot and maggoty and her eyes were eaten away by ants or something else small and insectish. Of course, some things are dead for eating, and that is just as well or I would be as thin as a twig. The fox's baby sucked on my fingers and scratched me until I bled, which made me remember that one day I will be hot and maggots will wriggle inside me. I put the little fox in my coat and tried to feed it from my teats like the cats and the mice do. After my dead brother was not-born they brought puppies in to suckle my mother's breasts until they were bitten and empty. The fox is my friend, but it will not do what I tell it. I have two friends and they are both like that. They are Grandmother Kassia and the fox. The fox does not have a name because its mother died before bothering to give it one. Grandmother Kassia says it is wrong to name wild things as though they are children, when they are wiser than we are and know how to live without war or warm coats. She says its name is *Vules vulpes.* Otherwise, she says, it has a name that only the wind knows. Secretly, I call it Anise, which was my mother's name. My mother is dead and maggoty, or she is a ghost with sharp teeth, like my fox, who hunts in the woods and does not leave footprints in the snow. When I call for Anise she will not come. She sleeps in my old cradle. Sometimes she pisses there and I have to wash out the sheets. Anise will come and eat from my hand if I have sugar or dried figs. Sometimes, she holds my hand with her paw and pulls it closer. I know this is not friendship, only hunger. A fox is a thing, like a moon or a tree, which does not know or care whether you are alive unless it can eat you.

ಛಾ

Each day Vivica and Kassia walked in the woods. Sometimes they were gone for just a few hours, sometimes longer. Occasionally I walked with them, but more often they went alone. I stood in the room where Kassia was meant to be sleeping, guarding the pile of blankets and pillows the two piled up beneath the covers.

Pietr used to keep bugs in his pockets, said Kassia, watching as Vivica knelt to see the black beetles disappearing into the dark rot of a log she had overturned. *At night, while he slept, we would have to go through his drawers and rescue them. Sometimes he put them in matchboxes and gave them names. Sometimes he ate them.*

Who? said Vivica, poking her fingers into the dirt, lifting a pink worm into the air. *Who did that?*

Your father, when he was little.

He's big, said Vivica. *He's the Consort; he doesn't play.*

Weeks went by while Vivica ignored me, keeping me in her sights but never approaching. Each morning she skated in the door, tugging at her grandmother's blankets until she woke, throwing open the heavy curtains to let in a little light. Slowly the room came to life: light, air, the rustle of twigs and the smell of fresh snow. On the windowsills they arranged their collections: leaves and twigs and nuts and the white bones of birds. Glass jars with spiders inside them. When it was too cold to play, when the storms came and blew snow up in drifts around the doors, they would sit up in Kassia's bed together, playing cards and drinking coffee. Cheating—both of them—and ignoring the court that swirled and gossiped around them.

At night, in the Empress Kassia's rooms, I stood watch over the two women whose hearts were at the centre of a storm. Pietr, the Emperor-Consort, fought wars, extended our territories, sent a generation of men to die in the soil and heat of foreign countries. He built monuments to his dead wife, burned churches, converted nations by the sword, by war and force, to the Rupettan Law. In my name, while I stood in the dark watching an old woman and a child sleep, he built the first Havens, and founded the Penitent schools and colleges where the Rupettans raised knowledge above faith. It was he, not I, who wrote his laws upon their walls and called them mine. The Fourfold Rupettan Law: Life is Death. The Earth is a Grave. The Body is a Machine for Dying. Knowledge is the path to Immortality.

For the Rupettans that grew up in the wake of Pietr's crusades, the life they were born to was a short, brutal imitation of my own. I was the symbol of the Penitent's sacred crusade for deathlessness. A thing of power, perhaps, but a thing nonetheless. I was a made, and not a born thing. A creature of art and science—of knowledge—rather than organic chaos, rather than birth. The Penitents and their followers aspired to be—like me—made of their own hands. Death was their only God, though she was not kind: merely a brutal, unconscious, unknowing opponent. Their crusade was deathlessness. They sought Eternal Life through Knowledge: a casting off of the pulsing, rotting bodies in which they had been born. They sought Transformation into the pure consciousness of a machinic life.

He hired clockmen, watchmakers, machinists and scholars, madmen and philosophers, doctors and naturalists. He founded Institutes within which the first Penitents—though untransformed—bent their lives to the task of transcending the flesh. They built fabulous machines—things of glass and wire, copper and steel, wood and water—into which they worked to channel the souls of thousands of men, women and children. For a while they thought that a child's soul—less attached to its mortal body—would be easier to extract. Ten thousand dead could not convince them otherwise.

In the end, it was a young boy who would give them the means of their Transformation into Penitents: the ordinary miracle by which they could remove the enervated hearts from their bodies. He would do it out of love, or pure inventiveness. He would do it without knowing where it would lead us.

Pietr sent the greatest scholars he could find to the Territories, where he founded the Oban College and made the Obanites the keepers of True History, the keepers of his wife's history, and of her false record of my past. He gave them Montane's Rupettan Annal—the Annal the Obanites guard so closely, against which all official history is tested. Upon which all this horror has been built.

Years later, he bequested land to those who swore fealty to his Fourfold Law, he sent generations of his followers to the Territories to found a new civilisation—like your Great Aunt Grace, Henri, whose job it was to populate the world with Rupettans, with lovers of his Law.

While Vivica played the world swung and changed. The old world —the world of grace, faith and uncertainty—died while the woods of the winter palace held her in their magical, timeless thrall. She never saw the world that heaved beyond the edges of her forest haven. Her world of hippocampi and mermaids, of dryads and angels.

At twelve she was long-legged, sharp-eyed. Her grandmother shuffled behind her into the woods, onto the ice, her bones stiff and sore. They ate dried meat and drank coffee, smoked fragrant cigars and fished. At night, when they returned to the palace, they sat in companionable silence, the doors locked against intruders, and played Oråki, read books, spoke of a world in which foxes and stones were as real as war.

One night, while Vivica slept, the Empress Kassia stood at the window, wide awake, watching the moon rise over her wild forest. I thought she had forgotten me. I stood over them, for months, perhaps years, in ready silence, though I was not weak as I had been after Margery's death. Mourning had loosened within me, perhaps, or perhaps I had already begun to change.

I will die tonight, she said. *You must make of her an Empress. A Wynder.*

She is frightened of me, I said. *She has never even touched me.*

Wake her.

She is just a child, I said.

She is the Wynder, and the world has need of her. Wake her now.

I carried Vivica from the bed, sleep-crushed and warm, and settled her on her grandmother's lap. She curled into Kassia's warmth, bringing her knees up to her chin, tucking the crown of her head beneath her grandmother's chin. Kassia lifted her chin, looked fiercely into her granddaughter's sleepy eyes. *Wake up,* she said. *You must Wynd Rupetta.*

I'm tired; I don't want to.

What you want is no longer my concern, or yours. You are the Wynder and must rule with Rupetta at your side; it is time you put away childhood. Kassia brushed the child from her lap as though she were a fallen leaf. *Here,* she said, *take the key.*

Vivica turned her sulky face away from Kassia. She moved as if to return to her bed. *I don't want to, grandmother.*

Kassia's hand lashed out and grabbed her granddaughter's wrist, wrenching her back towards us. She pressed the key into Vivica's hand and closed her tiny fist around it. Her other hand was tight as a claw around Vivica's wrist, rubbing the bones, reddening the skin. Kassia's breath was short and rasping. *I have no time for arguments. You will Wynd her.*

Vivica twisted her hand in her grandmother's fist and snapped away. The two stared at each other. Vivica straightened her spine and faced me. She placed the key into the lock and opened the chamber. Inside me cogs turned, pipes jumped, the several chambers of my heart swelled and sucked in even, perfect rhythms. She reached up her hand and slid it into place.

Vivica's life thundered into me: hot, fast, frightened and determined. I felt her sharp fear of death, her hatred of closed spaces, her love of the forest, for the tall pines and the deep, cold waters. For the fox who had been her childhood friend, who even now she saw sometimes, flashing through the forest like a lick of fire against the snow.

And death, resting inside her like a maggot. Her fragile heart and the virus within it wedding its frailty to my own.

Kassia died that night, after the Wynding, while her granddaughter slept in a tent in the forest. Angry at her grandmother for forcing her to change, to grow, she had stormed out of her grandmother's room after the Wynding. Perhaps, too, she had felt the change in herself, had felt my life and hers twine together and did not like to be so known, so interdependent. She went to her own rooms and sat at her desk, where she wrote a note to her grandmother.

> *Dear ~~Empress~~ Kassia,*
> *I hate you and banish you.*
> *Sealed under my hand,*
> *Empress Vivica Wynder X.*

As Vivica left the palace, wrapped up in her boots and coat, all her worldly possessions tied into an old blanket, she paused to slide the note under her grandmother's door. Kassia was already dead.

I let Vivica sleep outside, even though she was too young and too sick and any true guardian of her wellbeing would have coddled her into her bed. It was to be her last night of wildness. Of childhood. At the time I didn't know what it was like for her, tucked up in the darkness, how the night pressed in while she was sleeping. How the creatures she knew by day lost their shapes and sounds, becoming mouthless things that moved about. How the earth under her bare feet was sharper and more mysterious: earth, stones, roots, grasses and other things, things she couldn't name, slid and scrabbled under her toes. By day the forest was her domain—a place of magic—but in the dark it swirled around her, smothering her with thick, black emptiness.

Vivica woke to me at her elbow, urging her to dress and come back to the palace. It was nearly dawn; we would sneak in through the kitchen doors, creep through the sleeping corridors until we reached her rooms and pretend she had never left. I washed her and combed out her hair, slipped a clean nightgown over her head, tucked her into her clean, white sheets and watched over her while she waited for morning to come.

When the bells rang out to announce her grandmother's death, we walked down to the front steps of the palace. The red and gold flag marking her grandmother's passing had been hung above the palace. Its bright colours flashed in the dim light.

Outside, the courtiers were assembled to greet us as we stepped through the wide doors and stood facing the crowd. We greeted Kassia's mourners, her people. Vivica, her face pale and determined, stood at my side and spoke of her grandmother's fortitude, her strength and determination. Her intolerance for fools. Her sharp humour and the long, richly-coloured years of her rule. Her ambition for the Empire, and for the future into which Rupetta urged us. The future we —Vivica and I—would fulfil.

We performed the already-traditional public Wynding outside, on the stairs of the palace, while hundreds looked on. There was applause, and tears. The great Empress was dead and her granddaughter had taken the throne in her tiny fists. We would rule, as Kassia had wished it, together—interweaving our age and youth, our knowledge and innocence.

℘

Each night, while the Empress Vivica slept, I stood or sat at her bedside watching the pulse jump unevenly at her throat. She could have been like all the others—Eloise or Elisabetta or Montane—whose bodies bore them through their lives like frail machines, but Nature had cast Vivica with her grandmother's flaw. Vivica's heart was weak: it fluttered in her chest like a trapped moth, its wings damaged and faltering. Death would have been cruel for such a young woman, but this half-life was worse. She could barely walk, some days, and instead spent all her waking and sleeping hours fighting for breath. While my own constant centre beat on and on, hers faltered, always on the point of breaking. Her lips blushed and turned blue, her hands fluttered at her throat. Her heart beat madly, but was as ineffectual as a wraith. At night, in the dark of our room, she faltered and died in my arms, again

186

and again, and I wrenched her back to life, pressing the bones of her chest until I believed they would break, forcing air into her lungs, calling her name as if it were my own.

The physicians came and listened to her poor, limping heart but could do nothing. Like her grandmother, the great Empress Kassia, and her father, Pietr, her heart was weak. But Vivica was young—filled with the dreams her new role as Empress had given her. She would build a world where childhood reigned, where wisdom was a gift. She had plans for expanding her father's heritage of colleges and abbeys, cities and circuses. She wanted to open them up to the people. Free education for those whose minds were supple enough to learn. Her child's hand signed bills for the funding of new colleges, new Orders devoted to Harmonics, Botany and Astronomy. She dreamed of great gardens at the centre of every city, forests of trees for her citizens to shelter beneath, walk within. She dreamed of an Empire free of fear, its people nurturing the tender fragility of the earth they lived upon. Listening to the trees that lay at their centres, whispering dreams of the earth. She dreamed of undoing the power of the Orders her father had founded, and which had wrested such power in a few short years. She wanted to divest the Obanites of their hold on History. She dreamed of a world in which every child wandered the rivers of their countries, lay upon the banks and looked up through the trees to the stars. A world in which every child wandered until life called them. She dreamed of schools and homes and cities where knowledge was not a weapon, but a source of nourishment and hope. Her father had written the laws of heaven and hell; she believed it was her destiny, her grandmother's unspoken intent, that she write the laws of the earth.

She wrought as much change as her thin frame could support. Each day she wrenched herself from sleep, had herself tied into her gowns and woke her court. She spent long days in what had once been her grandmother's rooms, with reams of maps and charts and accounts, mapping trade, tracing the lines of the Empire on the table with a finger that was blue with cold and lack of circulation. She barely looked up at the adults who surrounded her. She barked out orders,

187

sketched plans, fought for her own vision, her own authority. The men and women of her chamber—fired with her passion, frustrated by her inability to stop, to ask, to consult with them—were loyal to the point of fanaticism.

Those who weren't were quickly dismissed.

There was no room in the Empress's life for doubt, for long and tiresome deliberations. Death hung in her chest. She lived and breathed and ate each day believing it might be her last. Determined to build an Empire of childhood dreams before it claimed her.

Late in the afternoons, when her white cheeks were sunken and the pulse jumped alarmingly in her throat, I would stand and lean to whisper in her ear. She would shake her head, hold up a hand as if to hold me at bay while she scratched her signature, pressed her seal onto another order, thrust it into a messenger's hand.

I insisted.

She turned and glared at me, stiff-spined as always, her fierce eyes flickering with pride. The messenger scurried past me, orders clutched in his hands. I dismissed the court. She would call them back when our business was done, she said. There was no time to waste with pathetic ailments, pointless rituals. People needed her. Their lives were short.

I put my hand on her arm, felt the clammy cold of her skin. Her eyes were wide, fevered. I led her to a chair and lowered her into it.

The future would have to wait.

I opened the chamber, let her in, but the flare between us was shallow. Her lips were blue, her skin so thin I could see the veins like a map of rivers beneath the surface. I carried her to her rooms, lay her down on the bed that had once been her grandmother's, called the physician. She looked as small as a twig half-buried in a bank of snow.

Six men and women came and hovered over her. Weighing her limbs, listening to her heart, bleeding her. This was their verdict: for months, Vivica must stay inside, alone. Hidden from the court, from the world whose great need assaulted and exhausted her. She must be still and listen to her heart. She must be quiet, and learn to die.

The Miracle of the Heart

Inside the Winter Palace, she was shut up like a wintering beast who could not sleep. The walls were too thick, the doors heavy oak sentinels. She paced like a caged bear through the wide, marbled halls: irritable, straining at the invisible collar that kept her bound. She seethed with impatience, her limbs too long, her eyes too bright for these dark, empty rooms. But to walk in the forest would hurt her. Vivica, Empress of the Rūs, daughter of Anise and Pietr, granddaughter of the great Empress Kassia. A warrior who rode astride, who had murdered her own father, who would eat the hearts of her enemies, build stone cathedrals with her own bare hands. The Child Empress who, at twelve years of age, argued on the lawns of the Haven and orated to thousands, to millions. Vivica, who had stood at the helm of her Empire as it lurched into her grasp, and turned it, by the force of her own will, towards a future only she dared name. She, who had transformed the Empire, who had been at once ruler, goddess, reaper, who had ruled the world from her cradle, was reduced to her body, like a worm.

She slept and I stood in the dark, watching the moon traverse the night sky, the Weaver following, pursuing her own death. I could see my reflection in the glass of the windows. I took the key, strung on its ribbon around Vivica's wrist, and opened my own chest. I watched my heart swell and suck, rocking in its leather and brass cradle. Its four chambers, like rooms, cycling through their constant beat. It beat on alone, unaffected by Vivica's weakness, unable to offer her its strength.

In the morning, when the physician came to test and soothe the Empress, she railed against her limits, clutching her coat in her pale, thin claws. *This is not who I am,* she said, barely able to find breath to speak. *I am Vivica, Empress of the Rūs. I am not this body.*

We are all our bodies, Empress, the physician said, trying to gentle her into the sheets. *The Law teaches us this—the flesh is weak, the body a machine. The spirit seeks Death.*

Not my spirit, she insisted. *I am the Wynder.*

There will be another, the physician said.

How will there be another if I die? The Wynder must be the daughter of my flesh, of my heart; I have not even chosen a Consort. Will you be Empress, old woman? Will you rule the world and Wynd the Great Doll?

Vivica . . . I said.

She turned towards me, her frame braced to fight any who dared contradict her. *Tell her to go,* she said. *What knowledge she has she learned in our Colleges. We don't need her.*

℘

That night, as she slept, I went down to the stables, where the horses had once been kept. Here, in a long line, were the carriages I had designed to bear Anise, and then Vivica, through the streets and rivers of their Empire. Here was the open summer carriage: a creature half-elephant and half-unicorn, who bore her on its back in a shaded palanquin. Here was the autumn carriage, drawn by snowy dryads, whose leafless arms bore the struts of an alder-wood cart. Here was the spring carriage—her favourite—a long, thin boat drawn through the rivers of the Empire by two pairs: mermaids and hippocampi, whose long tails gleamed with brass scales. At the end was Kassia's favourite—a creature of her own design—the winter carriage was a sleigh-footed dragon whose long rails sloped over snow and ice. The dragon's scales were silver and jade, its long neck curved around as it lay in the stable, as if it were sleeping. I lay my hand on its cool haunch, ran it up the roughness of its needled spine. It had, of course, no heart. It moved and rested but could not die. Inside its breast was a storage space for blankets and whisky, mittens and books. I opened its stomach and peered in at the mechanism that drove it.

At the end of the row was a long workbench, a cabinet full of keys, a series of shelves where tools and parts were kept. A half-made mechanism lay on the table; a thing of glass and blue stone, small enough to carry. In the corner, asleep at his work, was a young boy.

What is this? I asked.

190

He barely moved; shrugging his shoulders in his sleep as a child shrugs off a parent's hand on the morning they must go to school.

Wake up, I said, louder now, nudging his blanketed shin with my foot. He shot up from the floor and blinked, rubbing his hands through his shock of dark hair.

I lifted a piece of the unfinished creation: a bowl-shaped piece of glass with thin tubes lining its innards. *What is this?* I asked.

I don't know, he said, though he stepped forward and moved as if to take it from me. *It's—I mean, I'm not sure what it is, yet. It just is, you know?* He tilted his head like a finch and looked up at me, his eyes blurred with sleep. Then, as if he had made up his mind, he darted across the room to the winter carriage and plucked something from the storage space. He darted back and held it out to me.

I placed the half-finished piece back on the bench and took the small closed ball he held out to me. It was a smooth, perfectly-round ball, covered in a pattern of red Chinoiserie. When I tilted it, it made a sound, like the tinkling of bells in a far-off field. *What is it?* I said again.

Rather than reply he smiled and cupped my hand in his own. He raised it towards my face. As it moved more sounds emerged—tinkling bells, a sound like rain, a plink of water hitting old stone. The boy stepped back and stood, a few feet away. *Throw it,* he said.

As the ball arced into the air, curving towards him, he did not reach up to catch it. I heard a faint click and the ball opened, in mid-air, like the petals of a flower peeling back. A blur of red and gold and then a pale shimmer of white as it began to spin. It landed on the boy's shoulder. When I moved closer to study it, to lift it from him, the mechanism lifted into the air, hovered for a second and darted forward. It plucked a single hair from my head and fled to the rafters, where it continued making its odd, tuneless sounds.

You made this? I said.

The boy nodded and moved towards the bench, picking up and gentling the half-formed glass mechanism as if it were a child, turning it over in his hands to check for flaws.

191

What is your name?

Luon, he said.

I am Rupetta, I said.

He nodded again as he put down the glass bowl and picked up a small pipette. *Is it true what they say,* he said, *that the Wynder will die?*

Who says this? I asked.

Luon shrugged. *Everyone, I guess. Why can't you fix her?*

She's not a mechanism, like these toys of yours. Like me.

It is her heart that's broken? he said. *Make her another.*

It's not that easy, I said. *She is not like me; a heart of leather and brass would rot and infect her. A heart of bone and wood would fail.*

I made something else, he said. *I'll show you if you'll take me to meet her.*

Vivica?

He nodded again without meeting my gaze. His shoulders tight with determination.

What is it you want to show me?

It's a secret, he said. *You have to promise. Swear on the Wynder's life.*

I swear, I said.

The boy met my gaze, measuring my honesty with his own clear gaze. *Alright,* he said. *Come with me.*

We went out of the stables, into the woods. It was dark, but there was a bright moon. We made our way through the trees, along pathways he had clearly walked many times before. He paused, occasionally, to peer up into the trees, to touch the bark of a tree as if it were an old friend who allowed him to pass. We reached a tree whose belly was hollow. Stretched across the mouth of this wooden cave was a tanned hide. He pushed it aside and gestured for me to enter. This was his home.

Inside the hollow of the tree it was clean and dry. The earthen floor was swept clean. There was a nest of furs for a bed. A box in which he kept his belongings. A shelf ran around the room just above the height of his head, along which were arranged more of his mechanisms:

wheeled and winged, blinking and exquisite. A clockwork mouse, a wooden frog, a tiny house whose lights blinked on and off as the shadows within it moved.

Luon pulled the small chest into the centre of the room and removed something from it, something small enough to hide in his fist, before he gestured for me to sit on the closed chest. *Sit quietly,* he said. *He's shy of strangers.*

I sat and watched as he went to his bed and turned back the blanket of furs. A smell of wildness, of life. He smiled and reached out a hand. Something rustled and moved. A flash of dark fur. A glimmer of bright eyes and white teeth. Something dashed into his arms and buried itself there, its nose pressed up into his armpit. Luon smoothed its ruffled fur, humming in the back of his throat. *Shhhh,* he said, *shh, Hanaso.*

Soon the creature was reassured. It spun in his arms, picked at the boy's sleeves like a nervous child before diving into his pockets to search for food.

It's a fox, I said, watching its tail curl around Luon's arm, tickling his throat. It twirled in his lap, nibbling at the food it had found with its sharp teeth. Luon nodded.

A fox is not a made thing, I said.

Hanaso curved around his arm like a furred vine. Luon made a noise in his throat, like a burred whistle, and the creature moved onto his lap and lay on its back, twitching happily as Luon smoothed the fur of its belly. The pale fur of its chest was exposed, which was strange enough, but stranger still was the glint of metal. High up on Hanaso's chest was a silver oval, bound into the skin as if a wound had healed over its edges. With his free hand Luon reached towards me. He turned over his closed fist and unfurled his fingers like a magician. There, on his palm, was a tiny silver key.

Open it, he said.

I gazed at the ellipsis on Hanaso's chest, with its pale ring of scar-tissue. On one side was a fine hinge, on the other a keyhole. I opened the fox and saw its heart. Luon clucked and murmured to the creature as I bent my head to see the glass pipes, the cunning silver chambers, to hear the shush and shunt of its heart's chambers work. To see the leaves and vines chiselled on its surface shine under their fine coating of blood. I touched it with my fingertip, felt the chamber quavering like my own. He was just a boy—a child—younger even than the Empress. His hands were small, his knuckles grazed, his wide eyes clear and dark.

Luon closed the chamber, turned the lock and pocketed the key. *I will show you how it's done*, he said, *I will make a new heart for the Empress, after you have taken me to see her.*

℘

Years later, when Luon and Vivica's children and grandchildren played in this forest, I often brought them to that tree, and showed them the toys that lay upon its shelves.

Rebecca and her brothers would take down the red ball, the snow-dome, the faeries' houses and grumbling wooden trolls and set them out on the floor to play. One by one, most of them were lost or broken. Each of the children had their favourites.

Mateo loved the tiny horses best. He played with them until their brass surfaces were warmly-golden and smooth, until their features were blurred and their forelocks rubbed flat. When the leg of his favourite broke off below the knee—the metal worn to thin fatigue—he buried it in a secret place.

Rebecca had two daughters: Emina and Judit. Emina's favourite was a piece of white stone carved in the shape of a sleeping dragon. It did not move or sing or fly, but she loved it anyway. As a child, she loved simple things. Things she could understand and control. The whirring and twitching of her grandfather's other mechanisms frightened her. She kept the stone dragon in her pocket, her hand often curled around its satisfying weight. Years later, when Emina stood on the throne as Wynder, beside the false Rupetta, the dragon weighted her dreams. She dreamed of opening Alazaïs's chest to find, not a heart, but a tiny dragon, a fist of white stained with her mother's blood.

Once, when they were young, they brought their grandparents to the tree—to their grandfather's own childhood home—and stood him in its centre, laughing at how his grey hair disappeared into the hollow above them. He was tall by then. A grown man who had seen the Empire swallow up the world. He had been Consort for more than fifty years. Hanaso was long-dead, though Luon's eyes darted to her nest when he entered, as if she might spring to his hand, to his pockets in search of treats. His eyes scanned the tiny, well-kept space: its rough walls and earthen floor, its box and shelf.

Here, in the hollow centre of a tree as old as I, was the Consort's childhood, here was the miracle of Vivica's reign: the miracle of the heart.

Outside, as the children whirled and laughed, wrestling each other in the newly-fallen snow, Luon took Vivica's warm hand in his own. He touched their joined clasp to the cool metal door of her heart and smiled. He had loved the heart he had made, and held it in his own hand long before it was hers. He had been a child when he wrought that heart—the first Penitent heart—and did not know it couldn't be done. He had loved her; he had made her a life. It was his miracle. It was never mine.

Henri's Story: Part Five

I woke in the dark and reached out towards Miri, sleeping beside me. Miri's skin was cool to the touch, though our sheets were rumpled and warm. She slept, as always, on her side, turned towards me with her hands folded beneath her cheek, and her knees drawn up like a child's. I reached out to touch her cheek, to brush back a thick lock of hair from her neck and reveal the frailty of her throat, and in her sleep she turned towards me, kissed the palm of my hand. Beside us, on the bedside table, Perihan chirruped. I watched the mechanical bird hop from the table to the bed and chirrup again, urgently. Its voice tight and high.

'What is it?' I whispered, wondering if the leather of its tiny bellows needed oiling.

Perihan moved closer, hopped onto my open palm and leaned forward to peck the pale skin of my forearm. A bead of blood welled against my skin, as red and shining as the bird's gemmed eye.

I sat up and sucked the tiny wound, eyeing Perihan as it hopped back and forth on the sheets. I stood and peered through the window of my childhood bedroom into the garden. Outside the moon shone, half full and still rising, in a clear sky. I could see the familiar formation of the spring stars: the kite and the arrow, the elm and the beetle. Beneath them the trees of my father's garden were dark-leaved and strange. I could see the path that led to the end of the garden, and the forest. I could hear the toll of my mother's grave.

I pulled a pair of socks onto my feet and slipped Perihan into my pocket, curling my fingers around its warm, familiar weight. I crept into the hall of the house, past the closed door of my father's room and down the stairs to the kitchen, where I settled Perihan on the

196

windowsill, filled a glass with water and stood at the sink to drink it. Perihan hopped up and down on the sill of the kitchen window, tapping the glass with its beak. 'Careful,' I said, reaching towards the bird. 'You don't want to break the glass.'

Perihan turned, twittering, almost singing as it stepped off the shelf and dropped towards the floor. Perihan could not fly—its body was heavy and solid. Its wings could unfold, as they did now to slow its descent, but its bones were not hollow and filled with air. It landed heavily on the stone floor, righted itself and skittered across to the door to the hall and out to the back door. Perihan paused near the door's opening, pressing its beak into the small gap between the door and the frame. I pushed open the door, watching as Perihan bolted down the steps onto the path, as small and glittery as a jewelled mouse, weaving and tipping on the uneven surface.

As I followed Perihan into the garden a tart smell of oak came to me, though none grew there, as if I were walking in the gardens at Salt Lane. The bird, slowed by the grass and dirt beneath its feet, lurched from stone to stone along the paths, past the old mango trees and the graceful pomegranates, whose leathery fruit hung low and heavy, until we reached the ancient fig tree at the end of the garden. She was the grand dame of the garden: a tree so old and heavily-limbed that as a child I had often climbed into it with a blanket and cushions, a box of bread, cheese and sweets stolen from the stash in my father's desk. The tree was not very tall, but it was wide and knotted, with thick branches that splayed out like the ill-formed fingers of a giant's hand. I had picnicked there, alone or with my schoolfriends, plucking ripe figs from the branches nearby whenever my plate was empty. Here, Perihan waited. Its small feet—one new and brightly polished, one old and blackened with age—were curved over the shoulder of a small girl.

I hesitated with my hand on one of the old tree's branches. Glanced at the bird's bright head, at the tree and the stars. Looked up towards the gentling moon. The child was dressed in a heavy white dress, like a character from a play. *Like Margause's sister*, I thought at first, *Like my mother*: a jumbled, sleep-sap thought that collided the child's dark hair

197

and white dress with our walk in the mountain that day, the gift we had left behind. But the child I discovered in the garden was so small and her bare feet were splayed before her. The soles dirty. A wraith among the dark limbs and whispering leaves. A ghost-child come out of the dark to gather my father home.

'Hello,' the child said.

I stood, smoothed down the old white shirt I slept in and tried to smile, counting seconds in my head, waiting to wake in my childhood room again, with Miri's heated breath spooling across the pillow towards me, waiting for the terror and awful, awful cruelty of the child's small, pretty face to fade.

'I am Perdita,' said the child.

'I'm Henri,' I said. Feeling the word bulk in my mouth before I let it go, wondering at the vividness of the dream I was having. Was I ill? Was it stress? For weeks, while we had worked at arrangements for my father's care, interviewing carers, making daily trips to the Haven for medical supplies, I had had trouble sleeping, heard in my half-dreams the toll of my mother's and my father's bells in the garden, his death's heart chiming above his grave like an angry, chittering clock while hers prettied the hours away.

The child nodded and reached across her chest, lifting Perihan onto her finger. 'I know who you are,' she said.

I stepped a little closer, watching Perihan preen and shuffle on the girl's hand. 'I'm Henri,' I said. 'I used to live here. Are you lost?'

Perdita held out her hand, with Perihan standing on it. She studied the bird and smiled as she shook her head. 'Listen,' she said. Perihan tilted back its head and let out a soft, ululating note. One I had never heard it utter before. Perdita smiled and tipped back her own head, her dark hair slipping over her shoulders as she did so. She opened her mouth and let out a sound almost exactly the same as the one Perihan had made: a threnody, a murmur that was both musical and mechanical. As though the leaves of the trees had been blown into song by a clockwork wind.

'That's very clever,' I said.

Perdita smiled the pleased and particular smile of a child who knows it is clever. Perihan sang again: a series of notes that rose higher and higher. As the notes swirled around me, Perdita's voice joined them. A fairy's voice, spined with light, with wind, with wilderness. The tree's branches above us seemed to shift, the leaves to thicken and curve around to frame them. I could smell the fruit, ready to harvest. I could feel the warmth of my father's hand resting on my head as I studied and felt tears, suddenly, thinking of his good hat held so lightly in his other hand. The felted brim of his hat was worn smooth. The steadiness of him settling a plate of toast beside me as I worked, but not saying a word, just smiling and leaving it there. The sound of his mumbled agreements with the past as he sat in his chair by the fire, reading the History books my mother had left behind. The splay-spined books piled up at his side, their pages sighing beneath his fingers. The slow, steady toll of his gravestone bell. How cruel I had been, his whole conscious life; how small my world would be without him. I would not weep. People do not weep in their dreams.

'I'm not supposed to be here,' Perdita said.

'I can take you home, if you like. I have a bicycle at the house.'

Perdita shook her head and sat cross-legged in the thin grass beneath the tree. Her skirt stretched across the triangle of her lap and she settled Perihan into the white scoop of it. I sat beside her, the damp of the earth soaking through my thin nightclothes. 'Don't you want to go home?' I said, remembering the times I had run away from home as a child, camped shoeless in the playground of the school, or up in the mountains. How my father or Old Paul had always found me and brought me home; how they never made me feel foolish for my tantrums, only brave and independent. How they would sit with me at the kitchen table afterwards, and ask how my journey had been.

'I came here on purpose,' she said.

I looked down at the bird, a jewelled comma in the child's lap. 'Do you know Perihan?' I said.

Perdita nodded. 'My mother made it,' she said.

'Where is your mother now?'

199

Perdita turned, lifted her head and looked back through the garden towards the house. 'She doesn't know I've come yet, does she?'

Perdita leaned closer to me; put her head against my arm. 'It was so cold in the mountains. And then Sparrow died. I was lonely. I couldn't wait any longer. When Giacomo died I wanted to stay at the College, with Margause. I like the College; I like the orchard and the stone floors in the kitchen, and the way my mother keeps lavender in the linen so it smells nice, and the way she laughs and knows things and isn't afraid. No matter what. Can you ask her to let me stay this time?'

I looked down at the sleek, dark head resting against my side, felt the unfamiliar weight of it shift as Perdita looked up at me.

'Your mother?' I said.

'You call her Miri,' she said. Her eyes were round and bright and green as the ocean. Her hands were spread on the ground, like tiny stars, milk-white and perfect, the grass a tangle of dark blades between her fingers. Her feet were pulled up towards her bottom and her bare knees shone in the light. She was so young. So small. I reached across and brushed the hair back from the child's face, felt the skin that was as soft and fragrant as candlewax. Her hot little hand curled in mine and I imagined—or remembered, as though it were true—my mother standing in the trees, singing me home. Something tightened and turned within me. 'I'll talk to her,' I said.

ॐ

The kitchen floor was cool beneath our bare feet. Perdita settled herself at the table. She lifted the figs out of her skirt onto the table one by one, arranging them on a wooden board. I spooned ricotta into one bowl, and honey into another. The bowls Margause had given me: from the potter who worked on Oikos Island. I lit the fire and put on the coffee, took down the familiar mugs from the shelf above the stove and warmed them on the hob. Light spilled in through the windows and across the open doorstep. When the tap was turned off I glanced at Perdita, who was busy setting the table for breakfast, kneeling up on a chair to reach the other side of the table. I had expected her to fade as the sun rose, like a ghost, flickering into spatters of light.

The door from the hall opened. Miri came into the kitchen with the back of her hand rubbing at her eyes. She was wearing an old shirt of my father's—thin and spattered with olive-green paint stains. One sleeve was rolled up above her elbow while the other cuff dangled past the end of her arm. She was seated at the table, reaching for the coffee, already talking about what we needed to do today: Old Paul was coming to sit with my father so we could take the train down to the city for the day, pick up some supplies we needed: medications, rails for the side of his bed. Perdita made a little noise—of alarm, or recognition—and Miri's head jerked up.

Perdita grinned at her and Perihan chirruped loudly, as though it were a dog that had brought a new treasure to its beloved master. Miri hesitated with the coffeepot in mid-air, tipping towards her mug. She stared at the little girl. Her daughter, who had drawn up a chair and was spreading a piece of toast with ricotta. Then she turned to me, standing back from the table, hands dug in my pockets, my gaze direct and furious.

'She was in the garden,' I said. 'Waiting for you.'

'I waited and waited,' Perdita said, 'and then Henri came.' She clutched my hand and smiled up at me.

'You're supposed to be in the mountains, with Sparrow,' Miri said to the child. 'I thought—'

'You thought what?' I said, my voice sharp and dark.

'It's not what you think,' Miri said.

'No? And what is it I think?' I said. 'Do you even care what I think, what anybody else thinks?'

'Henri. Please. We had to protect her—'

'Protect her from what, exactly? She's just a child, Miri. The only protection she needs is to be with her mother: with you.' The house whirled. I heard my father call out from somewhere deep in the house. Upstairs, he was upstairs, waiting for me. Helpless and afraid. I gripped the bench as tightly as I could, and closed my eyes as he called out again.

Old Paul knocked at the back door, and came in and said hello to Perdita in the special voice he reserved for stray dogs and small children. With awful suddenness I recalled Old Paul coming to bury my mother, his familiar face suddenly strange above his moth-pocked Penitent's robes. Watching him wind the bells at the head of her grave. Of lying awake that first night, listening to the bells peal in the darkness, my arms and legs held stiff and flat beneath the sheets.

'Henri,' said Perdita. 'Sit down.'

I swallowed hard, stepped back from the table. Studied Miri's face for some sign of what she felt, what she was thinking. Who she was. 'How many lies are there, Miri?'

Miri looked down at her hands, gripping the chair on either side of her thighs. 'That's not my real name,' she said.

I nodded, once, and wiped my hands down the sides of my shirt. My voice was quiet, as thin and shaken as a leaf. 'So,' I said, 'it's all a lie.'

Miri shook her head. She put her hands on the table. She smiled at Perdita, just a little curve that didn't mean anything: the smile of a liar. 'No,' she said.

'You could have told me the truth,' I said. 'You could have trusted me.'

'She couldn't tell anybody the truth,' said Perdita.

'We needed to wait,' Miri said. 'We needed to be sure it was safe for her, for all of us. We didn't know if—'

I shook my head, 'If what? If you could trust me? Did you think I'd betray you? Run away? I told you everything and you—you lied to me. About everything. She's a child, Miri—whoever you are—a little girl. Look at her. *Look at her.* How could you not tell me about her? You could have told me, trusted me. I would have done the right thing. I would have protected you both from whoever it is you think is after you.'

Miri shook her head. 'Would have?' she said. 'Past tense.'

'How can I trust you? How can I believe anything you say? It's all been lies. All of it.' I looked at Perdita, who was seated at the table, fidgeting with the hem of her skirt, waiting for it all to end. 'Would you leave me, too, when I became inconvenient?'

'I never lied to you, Henri.'

'You never told me the truth.'

Miri hung her head again, breathed in, and then nodded. 'Henri,' she said, her voice low and broken. 'Please. Sit down. It's a long story.'

I stared at her, at the way her throat and shoulders and arms were still the same. Even her face: her eyes and nose and mouth, the way they were held—just so—without giving anything away. No blush of shame on her throat. No new cast to her face. Last night I had lain down beside her. Had kissed her and held her and breathed in the scent of her. She had closed her eyes as I kissed the curve of her throat.

My stomach knotted; I felt the salt of grief and fear and loneliness bloat inside me. Had Miri closed her eyes, last night, to hide what she didn't feel? Had she turned away afterward, curled up with her back towards me, not for the comfort of being held, but so she didn't have to look into my face? Was she here out of guilt, watching me grapple with my father's illness out of some sense of pity?

I shook my head, moved towards the door. The handle was smooth and cool and familiar in my hand. It was an old brass knob: well-polished but dinted, the ridged circle around it slightly blackened. This much was true: the weight of old brass, the turn of the tongue in the lock. This much I could rely on. I held onto it, pushed open the door. 'You said you loved me,' I said, the words blooming like stones in my chest. Wanting them to hit her. To hurt her. 'I guess that was just another lie.'

∞

I climbed the back stairs of my father's house with the last box in my arms. My clothes and books and photographs. My father's face peered up at me from a picture balanced on the top. He had loved History—

when he still knew what love was—even if he had never loved Historians, not after my mother died.

I put my hands on the desk, one in the dark, one in the light that fell through the window in a gold square of warmth. There were eight folders. I had six pencils. A wooden jar of pencil shavings. An eraser and a ruler and a slim box of photographs. Twelve books, their spines aligned, lay in four piles of three on the desk. I could measure and know these things: Mathilde had waited for forty-nine years. She had educated and housed 263 children. These things were knowable, measurable, and true. My mother's death, Miri's daughter, were historic riddles, like the rediscovered pages of a ruined diary. I could barely read them, but I kept turning them over and over in my hands, as if the warmth of my attention would reveal their hidden, inky truths. As if their lives were gestures still being made; a heady breath of movement still turning in the summer air.

Eight folders of research. I opened my notebook. Sat at my childhood desk. Laid out the pencils and felt heartsore, weary comfort at the sight of them lying there in a row. Opened my notebook and pressed the pages flat. The neat lines of notes: the whiteness of the still-unwritten page. I opened the second folder, flicked over the folioed notes until I reached the section where I had left off yesterday.

I had barely three months until my thesis was due. Jenon had been visiting me when he could, asking about my father, cursorily, but also asking to see my drafts, notes, methodologies. Poring over my lists of references, the draft catalogue of the Oikos and Salt Lane Archives, asking difficult questions, and watching my pinched face keenly as I stuttered my way through my answers. A week ago, he had posted out a copy of the schedule for final defences. There were twelve spaces—twelve appointments. Each student had been allocated a date and time for their oral defence, and was to supply a full draft of their thesis material a month before that date. My name was listed against the last possible date. I had gone down to the College one last time, packed up my desk in the library, and my papers, and brought them home.

I could not work at Elm, in the glasshouse, where Perdita's small cot now sat beneath a canopy of thick-leaved palms on the other side of the room. My old desk was still there, but it was too hard, each day, to sit and think and write with Miri wandering in and out, pretending to have tasks, to have forgotten her shoes or hat or pens as if it were an ordinary day and she was an ordinary, honest woman.

I knew now that love did not require honesty—that that was just a lie—but my anger wouldn't allow me to confess my mistake, or forgive her too easily. I wanted her to be sorry. I wanted her to be afraid that she might lose me. I wanted her to want me and fight for me and long for me. I wanted to feel the shape of her longing wrap around me like rough comfort. I wanted to keep her secrecy in front of me. A live twittering bird. Her voice in my throat, the weight of her fingers on my wrist.

At Elm, Miri was always coming in to stand near the desk, ask me if I needed anything. Bringing cups of tea and squares of chocolate. Offering to help. I could not turn her away, or turn towards her. I would lean forward over my work, refuse to meet her eyes, refuse to surrender to the false comfort of her hand on my shoulder, the promise of her arms around me.

Each night we lay down together in the glasshouse, or at home, after a week in which I had been unable to do even that, but the expanse of white sheet between us was a continent as vast and cold and uncrossable as the Antarctic. I held myself still and stiff on my side of the bed, watched the stars, listened to Perdita's breathing and ticking in the next room, to the familiar creak and hush of the trees outside. I thought about Emmeline, about all those years she spent alone at Salt Lane, waiting for something to change. I pictured her getting up every morning, making tea, packing something to take to the Haven—anything, it didn't matter—and cycling down there each day, as though she were delivering eggs to the market, as though it were as simple and ordinary as that. She had kept faith with Mathilde when there was no word, when she did not know whether there was anything—anyone—left to keep faith with.

205

I closed my eyes and feel the weight of Miri's sleeplessness beside me, of the stranger beside me who both was, and was not, Miri. I tried to imagine she was still the same woman I had loved so deeply, so innocently, and that we could find our way back to each other. Sometimes I fell asleep, just for a moment or two, and woke to the weight of Miri's hand on my belly, on my thigh. I would lie there, in the milky sleep of the past, and wait, holding my breath to still time, to believe again in the easy closeness we had once had. But it would always slip away and I would find myself lying there, with a familiar stranger in my arms. I did not even know her name; refused to ask what it was, refused to hear her say it.

The last chapter of my thesis was still unwritten. I had all the notes in order, the files and resources annotated and waiting. The chapter itself was two handwritten pages—a few references, a spiked, angry doodle, and a long list of questions. Three months. I could apply for an extension, but doing so meant making an appointment with Jenon, bringing in what I had done so far, coming up with a new timeline for completion, hobbling together reasons for my slow progress. *I've been a fool*, I imagined saying to Jenon. *My whole life is a lie.* Getting approval for an extension would require more lies. But if I worked hard I could get it done in time. Three months, and then there would be no more need to take the train down to the College at all. I could stay here and care for my father, wait for him to die: offer back the days he had offered me as child. Perhaps I would re-open the school, after all, as he had suggested in so many of his letters. Join the Historical Society, after all. These days, it didn't seem like such a bad thing.

I opened the window and picked up the pile of papers that would— somehow—become the final chapter.

Three months, I thought, and then I would be ready to say goodbye. To walk away from the future that had gone sour in my mouth before I had even tasted it. I could imagine finishing my thesis, doing the oral, submitting the final, bound copy for examination.

I could not imagine going back to Elm, walking through the orchard, through the kitchen, into the glasshouse to find Miri. Smiling at her, holding her in my arms, feeling the smooth weight of her head resting beneath my chin. Could not imagine what we would say to each other, when the only words we had now were so broken, so unsure. Here—in my childhood room, with Perdita playing in the garden and my father sitting in the sunlight on the back deck—I could work. I could forget, for moments at a time, that Miri was not who I had thought she was. I could begin putting her back together in my mind, piece by piece. Here, listening to Perdita playing in the garden, seeing her pass by my window—I was connected to Miri without being able to speak to her each day, without having to weigh each word she said and wonder which were true, and which were not, and whether there was any way to tell the difference. Whether a life lived in the shadow of lies had made me incapable of knowing truth or love or anything else, anything real. Here I did not have to be kind, or patient, or forgiving. Not for her, anyway. If I thought of her at all, I could remember her as she had once seemed to me: a woman complete and mysterious. A woman whose secrets could not damage me, wandering across the forecourt to the library and back, her head bent forward, her hands dug deep in her pockets. I could love her, from this distance. And would learn to love her from further and further away as the months turned.

℘

I put my father's picture on the table in my childhood room and lifted out my folders, laying them out on the table. He hadn't needed to tell me about my mother's bodily heresy. He could have left me with the lie they had manufactured in its place. He could have taken the truth to his grave, but he had given me a partial truth—a story that was true but which I could not fit inside the other truths I had about myself, my family, my past. I had searched and searched the shelves of my child-hood consciousness; I had nowhere to put what he had told me that did not warp everything. No sense of what to do with it. I was a hollow child, without a centre. The child of a weak-hearted woman; the child

207

of a woman whose body had cast out her Penitent heart, Rupetta's gift, and I hadn't even known it.

I had punished him the only way I knew how: I had stayed away, hating him for the years of innocence, for the pity he showed me, and for his awful tenderness.

But I had loved him, too, when he told me. I had watched his hands shake as he spoke, seeing what it had cost him to bear her heretics' death alone so long, and what it cost him to share it with me. How long and heavily he had debated with himself whether it was better to let the truth die with him, or release it into the future; into me.

I went over and over what he had said, pulling the sentences into pieces: nouns, verbs, prepositions, clauses. Unpacking and re-packing them. Imagining them as artefacts that needed to be labelled and packed into glass-fronted drawers. Or wrapped in acid-free paper and filed away. Wanting to feel him lean over my shoulder and put his hand on the page, take up the pencil and make one strange and perfect mark that would make it all fall into place.

I could hear him downstairs. Old Paul's voice murmuring to him, my father's short grunts and whistles in reply. Could hear his voice rise in aimless panic, and sink again. Old Paul shushing him like a child. I heard him cry like a lost child and went to the door, looking down the hall, not strong enough to go to him. Not yet. I closed the door, went back into the room, sat on the bed, put my hand flat on the bedside table. My childhood books in rows on the bookshelf, my old wooden pencil-box. I knelt on the floor, put my hands flat on the timber. I had sat here for hours as a child, knees drawn up to my chest, a book resting on my knees. For a moment I heard him in the hall, his steps sure. I had such a strong image of him standing—healthy, strong, clear —at the door, smiling down at me, telling me to come to the table for dinner, glancing at the book in my hands and reciting—from memory —his favourite passage. What had that book been? That passage? Something about trees and winter and a child. He would know. Would have known, once.

All my childhood was gone with him into that strange and secret place where he now dwelled. My father, who had been my only true parent, the only one who had known me. I had been forgotten so completely, so suddenly, I felt loose-boned. I had presumed there would be time to forgive him, or forgive myself, or whatever it was I needed to do: unravel the knot of panic his story had placed inside me like a tapeworm.

I had thought there would be time for a great many things. But now he was gone into himself, into the true Land Between where we all travel eventually, and he had taken the meaning of home and family and Henriette—his little Ettie—with him. He was travelling down into his paper grave with it held to his chest, a moon-pale globe of secrets I would never know, lighting his way into death.

ℴ⅋

I woke, in the dark, to the sound of footsteps out in the hall. I had sat on the bed in the late afternoon to read and edit the day's work, a sheaf of papers leaning on my knees, and fallen asleep. The afternoon had been warm and my head swam with dates and references and images. I had given up on the ending, again, and gone back to fine-tuning the beginning of the thesis. Revising the first chapter was easy—old ground—a litany of facts that were already well-established, but I was deliberating over my thesis statement, and the section where I out-lined my research question, unsure how much to say. I had stumbled here, as I did again and again, over having not discovered much of anything at all. Over my conviction that after all this work, more than two years of reading and writing and thinking, the work I had produced was inconsequential. I had found no startling new evidence, nothing to shift the world of the past or the present. The paper was dull, and pointless. I wanted to weep and tear apart the pages and start again, but I had no time.

I listened again: there was someone out in the hall, down at the other end, perhaps, near the stairs to the back deck. I heard them

209

hesitate at the door and push it open. I glanced at the window, at the blue light of early evening falling through onto the desk. It was too late for it to be Old Paul, who came each day to visit with my father, to talk with him and bring small gifts: food, seedlings, books. Who sat on the back deck and set out the old Oråki board and moved the pieces and told the stories as though nothing had changed. Who made tea and washed the dishes afterward and sometimes left a vase of flowers on the kitchen table.

I swung my feet onto the floor, picked up the papers that had fallen to the floor and lay them on the bed beside me. Two of the pages had been crushed beneath me while I slept; I flattened them with the palm of my hand and frowned when I noticed the smudged reference at the bottom of the second sheet, the scribbled addition I could no longer make out, dribbling up and around the side of the page. I brought the page closer to my face, tilted it towards the light and squinted, trying to make out what I had written.

'Why don't you light the lamp?' Perdita said.

I looked up and saw her standing in the doorway, Perihan perched, as usual, on her shoulder. 'I was sleeping,' I said.

Perdita nodded and came into the room, set the small box she was carrying down on the desk and lit the lamp. 'I made us some dinner,' Perdita said.

'What about Dad?' I said.

Perdita nodded and set down the tray she was carrying, lifting a green ceramic bowl and handing it to me. 'He's sleeping,' she said. 'He ate a little bit, earlier.'

I took the bowl Perdita offered me. Saffron rice, with fish and beans. The bowl was warm in my hands. 'I see,' I said.

'I like it here,' Perdita said, 'with you and Oliver. At Elm, they treat me like a child,' Perdita said, settling beside me on the bed with her own bowl in her hands. 'As though my opinion doesn't count.'

I nodded. 'They're used to keeping things to themselves.'

'Perhaps we should have some secrets, too. Maybe then we'd feel better. At least one secret.'

'One would be enough, I think.'

'What should it be about?' said Perdita.

I shrugged. 'You could tell me something only you know: about being in the north, about your guardian, about why she sent you there on your own.' I was aware, even as I said it, that I was treating her like a child, too, wanting to trick her into telling me things I needed to know, not playing the game of secrets with honesty, but using it for my own ends. I was too small and pathetic to ask Miri these questions; so small that I would play mind-games with a child to find out what I did, and did not, want to know.

Perdita tilted her head. 'I'll tell you that stuff, but it's not a secret from them: my guardian wrote to Margause every month. That was the promise she made when they left,' said Perdita. 'It's not much of a secret.'

'Did they ever ask you what you wanted?'

'I liked it in the mountains, mostly. It was quiet and I could go for long walks. And in London, when we lived there for a while, I liked the bookshops, and the museums.'

'And your guardian?'

'I guess she liked it: she always liked to walk outside when it was snowing, or when the wind blew. She said she liked the tangle of the north in her hair. It was cold, though, and dark in the winter, and sometimes we stayed inside for a long time and didn't see anyone else. The last guardian sometimes seemed sad, but she never said anything about leaving.'

'Would you like to go back there?'

Perdita put her bowl down in her lap and looked out the window. It was growing dark, but we could make out the familiar shapes of the trees near the window, and the mountains in the distance. 'I like it here,' she said. 'It must have been nice, growing up here with Oliver and Old Paul, and the garden and everything. I would have liked that.'

'I thought you wanted to stay at the College.'

'I like it, but we can't stay there. There are too many Penitents in the other Colleges. They'll find out about me, and about the others.'

'Where would you like to go, then?'

Perdita tilted her head, as though she was thinking, very seriously. 'I liked it on Oikos Island,' she said. 'That was my favourite home. Where we were a family. There weren't many other people, but they were different, when we were there.'

I nodded. 'I knew some Oikos when I was little,' I said. 'My Great Aunt Grace had made friends with them, and we shared land with them until my mother died.'

Perdita nodded, 'I liked the trees on Oikos: they are so tall and old. And the houses along the water with decks all around them. And the water is warm and so clear you could always see the fish and sand beneath you.'

'It sounds perfect,' I said.

Perdita stood up and put her empty bowl on the tray. She set the cups side by side on the desk to pour the milky coffee into them. When she handed one of the cups to me a little of the hot liquid sloshed over the lip. I started and my bowl rolled forward on my lap.

'That could be our secret, then, if we went there together,' I said.

Perdita frowned at the grains of rice that had spilled from my bowl, some of which had scattered across my fallen papers, making small yellow stains. She leaned forward to pick up my pages from the floor, scooping the rice off the page into her hand. 'What's this?' she said.

'Notes. Rubbish. I'm supposed to be writing up my research paper.'

Perdita squinted at the page, turning it over to read through the notes on the other side. 'What's it about,' she said, 'your research paper?'

'Two women who lived near the Colleges once, a long time ago. Mathilde and Emmeline Salt. They opened a school on their property —a hedge school for Oikos children during the time when they weren't allowed in the ordinary schools. Mathilde was arrested, imprisoned for more than twenty years for supporting the heretics. When she got out she disappeared. I'm trying to find out what happened to her. There was a theory that she went to Oikos, but I've been through the archive: I can't find anything to support that.'

Perdita smiled. 'That's a good secret,' she said. 'Mathilde's secret.' Perihan twittered on the desk, skittering along the edge towards us.

'It would be if I knew what the secret was,' I said. 'I haven't been able to find out very much.'

Perdita settled back on the bed and snuggled up to me. 'I know where Mathilde went when she came home,' she said. 'She stayed in the treehouse, with me, for a little while, and then—'

'The treehouse at Salt Lane?' I said.

Perdita nodded and sipped at her coffee. 'It was like two ships, moored in the trees. I can take you there, if you like. I can show you our room with the sails to keep out the sun, and the platform where we watched the clouds, and the ladder to the stars. That's where we kept our secret things, in the cupboard at the top of the star-ladder.'

'I've been to the treehouse,' I said, 'but there was only a rope, no ladder. The treehouse has weathered more than a few storms; it's more like a wreck than a ship now, perhaps the ladder isn't there anymore.'

Perdita smiled, swinging her feet beneath the bed, knocking her heels against the cardboard box beneath it. 'The rope,' she said, 'is just the way you get up to the first ship. The ladder's in another place—a secret one—but you have to swing out into the air to get to it. I'll show you,' she said, tucking her hand into mine, leaning her dark head against my arm, 'We'll go there together. Then we'll be real friends. Then we'll have two secrets.'

The Miracle of Beauty
Rūs: 1895

The sixth orb of the chronometer; the miracle of the Beautiful. I weigh it in my hands, turn it over and run my thumb over the worn edges of the image. The orb is etched with the image of a clockwork tree, its arms twining out around the orb. Two tiny fruits are suspended in its arms: a silver apple, a golden pear. This is Emina's false miracle—the thirteenth Wynder, the false Wynder—who took her place as Wynder by force. And stood my false twin at her side.

Rebecca had been dead for a month the day that four Penitents followed Emina to our rooms. The Penitents were men we had never met. They had rifles slung across their backs. Their mounts stood stiff and gleaming in the hall behind them.

Judit was at the window, watching the first snow of winter fall.

Give me the key, Emina said.

Judit turned and smiled at her sister. *Emina*, she said, *this is so unnecessary. I have no wish to rule, but you are not the Wynder. Surely we can find another way.*

Emina held out her hand, but Judit turned away. She pushed open the window and held out her hand. Snow fell and melted against her palm.

You are not fit to be a Wynder, Emina said. *Our mother would have named me her heir if she had lived another day.*

If you and Mateo had not murdered her, you mean.

Emina peered at Judit, as if she were a child who had said something foolish, something outside their understanding. *Is that what you think?*

214

Are you going to deny it, now? That alone marks you as unfit; a Wynder cannot lie, least of all to herself; a Wynder would never take another's life.

You think this honesty of yours is a mark of goodness, a mark of a fit ruler? The people don't want your petty honesty; they want strength, vision, wisdom. A ruler must be willing to make sacrifices for the greater good.

Is that what you tell yourself, Emina? Is that how you ignore the blood that stains your hand?

It was not my hand . . .

But you wanted her dead. You ordered it done.

Emina straightened herself, refusing to glance at the Penitents who flanked her, whose eyes sharpened themselves on her sister's tongue. *Give me the key.*

There is more to being Wynder than possessing a key. No key will reveal Rupetta's secrets to you, or admit you to her heart; those are the Consort's lies. His myths.

Emina's face was white with rage. *I will have all your secrets,* she said. *I will have them torn from you.*

They are not my secrets, little sister, any more than they are yours.

Emina pulled the glove from her right hand. The two mounts that had stood by the door since she entered hissed forward, their jaws sliding backwards, their bladed shins snickering against the floor. She caught her sister from behind, holding her about the waist and shoulders. There was a blade in her hand, pressed against her sister's throat. *I don't want to hurt you,* she said.

Judit gestured towards the ruined city, the burning forest where they had played together as children, where their grandmother had fished and hunted, and their grandmother's grandmother had played. *It is too late for that.*

Where is the key? Emina said.

I stepped towards them, stood before the two sisters and reached up to open the unlocked chamber of my heart. Emina pushed Judit aside.

The tips of Emina's fingers were blue with cold as she reached towards me. She glanced at Judit, whose face was flat and proud, before she pushed them in. Her fingers found and rested upon the crown wheel, sliding across to the arbour.

Nothing. Of course, nothing. She pushed further, her palm resting against the upper tip of a torsion pendulum. The edge of her sleeve caught and tore on an overcoil. It scratched the back of her hand. The mounts snickered and boiled at her feet like a swarm of bees.

Fool, she hissed, turning, wiping her hand against her skirt as though it itched, pulling on her fallen glove. With her back to us, she nodded to the Penitents. As one, they unslung their weapons. The mounts slinked at their ankles like dogs, their lips curled back to reveal teeth that glittered with oil or blood.

෨

Judit and I were taken to an old part of the Winter Palace: to a suite of cold, stone rooms at the eastern edge of the building that had once been used to house the laundries and storage rooms. The windows had been barred with iron in preparation for our internment there. The doors were locked and barred behind us. Sometimes we heard men outside the rooms. Judit tried to speak with them—reason with them—but they had been warned against us. Occasionally, we heard gunshots and shouting, and sometimes saw Penitent soldiers and their mounts moving in packs through the streets. One night we watched a cathedral burn on the outskirts of the city, and heard the soldiers' booted feet march past below. Through it all there was a sense of frenzied celebration. Revelry. A kind of blood-furied madness.

One bright, spring morning as we stood at a window, we saw the gates of the palace opened, saw the flags go up and heard them snap brightly in the cool air. The mounts lined the streets, which swarmed with people. Finally, the Penitents came out, followed by Emina and Mateo. Alazaïs stood in my place, the boy-Consort Mateo in his, and Emina, the false Wynder, proud and unashamed at their centre. Alazaïs was silent, stiff. Had I ever seemed so strange? I looked out over the sea of people, willing them to see that she was not me.

Mateo stood on the steps of the palace and orated great lies, thick as the midwinter snows that had melted beneath his soldiers' boots. He spoke of Judit's treachery, her hard-hearted pursuit of power, her disbelief in—her flouting of—the Rupettan Law by which she was bound. Mateo, who had wept false tears for their mother's passing, spoke with passion and conviction. His voice swung and softened. He opened his arms as if seeking their love, their understanding.

She has fled into the north, he said, *ashamed at having destroyed the city, the cathedrals. Ashamed at the blood she has ordered spilt. Unable to face your fury. Too weak to face her punishment. Women,* he said, *are only half the world.* Now, he proclaimed, it was time for the Age of the Consort, when falsehood and contrivance would be sought out and illuminated, when dishonesty and corruption would be punished. He promised to continue the work of his grandfather—the great Emperor Pietr—whose Colleges would once again flourish, whose campaign against superstition and the heresies of the Oikos would be resurrected.

Emina smiled prettily beside him. Tucked her arm into Alazaïs's and strode slowly between the two rows of mounts: up to the city gates, where she was handed gifts by small children, then they turned and moved slowly back. Once, she raised her chin, as though tilting her face into the sun to warm it, and smiled up to the windows where we stood watching.

I turned to say something to Judit, but she had moved away from the window into one of the dark inner rooms.

Later, there were celebrations. Fireworks burst over the city, and carriage after carriage pulled into the palace. I imagined Emina swirling through the rooms below us, dancing in the halls, parading herself along the hallways with my dumb, clockwork sister.

The guards told us that she commissioned great follies for the city centres: clockwork angels that fled before the dawn, dragons whose eyes lit up the harbours and guided the great ships home, copper mermaids who swam through the rivers, towing cargo-carriers along the watery routes from one walled city to another. Occasionally, we saw one of her strange monsters pass in the street, or set up in the palace gardens so that people could admire them through the tall fences.

At the beginning of spring, to celebrate the razing of the last Oikos village, they held a celebration. Emina and Alazaïs were dressed in twin gowns of pale green with swooping necklines and wafting silk skirts. They paraded on the lawns of the palace, beneath newly-planted pear and apple trees that had been forced into bloom. At the centre of the garden was a clockwork tree, whose hand-carved fruits were gold and silver. At the end of the parade, Emina reached up into the branches and plucked a rose-gold apple to lie in Alazaïs's hand. The court stood at a respectful distance.

The carvings Eloise had made on Alazaïs's hands and arms unfurled across the apple and wrote themselves onto Emina's skin in thin, dark green lines. Dragonflies and apple-blossoms, vines and flowers, spiraled up from Alazaïs's fingertips, across the fruit and onto Emina's skin. They bloomed, too, from the neck of Alazaïs's gown, across her breasts and throat. A thin tendril curled out from beneath her lip and unfurled to form a half-open bloom, a thin leaf. A dragonfly spread its wings across her cheek. It was a conjurer's trick: a performance of chemicals and light, which revealed the tattoos so carefully hidden until that moment, as ash will reveal a message written in lemon, but the court was ablaze with obedient fear, with fawning wonder. As the vines wreathed themselves along Emina's arms they gasped and applauded.

፠

Once, Emina came to our chambers. By then, we had no matches, and no wood left to burn. Every stick of furniture had been broken apart and fed into the fire, as had most of the books we had found, the old paintings, the hoops of my skirts; the slivers of pale timber that had ringed my throat. I had scoured the rooms for blankets and tapestries to line the walls while winter snuck its fingers between the cracks. At night, Judit lay swaddled in everything we owned, a tiny bead of warmth, while I stood by the windows, whittled down to the rude shine of my metal skeleton, and watched the city boil beneath her sister's hand.

We welcomed Judit's sister as though we were still holding court in a sparkling palace with heated rooms and silver chandeliers, as though we were free to pass through the doors at any time and ride out into the forests where their mother's body lay, eaten by foxes, torn apart beneath the heavy snow. Emina's eyes scanned the stone walls, the threadbare tapestries that hung there: my face was repeated in them, again and again, amid the images of clocks and mounts and miracles. She smoothed her hand over the pale silk of her dress. *Are you comfortable here?* she asked.

We have what we need, Judit said. The cold had settled in her bones, whittling her cheeks into roseate ice. It echoed in her voice, too, the bite of frost.

Mateo wanted to have you executed for your false accusations, your heresies, Emina said. *I saved you. You should be grateful.*

Why have you come here? Judit said.

There are rumours about a child, she said.

Judit did not flinch or stiffen, though I felt the sudden flash of fear shoot through her like a blade. *A child? Whose child?*

Some of the Oikos have come forward and told us stories about a child, hidden away in the north. Emina glanced at me. *A deathless child with a copper heart.*

Come forward?

Emina smiled. *We have been conducting interviews. Trying to understand the Oikos, trying to show them the Truth.*

I don't know anything about a child, Judit said.

Emina leaned forward into her sister's face. A sudden echo in her face of the sweet, adoring little sister she had once been. *Please,* she said, *don't make me do this.*

Judit flattened her palms against the sides of her skirts and stood tall. She arranged herself precisely, like a statue.

Emina stiffened and nodded. The little sister fell away as she gestured towards the mounts behind her. One of them came forward and embraced Judit, almost tenderly, folding its chitinous limbs around her until she was cocooned in gleam and sharpness. Three other mounts stood between her and I, their teeth chittering in their maws. When I moved towards Judit they slithered onto me, pushing me to the ground and holding me there, though they did not harm me. I watched her carried from the room.

Every day I thought she must be dead by now, and wondered that my heart did not shudder and stop. Outside the palace the riots had started up again—sometimes close by and other times at a distance— though there were more of them each day. The roar of people shouting, of weapons being fired, of windows shattering, of wood being smashed and burned, was softened by distance and the thick walls of the palace. If I stayed away from the windows, it sometimes seemed like the sounds of a dream.

The silences were worse, as if the old city were finally dying. Was dead. And I alone lived on.

At the end of the second week after Judit was taken from me the guards outside the room disappeared and did not return. I heard a stone wall fall, felt the walls of my own room shudder as it went, crashing onto the street, and wondered how long it would be before the whole palace fell. I spent my days working at the door, as Kassia and Vivica had done in the fisher's hut, removing the pins that held the hinges in place.

80

How long had it been? The city was quiet. Far away a sudden roar, then nothing. At night I heard noises, like rats. A frantic scuffling in the walls. Finally, the doors were broken open, but I had nowhere to go. Two men came to the door. Strangers. They were not wearing the Penitent uniform, but wore the long, tangled hair and rough clothes of Oikos. One of them had a wound in his upper arm, and the other smiled at me as he entered, ducking his head and muttering something I could not understand. Between them, smiling grimly through her broken mouth, stood Judit.

Judit's head was shorn, her knuckles and knees and elbows bloodied and raw. She held one arm cradled in the other. It looked like a dark, thick sock filled with rough stones. The fingers of her right hand had all been broken: the smallest finger cut away. One eye was swollen shut. She was wrapped in an old Penitent's robe, which was glued to her back by dried blood. She stood upright, though it clearly pained her, as I did what I could to clean and bind her wounds. She would not speak about what had happened, what they had done to her. There was no need.

There is no child, she said, the lie decanted from her over and over, like a prayer falling from her blue mouth.

℥

We fled into the north; the Oikos soldiers our guides. There is no room in the mountains for regret. No air for it to breathe, no soil for it to turn. Instead, we laboured with stones and clouds, our vanity a spade driving us deeper into silence. When Judit pressed her grazed hand into my heart I saw the clouds as she saw them, puckered against us. I felt the mountains writhe; their ridges rising like a dragon's spine. I carried the dragon's dreams in my body. They are jagged and cold. My stone children.

Out there, where the air is empty and cool, free of smoke and light and the weight of a thousand whispers, Judit's body should have been still. Instead, she fell, as ever. Her body writhed on the frozen ground, her mind filled with flashes of light, of memory, of prescience. When the spasms ended, I knelt beside her, lifting her from the ground as her head turned into my shoulder. Afterwards, as she slept in a dark miasma—her skin pale, her freckles bright and dark on her skin—I picked the stones from her palms, her knees, wherever they had lodged, and rubbed ointment into the red wounds.

221

The world, it seemed, had been made to penetrate her.

We followed the last of our Oikos guides into the White Mountains. The jagged fingertips of winter and fear drove us onward. When it was clear, hoarfrost shimmered whiter than the snow. The light of the sun, brighter than midsummer, melted nothing. The light burned Judit's pale skin. There was whiteness everywhere; snow-blind polar bears howled in the distance.

I walked close behind her, watching for the twitch of her hand, the telltale spasm that moved through her shoulder, flickering across her throat before she fell. The ground was thick with snow; it squeaked and crunched beneath our feet, hiding the stones, hiding the knee-deep sinks into which she stumbled. Beneath the bulk of her winter clothes, it was hard to tell when a seizure came over her. When she fell I moved to catch her; often, I was too late.

Our guide bid us climb higher, faster, until there was hardly any air to breathe. Judit's breathing grew laboured, her face red and raw with cold, her lips bloodied, cracked. We saw the hunters in the distance, dogged black forms moving in the snow. Sometimes they seemed far below us—behind us—other times, looking down, I could see details: the pink moons of their faces, the eyes that peered towards us, the rifles at their backs. I heard them shout, pointing up at us, and heard the strange punctuation of their weapons being fired.

When I looked back towards Judit she lay in the snow. She was not an innocent child any longer; we were not making snow angels in the garden of the Winter Palace, with Luon and her mother. I leant towards her, felt her breath stutter against my cheek. When I said her name she turned towards me, her face pale, her eyes shut. I could see the blue veins in her eyelids. I slid an arm around her shoulders, another under her knees, and lifted her up. The blood, like liquid rust, flowed down my arm to my elbow as I lifted her.

The blood of a wounded animal, shot by hunters, stained the clean snow.

The snow was blinding, blowing into my face as I carried her up the face of the mountain, sharpening and stiffening my features. The guide paused at a place where the path—what path there was—split in two. He bound Judit's wound, packed it with strips of cloth and helped me wrap her more securely. I shouldered our supplies, thanked him, and hoisted Judit in my arms. He took a blade, cut open his palm and held it out over the snow as he walked away, taking the path that led away around the mountain, to the east: a distraction, a decoy. When I turned back I could see, but only faintly, the blue mouths of my footprints and his, leading away from each other. His blood, stark red, frozen, a line of gleaming beads beside his trail. I turned Judit's face towards my chest, pulled the heavy cloak up and over her to shield her from the wind. *Not long now*, I said. I don't know if she heard me.

When we reached the cottage I built a fire, stripped the cloaks and clothes from my body and bundled Judit into them. She lay cocooned while I dug through the snow for stones to repair the ruined walls. It was not perfect, but soon the single-roomed building was solid enough to keep out the worst of the wind. It blew without cease for five days —a cold north wind. Each day I cleaned and bound her wounds. When the wind stilled I could hear the hunters—a shout across packed banks of snow, a shot echoing across the thickened brightness. It was time, again, to leave.

We walked, and were pursued. I carried her further into the north, places I had never been—vast tracts of snow and forest and stone across which, it seemed, no eye had ever been cast. Our hunters came on, one after another, in groups and individually, each more strange than the last. Their uniforms faded, their guns misfired, their faces were burned almost skinless by the cold. They shouted across the divides, their voices winnowing across the distance, whispering of our death. We sought shelter in caves, in hastily-constructed cottages, in abandoned fishing huts or hunters' homes. Her wounds healed, but her face was pale, her eyes fever-bright. We lay beneath the stars, watching them picked out like diamonds in the crisp sky as the light faded, and she wept for what we had left behind: for her home, her books, her dresses and halls, for all her lost, loose hope, for her brother, Mateo, who had grown into a stranger, for the forest where her mother and great-grandmother had wandered, for the people who had died, for the family who had turned against her, who had wanted her dead, for her father whose warm, callused hands had softened the stone world of the palace, had made it a home, and then closed around her throat.

Judit was not hard-hearted, but I never saw her weep for her lover, whose blood had been among the first to be spilled. She never spoke the names of her son once he was gone. Instead she wrote poems about the stones, about the snow. About the great trees that drew in around us, who offered us comfort and shelter, who whispered their names—over and over and over again—in the ruined winter of her dreams.

All through the years we lived in the mountains we imagined the hunters turning back to a ruined world, Mateo's and Emina's ambition spreading across the snow in our wake, seeking us out. We were foolish enough to believe we were the only ones whose hearts and minds they wanted stilled, that we mattered, even in our absence. We walked away and saved ourselves, and countless thousands died in our wake. Silence closed its arms around us like a protective blanket; until we heard only the twittering of birds, the fall of snow.

After all of our elaborate and civilised defences we found refuge in the weather, in Nature, whose hoary silences the Penitents and their mounts could not cross. I built another cottage—stone and timber, a single room whose walls were soon thickened with ice—at the furthest edge of the world. So remote that, most days, even the wind could not reach us. Behind us—around us—was the blue-black forest. As thick and crisp and quiet as a secret. The needles of the ancient trees crunched beneath our feet, releasing their scent into the air. We walked onto the frozen fjords and gazed down at the shadows of leviathans, trapped in the ice many miles beneath us.

In the White Mountains I was nothing. Even if our pursuers reached us—crossed the fjords and mountains and forests and thick-ribbed darkness—they would not find what they sought. A one-roomed cottage, a slight girl and her companion, a stock of dried fish and ice, a single table, a single chair, a slim bed. They would see, if they came, the hollowness of the threat I had become. In the mountains of the north I was less than nothing: a whisper, a story, a shell.

There were birds and winds and stars—trees whose arms rubbed together, creaking like footsteps in the darkness. Sometimes a great crack rang out—the ice moved, shifted—or snow fell like the smoothing of a mother's hand across her child's cheek. Storms rippled through the forest and across the green ice. We forgot music, forgot the sounds and smells of gaslights and horses, of streets and doorways, of silk skirts rustling in the darkness, of gunshots and needlework and boots. I heard Judit breathing, and learned to measure the day by her heartbeats. We were in the arms of the forest—of Tapio, the god of forests—who had no shape, no substance, who was given a name only to comfort the humans who walked through the corridors of his body. The lakes were his sightless eyes, the forests his dreams, the wind his beard. When he stirred great storms rippled through his cloak, shuddering the earth beneath our feet. When he sighed the snow fell; when he wept our hearts were cold.

One day we stood above the great frozen shape of a dragon deep in the ice. *Is it real?* Judit asked. *Am I?*

Perhaps, I said. *Though it could be a drowned tree. A rock.*

She looked at me as though she had not known I would speak. As if I were, once again, a miracle. *It could as easily be a dragon, a whale, a gryphon, a house.*

There, I said, *is that a wing? It could be the hair of a giantess. Here is her hand, her claw, her foot rising towards us. She has fallen down from the mountain and is falling still.*

She has fallen out of time, Judit said, walking around the shape, across it, peering down through the shadowy green ice. *Is there only us left? It seems as though it was all a dream. The world—the world is so very empty. Are they all dead? It is easier to think this is all there is of the world: the forest, the ice, the air.*

There are two people here, I said as she knelt and splayed her white hands on the ice.

She breathed on its surface and rubbed it with her sleeve, pressed her face close and peered through the ice as though it were a window. She shook her head. *It is nothing,* she said. *An illusion, like seeing a woman's face in a cloud, or the weaver in the stars. There is nobody here.*

She stood and shrugged her shoulders deeper into her coat, thrust her hands into her pockets. *What use is there in talking, if I am only talking to myself?*

ৎე

He came into the mountains, walking across the fjord towards us, when the seasons shifted, from snow to sleet and sullen sunlight. Judit had been silent for five years. When men passed us in the woods— hunters, trappers, naturalists—she watched them without a word. She studied the birds, the trees, the movement of the stars, the shapes of clouds. She wrote and, in the evenings when she Wound me, I knew the unspoken words flurried inside her like snowstorms.

When the stranger saw her, he called out and raised his hand in greeting. She watched him approach from just outside the door of our home. She stood as still as the trees, her companions, the only ones she trusted, her eyes fixed on the weapon slung across his back. When he had come near enough she stopped him with her clear, crisp voice.

Why have you come here?

I am Giacomo, he said, his gaze moving to study my face. *I am an Oikos—the last of the Oikos. I have come to tell you that you must return.*

I stepped forward into the doorway and stood beside Judit. *You know who we are?* I said.

Judit, the true Wynder. And the True Rupetta.

There is a false Rupetta? I said.

Alazaïs stands in your place, the Consort is dead, the false Wynder is sick. Soon she will die and there will be war between the Penitent Orders. Another war.

226

I glanced at Judit, who stood beside me with her pretty face still and smooth, as though it were made of porcelain. *Mateo is dead?* she said, finally.

Executed. By order of the Empress Emina. Giacomo spat on the ground before he looked up, caught and held Judit's gaze. *Mateo gave his false Wynder and the Penitents power to give and to take life, and they have used it many times. It is not the true Way of Rupetta to conjure Death, only to respect it, and await its comfort.*

What good would it do for us to return? We are heretics, exiles—

Judit gestured for me to stop. *My sister is ill?* she said. *Dying?*

Giacomo nodded. *There is more,* he said, meeting my eye finally. Perhaps I knew then, felt the shadow feathering through the snow. *They know about the child.*

Emina stiffened beside me. I felt her resistance, her refusal to look at me. *They suspect something, you mean.*

No, he said, his eyes sought out mine and held them, seeking some forgiveness for the things he needed to say. *We were careless. We were travelling to Paris; she wanted to see the Great Exhibition. Her mother* —his gaze twitched; he corrected himself—*her carer thought we could disappear in the crowds, but we were seen. They knew what they were looking for. A man approached us outside the Palace of Electricity—an old man—he remarked on the statue of La fée de l'électricité at its peak, bursting from a golden star of light, saying that it was very beautiful, at night, when the fée's chariot and prancing hippogryphs appeared to ride the fountains of the Chateau d'Eau. He wondered aloud if the Spirit laid down the reins at night and stalked the streets of Paris, sparking the moving sidewalks, kissing the streetlights into sharp and scentless light. He spoke kindly to her, as if she were truly a child, enchanting her with his stories of the imagined, secret life of the Exhibition. He showed her a strange toy—an iridescent black beetle the size of a peachstone—said he had bought it after seeing the Lalique exhibition, with its myriad of insects, and invited her to hold it, and when she did . . . she was revealed.*

Is she harmed?

She is safe, but not for long. We got her out, though the carer was wounded. Captured. By now, she is probably dead. The word caught in his throat like a barb. I saw how it must have been between them; what he had lost.

Will she speak? Will she give Perdita away? I said.

He shook his head. *She has been the carer for over forty years. She was born to it; raised to it. But this thing he had: it had led him to Perdita. It recognised the child; tried to penetrate her. We destroyed it, but there will be more of them. And other things we don't know about. Other weapons. We must get you both to somewhere where you will be safe. Somewhere far away.*

You could bring her here, I said.

He shook his head, looked backwards, as though the hunters had pursued him. *They know where you are. They have known for a long time. It has suited them to have you at such a remove, observed and contained. They have made stories out of you. Mothers at their firesides describe you as thin, bony creatures dressed in tatters, wandering in the wastelands of the north, eating stones and praying to the ghosts of gods and trees. You are legends, spirits who fly in at the windows to snatch babies' spirits, whose breath frosts the glass with curses. You are the witches at the heart of the woods: children watch for you—fearfully, gleefully—in the winter dark. But things are changing; the people no longer believe in fairytales. It is time to move on.* He met my gaze again, then turned to Judit. *You are no longer safe here,* he said.

Judit took a step forward and put her hand on Giacomo's arm. *We will leave tomorrow,* she said and turned away. She stood at the edge of the fjord, complete and isolate as a mountain, and tilted her head towards the sun. In her eyes, the ice shifted, as though a cloud had passed overhead. *Beneath the ice the giantess sleeps/She has fallen and is falling still/Beneath the ice Death is waiting/Its arms are wide and empty.*

Henri's Story: Part Six

Perdita sat at the edge of the upper platform, her chin resting on a rail and her feet dangling over the edge while I leaned against the trunk of the tree, reading through the final draft—the final printout—of my thesis. The sun had swung around us, the clouds thinned in the late afternoon, while we ate our lunch and played a game of Oråki using leaves and seeds for playing pieces. As the afternoon settled into place Perdita had dozed and I had taken out the printout and started going through it, one page at a time, checking for the last time it was as I had imagined it; there were no more spelling mistakes, missing page numbers or misattributed references. It was too late, now, to focus on anything larger. It was difficult to read my own words, difficult not to cringe at the passages that were clumsy or poorly-written, difficult not to wish for more time to check just one more source, try a little harder. Reading it now, in its finished form, I understood for the first time what it was truly about, and where I should begin, though I couldn't really make myself believe that anyone else would read it. Though I tried, I couldn't picture the pages open on Jenon's desk, his head bent over it to read.

Hours passed in idle, sun-swooned silence. Soon, we would pack up the picnic, climb down the new, thick ladder rope and return to the College. The trees below rippled like a field of green wheat, or the wind-worried surface of an ocean. Perdita had told me about the white sails that had once been tethered above the platform. How they had filled with wind, stippled with grey shadows, stretched and bowed in the breeze, snapping like thick whips when the wind was high. I lay back on the warm boards and looked up, squinting into the sun, imagining the snap and shift of the sky-bound ship as it had been back then;

imagining myself at the helm, a wheel in my hands, clouds scudding beneath my feet.

'Bored?' I said.

Perdita shrugged and tipped her head backwards, arching her back and neck to peer at me upside down. 'Are you done yet?'

I nodded, holding up the thin sheaf of papers in my hand. 'Nearly,' I said, 'two more pages.'

Perdita rolled onto her belly, laying her arms flat on the timber. 'Is there any food left?' she said.

I laughed and pushed the satchel closer to her. 'One peach,' I said, 'but that's about all. Maybe some of Margause's biscuits.'

Perdita crawled over to the satchel and took out the peach and small packet of biscuits, wrapped in wax-paper. She turned them over in her hand and set them down on the floor before biting into the peach. 'Does she even eat them?' she said.

My brow furrowed as I turned to the last page of my thesis. I shook my head. 'She's still alive,' I said, 'so maybe not.'

Perdita picked up one of the pages lying flat on the timber beside me and scanned it. 'Are you worried?' she said, 'About the defence?'

I placed the last page face down on top of the others, picked up the whole bundle and slid it into a cardboard wallet. I slid the elastic around the bundle and held it on my lap. 'No,' I lied.

Perdita nodded solemnly, rolling the peach stone into her cheek as she did so. 'Me either,' she said.

I looked at her, at her rumpled clothes with dirt and juice stains down the front, at her knotted hair and the small bulge in her cheek. I would miss her, when I went home, and would perhaps have no way of knowing what became of any of them. 'Gooseberry,' I said. 'We should go back. Miri will be wondering where you are.'

'Why do you still call her Miri?' Perdita asked.

I started and turned away, sliding my thesis into my satchel and looking around the platform. 'Where are your shoes?' I said.

'You know her real name now; why don't you use it?' said Perdita.

I sighed and leaned back, pulling Perdita close and dropping my chin to rest on her head. 'I know who she is,' I said, closing my eyes and breathing in the leafy scent of Perdita's hair, the sun-warmed flush of her skin.

Perdita squirmed in my arms, pulling my arm around to encircle her belly. 'Did you know,' she said, 'that I can't feel a person's pulse with my thumb? Do you know why?'

'Why?' I said.

'Because,' said Perdita, pressing two of her fingers against the faint blueness at my wrist, 'there's a pulse in my thumb.' She tilted her head to the side, her lips forming a rosebud O of concentration.

'We have to go down,' I said, feeling my pulse jump against the pressure of her fingers.

'Shhhh,' said Perdita. She waited a moment, her eyes pinched shut, and then smiled, her eyes flashing open as she tilted her head up to look at me. 'I can feel how fast you love me.'

∾

I had given Miri the finished copy of my thesis earlier in the afternoon, when Perdita and I had returned from Salt Lane. I hadn't said anything, just laid it down on the kitchen table in front of her, careful not to hold on to it for too long. Miri had turned, smiled in the sad way she often did these days: a smile that was partly affection and partly sorrow. *Do you still love me?* the smile asked. *Do you forgive me?*

Saying no would be a lie, and I was so tired of lies.

I looked away, unsure how to arrange my face. It was easier in the dark, to hold each other. To pretend. In the dark, in our bed, we were learning to turn towards each other, learning again the shape of each other's hands, the weight of each other's bodies. Our bodies were forgetting. They knew how to forgive, even when we did not.

In the daylight, our arms and wrists and hands were always in the wrong arrangement. The light undid me: it opened the world too wide. Shone too sharp a light into our lives. My bones were too heavy.

My knees too sharp. I could only concentrate on small things: on Miri's hand curved around her cup. This much, and no more, I could understand. This much I could love without a sharp stab of pain and anger. Tomorrow, I would love Miri's wrist again—the memory of it— the next day her arm. And so on and on, until Miri's whole body unspooled into my heart. A memory. A ghost.

I put my hand on the top of the folder. 'It's done,' I said.

Miri wiped her hands dry with a towel, lay it down on the bench and moved to stand beside me, looking down at the folder. She did not touch it. 'Two years,' she said. 'You've worked so hard.'

I nodded. 'Will you read it?'

I felt Miri look at me, felt the sudden flash of heat rise along that side of my throat, as if she knew what I had written, and what I was planning to do with it, even while I was still unsure. Miri wiped her hands down the sides of her pants and laid them down, one on each side of the folder. She lifted it up, smoothed her hand over the blank cover. 'Now?' she asked, and I nodded and left.

I took Perdita off to play in the orchard while Miri read. I made dinner while Miri turned pages at the kitchen table; I had prepared a meal for her, and Margause and Perdita, but couldn't watch her frowning so intently over my work. In the end, I had taken the others off to the glasshouse, where they had played a game of cards at the old table while I tried to read.

After dinner, I had taken Perdita up to Ahkronova's room, her favourite room in the old building, with its low ceiling and dark, age-softened timber floor. I sat on the end of the bed in Ahkronova's room, my knees drawn up to support the book I was reading. Perihan was perched on the bedhead. Every now and then it would hop along to stand behind my shoulder and chirrup, as though commenting on the story. Perdita lay beneath the sheets at the other end, her pillow plumped up, her hair washed and plaited, ready for sleep. I opened the book, removed the bookmark, and smoothed down the page.

'Are you really going tomorrow?' Perdita said.

'Home?' I nodded, feeling the terror of it clutch me. The house full of empty rooms, my mother's grave tolling in the garden. And my father, lost inside himself. His slumped body just another piece of furniture that needed to be dusted and re-arranged. The possibility of being alone, and for so long. I pulled her to me, felt her snug body settle against my own.

'I'll go with you,' she said. 'If you want.'

I closed my eyes, breathed in the powder-soft scent of her clean hair and skin. The childlike breath that smelled of apples and wild earth. 'Okay,' I said. 'Okay.'

'She'll come too, later.'

I shook my head, trying to clear my head. I couldn't think of the future now: only today, perhaps a tiny sliver of tomorrow. 'Chapter One,' I read. 'There's an illustration.' I tipped the book to show her the colour plate, with its faded, sepia-outlined shapes and twining, scrolled border.

Perdita nodded. 'The Bear,' she said, 'lumbering through the snow. And Rose Red waiting for him with her shotgun.'

'Will she shoot him this time?'

Perdita laughed. A burst of bright noise in the quiet room. 'Only one way to find out.'

The Winter Bear was Perdita's favourite story, the one she requested over and over again. The one whose illustrations she knew, whose words she could recite. I smoothed down the page and read:

Snow White heard Rose Red open the door and, a few moments later, she came into view, just outside the kitchen door. Her red coat swirled around her, her hair flying about her head as she struggled through the knee-high drifts, the shotgun clamped to her side. Once more they both heard the terrible, desperate roar somewhere in the snow and this time Snow White's heart leapt with fear. Before it had been a mere curiosity, a perhaps, a notion of something other than the long, dreary days and bitter tulip-bulb soups, but now Rose Red was out there in the storm, half-blinded by the wind and the snow, flailing about searching for a nameless, faceless, ancient creature whose roar shook the walls of the house.

Snow White watched Rose Red trudge through the snow, raising the barrel of the shotgun to hip-level and twirling awkwardly at each fresh flurry of snow, each sigh of the wind, as though she were the one being hunted. Once more she heard the howling—this time nearby, quieter, a rising tone like a question. Rose Red spun and fired off a shot, releasing a clump of snow from the nearest tree. A dark shape reared behind it and seemed to fall, rolling like a wave across the snow towards the stable. Rose Red lowered the shotgun, reloaded, pulled the gun up to her shoulder and fired once more. The beast paused and looked up at Snow White, standing at the bedroom window, her hands pressed to the glass. The creature's shape was like that of a small, dark mountain.

Rose Red poured gunpowder into the gun, tamped it and took aim. Snow White heard another shot, strangely muffled. The creature moved towards Rose Red—unhurt—and Snow White's gaze shifted from it to Rose Red, lying spread-eagled in the snow, the gun in her arms and a bright circle of blood seeping into the snow at her side.

Then she forgot the creature, and the snow, and the fear that held her at the window. Snow White bolted down the stairs, tripping down the last few onto her hands and knees and clambering on her knees towards the open door, through the snow that had blown in, onto the front step and down into the snow. She did not feel the cold as her feet—shod in thin stockings—sank into the snow. Nor her hands as she clutched at the snow and dragged herself through it to where Rose Red lay, the creature lumbering towards her, snuffling and snorting, its breath pungent and warm.

'Rose Red,' she screamed, her eyes pinned to the beast's as it paused in its tracks, reaching out a paw to flick the gun away from her out-stretched hand. 'Please,' she said. 'Please. . . .'

The creature turned its great bulk towards her, lowering its head and dropping its shoulders. 'Snow White,' he said, or seemed to say, his breath hot and rich on her cheek. The smell of him was warm and damp as he closed on her. She glanced down at Rose Red, whose head he clasped in his arms, her form laid out in the snow before them.

And then nothing; the white fields, the white snow, the white sky melted together. Rose Red and the creature faded as though they were clouds chased across the sky by a stiff wind. She felt herself drop to her knees, felt the coolness as the snow seeped through to her skin, and thought only of the tulip bulbs steeping, forever, in their little pot on the kitchen table.

When I looked over the top of the book Perdita's eyes were closed and she had turned onto her side, tucked her hands beneath her cheek. Perihan sat on the desk, its legs tucked away beneath it as it curled into the nest of sticks and leaves Perdita had made for it. I closed the book and stood, leaning over Perdita. Her breath was slow and measured. Her slippery hair already untangling from its neat braids. In the felted quiet I could hear the familiar swoosh and tick, swoosh and tick, of Perdita's heart. I pulled the sheet up, over Perdita's shoulder, and turned out the light, leaned down and kissed her brow, brushing the hair back from her sleeping face. Perdita frowned and turned over in her sleep, curling her knees up until she was a firm, round ball of unapproachable softness with one pale arm flung out across the sheet. Outside the window, down on the ground floor, I could see the spill of light from the kitchen where Miri sat, still reading. As I watched the light flicker, I saw her hand come out into the dark and empty the teapot of its tired, wet leaves.

I made my way down to the glasshouse, feeling the rawness of the air I was leaving behind. The old familiarities chafing as I tore myself away from them, thread by thread. I pulled an old cardigan from my suitcase and drew it closed around me. On the other side of the room was my and Miri's bed, my old desk, empty now, and the long rows of shelves on which lay pots and shards and buckets and jars. The air was cool, but the scent of the compost in the newly-planted seedling pots was rich and heavy.

Outside the moon shone, half full and still rising, in a clear sky. I could see the familiar formation of the spring stars: the kite and the arrow, the elm and the beetle. Beneath them the trees of the orchard were dark-leaved, thick with pale fruit. Miri wasn't out there, walking through the orchard like a ghost, thinking her private, unfamiliar thoughts, waiting for me to come down and lie in our bed, to close my eyes and sleep as though it would always be like this. As if it ever had been.

The stone floor of the glasshouse was cold beneath my bare feet. I slipped into the hallway, past the closed doors of the workrooms and down the hall to the kitchen. Light bloomed in a pale halo from beneath the kitchen door, making the tiles appear warm. Soon, in the shifting darkness, I heard Miri turn over a page, heard her shift in her seat and pour more tea. I had tucked Perdita into bed, read to her from her favourite, familiar story. I had done all the things I understood, and felt I could do, and tried to do them as if they would be done again. As if they were not ending. And now I was here in the hallway, with the low light that escaped from the kitchen door spilling across my toes. I closed my eyes for a moment, took a deep breath and opened the door.

ℂ

'So,' Miri said, smoothing her hand over the cover of my thesis as though it were the pelt of an irritated cat, 'you know everything, then.'

'Not everything,' I said. 'Enough.'

There was a pause as we sat, each contemplating the texture of the table, the pale, slim bulk of my thesis on the table between us with its barely-read pages, still white and crisp and square, as we each considered what it was, what it said, whether it made any difference. I reached towards the manuscript, but did not touch it.

'I'm going to submit tomorrow,' I said. 'I think you should go back to the Haven, with Perdita, make public who she is, use your status to ensure her safety. She's in less danger in the open, and so are you. The world is a broken thing; half-wound and rusted, the Penitents have too much power, the Alazaïns—the false Rupettans—have wrought Horrors in your name once and will do so again. There's a false Wynder where Margause should be, dealing lies instead of honesty, and there's an empty doll in your place. You can't just hide who you are.' My hand moved to cover the place where my old Bellmer heart still beat. 'You can give us back our humanity. Perhaps even find your own.'

'I'm not Pinocchio,' she said, 'I'll never be a real boy.'

'You're real enough, Rupetta, and so is the world that has sprung up in your wake. The world you made.'

'You called me Rupetta,' she said, her voice low, almost shuddering.

I nodded and reached across the table, took her small, cool hand in my own. 'Like I always told you,' I said, 'I know who you really are.'

'Will you come with us?' Miri looked up at me and, for the first time in a long time, we held each other's gaze, saw there the familiar echo of the stars we had gazed at through the glass panes above our shared bed, the orchard we had tended, the child we both loved. It still hurt, but the hurt had waned.

'We'll leave in the afternoon, when you come back from Jenon's office.' She hesitated, gripped my hand, her head and mouth and lungs full of the things she knew and could not say, full of the lack that hung so heavily in my silence. She would go back to the Haven—and from there to the Winter Palace—with its muted corridors, its sullen, silent, daily betrayals, the air full of ambition and rot. The quick looks and protracted politenesses that only played at hiding the knives they all wore beneath their robes.

'You could choose not to submit the thesis,' she said, as if she could slide into my head, after all, and read my muddled intentions there, my doubts. 'You could slip away tonight and go somewhere else. Go home, perhaps, or to the island with Perdita—to Oikos. Margause could arrange for your degree to be awarded—we can do that much—and you could find work, live a quiet, ordinary life.'

'Is that what you want?' I said.

Miri turned my hand over in her own, studied the delicate pattern of blue veins on the underside of my wrist, ran her fingertip along one. 'I would like you to be safe, and not to become like us—caught up in all this. That is what I wanted for Perdita, too. I would like to think of you out there, on the island where we were happy, once, reading and looking up at the stars. Gardening and cooking, as you said. Wasting your lives. But then, I'm selfish, too. I want you both to stay with me. I want that very much.'

'I've left Perdita sleeping in Ahkronova's room,' I said, squeezing Miri's hand a little before I released it. I stood and kissed the crown of her head. 'I'll go up and check on her, spend the night up there. In the morning, I'll pack up what I need to take with me, then I'll go to Jenon and submit my thesis.'

I put my hand on the doorknob, pushed it open and felt the cool, crisp air of the corridor meet my face, smelt the ochre of the old brick floor and, faintly and not-far-off, the earthy scent of the glasshouse— of the glass walls and iron framework, of the earth and clay pots and loam—of my old life, already slipping into the past tense. 'Then,' I said, 'we'll leave.'

℘

It was autumn, and the orchard half-slumbered in the old light. I walked beneath the trees, their familiar branches leaning down towards me like the arms of sorrowing friends. I reached out my hands, felt the waxy patter of the citrus leaves against my fingers as I passed. I could see the light in the kitchen; see the shapes of Margause and Miri—of Rupetta—moving in the old room, making tea, making plans. Above them, in the corner window of Ahkronova's room, Perdita's night light glowed.

As I turned towards the building I saw someone come out of the College's side entrance—the door that led most directly to the resident's rooms. I smiled, watching them huddle in the doorway, imagining where they'd been: studying was unlikely, it was far more probable they had been visiting a lover, lying together in the dark of a student's small room, exchanging hushed kisses and whispers. They opened the door; light spilled across the doorstep and illuminated their robes. Obanite scholars.

I frowned and moved a little faster. Strictly speaking, visitors were not allowed inside the College Dorms after 10:00 in the evening. And none of the residents were seeing an Obanite: I would have known. The Elm College students teased me enough about my loyalty to History: my conformist, ordinary studies. Some of them went so far as to click their tongues to imitate the stilted beat of the Penitents' hearts when I came into the greenhouse—a mild and affectionate ribbing. But the Obanite students and those at Elm were not usually so friendly with each other. There was no reason for one of them to be at Elm so late.

As I reached the edge of the orchard—still too far away to make out the visitor's faces in the darkness—I saw another figure move towards the door. They had been hiding there, waiting in the shadows by the stairs. The second figure sprinted up the stairs to join the others. And now, suddenly, as I began to run, I saw what I had been unable to make out before. There were three of them on the stairs; two of them had come out close together, as if in an embrace. The second of them carried something in his arms. The bundle was large and awkward, wrapped in a dark sheet, and clearly heavy. As the three came together they distributed the weight between them and moved off.

I began shouting. Running. Feeling my breath shunt into my mouth, my lips dry, my heart banging. Noises came out of my mouth, but it was as if they were the wrong words: an unfamiliar language. The three figures turned, their faces as indistinct as three blank white coins in the half-dark, before turning away and moving faster, running away from me despite the burden they carried.

'Perdita!'

I screamed, finally finding a word, a shape, which made sense of the heavy bundle in their arms. I was running across the open square, seeing the bundle shift a little, seeing—I thought—a small hand reach out like a star from within the swirl of black robes, around the shoulder of one of her bearers. For a moment, I saw Perdita's face: the short flag of her hair whipped across it by the wind as I called out. A word. An exclamation. A sound: soft as a bird's feather. Airless with fear.

One of the figures sheared off from the group, turned in a full circle and started running back to meet me. I thought then I must have been mistaken about what they were doing—why else would one of them come to meet me other than to apologise, to make sense of the running and the sweeping gowns and Perdita's pale face? Why else turn and move towards me? As he neared I saw the Obanite's face and hesitated. Jenon, but his face was transformed, the angles and surfaces all wrong. It was Jenon, I was sure of it, but he seemed unfamiliar. The two more distant figures carried Perdita further and further away, wheeling around the side of the library building like a diminutive flock, their robes and the sheet they had wrapped around Perdita flaring behind them like birds' wings. I heard her cry out and lurched forward, a sob rising in my throat.

I raised my hand as if to grasp them and pull them back, though they were so far away. I veered, trying to step out of Jenon's path and go around him, but he raised his hand, as if in reply to my gesture. 'You should have trusted me,' he said.

I frowned, kept moving forward, my eyes on the others. Joaquim, I saw now, the caretaker of Ahkronova's room. A fool, Jenon had called him, but now here he was. Here they were together.

'What are you doing?' I said.

Jenon smiled, his teeth precise white bones in the dark. He tilted his head and smiled, raised his hand and pointed it at me.

There was a short, sharp barking noise, as if a great old tree had fallen not far off, and then another. I felt heat rush past me, like a hot bird, tangling itself in my hair, and then a thud of warmth in my belly. A slick of starlight sparkling down my leg, then more heat, a kind of splitting in my left shin as I slipped on the dry stones and fell. *Not now*, I thought, *don't be so clumsy*. Get up. Don't fall. Don't be a fool. I half-rose to my knees, frowned when I discovered my leg was suddenly too short, as if I were a paper picture of myself, cropped off at the knees. I grimaced, looked towards the corner of the building where Perdita had disappeared and tried, again, to rise and follow her. Another short bark in the darkness, echoing against the stones and the bricks of the buildings and the hollow dome of the sky.

I lay on my back, a smell of hunting rising around me, and blood, as Jenon's footsteps faded.

The old moon was slim and distant above me, peering down, curious, as I put my hand against my belly, felt the warmth of my own blood and understood that the stones were cold and the sky was dark and merely watching. I lay there, unable to fly, or even to walk, as Perdita—borne by some dark Autumnal bird—was winged away.

෨

Two of the residents found me and carried me into the College. Dark-haired girls with hands roughened from the daily digging and turning and harvesting work of Elm College, their voices familiar despite the whispering as they laid me out, like the newly-dead, on the kitchen table. I stared up at the ceiling, seeing the cobwebs and dust and lizard traces that littered the beams, thinking it needed cleaning, this room, before we went away. Thinking there was so much to be done; I had no time to lie there like the dead, right now. Things needed to be in order, in their places: the rooms and buildings and I, and Miri and Margause, and Perdita, too. They all needed to be clean and true and strong and put back where they belonged.

Margause came into the room, and then Miri, rushing in, her face as distant and abstract as a painting as she leaned over me, pressing gently on my cheek and shoulder. Margause cut open my damp clothes, peeled them away like dead leaves that had rotted against the stalk. I was shedding my heretic's body, there in the kitchen, being peeled open in preparation for the Transformation. I put my hand up to stop Margause, to protect my poor, muscled heart from the knife.

'Jenon,' I said. 'It was Jenon.'

Margause nodded. 'Don't worry,' she said, leaning close, wiping my forehead with the flat of her palm as if I were a sick child in need of being soothed and comforted.

The clutch of nausea rose up through my gut, spooling outwards into my chest and mouth and nose, pushing down to meet the other pain that had taken root inside me. I could not breathe. I opened my mouth and felt my father's tongue in my mouth, tangled and imperfect, the words like stones. *Perdita,* I said, feeling my lips open and clap together. No sound emerged.

Margause and Miri lifted me, whisked the shreds of my wet, discarded clothes from underneath me and dropped them to the floor.

Margause pressed a clean, white cloth to my mouth, whispering something—a prayer? A nursery rhyme?—and I breathed in without knowing what any of it meant: I tasted apples, rotting in rows in the cellar, cidering away the winter while the Autumnal birds moved further and further away. What were they carrying? It looked so heavy, and its clothes were wet, dripping tears onto the orchard, onto the snow that capped the mountains. I tried to breathe upwards, to arc into the light and air, like a whale breaching the surface of the ocean, but could not.

When I woke my wounds had been cleaned, emptied, dressed. I breathed in and felt the stab in my chest, as if my bones were knives pointed in towards my heart.

Miri lay curled on the hard table beside me, her hands folded beneath her cheek.

'Perdita,' I said, and this time sound came out of my mouth, though it was stretched and thick as toffee. 'They've taken her.'

Miri nodded, reached out and stroked my cheek. Her hand was hot against my skin. 'Shhh,' she said. 'We know. It was Joaquim who found her; he came to check the room, after all, though why now, after so long? Why now? He saw her sleeping there. Margause's trying to find out what she can but you have to lie still. You've been shot in four places; five of your ribs are broken. You are hurt, my love, hurt badly. Margause has done what she can and someone is coming to stay with you, to care for you until you're well enough to travel. You have to listen, my love, you have to lie still and listen, and remember everything I say.'

I nodded, though the words were separate and heavy. It was my father who needed to be cared for, not me. Miri's hand was wintry on the hot skin of my cheek.

'We're going after them. I don't know where they've taken her. I don't know how long it will take to find her, but we need to leave tonight. You'll have to stay behind, Henri. We have to travel fast. We have to go before she disappears completely. When we find her, when we come home, all of us, we'll go to Oikos Island again, like she wanted. We'll do everything just like she said. While you wait, you can stay here, at the College, or go home, perhaps. It's safe there.

'Henri, my love, my historian, my keeper, listen carefully, remember: I've put your thesis in the stacks, where you used to hide, in Perihan's old nest. You must go down there and find it when you wake up. And burn it. Nobody can know what you know: you're safe while they think you were just in the wrong place tonight, just a bystander who got caught up in it all, but . . . you understand, don't you? You have to let them think you don't know who she is, not really. I'd destroy the manuscript for you, but it's your work, not mine. I'm sorry, Henri. So sorry.'

I rolled my head towards the face that hovered beside mine: the mouth that opened and closed like a fish. *Jenon*, I wanted to say. *Jenon understands*. Miri nodded as though she was pressing her thoughts into me and I followed the bob of her head, nodded, too, as if in response.

Miri closed her eyes a moment. Took a breath. Pressed her cold, wet mouth against my forehead. Outside the kitchen there were footsteps. Margause came in and shut the door. She smiled at me, pulled away the sheet and checked the wounds, touching the flat of her palm to each in turn. 'You'll be fine,' she said, and smiled again as she tucked the sheets around me. 'They're taking her to the Haven in Portugal. There's a boat in an hour, but we have to leave now to get to the harbour in time.' She glanced at her chronometer, frowned and leaned close to me, as though to smell my hot breath. 'Is she awake, do you think?'

'I don't know.'

'Old Paul will be here by morning; he'll take her home and care for her until we get back.'

Miri slipped off the table and looked down on my long, flat body. Would she eat me now, tear out and eat my weak heart, and take me with her that way? She put her hand on my wrist, ran it up along my swaddled arm to my shoulder, the curve of my throat, the damp clot of hair at my nape. 'Can we trust Old Paul?' she said.

Margause nodded. 'We have to. Say goodbye now.'

Miri nodded, as though she was not sure what she was agreeing to. How many times had she lived through this scene? How many times had she lost everything and had to run, pursuing her daughter, running from the hunters?

Margause pressed her palm once more to my forehead, leaned close and whispered words I did not recognise, could not sort out from the breaths and tinkles of the wind and trees outside, the shunt and shuffle of pain inside me. 'I'll pack a bag—some things we'll need for the journey. Five minutes. Ten at most, and then we have to go.'

Then it was only Miri leaning over me, smoothing the sheet over my chest, straightening my limbs and neck, smoothing down the tangle of my hair. She ran her hand over my eyes and nose and mouth, as if she were a blind girl trying to remember the shape of my face. She leant down and kissed me. I felt tears like star pickets wounding me. 'I'll be home soon,' she said, 'don't forget me.'

I breached and breathed. I wanted to tell her to bring Perdita home. I wanted to tell her I loved her, absolutely, terribly, without fear any longer, or any need to understand how or why, to forgive or forget, or even to understand. That loving her was like a disease in me, something I would never recover from, could never hope to cure. That no matter how strange we had become we were a single thing, the three of us, however many we became: leaf, stem, limb, trunk and root of a single tree. I wanted to tell her it didn't matter where she went or who she had been or who she might become. I wanted to ask her to go, to stay, to come home. To kiss me. To hold me. To know me. To let me go. I wanted to tell her that I knew who she was, what she was, and loved her not despite of it, but because of it all. I wanted to say her name.

'A green thought in a green shade,' I said.

The Hidden Miracle
Oikos Island: 1936

There are things I haven't told you. Gaps in this history, which is like a spider's web of hair-thin lines that connect across gaping silences. I promised to tell you the truth, and I have not. Centuries of silence about Perdita, my daughter, have become a habit it is almost impossible to break. I have learned to believe that my silence buys her safety. That not speaking her name is a kind of magical protection against discovery. But it is time, now, to break that ancient, foolish bond.

We had lived separately for centuries, though I had seen her sometimes, at a distance, walking in the forests near the Winter Palace. She had left messages in the woods: strange arrangements of bird-bones and leaves, feathers and fox-fur. I would take them home, these nests of ribbons and sticks, and arrange them on the windowsills of my chamber, replacing them with my own gifts. Things I thought a child would like, though she was not a child: gold bangles, ribbons for her hair, fine red leather shoes.

I met each of the caretakers. They were a family who became like a second clan of Wynders, though they were kinder, softer, more strange. The first carer was a man—Oliver—a scholar who had been thrown out of the academy. He was living in the mountains, solitary. We found him there, wandering like Odysseus, reciting the works of Homer as he hunted pigeons. He became her teacher and her friend. They lived in Portugal then, in the mountains above the city, growing oranges and reading poetry. She studied mathematics with him as well as poetry, philosophy and botany. Learned how to be a child, perhaps forever. Or at least to put on the appearance of a child.

I can well imagine her in Paris, at the exhibition. Riding the moving sidewalks, jumping from one to another, laughing at her carer's slower movements. I see her eating ice cream, sipping at *citrons pressés* in a crowded café, practicing her schoolgirl French on the waiters and demonstrators. It is harder to imagine him—the man—who came to stand beside her that late afternoon, and put the beetle in her small white hand. It is hard to imagine how they dared, in that crowded square, with Paris lit up so brightly, awash in visitors, to try to steal— to murder—a child. Did she cry out when she saw her carer wounded? Taken. Did someone in the crowd—anyone—move to help her, think- ing her a child whose mother had been snatched away? I closed my eyes and saw my daughter's dreams. Saw her carer taken down into the belly of the Palace, where the terrible dynamo shuddered and stank like an oiled, black beast. Down into the gaping darkness beneath the glitter; down into the cellars where a hot, awful cylinder housed the Exhibition's coal-driven heart. Burning darkly, thickly. Did they murder her there, stoking the heart of that sparkling, imaginary city with her bones? Would they have murdered Perdita there, too, dismantled her piece by piece to see how she worked, as though she were one of the strange machines that lay in the glass and gleam of the Grand Palais, her innards exposed.

Giacomo laid out his plans for us to travel south, to find refuge on Oikos Island, which was a small—barely populated—island off the coast of the southern continent. There were Penitents on the mainland —a few small havens, and a school of Obanite scholar-soldiers—but the island was isolated, and unremarkable. It could only be reached by boat. A service came out once a week to deliver the post, news and whatever small luxuries the islanders required, but there were few visitors. He pointed it out on the map; Judit and I leaned over the paper, imagining the warmth of the blue seas, the white sand, and Perdita, playing in the shade of the tall pines that soughed and sighed in the ocean breezes.

Perdita would travel there separately, by a different route. We walked down out of the mountains until we reached the edge of the first unfrozen fjord, its water deep and green. Here, Giacomo had moored a small boat, and sunk two addled hippocampus beneath it to wait for us. When he raised it—inflating the bladders that made it float with a small footpump, forcing the water out of its cavities—and primed and wound its motor—it chuddered smoothly though its surface was starred with age. It had belonged to Giacomo's father, he told us as he wiped down and oiled its surface, who had taught him how to care for it, how to mend and maintain it.

We travelled by night, and in silence. The hippocampus drew our craft patiently, its tail weaving like an eel's body through the water. Two days journey, through the tangle of the fjords, sinking slowly down from the mountains into forested lakes and rivers. Jetties began to appear, and sometimes small towns. We saw the lights of them, spilling down through open fields towards the water. Each one we passed in silence. Sometimes, Giacomo gentled the hippocampus. I would step into the water and tow the craft through the dark water.

Each morning, as the sun threatened to rise, Giacomo steered us to the shore and we lifted the boat out of the water. The first day we upturned it in a field, sleeping beneath its grey hull. We moved further south. One day, when we stopped, there were no fields. The river ran through a gully etched out of a rocky, white hillside. We upturned the boat and sheltered beneath it while the sun passed over our heads. As soon as night fell we set out again, leaving our boat behind. We walked for two weeks, following the same pattern of nightly movement and daily sleeping, huddled in caves, or digging holes in the earth like moles, until we reached a small plateau, at the edge of which was a sudden, sheer drop into the sea.

It was nearly morning; though the sun had not yet risen the sky was suffused with light. Judit's knees were swollen, her feet blistered. She sat on a large rock and removed her shoes, easing them off with a grimace. Giacomo stood at the cliff-edge, watching the dawn light spread like honey over the horizon.

'Nearly there,' he said, and, turning to his right, disappeared over the cliff edge. When I walked over to where he stood I could just see the slim path that cut down across the face of the cliff. Five feet below the edge I could see Giacomo holding onto a rope, anchored in the cliff-face with thick iron loops. He gathered another rope and a set of leather belts, hidden under an outcrop, before returning to the clifftop. He secured our packs to the second rope and cinched a belt around each of our waists. The packs went down first: Giacomo lowering them onto a rocky platform at the base of the cliff. The rocks where our packs landed were pocked with holes, many of which were filled with water. Waves crashed against the rocky outcrop, sending dramatic surges of spray over the pools.

Giacomo clipped the rope to my belt. The first ten feet were easy: I followed the path that cut across the face of the cliff until I reached the outcrop where Giacomo had retrieved the supplies. From there I could see that the outcrop concealed a small cave, carved out of the cliff-face. Piles of looped ropes were lined up in the cave, alongside heavy baskets for winching supplies up and down the cliff. All along the wall were hooks with leather belts, like my own, and on the floor lay boxes of iron loops and clips, heavy hammers and boots with speared toes, all neatly arranged.

When Giacomo and Judit reached the cave, Giacomo hooked up a basket to a winch secured in the ceiling of the cave and buckled Judit into it, as though she was a child on a fair-ride. Her face was white and she clutched at the rope as we lowered her over the edge.

'Look at me,' he said to her, 'and keep your face to the cliff. Palm your way down. Good. Good.'

'Will you need the cradle, too?' he said, once Judit had landed on the rocks far below. 'Are you afraid of heights?'

I shook my head and Giacomo nodded; relieved. I noticed only then the strain in his face—the sweat that had formed on his forehead and chest as he took the strain and lowered Judit down. It had not taken long, and yet the tide had clearly started to come in while he lowered her onto the rocks. Already, the rockpools were awash. The waves crashed onto them with steady, hushed roars. The rope Giacomo pulled up, with Judit's empty cradle attached to it, was wet with saltwater. I peered out over the edge, trying to see where she had landed, but the cliff bowed out between where we stood and the ground far below.

'We'll go down together,' he said, once he'd looped and stowed Judit's rope, and the cradle-basket. He secured our own ropes to two of the heavy iron loops evenly spaced out along the edge of the cave's mouth and stood beside me, facing the cliff, his back to the ocean, each hand on the rope—one above and one below his body. He showed me how to swing out onto the cliff-face and rappel down, like crawling backwards, with the rope hissing through the iron mechanism at the front of my belt. He showed me how to pull the rope to the side, to slow the rope sliding through the iron mechanism, how to twist the iron loop so that it cinched the rope tightly to stop, if need be, hanging suspended between earth and sky. Soon, I felt the ocean's spray at my back, smelt the wet rock.

When we reached the surface I saw, for the first time, the mouth of the hermitage: a narrow slash of a cave-mouth, its edges worn smooth by the ocean, its floor a cup of rock in which crabs and pink weed swayed and scuttled. Water washed in and out of the cave-mouth, filling the pools inside it, swirling up the walls before it receded. Two small wooden boats were moored inside the cave, though one was clearly not sea-worthy. Towards the back of the cave I glimpsed a man, holding a softly-glowing torch, standing on a set of stairs that disappeared upwards, into the dark interior of the cliff.

℃

We followed our guide into the caves, up through stone hallways and stairwells that grew smoother and cooler and lighter as we climbed. Thin wormholes let in the light, spearing the darkness with milky threads of brightness. Soon, we reached an open space, cut into the face of the cliff, facing north across the ocean. The floor was tiled with thick terracotta tiles. Tables and chairs were set out around the space, and daybeds—wide, low-backed platforms covered in cushions on which the inhabitants of the hermitage reclined: talking, eating and reading. For them, the day had only just begun.

Giacomo ushered me towards one of the daybeds, nestled into a cool, dark corner of the chamber. I could see Judit leaning back against one of the cushions, her feet being washed and wrapped in white cloths. A young man brought us a dented silver tray of tea, fruit, bread and yoghurt, which he placed between us on a low platform.

Giacomo knelt beside the daybed to wash his hands and face and feet in a bowl of clear water. A young man handed him a cloth, with which Giacomo dried himself, smiling and thanking the boy when he handed it back. 'I'm tired,' Giacomo said. 'I need to eat something. Rest a little.'

I looked at our guide, whose eyes were ringed with dark, whose voice was rough with tiredness. Judit's blistered feet rested on a cushion as she sipped at a warm bowl of tea. When she closed her eyes I saw the effort it took to open them again. 'Good,' I said. 'We should all rest.'

Giacomo eased himself onto the daybed, sliding back towards the cushions, taking the bowl of fragrant tea Judit had poured for him. 'Sit for a moment, Rupetta,' she said. 'We have been travelling for weeks. Months, perhaps.'

Reluctantly, I perched on the edge of our platform to wait. Giacomo and Judit ate and drank, discussing the hermitage's work, the raids, the weather. As the sun swung into the sky the chamber was flooded with warm light. Two young men lowered thin cotton blinds at the far north of the cave's mouth, filtering the light. The hermitage was the home—the refuge—of Fallen Penitents, their mechanical hearts concealed beneath white robes. They had once been Penitents, but had seen too much of the Penitent world and fled.

They wandered and chatted, read and wrote. For a while, one of them took out a small wind instrument and played. A few played cards, or Oråki. There were bursts of laughter: a low, warm rumble that echoed around the chamber. The young man who brought us our breakfast moved among them—one of a handful of helpers—delivering small means of comfort, doing rounds, listening to their hearts. Many of the Fallen were frail. Their skin papery and blue, their breath short. They shuffled over the floor in soft shoes. Giacomo and Judit dozed. A young boy took away the tray with their cold, half-empty tea bowls and the inverted, empty skins of oranges.

While they slept I crossed the room to the edge of the cave-mouth and sat on the low stone wall at the edge. Below me the sea pounded against the wall of a sheer, rocky cliff. There were no rockpools there, no landing place. A handful of birds hovered over the water. As I watched, one of them dove. When it rose again it had a bright fish in its beak.

One of the young men approached me. 'Excuse me,' he said. 'I'm sorry to disturb you; I know you must be tired, but Kapil, he asked me, you see, and he's not well. You know? He wants to know if you will play. If you will join him. He's tired of the others, you see, tired of beating us.' The boy tilted his head and smiled, shrugging.

'Play?'

The boy held out a small, tin playing piece: the weaver. The piece's face was worn smooth, featureless, and her skirt dinted. One of her hands, perhaps the one that once held a tiny shuttle, had been snapped off. 'Which one is Kapil?' I said.

The boy led me towards one of the daybeds, on which was already laid out a small tray of wine, silver glasses, cheese and dry bread. The mattress of the daybed was thick, wrapped in dark blankets with faded silver stitching. It was scattered with purple and white cushions. On a small wooden table in the centre of the daybed was the Oråki board, with its mismatched pieces. Kapil sat on the edge of this daybed, his small kingdom, his dark eyes glittering as I approached. He stood to greet me, took my hand in both of his and held it. 'It is you,' he said. 'I knew it was you.'

We slid back onto the daybed and I settled the Weaver in her place at the edge of the board. 'I am Rupetta,' I said. Kapil smiled and poured the wine, he glanced over at the platform where Giacomo and

Judit were sleeping, wrapped now in a screen someone had set up to shield them from the light streaming into the chamber.

'Your companions are tired,' he said. 'They are not journeymen like you and I.'

'We have come a long way,' I said.

'And you have further still to travel.' Kapil took a sharp breath, leant back against his cushions. His face was pale, his lips blue. He drank from a small philtre. 'Unlike myself,' he said. 'I fear my journeying days are over.'

'How long has it been since you were wound?' I asked.

'Two years,' he said, grimacing. 'I never thought I'd last this long.'

'Penitent hearts must be wound monthly,' I said, looking about the room again, at the weary men who passed the time in this rocky eyrie, waiting for their hearts to stop beating.

Kapil nodded, sipping at his wine, rolling the copper Fisher King in his hand. 'So they say. It would not be the first lie the Penitents have made, though, would it? For the first year I wound it myself, with a false key carved from a piece of wood. Not well, it seems, but well enough.' Kapil placed the Fisher King on the edge of the board. 'You are looking for someone. For the child.'

'You know about her?'

Kapil nodded, poured more wine into his silver tumbler. When he moved to pour some into my tumbler there was only enough for a thimble-full. He smiled his strange, sad smile and moved another piece. 'I am thirsty, this evening. Where is that child? Ask him to bring more wine.'

'Have you seen her?'

'They came to my brother's home looking for a guide: someone who could take them into the Ayr Mountains, make contact with the Ramocca. They murdered his wife. They have taken his sons and will murder them if he leads them astray. Every night the children sleep surrounded by knives.' Kapil drinks off the last of his wine and, when the boy comes with a fresh carafe, pours a fresh glass for himself, and for me. He will not meet my eyes. 'They took my daughter, Meladi. She was the first to die.'

∽

We spend one night in the caves. Kapil sleeps while I oil the hinges of his heart, file off the rust of disrepair, and open him up. His heart is a cheap thing; tinny, thin-walled. The heart of a man who has been ill-used by the Order to which he devoted his life. I send Giacomo to scrounge for whatever parts he can find—for copper pots and leather shoes and tin spoons to beat into new shapes, new purposes—and we do our best, Judit and I.

All around us, in the cave, I hear the tick of old men's hearts, worn smooth and uneven, unwinding into death. As they stir in their beds, as they cough and turn and wake, the sound of their dying is muffled but persistent.

One by one Judit and I go to them. We sit on their beds and speak with them, ease them into dreams with a dark spirit-laced tea, and pick open their hearts. We oil their glutted cogs and polish their blackened pipes, straightening and smoothing and tightening the tiny mechanisms, repairing and replacing the bent pins that hold the cogs in place, aligning the wheels more precisely, and winding up the springs that have stiffened and uncurled within them. When they wake, we show them how to break open the locks of their own hearts and make a key by pressing or dripping warm wax into the crenellations, how to use the hardened wax as a mould. Some of their hearts we cannot mend; the parts are too old and worn, or the rust has settled into them like cancer, weakening the joints and thickening the slim pipes through which the blood beats in niggardly flows. We do what we can.

By morning Kapil's heart, bright and newly-polished, beats as though he has just been wound. I string the key on a piece of leather thong long enough that it will be well-hidden in the folds of his travelling coat. At breakfast we serve him oatcakes and honey. Giacomo shows him the key and Kapil weeps and kisses our hands. Swears that he will stay faithful to our cause; that we can call on him, on the Fallen Penitents that live in his strange hermitage, whenever we have need.

Our eyes and hands are worn, scratched, well-used. Giacomo is tired, but smiling, moving among the men, offering them small cakes and bitter tea, speaking with them as though they are his sons and brothers and fathers. This is the last time he may see them. Kapil comes and sits with me, watching a small coracle cut across the water towards us. Light spills over the edge of the earth, lighting the rocks at the base of our cliff. Kapil puts his hand on the back of my shoulder and I turn towards him, seeing his eyes drop down rather than meet my gaze, seeing the flush and pinch of gratitude and something like wonder rise in his throat. A shame; I had hoped we would be friends.

Giacomo, Judit and I make our way down through the cool caves to the rockpools, drag out the small rowboat and load it with supplies—not many, but enough—soon we are in the coracle. The cliffs recede behind us. When I look back, I cannot see the cave, the carved stone balcony, or the winged blinds that shut out the light. Judit is seated at the prow, watching the boat's sharp breast slice the water into twin curls. Her bare feet dangle above the waterline; the spray cooling her skin. I sit beside her, dangle my feet and look out, as she does, at the low, gold horizon that shimmers hazily in the distance.

৪৩

I had forgotten how small she was, how perfectly made. She stood on the dock of that tiny harbour—on the wooden pier—with her hair fluttering like wings around her face and her serious eyes peering out to sea. It took us too long to reach her, and not long enough. I could have spent a century learning again the shape of her face, the way her shoulders were curved, the way her little knees peeked out from beneath her skirt when it was whisked to the side by the breeze. The way she held herself, so neat and patient. I could have spent a decade studying the tiny furrow that formed when she looked at us all, standing on the deck of the boat, as her gaze moved from face to face.

Then she saw me, and her face was transformed again. She put back her shoulders, and waved.

Time can be such a soft animal. It can lull and comfort. In the wet heat of that first summer on Oikos Island we learned to forget the things we had seen. Or not to forget, but to think of them the way you think of something you once believed in—hotly and desperately—but have since given up on.

We built a modest, air- and light-filled house to live in—Judit and Giacomo, myself and Perdita. An open, white-walled room in the middle opened out into the back garden through wood and glass doors that folded back so that it seemed the third wall of the room had been removed altogether. Three interior doors led off that large central room to Judit and Giacomo's bedroom, and Perdita's room. On the other side of the house were the kitchen and a study that we soon filled with books, though Perdita didn't really use the study, preferring to work at the round table under the shade of the Jacaranda or in the small sukiya we built for her during that first summer on the island. She liked, so she said, the smell of earth around her when she was working.

Perhaps nothing marks the passing of that time so much as the books we each wrote during those years. Our days circled and bloomed with laughter, with light. We swam in the warm ocean, grew herbs and fruit, learned to bake bread and preserve lemons. Judit spent her days in the garden. Her face grew warm and brown, her hands long-fingered, almost rootling in the soil as she planted out her seedlings. On the shelf in the kitchen we kept the books we wrote: *Fresh Longing; A Cookbook for Gardeners; Milk and Honey, An Islander's Year; The Agony of Leaves; Small Stones and Red Feathers.*

The last was Perdita's work: a book of stories she wrote for Judit's daughter while Judit was still yeast-plump, the child tumbling slowly inside her. They were tales she had heard, tales that had been told to her by her generations of carers: tales of hedgehogs and bears, snow and stone cottages. She would often take the baby out into the sukiya and lay her in the rush-basket Giacomo made for his daughter. As

Margause grew, the two became fast companions. Perdita held Margause's hand when she took her first steps; ran beside her as she cycled along the harbour path for the first time, taught her to read and write and draw. In the evenings they would lie on the floor in that great open room, playing the games nobody else knew or understood, in which the flat white stones they collected were piled up and tumbled down. Perihan was part of the game, hopping and chirruping between the small stone towers. When Margause grew too big for her rush-basket, Perdita built a driftwood bed, where the two of them sometimes dozed together, curled like two dark commas, with books and papers strewn about them.

We heard things, of course, about the outside world. Every few months, Giacomo would travel to the mainland and return ashen, withdrawn. He would tell us a little of what he had seen and done—but it was as if he was telling stories out of Perdita's fairytale books: evil princes and princesses, strange storms and ships, men that wept and held out their hands, cities that burned. We talked about going back, when the time was right, finding a way to change what was happening, but there was so little we could do. Sometimes Giacomo brought children back to the Island—the sons and daughters of so-called heretics—from the house of the Salt Lane Witches. They stayed a few weeks or months, sleeping in makeshift beds on the deck, swimming in the ocean, playing in the garden with Margause and Perdita, before Giacomo found other places for them to go and took them away again. Mostly, we watched, and waited, and did what we could.

Twice we were visited by people from that other, distant world.

The first visitor was a young man. He sat at our table, urging Giacomo to make contact with the true Rupetta. His mother and father, and two older sisters, had disappeared into the Haven, and died there. He spoke urgently, his hands restless, his body charged with fury. He spoke of Rupetta's body—of my body—as though it were a weapon, as though my reappearance would be the match-strike of a thousand burning years of revolution.

The night grew dark; I tucked Perdita and Margause into their driftwood bed, with the white net curtain draped around them and Perihan hopping restlessly up and down the bedhead while they slept. The glass doors of the great room were pushed back; we could see the ocean, hear her subdued roar. It was a warm evening. We poured more wine, took off our shoes, walked down to the sand. Our visitor was furious, intent. Tears leapt in his eyes. In the morning, Judit took out Giacomo's travelling boots and backpack. The leather was softened with age and wear. She lay the palm of her hand on his chest and cheek and heart, and kissed him. The boy stood impatiently on the deck, waiting, watching the boat.

Giacomo was gone for two years, that time. After he returned he would sit on the deck and stare out to sea, watching the tide, the waves. Sometimes, I would come out and sit with him. The moon would rise up and over us, swinging away over the Norfolk Pines. We would set out the old Oråki board and play a game or two. When we were sure the others were sleeping, when the sound of their dreams tangled with that of the sea and the pines and the dune-grasses, we would talk about what he had seen, and what could be done. We made plans for his next trip to the mainland, about who our supporters were, and what work they could do. Who could be saved. And who could not.

The second visitor was a travelling Penitent, an Obanite historian who had come to Oikos Island to visit the remains of the Haven a few miles north of our home. The girls were away, camping together on the other side of the island, as they sometimes did, retreating into their shared, imaginary world of dragons and sea-sprites. The Penitent and Giacomo sat on the deck all afternoon, watching the tide seep in and discussing the finer points of Rupettan history over a seemingly endless game of Oråki. I had wandered off after a while, bored with the same obscurities, the same strange sense of hearing a story about a woman or creature I perhaps knew, of a life I had almost lived. I went down to the beach and collected shells and stones to show the girls, checked the pots for crabs and filled a small creel with seaweed for the garden.

258

I was still down there, standing ankle-deep in a rockpool of blood-warm water, watching a tiny crab wave its pink claws in the tidal drift, when I heard Judit cry out. She had been sleeping while the men sat and talked, and had woken when the house fell silent. She had come out of her bedroom without turning on any lights. The moon was fat and candle-white, throwing drifts of grey light across the deck and into the house. She shrugged against the sudden cool, took an old blanket from the lounge and went out onto the deck where she could see Giacomo sleeping in his chair. The Penitent was gone, but he had left a gift curled in Giacomo's lap: a silver Penitent's chronometer. She put the chronometer on the table beside him, curling the length of it like a bright snake. She put the blanket over Giacomo and bent to kiss his cheek.

She said his name, and brushed the hair back from his forehead, willing him to wake and smile and pull her down onto his lap with that familiar, sleep-addled smile warming his skin. She was still imagining the way she would curl into his lap as her hand moved down across his cheek, his throat, onto his chest. She stood with her hand pressed against his heart, convinced she was dreaming, and that soon it would begin to beat.

When I reached them she was sitting at his feet, her head resting on his knee, holding onto his bare foot. She barely made a sound as I knelt beside him and pressed my hands against his heart and belly and neck. There was no wound: if we hadn't known better we might have believed he had drifted gently into death. But the Penitent was gone: when I reached the pier I could just see, like a moth drifting into the light, the boat on which he had come.

In the morning, when I was clearing away the teapot, the cups and the unfinished game of Oråki from the deck, I picked up the chronometer. I planned to get rid of it, perhaps throw it into the sea or bury it. The stones that marked each miracle were solid and finely engraved, except for one, which had a hinge and a tiny latch. Inside the ball there were a few small hemlock seeds. I tipped them into my hand. Such tiny things, they were. I put one on my tongue. The seed was small and curved and bitter. I swallowed it down, and another, and then another, wondering what it would feel like for the poison to take effect. Heaviness drifting through the body. Perhaps at first Giacomo had thought it was just exhaustion, or old age. Perhaps he had laughed a little, as he sometimes did, and told the Penitent about how as a child, when his foot or hand went to sleep, he had held his breath and waited, believing he was about to be transformed into stone. His feet would have fallen numb, and then his knees. Perhaps he had adjusted in his chair, feeling the sudden heaviness of his limbs, their alien weight. He had not cried out, as far as either of us could recall, in fear or shock. Had he been sleeping when the poison reached his hips, his groin? When it rose to his belly and swirled coolly beneath his ribs. Had he been dreaming while cold and stillness fingered their way up through his body, like a gently rising tide, until they found his heart and stopped it.

ℰℛ

I want to stop here. I want to tell the truth. Giacomo's death was one among many. The weight of his body as I carried him into the house, and laid him on his bed, was not strange or unusual. The stiffness of his limbs, the slackening and strange sharpening of his features, the way his nose and mouth and eyes shifted so that he no longer looked like Giacomo at all, but like a wax doll with Giacomo's features. Or like a perfect, dead statue of Giacomo, who did not know—had never known—how to kiss or laugh or cry. A Giacomo who had never loved his wife, never held his daughter in his great, rough hands as though she were an egg. None of these things were unexpected or unusual. Nor was Judit's grief; how when she put her cheek on his knee and her hands beneath his foot that night she seemed to soak up the cool, stiff breath of the hemlock. How her heart stopped and her face became carved and distinct. How when her daughter came into the house with her tousled hair and her dirty clothes, with Perdita tailing behind her suddenly smaller than her playmate, she looked up and said, 'He is dead,' as though that was all that needed to be said. How the world fled out of her fingertips, her ears and eyes and open mouth. How she was a streaming, silent emptying out. An echoing hollowness. How her daughter ran past her and she stood and felt the wind of her daughter's grief pass through her and could not move. Could not speak.

None of these things were unexpected.

Perdita picked up the dropped tent and packs and took them out into the yard. I followed and knelt beside her as we rolled out the oiled canvasses and scrubbed them clean and rolled them up again. We made piles of clothes to be washed, took the pots into the kitchen to be scrubbed. We hung the empty packs on the line and took the supplies they had not used into the kitchen. We made tea and baked bread and washed the windows and swept the floors and changed the sheets on all of the beds, save one. We worked together without speaking, knowing what had to be done. Our movements were precise, as though choreographed. We moved outside the circle of their grief, circum-navigating it as if it were not our own. Once, while I was passing her a folded blanket, our hands touched. I felt my fingers graze against the living warmth of the back of her hand. It gave me a shock—sharp, exploding, earthy. Like a seedling shooting out of the seed in which it has been contained. I knew I would never be able to lift her cooling body out of a chair and carry her into the house and straighten her limbs beneath a grieving sheet. Would never be able to bear the weight of such a thing.

I grasped her hand, her wrist, pulled her to me, up onto my lap, and put my head against the silk-slip of her hair. I could smell the wildness of the woods on her, as if grasses were growing in her scalp. She put her arms around my shoulders. I could feel the supple weight of them: their warmth and smoothness against my neck. I wanted to tell her something, perhaps that I loved her, though that didn't seem enough. Words were such small containers, such inadequate, abstract things within which to live. She was curved into my lap, her feet dangling. I could feel her bare heels knocking against my shin.

Finally, we sat at the table, all four of us, and pretended to eat, pushing the food around on our plates.

'Of course,' said Judit, without looking at either of us, 'you'll have to leave this place.'

I nodded.

'Giacomo had a friend—a contact—at the Haven where they took the Salt woman. I'll go to the mainland and see her. She will help us find a new carer for Perdita; somewhere for her to go. Then you and Margause can move to the mainland, find a home. It's time Margause went to school, anyway.'

'We can stay together,' I said. 'We can find another place.'

'There is nowhere we could go together. Nowhere where we would be safe and our daughters would be safe. You are fools: you and Giacomo. You think they will forget that you exist, and leave you to live out some utopian eternity of gardening and swimming and story-telling. You think you can slip out of the world, into a fairytale, and grow mossy with age. You think this is your afterlife, your reward for all those centuries of fucking life. You think their memory is not perfect, like yours, that it does not itch at them, but no matter how long you live they will not forget who you are or what you mean or what you might become. They will never give up searching for you; wanting to have you and contain you—to hold you in full sight—or destroy you. They are terrified of what you are, because they don't understand that you are less than they are. They would like to tear you apart, just to prove that you are fragile. They would like to make you a god, and have you fail them, just to prove that you are not a god.' Judit put her fork and knife down on her plate and pushed it away from her, into the centre of the table. 'You will care for my daughter, and I will ensure yours is cared for. That is all we can do for each other now.'

❀

I grope my way back along the thread of my life, like Ariadne making her way through the dark of the maze, step by step, knowing I laid the thread down surely, knowing it will lead, eventually, into the future, but never sure which step in the dark will be a misstep, which step will lead to death and which will carry me out in the sharpening light.

Here are those last days in the house on Oikos Island. The summer breezes sharp with the scent of sand, of waxy frangipani, of death. This is the key, this is the lock, with which we shut up the house. Here is the rush-basket in which the baby Margause once slept, rotted to nothing and burned in the final cleaning out of our lives, along with the driftwood bed, and the chair in which Giacomo died. Here are the books we wrote—too dangerous to keep—wrapped in oiled cloth and buried in the old Haven. Here is the house where we played and ate and laughed, locked up. Its windows blinded, its mattresses rolled and tied like fat snails. Here is the path, which points the way to the gate, and from there to the dock.

Here is my daughter, standing on the dock with Margause beside her. Two little girls in twin coats, their pockets filled with flat white stones. Margause and Perdita in their red and green coats. I am caught by the very word 'girls', and caught all the more by their form. By the beautiful image I have of them standing there, waiting for the boat that will take us to the mainland and sever us from that place, perhaps forever.

I have always understood and trusted images more than words. A white bird on a blue sky; a red coat and a green coat; a woman's hand cupped beneath her dead lover's foot. Perhaps you will find this strange, incompatible as it is with your own vocation of rendering the past into strings of sentences, paragraphs like stone blocks; but I no longer trust words. The last thing in my life will be a picture, not a word.

Judit and I went to the Haven, to find Mathilde, knowing that we had not yet seen enough.

I am faltering.

For so long I have avoided speaking of what I saw there. I do not want to speak. What words are there that would be the measure of that place, that would truly mark it? It is pure vanity to speak. To think that these words—my words, or any others—can mark the place where those bodies lived, suffered, died. All of the vanity and certainty inside me has been stripped away by what I saw. I was gutted, eviscerated. A sharp hook went in through my eyes and tore out my gut, my heart, my lungs.

I walked through the halls, with Judit at my side, silently. We went into that room. We sat in those simple wooden chairs. The stench overwhelmed me. Burned my mouth, my nose. I looked at Mathilde. This place had given her its shape. I do not want to remember her that way, as she was made and shattered.

Afterwards, Judit and I walked through the streets to the house where we were staying. The girls were outside, playing in the garden. They had perched Perihan on a thick branch and were taking turns climbing up the old tree's trunk, perching on the branch like oversized birds. Their pretty coats had become wings; they were showing Perihan how to spread them wide, how to launch off the branch into the air. How to fly.

We set out tea and cake and called them in to sit at the table and eat. We said nothing about where we had been or what we had seen. We sat, exhausted, and lifted the cups to our lips but the tea was bitter, the cake like dust in our mouths. Like the flesh of the dead, rotted to sweetness. And our exhaustion was nothing; we were ashamed of it, and ashamed, too, to smile at our daughters. To remark on their beauty, or to smile when they set Perihan on the table, among the cake crumbs, and stood together and sang for us. We clapped when they had finished and sent them back out into the garden. We tried to love them, without shame, without fear, but there was no language left to do so except the language of the past. The language of the present had shrunk to the size of that small, stone room where Mathilde sat, to the shape of her bones, shining out from beneath her skin.

The last day I saw Perdita, we were in the treehouse at Salt Lane. The others were sleeping, and we had gone up to the top platform— the highest layer of that strange, leaf-sailing ship—to watch the light slip out of the world. The next morning Perdita would sail to Lisbon, where Judit would hand her and Mathilde over into the care of the Fallen Penitents. From there, I did not know where they were headed. It had been decided—we had all agreed—that it was better if nobody knew.

We sat at the edge of the platform, our legs dangling in the air. Perdita's chin propped on a low railing. We fought. I wanted to know where she was going and she refused to tell me. I could not bear the sense of panic at not knowing where she would be. I knew I could not save her, could not keep her, but I wanted at least to know that I could find her if I needed to. When I needed to.

I tried to order her to tell me, as a mother orders a small child to confess to hiding sweets under their bed, or having not brushed their teeth. I had forgotten that she was not a child; that she only played at being a child for my sake, and for Margause's. I was stubborn, and foolish, and afraid. I should have offered her comfort, but I could not say what would happen to her, and I would not lie and say that I knew what was to come. Or that I could protect her. She knew as well as I did that we had no chance against a world that thought of us as both goddesses and monsters. I pressed Perihan upon her—an apology, a connection—and she put it in her pocket. Later, I found out she gave it to Emmeline; a poor substitution for taking Mathilde so very far away, without knowing what lay ahead.

I stayed behind with Margause.

The pain reminded us of each other. When we met later, if there was to be a later, we knew we would recognise each other by that pain.

The light let go of the world, as if it had been shrugged off by the earth as she turned over in her sleep. We fought, and then fell silent. We had nothing to say: no promises, no lies, to offer each other.

Henri's Story: Part Seven

Mathilde and Emmeline Salt:
An Account of Their Lives from 1895-1946

Submitted by Henriette Francine Bellmer in accordance with guidelines for the presentation of theses at Obanite College. Completed under the supervision of Master Abel Jenon.

Chapter One

The Salt Lane School was founded in 1904 by Emmeline and Mathilde Salt. The two women had lived on the property, prior to opening the school, in almost perfect solitude for nearly ten years, having inherited the property without encumbrance from Emmeline's uncle, Charles Birney, in 1895. There is evidence to suggest the women were involved with the fledgling Oikos movement from its inception, that Mathilde, in particular, played a key role in the operations of the movement during the height of the Oikos heresy, particularly in the years after the Rupettan re-settlement of the Territory began. This thesis explores some of this evidence, and draws modest conclusions concerning the centrality of the Salt Lane Women to both a history of the Oikos, and to the history of Rupetta and the Wynders.

Both Mathilde and Emmeline kept extensive records of their work at Salt Lane: records concerning establishing and managing the gardens, their work with the children who attended the Salt Lane School and, later, sometimes in a mildly encrypted form, of their activities as part of the Oikos heresy. While these records had been preserved in the stacks of the Obanite College, they have never before been catalogued, folioed or studied in detail. This thesis, then, is the first to explore the lives of the Salt Lane Witches in any detail, and to begin to appreciate their significant contribution to History. The thesis details some aspects of the operation of the Salt Lane School, and includes two detailed appendices listing the primary sources that were retrieved, archived and folioed as part of this research project, and which might be used to write a more detailed and comprehensive history of the school, of Emmeline's extensive work in education after Mathilde's disappearance, and so forth. The thesis also explores the extent of Mathilde and Emmeline's involvement in the Oikos heresy in the Territory, and of the centrality of the Territorian Oikos, particularly those who made their home on Oikos Island, to the ongoing attempts to overthrow the Rupettan Trilogy since the rule of the Consort Mateo, drawing on a range of sources from the Salt Lane Archive. Again, this work is supplemented by two appendices: Appendix One, which details the primary sources, including diaries, journals, gardening journals, correspondence and occasional writings, and Appendix Two, which is a linguistic map of the various encryption codes used in both Mathilde and Emmeline's papers. The final section of the thesis brings the two threads of the women's work and lives together, introducing connections between the aims of the Salt Lane School, the identities of its students, and the previously unsuspected and perhaps deliberately-suppressed nature of their involvement in the Oikos heresy.

Mathilde's diary for the year of 1895 (D4:ff1.1-12.54) documents her growing despair at the changes being made under the rule of the Consort Mateo in Europe, particularly those that had begun to be felt in the Territories—the Oikos Territories, as they were then known—as well as documenting the work she and Emmeline were undertaking to develop the site at Salt Lane for use as a school. The entry for May 14th, 1895, for example, includes details of purchases of '12 pillows, 12 sets of white sheets (cotton), 6 metres oilcloth, 20 straw hats (various sizes)' (D4:ff5.16).

At first, Mathilde and Emmeline's response to the political upheavals of the time was to retreat from the city and to think, increasingly, of ways to diminish their dependence on the Penitent Orders and Rupettan technology. After moving permanently to the Salt Lane Property in 1894, they became increasingly self-sufficient: adding to the existing, established orchard with new plantings, building two extensive greenhouses in which to strike and nurture seedlings, converting the old milking sheds to an extensive if primitive storage facility, and establishing the extensive kitchen gardens that are, to this day, a feature of the Salt Lane Property[1].

The following extract from Mathilde's journal (J5:ff1.1-250) is a typical one for the year preceding the opening of the school, reflecting both her intellectual, and domestic/agricultural interests, and also revealing some sense of the political discontent, the heretical doubt in the Fourfold Rupettan Law, which would later contribute to her arrest and imprisonment:

> Centuries ago, living in a world that did not value women, and in which nearly everyone in Europe was bewitched by the mythology of a single, mysterious god who had gifted them with life, a sexless, ageless creature who sat outside of both Natural and Mechanical Creation, who was the source of all things, who gave and took life both mortal and eternal, the mystic Hadewijch, a Beguine recluse and mystic wrote: *we all indeed wish to be God with God, but God knows there are few of us who want to live as humans with humanity*. And it strikes me that though humanity is no longer enamoured with God, but with, instead, a mechanical goddess, it is perhaps true that the great mass of humanity still does not wish to live *as* humans *with* humanity. Perhaps part of this is, as Emmeline often says,

[1] See illustrations 1, 2, 3, 4, 5 and 7 (images of the grounds during the years 1894-1896), and map 1.1 (map of the grounds drawn by Emmeline in June, 1895: SB7:ff8).

that the mass of humanity is just too overwhelming. She is fond of Teilhard du Chardin's way of putting it. He wrote of *the whole vast anonymous army of living humanity . . . this restless multitude, confused or orderly, the immensity of which terrifies us, this ocean of humanity whose slow monotonous wave-flows trouble the hearts even of those whose flame is most firm*[2]. Certainly, though our flames are firm, they have burned low these past months. We have had no wish to live among a humanity that treats its own kind so ill: a humanity that includes the Consort Mateo and his Obanite soldiers.

The Consort and the Penitents seek knowledge at all costs, persecute and silence those who value this life, this earth, this body, as though the eternal life they seek is the only life. As though to speak of joy and pleasure and love and friendship in *this* life, in *this* body, were to deny the possibility of the other, eternal life they seek so violently. They insist on a literal, limited, hopeless interpretation of the Law: they insist Life is *only* a kind of animated death. And yet, I cannot believe this: Life is not only death, though death is an essential part of our existence. Life is also birth and hope and love and joy and pleasure: the breathtaking, exhilarating [sic] suck and sap of time, of our bodies stretched in movement, of our lips joining to kiss, of our hearts beating towards each other against the endless current of the wind.

The ancient Greeks had a word—Oikos—which is the ancient word at the root of *ecology* and *economics*. It meant simply household. Life is the house in which are held, perhaps while we search for and await immortality, the cessation of pain and uncertainty, the cessation of change, but—perhaps—oh perhaps!—Perhaps not. Perhaps life is the house in

---

[2] Check this source—ESP check it doesn't predate the entry in Mathilde's diary

which we will always be held. Or the only house in which we will be held. Perhaps life is our household/Oikos.

Hildegard of Bingen, another mystic, wrote about the ways in which our bodies—those cages of flesh the Consort despises, the organic prison from which the Penitents seek to free us—was not—is not—a cage, but a gift, a home. She writes: *It is the senses on which the interior powers of the soul depend . . . a person is recognised by her face, sees with her eyes, hears with her ears, opens her mouth to speak, feels with her hands, walks with her feet, and so the senses are to her as precious stones and as a rich treasure sealed in a jar*[3]. This last, it seems, might echo the Consort's beliefs, his interpretation of the Fourfold Law—this notion that we are 'sealed in a jar'—and yet I think Hildegard did not mean to conjure up the image of a soul trapped like a butterfly in a killing jar, but of a soul safe and nurtured within its home: a soul held as a child might hold a bird in its hand: with wonder, awe and grace.

Oikos: the house in which we are held, is the body.

Today, as I harvested another basket of tomatoes, as I sliced and boiled and canned them for use throughout the winter to come, I felt such gratitude for the dark earth that has held these seeds, nurtured them, fed them. Gratitude to the sun and rain and wind and—yes—even the blasted turkeys that dug up the early seedlings, teaching us that the earth—even this small corner of it—is not ours alone. I wandered through the orchard, plucked three heavy, ripe pomegranates from the tree. As I sit

---

[3] Mathilde here translates Bingen's work in the feminine, whereas the original and most translations record the quote as: *It is the senses on which the interior powers of the soul depend . . . a person is recognised by his face, sees with his eyes, hears with his ears, opens his mouth to speak, feels with his hands, walks with his feet, and so the senses are to him as precious stones and as a rich treasure sealed in a jar* (from the Scivias: 1.4.24). Throughout this work, where Mathilde or Emmeline misquote sources in their letters, journals, diaries, etc I have preserved their wording in the main body of the thesis and supplied, in the footnotes, details of the quote as it more usually appears.

here and write, before me on the desk are the sweet, fleshy kernels of one. My fingertips are pink with their juice. Outside the window I can see the yellow-tailed black cockatoos pass over the house, dropping heavy cones onto the tin roof. I am struck by how the walls of the house are merely the walls of a room: how our home is the land in which we plant our seeds, reap our harvest. Our home is the wind that ruffles the leaves, that lifts the birds. Our home is the light and the darkness, the whirling earth.

Oikos: the house in which we are held, is the earth.

While the women were politically engaged at this time—interested in, and critical of, the Consort and his Penitents, though only privately— their attention and energy was principally taken up with the establishment of the Salt Lane School. The official schools appalled them both, and were at the time determined not to provide educations for Oikos children. Emmeline wrote, in 1894, of the rigid, long days:

> Who could learn anything of use to the heart, mind, or spirit in such a room: windowless and crowded, underheated in winter and overheated in summer. Each child is loaded down with books that weigh more than they may ever attain on their poor diet. Their desks are arranged in tight rows, and the children dressed in cheap, identical uniforms that itch and stick against their skin. I visited one, 'progressive' school in which the children were allowed to select their own seat at the beginning of their year. This was considered a great moral laxity by the Penitent Inspector, who informed me that the practice would not be continued. Each child learned pages of useless information by rote: Histories, Laws, Mechanics, and Harmonics. The children were tired, pale, bored. During their fifteen-minute break, in a paved courtyard at the centre of the school—treeless, shaded, supervised from the second floor by an invigilator with a loudspeaker—they sat in pallid rows, drooping like plucked

flowers left too long in the sun (September 11, 1894: D3:ff9.11).

The women had decided to open a school of their own; a 'hedge school' as Mathilde called it (Letter 37:ff2), in which rote memory and desks would be forbidden, and the 'natural wildness' (Letter 37:ff4) of childhood encouraged, and within which, Oikos children would be permitted to learn alongside any others that came. They sent out letters of invitation to a select group of families, offering a free education to those who, under the Education Law of the time, were not entitled to an education at all in the official system. They received letters of interest from at least thirty families. Twelve children were selected, largely on the basis of need. Emmeline wrote in a letter to her sister, on November 13, 1894: 'We have cut the list down to 20 thus far, but it is so hard, Ellen! Each of the children are bright, strong, dear creatures. I hate to think of the cramped childhoods they will lead if we do not take them. Those windowless rooms, and cheerless instructors. It is too awful. One child—Imogen—climbed each of the trees in the orchard, one by one, testing to see which was best, she told me, for reading, or naps, or hanging upside down. She is on my shortlist. We can only take so many; and the first of our "seedlings" arrived today: lusty, hungry, his limbs still green. He is such a cunning creature: our little yew tree will be planted tomorrow' (Letter 42:ff5).

This is one of the first documents in the archive that mentions the 'seedlings'. While most of the children taken into the Hedge School were official registrations, housed, fed and educated for free, it appears there were other children—newborns and infants—whose provenance they guarded jealously, of whom they kept little, if any, records. I had thought there was no record of them at all—that the brief and veiled references to their arrivals and departures were all the evidence I would locate. I could not, through these sketchy asides, compile an accurate picture of who the children were, how long they remained at Salt Lane, or how many there were of them in residence at any one time. At first, I suspected the children were being disposed of: that the planting to which Emmeline refers in her letter, above, was a cruel internment. Or perhaps, more kindly, that the children were sickly on arrival and failed to thrive under the Salt's care. Finally, I revisited one of the earliest sets of loose-leaf folios (LL1-57) and made a connection between the yew tree of folio LL3[4], and the male child in Emmeline's letter. For some reason, I concluded, either the birth of each child who came to Salt Lane, or their arrival date, was commemorated with the planting of a tree, which was then named for them. Map 2 details the site of each of the 57 trees represented in the loose-leaf folios. Five of the trees are deceased: two through some kind of natural death (for example, LL45: *Snow Mahogany*, appears to have been prey to termites, become weakened, and fallen during a storm: the trunk lies across a slim waterway and is now home to a colony of small frogs). Three of the trees appear to have been chopped down, though it is unclear why: none of the remaining stumps show signs of disease or damage. There is no sign of the fallen trunks, and their stumps appear to have been transformed into shrines of some kind. LL23, for example, is covered with a hardenbergia, planted at its base around the time it was felled. The hollows within its roots are home to small piles of river stones, carved or painted with abstract images of leaves, flowers, fruit, frogs and birds[5].

The Salt Lane School was opened in late February, 1895. A sign was hung over the door of the schoolroom—a large room with sliding doors opened onto a shaded deck and furnished with large floor cushions, low shelves full of books, and low tables on which were arranged, each morning, coloured pencils, inks, papers, scissors and such. The deck at the edge of the room led into the vegetable gardens, and from there into the orchards. The small scholars—some still unable to crawl—spent the larger part of their days in the garden and the forest, among the trees, the herbs, and the vegetables. They planted trees and watched them grow: their copybooks show records of wind

---

[4] See illustration 8
[5] See Illustration 9

and rain, sun and worms and leaves and soil. They wrote poems about the weather, drew pictures of root systems, of spiderwebs. Pressed flowers and leaves between the pages of their copybooks, and pasted in small, clear packets of seeds.

There were no lesson plans, no closed rooms, no set curriculum. Each child learned to read, write, count and think. To grow and harvest. To cook and build. They made treehouses and coldframes, baked apples and bread. They learned to harvest and store seeds, to mulch the vegetable beds and fly kites.

In the evening, Mathilde and Emmeline built a fire and drew their armchairs up to it, or slid open the doors and dragged their old sun chairs onto the deck—depending on the season. The children sprawled on the floor, on piles of thick cushions. They brought pillows and blankets and soft toys down from the dormitories to lie with. To listen. The women talked. About the future. About trees and water, tides and stars. About dragons and mermaids and clouds. Bears and box hedges. Late at night, they would speak of ghosts, of lost ships and stolen treasures. The children drifted into sleep, one by one, and were carried to their beds.

Sitting on the deck with the older scholars, as the stars broke out and the moon drifted closer and closer to the roof of the sky, Mathilde would talk about her intention of giving up the land, their home, in the end, into the care of the wind and the rain, the seasons and the sunlight. To you, she would say to her charges. To the future.

Chapter Two: The Arrest

Haven records indicate Mathilde was arrested, along with thirty other suspected or confirmed Oikos heretics working against the repatriation of the Territory, on June 20, 1914. She was taken from her home in the early hours of the morning. Emmeline writes that Mathilde was taken before sunrise: that she woke first on hearing someone outside the house. She woke Mathilde and the two of them put on the clothes that were hung over the end of the bed. Later, Emmeline discovered she had put on Mathilde's shirt by mistake and wrote that she 'took some little comfort' from it as it 'stank of [Mathilde's] garden-self'.

They went downstairs and opened the door, thinking to find some of the older children at some prank in the night-dark garden. Instead, there were three Penitents on the doorstep. One of them held a gun. They smiled at Mathilde and nodded. 'It is time,' one of them said, and Mathilde nodded in reply.

'One moment,' she said and turned back to Emmeline, and took hold of both of her hands and held them fast. 'Do you remember,' she said, 'Marvell's *The Garden*? I gave a copy of it to you, that first summer.'

Mathilde nodded and quoted one of the stanzas, the last line of which they appear to have often quoted as a kind of mnemonic indicator of their relationship. I found the phrase engraved inside a ring Mathilde wore:

> *Meanwhile the mind from pleasure less*
> *Withdraws into its happiness;*
> *The mind, that ocean where each kind*
> *Does straight its own resemblance find;*
> *Yet it creates, transcending these,*
> *Far other worlds and other seas,*
> *Annihilating all that's made*
> *To a green thought in a green shade.*

The taller of the Penitents took hold of Mathilde. Unlike many of those who were arrested, Mathilde did not struggle. Emmeline records that she walked unaided between the two men, that she was taller than them both, and that she never turned back.

Chapter Three: Visiting Hours

Every morning, during the years of Mathilde's incarceration at the Haven, Emmeline made tea, packed up a parcel of food from the garden, paper, pencils, bread and fruit, a flask of soup or tea or wine. She labelled each of the parcels, *For Mathilde: a green thought in a green shade.*

She rode her bicycle down to the Haven where Mathilde was held. She would have passed the window of Mathilde's cell and perhaps looked up in hope of seeing her there. The windows were far above the street, and lidded with rough boards during those years.

At the entrance window, where the guard sat to receive and inter-view visitors each day, she stood in line with the others—those familiar strangers—each with their own parcels wrapped in cloth or brown paper. When it was her turn, she handed over the parcel, watched with avid, pretended patience as the guard sniffed the liquid, ruffled the papers, bruised the fruit. Behind the guard, the room was lined with shelves, along the front of which were pinned numbers. The shelves were heavy with fruit, cake, soap, blankets, shoes, glasses.

'For Mathilde Salt,' Emmeline would say, watching the guard run her finger down the page of the record book, turning the pages with her pen poised. How grimly bright and festive the shelves must have seemed: the gleaming jars of preserved fruits, the baskets of oranges and boxes of lettuce. As if they were preparing for a feast or a holiday, a fete of some kind. Emmeline would have waited—it was the habit of the guards, so she wrote, to drag out each 'interview' for as long as possible, to make the visitors wait, shifting from foot to foot while they struggled to reveal nothing, to give nothing of their desperation away. Finally, the guard would nod and move Emmeline's bundle from her desk to a numbered shelf. The guard never looked up from her book; never met Emmeline's eye. Never said anything. Once, Emmeline wrote, she leaned forward, pushing her dirt-stained fingers in under the glass barrier towards the guard, palms up in supplication. Calling attention to herself in this way, calling attention to her heartache and desperation, was a risk. There were many, at the time, who did not even visit those they loved, believing it put them and the others who remained free at risk, exposing them. Rumours abounded that records were kept of those who came each day, that they were followed and watched. That disappearances followed them like the bloom of a viral infection. Emmeline must have known all this, must have been well schooled in the careful ways the Oikos and those associated with the heretics managed their affairs. She would have seen visitors who wept, who called out, who argued with the guards, and begged to see their loved ones. Only a month before her own protest she had seen a young man bang on the glass, demanding to see his sister. After a few minutes two Penitent soldiers had come out, their black boots shining in the light, and taken hold of the visitor, one on each side of him. They had taken him away. Supporting him between them as though he were ill.

He and his sister were never released.

Nevertheless, after six years of unremarkable visits, Emmeline lost patience. Whatever the reason, she attempted, just once, to break the visitor's protocol, as recorded in her journal:

> I pushed my hands in under the glass and tried to grasp her hand, her pen, her book, anything. I wanted to make contact. I wanted to make her feel the coldness in my fingertips. 'Please,' I said. Just that and no more. I leaned forward. I could see I was too close, that my breath was fogging the glass, but it had been six years, Mathilde, and I had had no word. Not a one; just packages and lists and silence.
>
> The guard looked at my hands as though they were worms. The guard was a young woman: plump-faced, familiar, young. Perhaps I had taught her once. I looked closer, trying to imagine that she, too, was still a person, with a name and a home and a lover and a heart filled with fear and hope and perhaps even love. *Imogen*, I thought. *Her name is Imogen.* I pressed my

277

forehead to the glass and peered at her. My heart was beating so fast I thought she would be able to hear it, see it jumping beneath my shirt. Imogen looked at me—steadily—and then glanced at the door behind her, as if to point to it. I heard a step in the hall outside her office—a boot on the old slate—and then heard a hand settle on the doorknob. It began to turn. I looked at Imogen. Her eyes begged me to go. She almost shook her head. I saw a shadow passing across her eye, and then she opened her mouth, looked past me. Her face shifted back into the coldness I had seen before: the grey nothing.

'Next,' the guard called, looking over my shoulder. A man stepped forward, shouldered me aside. He pressed the back of his hand against my own as he passed—a quick flash of human contact, a sign of something: of complicity, of comfort. And then it was over. My little protest. So futile. So childish. I walked away. I am ashamed that I tried. That I failed.

Every day I went there and handed in a parcel. I played games, sometimes, filling the parcels with leaves, with stones, with seeds. I had no way of knowing what you needed, Mathilde, no way of knowing what your days were like in that place. And yet every day I came and stood in the queue and passed over a parcel and was made to wait while the guard scanned the book for your name. I tried not to shuffle and fidget while they searched. I tried not to hold my breath as they ran their fingers down the page. Was it better, in that place, to be alive? Or better that your name be scratched out? Every day, when they found your name in that long list, when they made the mark beside it that indicated you had been left a parcel and that it should be taken to you eventually, wherever you sat in that labyrinth of rooms, I let out my breath and turned away. I wheeled my bicycle along the path, out into the street. I rode happily through the streets towards home, feeling lighter, feeling bitter gratitude to think—foolishly, hopefully—that you were, that you *are*, still there. I was selfish, Mathilde; I wanted you to live (D26:ff189).

Chapter Five: The Release

Mathilde was held in the Haven for just over 22 years, a prisoner of the Obanite Order, under the rule of the Consort Mateo. Every week, for 20 of those years, she was interrogated for several hours by the Penitent clerk who was designated her 'Assistant'. For the first five and a half years her Assistant was the Obanite Penitent Bonnard, under whose hand at least 200 souls were Assisted into death. For the latter 17 years of her time in the institution, Mathilde's Assistant was a woman by the name of Kamila. Each week, on a Wednesday afternoon, Mathilde was brought to Kamila's rooms. She was given a physical: her weight, height, blood pressure, and pulse were recorded. Her blood was tested, as were her strength and reflexes. She was often given vitamin supplements, usually by injection. And, though her menstrual flow ceased after the second year, and she was kept in almost complete isolation, she was tested for pregnancy and syphilis. After the physical examination she was dressed in a clean robe and taken into Kamila's office. Each interview took place over at least four hours. Records were kept by the Assistants, but they are sketchy at best. Kamila's workbook, for example, records the following details for one day of Assistance:

Client: GU412 [*ed: Geralda Ulrick*]
   Interview GU412.98: Four hours in west wing. Client non-compliant. Applied test of Piety. Unreliable confession of Oikos coven location and of heretics Heloise Errata and Abel Errata: to be cross-checked against interview AR326.32.

Client: MS843 [*ed: Mathilde Salt*]

Interview MS843:345: Six hours in west wing. Client's speech incoherent after test of Honesty applied. No new information (File 298 of Penitent Kamila. FN298.334).

Each client was given an identifying number: Mathilde was identified, during her time there, as client MS843. Each interview with a client was then numbered—so the record above is of Mathilde's 345th interview. Various tests were applied to each client by the Assistants, in a cycle of 'Support' designed to elicit information regarding the Oikos heresy. The test of Honesty involved the client being forced into a kneeling position on the floor. Their thighs were bound to their ankles and their wrists tied behind their backs. The client was then tested by the application of a heated set of tongs, which were applied, in turn, to the tongue, the base of the throat and the soles of the feet. Between each application of the tongs by a young Penitent—often an Assistant in training—the client's wound were bathed with cool water and their head was held by the Assistant, who might speak words of comfort to their client, or gently stroke their temples with a sweetly-scented, damp cloth. Assistants were encouraged to 'weep tears of empathy for the Oikos, who knows no better than to hold sacred the horrors of the flesh. Offer them the pleasures of the Penitent heart, the Penitent deathlessness, which knows no pain, which cannot know Death, if the heretic will honestly and with passion and a clear voice renounce the horrors of the flesh that so betrays them into pain, and speak truly and with common wisdom of their True and Honest understanding of the Fourfold Rupettan Law' (Herault, 1893: 245).

On September 10, 1936, Mathilde was released. Nothing in the record of her interviews, or any other official record of Mathilde's incarceration, gives an indication as to why her release was made on this day. She had not revealed any new information in her interviews for the 12 years preceding this date, and so was not considered 'Cured' of her heresy: a candidate for release. Four others, however, all women of a similar age, were released from the same institution on this date. Records for the institution indicate ten new heretics were to be Assisted by Kamila from the end of September. Until now, this has been offered as the reason for Mathilde's release; that she and four others were released to make room for more recently-arrested heretics.

As usual with both internments and releases, nobody was notified that Mathilde had been released. The things she had been wearing at the time of her arrest were returned to her, including her hair and the teeth she had since lost, and she was let out at the main gate. There are no records of where she went, or of what became of her. Official History records indicate she disappeared, as released heretics often did. Suicide, by drowning, was a common enough end to a heretic's first day of release. Three of the others released on the same day as Mathilde were found drowned within a week of their release. One left a note citing her inability to live alone, without the 'succour, comfort, and life-preserving cruelty' of her Assistant, Kamila (Intaft, 1988: 125).

According to Emmeline's diary for the day of Mathilde's release, she arrived at the Haven at around 10:00am for her usual visit, with a satchel of goods for Mathilde, and queued with the other visitors. When she reached the guard's window she was told Mathilde was no longer held there. Emmeline tried to force the guard to take her parcel, beating at the small door through which parcels were passed until the glass broke. A guard came out and walked with her to the main gate, asking her not to return to the premises as Mathilde was 'no longer in their care' (D48:ff567).

Until recently, it was assumed Mathilde never returned to Salt Lane. Indeed, Emmeline's journals during the eleven years after Mathilde's release are filled with indications they were never together again. Entries such as the following, written five years after Mathilde's release, are typical:

> She walked out, into the darkness and comfort of someone
> else's garden, and never returned. Time continued to flow, seeds
> to grow, trees to turn their long, leaved arms to the sun. I never
> saw her again, not in my waking life. Somewhere, some when,
> however, she is always in my dreams. She is always in a garden,

her hands in the soil, her old hat, with its too-wide brim, tipping forward over her face. She is always bent on growth and change. There is always soil beneath her nails, staining the knees of her pants. There is always a child kneeling beside her, bright with promise, plump with questions, chattering away while she works silently, patiently, along the row. They are planting seeds in even-keeled rows, moving along, troweling the soil into the grooved earth as they pass. At the end of the row she stands and turns towards me. I can almost see her face. Almost. Oh, almost. I can almost smell her sun-warmed skin. Beneath the shadow of her hat her eyes seek me out here, at the other side of the garden. She presses one hand to the small of her back and raises the other in a greeting (D49:ff354-5).

During my research, however, I uncovered evidence of another truth—and of a secret the Salt Lane women kept from the Penitents, and perhaps even from their Oikos friends, for their entire lives. During explorations at the Salt Lane site, I discovered a treehouse. Access is by means of a rope ladder, which cannot easily be seen from the ground. The platforms of the building are screened by foliage from surrounding trees and cannot be seen from the ground. This site, though much degraded by the years, was clearly once a residence of some kind. It includes two platforms, at different levels, joined by a steep set of stairs. The higher level is a sleeping area with accommodation for two or three people—one or two adults, and one child. The lower level has a living area, which contains the remains of a table, desk, and chairs. It also houses storage facilities, including cupboards and shelves built in curves around the trunk of the tree. Most of these storage spaces were empty when I discovered them—though there were some remnants of the people who had once lived there: eating utensils; a child's picture book; a broken coffee cup and a pottery bowl with a sea-themed design painted on it.

During my fourth visit to the Salt Lane treehouse I uncovered a hidden storage area; a kind of false floor between the living area and the sleeping area above. The space contained three jars of seeds, label-led in Mathilde's distinctive hand, a leather necklace thong with a silver medallion[6], and a journal—only partially filled—with entries that cover a period of approximately one month following Mathilde's release. The first entry, for September 11, 1936, is as follows:

I was released on Wednesday—yesterday—and showed up at the house with my charge. I had no sense of what to expect. I had a month to prepare; a month to learn the measure of my duty, a month in which to live my own life before I had to leave again, to travel north and disappear. As I approached the house I heard laughter—Emmeline's laughter: such a shock after so long that it knocked me to my knees. I sat on the back step, listening to her move inside the house as though the rooms were just rooms. As though our home were just a house. She did not laugh again but I heard tea being poured, heard her tell one of the old stories, heard unfamiliar voices speaking with her, child-ren softening into sleep, footsteps on the stairs. The same creak in the third board as they crossed the landing. Everything was different. Everything was the same.

The trees made me weep: they had grown so old and tall and strange. The spotted gum I had loved so well had fallen, the Bloodwood I had watched from our bedroom window still twir-led its arms in the air, but its limbs were heavier, longer. I did not know who I was or why I was here. I waited for someone to come out and recognise me, but nobody came. Perdita put her hand on my knee and we watched the moon slowly rise and swell.

The day before my release the Wynder—not the false Wynder, but the true one: Judit—had come to my rooms with the child, Perdita. In dealing with Kamila she had pretended to be a visitor—a stranger with money to pay the usual fee to see a

---

[6] See Illustration 10

Heretic. This was not common or uncommon—it happened, occasionally, that ladies of leisure would come to see the Fallen and the Heretics; to see the Freakshow Horrors of their times and recoil in genteel distress. In this guise, she had spoken to Kamila, claimed she wished to show her daughter the cost—in liberty and madness—of heresy. The child was a tiny thing, seeming no more than five years old, but quiet and composed in a way I had never seen before. When Kamila left my cell, the child sat beside the Wynder with her hands folded in her lap while we spoke. In truth, I did not say much. The Wynder quickly dispensed with the lie she had told Kamila, and bid the child open her heart and show me what she was. When I had recovered my dignity, the Wynder leaned close, took my hands in her own, and told me she had come to offer me freedom. If I chose it I was to be released. I was to take this child—Perdita—into my care and protection. I was to go somewhere nobody would find us: I would be taken into the wilderness. The Wynder would travel with us, would show me the means of living in the place, of caring for the child, and then leave us. Perdita and I would live alone until such time as Rupetta came for us. Perdita was, I was told, a special child. Rupetta's child. A miracle and a heresy whose whereabouts were to be kept secret.

Alone, I said.

The Wynder nodded and looked into her lap. *You may go home for a month; we have built a place for you and the child to live—near Emmeline—for a time.*

Not true freedom, then, I said.

The Wynder shook her head. *We cannot risk it,* she said.

And so I had been released. And had come home.

As I walked in the garden Perdita waited. When I returned to the back step she bid me take the bird out of my pocket and hold it on my hand. She stroked its beak and it sang—a strange song, but true and clear. Inside the house silence fell, and then I heard her come to the door, saw her shadow outlined against the light. My throat was dry. I could not weep. I had grown so old. So old. I had never been a beauty, but now I was a woman marked by the tests of Piety, Honesty, Fortitude, Fealty and Love. Emmeline opened the door. She came down the stairs into the garden and stood before me. She took my face in her hands and smiled. We are old women, marked by time and grief, but she kissed me, then, as though we were still young.

She does not know I will leave again, so soon. I should not have come home (D54:ff1-3).

Later entries in the diary indicate that Mathilde stayed at Salt Lane for just under a month, though she and Perdita lived in the treehouse in order to conceal their presence. The Wynder visited them there and trained Mathilde to care for Perdita. The details of the child's care included instructions on the maintenance of each of her systems: nervous, circulatory, harmonic, skeletal and mnemonic. Descriptions of the child's nervous, circulatory and harmonic systems, in particular, indicate the child is both Organic and Mechanical. Her skeletal system is formed of both bone and copper, and grows in an ambient, Organic manner, though it grows slowly. Even the Wynder was unsure about the child's physical and intellectual potential.

The folios 98-104 are the most intriguing, relating as they do to the child's birth and parentage. Mathilde writes that, according to the Wynder, the child is anemophilous—that is, wind-fertilised—and that she is the child of Rupetta.

Mathilde writes:

Another day of miracles and lessons that seem the stuff of fairytales rather than reality. Today, Judit instructed me on the history of Perdita, reading from a document Rupetta herself recorded, and which they carried here, stored inside the child Perdita. I have listened to it several times now, and am each time alarmed, amazed, distressed, disbelieving, appalled and awed. Is this truth, then? And if it is, what does it mean? According to

Rupetta the child was conceived within Rupetta, delivered in the form of a seed, nurtured in the earth and born in the river. She is the child of 'the wind, the ocean, the flame and the earth'. Rupetta records that, prior to the production and planting of the Perditan seed, she had spent a period of time alone, and in silence, and that in that time her body was visited by each of the elements: fire, air, water, earth, and that out of these—and out of herself—the seed was made. The Annal does not indicate a time period for the conception, planting, gestation or delivery, but I have learned enough now not to judge Perdita's age by her form. She has been raised in the company of women, like me, whose lives were given over to her care, maintenance and tutelage. She has been trained to speak of these guardians as though they are one woman, with one name—the name I, too, must adopt when we leave this place. She has been kept in virtual isolation with these women, and often in silence—in various monasteries, hermitages and libraries—throughout her entire life. She has been trained to keep the secret of herself, to guard her strangeness, and her seeming immortality, as her life. I listen carefully, speak only a little, pay attention to the silences and omissions in the tales she and Judit and the Rupettan record tell. Occasionally, some evidence enters Perdita's speech of the guardians' differences, their individual times and lives. She is careful and ancient, but she is still a child, with a child's incapacity for true deceit. From these gaps and silences and small betrayals I have garnered enough evidence, I believe, to indicate she was born at the end of the hundred years of silence. From all I have learned from Judit and the Rupettan Annal of the true Rupettan history, rather than the false narrative composed and distributed by the Consorts and Alazaïns since the time of Eloise IX, it is perhaps this time alone that would account for Perdita's gestation and birth—a time of solitude, silence, almost-death, a time outside of time, or, at least, a time outside of history.

It is only my surmise, and I am new to the vagaries of Rupettan time, to the mystery of time lost and time saved, of a child
who was never born and a future that is as uncertain as the past
out of which it arises (D54:ff103-5).

From this and other evidence contained within the record, it appears
Perdita is, then, the heretofore undisclosed eighth miracle; perhaps the
only heresy Mathilde was a part of—a union of the Organic elements
of the Natural World and the Mechanical elements of Rupettan Life. It
also appears Mathilde was released from her incarceration under the
aegis of a large bribe, paid by the Consort Judit to the Penitent Kamila,
and that after her release Mathilde travelled north, with the child
Perdita, to act as her guardian. It is unclear from the diaries and records
I have located whether Emmeline knew all of this, or some of it, or
none. It appears to me now, as I read the entries in Emmeline's journals
for the years between Mathilde's release and Emmeline's death—
suicide by drowning, in 1947—that she did know at least some of what
I have since re-discovered. I have no hard evidence to support this
claim; it is merely a Historian's intuition. Emmeline's diaries record
her loss; it is true, but also her peacefulness, her sudden equanimity in
the face of that loss. It is as if she knew that Mathilde had not
abandoned her, had not disappeared, but had passed into History, was
doing good work and was safe, well cared for and, perhaps, content. I
have come to believe, also, that Emmeline received, occasionally, word
of Mathilde. Again, there is no concrete evidence for this contact
except that every three months, almost exactly, Emmeline writes of
Mathilde in her journal. These entries are similar in tone to those of
the entry cited earlier, in which Mathilde is gardening with a child, and
each is specific and seasonal. Selected out of the journals and read
together, sequentially, they form a schematic and yet cohesive narrative of ten years in a northern climate—in a small stone cottage, in a
quite isolated location—mountainous and cold, on the shores of a lake
that is frozen over for the better part of each year—and of the life of a
woman and a child, each of whom grow and change as the years pass,

though the woman ages far more quickly than the child. This is slim evidence, and yet it is compelling. The Mathilde that Emmeline draws in these entries grows older, thicker, sickens and regains her health, she breaks her arm while walking on the ice one winter, and afterwards suffers arthritis most particularly in that once-broken joint. She fears dementia as she ages, and increasingly longs for home. The child, however, is always a child, though one of a particular and odd nature. She is composed and often silent, self-contained and physically adept. She fishes, plays chess, climbs mountains and plants trees, always assuming she will see them grow into old age while her guardian—Mathilde—will fade into a shade: as light and cool and insubstantial as falling snow.

The Search for Perdita
The City of Bridges: Present Day

Somewhere, Henri, at some moment in this vast catalogue of disordered time, I am always travelling towards you, travelling day and night to lie down beneath a glass roof and look up at the stars from within the circle of your arms. At night, while you sleep, my footsteps echo down the corridors of the world, along the paths that lead to you. I hesitate at crossroads; lift my head to hear your name carrying on the wind, like the scent of a forgotten season.

Behind every door you do not open my hand is resting, my heart beats.

Margause and I find a room outside the city. She borrows two second-hand bicycles from the landlord so we can travel back and forth to town. She brings back newssheets and gossip, spare parts and second-hand clothes. Traveller's boots, traveller's clothes: loose pants, warm capes that can double as blankets. Groundsheets we roll into tight cylinders and strap to the bases of our backpacks. Dried meat and fruit tied into waxed paper packages. While she scours the city for supplies, trying to procure everything we will need while passing unremarked through the markets, I work, stripping back my frame to its essentials.

I become leaner and slimmer. I dismantle the hoops of my skirts; refashion my chest, my face. There is something of you, Henri, in the new cast of my eyes, in my new arm, with its unpatterned surface. There is something of Luon in the smooth swoop of my chest, in my flat hips and loose, woodsman's walk. There is something of Giacomo in the squareness of my new hands, in the worn knuckles of my fists. My hair is short, dark, cropped close to my head: a mat of tight curls.

My new skin is a warmer, slightly darker shade—the warmth of polished jarrah. Removing my skirts, which for so long hid the clumsy, wide wheels of my hips and knees. I made slim legs for myself years ago, but the old habit of belled skirts has stayed with me until now. I have become taller. It is most of two days' work to fashion more sturdy knees, longer, thicker thighs and narrower hips with tensely-coiled joints. I stand a half-head higher than Margause. I can walk more easily, more naturally. I am taller, but my centre of gravity seems lower, more sturdy and certain.

I am a man with a crinkled smile, the open, easy grace of a farmer or a traveller. I am a stranger, even to myself.

Margause studies me in the fading light: walks around me, touches the skin of my back, the scoop between my shoulderblades, the curve of my cheek, the flat of my belly. The door of my heart. She asks me to walk across the room. I turn and face her. She is smaller, frailer than I remember.

She nods and picks up the bags she has bought for us: one each of old leather, already well-worn. Mine has been broken and repaired: mismatched buckles fasten over the pocket on its front. She picks up the last of our supplies from the table and tucks them into the bags: water bottles and maps. We will take only as much as we can carry, no matter how far we travel. We will be strangers to everyone, even ourselves. Nothing we carry ties us to home. If we are caught on the road, if our packs are taken, if our bodies are broken, there will be nothing to indicate we are anything more than lost souls, itinerant workers travelling from place to place in search of a bed and a meal: a day of work, an hour of pleasure. There will be nothing to lead them back to you.

Margause hoists her pack onto her back and watches as I lift mine; the straps settling against the new contours of my shoulders. It is late afternoon on the second day, time for us to leave again. I press my hat onto my head.

'What is your name?' she asks.

'Volta,' I say.

ళు

Late in the evening the river is flat and dark. We ride our bicycles along the riverside path, past the College buildings where music flits in and out of the open windows, until we reach the boatsheds. The wharves are old, the wooden slats and posts worn smooth with age. Kapil—our old friend, the Fallen Penitent—is sitting on the end of one of the wharves, watching the water beneath his bare feet. His pants are rolled up, as if he has been wading in the shallows. There is a small pack at his side, which he drops into the boat as we approach. It is a slim craft, with cradles for oars and graceful, curved sides. Over its pointed prow are slung two slim ropes.

Kapil climbs down into the boat and turns, reaching up to offer Margause a hand. It is only then, looking up from the boat as I bend over the lip of the jetty, that he sees how much I have changed. He peers behind me, takes back his hand and speaks to Margause. 'Where is the girl?' he says.

'This is Volta,' Margause says, easing herself down the ladder without his help, stowing her bag under the plank seats.

Kapil hesitates. Squints up at me in the half-light. 'It is you,' he says, and smiles. 'You have changed a lot since I last saw you in the caves.'

'I have become more like you,' I say, lowering my pack into Margause's hands, slipping the shirt from my chest and tying it at my waist. 'But I am not like you. I am still made, and not born.'

I turn and descend the stairs, sit on one of the plank seats and take the key from Margause's outstretched hand. I unlock the chamber and show him my heart. He peers inside me, sees the tubes, blackened with age, the thumping of my heart in its worn cradle.

ళు

It is so very unlikely, life. Such a strange, flawed miracle of chance and circumstance, of cells and sinews and viruses and carbons flowing into and out of each other. Each insect, each blade of grass, is more complex than any machine any of us can make or imagine. Each stone and tree and child is so strange, so appallingly unique, that it is, perhaps, hard to believe they can end.

Until you have seen them end, as I have, again and again.

Our fourth day in the desert. One of the camels breaks down and we stop, in the middle of a wide expanse of sand, stone and stunted shrubbery, wilfully growing in the almost-desolate terrain. Within an hour Kapil and I have helped our guides put up our five tents. They are low-ceilinged affairs within which we can sit and crawl, but cannot stand. Four of our camels are settled in a circle around us, facing towards the desert like sentinels, though their eyes are dark and sight-less. The fifth is folded down inside a tent, awaiting repairs, while our guides kneel at the outer edges of our camp, watching the sun set over the edge of the extinct volcanic calderas that surround us. The stony mountains of granite and sand—gold and yellow and autumnal brown in the day—turn blue as the light fades. We can no longer see the ribbons that winnow out from their tips in the wind, nor feel their heated, sandy breath blowing at our backs. As night settles, as the guides bury stone-winged beetles in the sand to protect us from harm, the temperature drops and the sky—burned white during the day—darkens to a blue that is as nearly-black as the ocean.

Margause and two of the guides unlock the hump of the copper camel, a brightly-polished surface carved with the face of the east wind: cumulus clouds and a beetle-swarm swirling down across its spine. Together they lift out from its vaulted interior a small stove and a bag of black rice, a box of spices and another of dried vegetables and fruits. Together, with much laughter and whirling chatter, they spread a felted rug in the centre of the camp, throw out pockets of cushions and short-legged wooden tables to work at, and begin the nightly ritual of singing up the meal. Each cook has a tune to sing, each spice a note.

Warming the oil in the steep-sided pan is a low hum of bass, slicing the dried purple onion grass is a bare, thready hum in an old man's throat, pouring in the rice is a patter like rain, the fingertips of the six chefs fluttering against the edges of their tables as Margause stands at their centre and pours the rice, in an inward-turning spiral, into the pan.

Meanwhile, inside one of the tents, the broken camel's load is first unpacked into the tent, and then it is opened. Four drivers, as well as Kapil and I, lean forward and shine our small torches into its mechanism. Each torch beam is a thin, wavering finger of light, crossing and re-crossing the encaved darkness in an almost reverential hush. The camel's driver sits at the door of the tent, holding open the thick flap to let in the moon's light. He has his back turned to us; like his fellow drivers, he has never seen the inside of his own mount.

'Here is the problem,' says one of the drivers, the one whose mount I ride. He points towards the back wall of the camel's innards. We each turn our lights upon the spot, like seven pale blades, and see the brightness of a broken pipe: its sharp edge glittering. Another guide reaches in with a long stick, on the end of which he has tied a damp swab of cotton. When he taps the end of the pipe with his instrument it sizzles. The guides mumble and nod, easing back onto their heels. 'Not too bad a wound,' says one of the guides, and I see the outward-looking driver's shoulders shift, settle. He lifts his head to the blue sky, to the bone-white moon. The young boy who sits at the camel's head strokes its forelock with a cloth, leaning forward to whisper comfort into its mouth.

A driver leans forward again; leather gloves on his hands, and reaches into the camel's innards. Gently, he fingers the broken pipe, pinches it closed. Another pair of hands appears to clip off the ruptured pipe—split and blackened with wear. Each driver cuts off a scrap of cotton from his gown and wraps it around the small piece until it is swathed in the shade of each of the camels that wait outside: copper, green, white, and grey. The bundle is handed to the driver at the tents' opening. Later, he will bury it in the sand at the centre of the camp, beneath the spot where the cooks now dance in a whirl of flame and spice. The camel's driver ties the flap closed and we pinch out our lights. The shadows of the dancers flash like smoky ghosts on the walls of the tent to our right, near the centre of our camp. To our left there is darkness and cold: the black wall of the desert. The men work quickly, without speaking, as if they have no need for words. In the half-darkness I see them pass instruments along the line, lean forward in turn. A hand takes mine and turns it palm upwards, writes a sigil in my palm. Their finger is cool; I feel the burn of the invisible mark for days afterwards. Finally, the job is done.

Outside, the camp is quiet; we hear bowls being set down on the wooden tables. Smell the spice and starch and heat of the meal being set out for us to share. Beside me I hear a woman's voice. A single, whispered word I do not know. And then silence. We sit and wait. The desert's darkness breathes into the tent, through its walls, bringing with it the scent of loneliness. I smell the silent, fearful tears of the camel's driver soaking into the felted walls of the tent. Finally, finally, the camel replies. A sharp, feculent note. I see white teeth in the darkness; a series of smiles, brighter than the torches, and the tent-flap is thrown open.

The young boy goes out first, crawling over our laps to reach the entrance. He pokes his head through the flap and disappears. Too quickly, as if dragged out into the light by someone tall and rough and strong. The camel's driver, still smiling, holds open the door flap to peer out at the camp, to see what the boy is playing at, and only then do we see the spilled food, the drawn faces of our guides and cooks standing with blades against their throats, the young boy sprawled across our entrance, his blood fresh on the blade of the Penitent who stands to greet us, mirroring the driver's smile with one of his own.

I scan the small, temporary courtyard and see Margause, held in the arms of a Penitent as if he is about to dance with her, spinning her out across the rice-spattered rugs. There is blood on her cheek, but she stands tall. A body lies sprawled near her feet; another slumped across one of the tables, as though sleeping. Two of the tents have been flattened, opening up a space within which the Penitent mounts stand:

294

sharp-fingered, dark and smooth-skinned, their eyes gleaming like wet rocks.

Behind me, I feel a breeze, and Kapil's hand against my shoulder, pulling me backwards. I look for Margause again; see her face turned towards the north, away from me, as each of the captives is bound together on a long rope. Two of the drivers in our tent signal their intention to stay behind; the others roll beneath the hem of the tent after Kapil and me. We raise the camels—the white and the green—by speaking their names, unearth the beetles that are their, and not our, guardians.

I turn back twice. The first time I turn I see the tents burning fast and hot and bright; see the thin caravan of Penitents moving away from our camp, their mounts stepping lightly on the massif, their lights swinging prettily in the darkness. When I turn back again they have moved in staggered formation up the side of a mountain; a ragged, migrating arrowhead of dark mounts heading southeast with their captives: a string of stumbling, broken ornaments, following in their wake.

§

We approach Nepholi, the city of bridges, late in the afternoon on the last official day of the dry season. Rain looms over the mountains in a mass of dark clouds and our mounts—heavy with produce and other trade goods—sway heavily, as though the unfamiliar humidity slows their blood, making their joints, as well as ours, swell and ache. Our guide leads us along a ridge, where the dry scrabble of stones replaces loose dirt, forming a road as seasonal and irregular as the path of a dry river. We wind upwards towards the city, its pale stone walls and rounded rooftops seeming part of the sand-coloured mountain out of which it rises.

With the rainy season come floods and the end of wandering for the tribes, so our arrival at the city is concealed in a tide of others, flowing upwards towards the city in an increasingly rich and unruly tributary. Tribes of herders, philosophers, traders, and storytellers, sages and assassins, converge on the city of bridges, one of the great wonders of the modern world. As we approach the city we fall in with another small band—a family who have come here, each year, for sixty generations. The old matriarch walks beside us, her gait steady and strong, herding the children as though they are goats. Sixty generations, she tells us, of foolish adherence to tradition. She would rather travel north, to Europe, to China, to the wide steppes on which her own family once spent their summers, swimming in the rivers, drinking horse milk and harvesting wild wheat. But no, her husband's family are descendants of the wandering Architects, and must return, year after year, to reclaim their ancient citizenship, to revisit their foolish heritage.

'Who are the Architects?' I ask.

'Listen,' she tells me, drawing a child up onto her shoulders, hooking another closer with the tap of her walking stick. 'I will tell you. Once the city was not a city but a single house—an outpost in which the younger daughter of a sprawling empire had been exiled with her husband, children, companions and servants. It was comfortable enough, this exile, except that each year the palace flooded, and the residents were forced to load their possessions into boats. The princess's servants and family were not, however, great boatbuilders. Being desert people, despite their long exile in the flooded valleys, they had never learned to build boats.' The old woman laughed and winked at Kapil. 'The first year all the boats were made of stone, and sank as soon as the rains came, swallowed up in the first flush of mud and silt. The second year they were made of rammed earth, and some of those lasted a day, maybe two, before they dissolved. The third year they made boats out of their beds, tied together, and some of those floated, though their linens were damp as old towels and the princess and her family and servants and goats dreamt unpleasant dreams of fish, swimming in their mouths. The boats rose on the floodwaters, higher and higher each day, until they were moored to the rooftops.

'Each year, when the floods receded, things were not much better than they had been when they were afloat: the palace's rooms would be buried in sand, awash with fish and weeds and shells and the bones of drowned whales. Each year they would have to rebuild. Worse still—those foolish exiles—each year they lost livestock and precious goods, seeds and stories, children and husbands, in the rising water. They were drowned, of course, or floated off. Some of the husbands may have deliberately unmoored themselves, perhaps even some of the goats. Finally, one summer after the princess lost two daughters, a goat, and six boxes of seeds in the floods, she sent out a promise that whoever could devise a home that would survive the floods—a way to stay in the valley of her exile without being washed away each year and having to begin again—could live in the palace with her. Would become a citizen of her exile.

'Many tried and failed. One man—a scientist, and a well-respected fool—proposed that the princess and her household become mermaids. He drew complicated tables, arranged marriages with the great house of the Eluin narwhals, showing that within three generations, perhaps four, the princess and her family might be like the salamander: a creature of two elements. Another fool proposed they become angels, bodiless and weightless, and live out their exile in the clouds.

'And then the Architects came. There were six of them—four men and two women. They designed a walled city, within which there would be a system of gates, levees, conduits and pontoons. Each pontoon would rise on the floodwaters and float when the rains came. The pontoons would become interconnected continents on a temporary sea, tethered to the submerged city's walls. And so it was done, as the great fools designed. Each summer the city of Nepholi rises above the circle of its stony anchor, and each spring, when the waters subside, the pontoons are ravelled back into the city, and moored on the desert floor.

'But, there is more. When the city of Nepholi was built the six Architects became its first citizens. Three of the Architects stayed there happily throughout the year, breeding goats, telling stories. They opened stores or sowed seeds or did whatever it is the still people do. Drank wine and married. Told tall tales to while away the time. The other three Architects had been wanderers before they came to Nepholi. After a year of life in one place—although it was a city that rose and fell it never wandered very far—their feet itched and their eyes could not cease from seeking out horizons when they spoke. After five years the wandering Architects and their descendants began to ramble in their sleep, up and down the city's bridges, making them creak in the night and keeping the princess and her children awake. Finding the edges of the city, the great stone walls, the wanderer Architects would often pace in great circles, forming troughs as deep as they were tall. Today, you can still see the moat their rambling made, a great empty river just inside the city walls. Their neighbours, desperate for a peaceful nights' sleep, tethered the wandering Architects to their beds, but during the nights the wanderers always managed to work their way free, or, if they were strong enough, they wandered despite their burdens, their poor restless beds dragging in their wakes. After ten years of containment within the city's walls the wanderer Architects' souls began to leave their bodies behind, impatient with the Architects' foolish immobility. The souls wandered the world, seeking adventure and change and movement. They returned only when the rains came. During the dry months, the Architects' empty bodies cluttered the streets and parks and other public places, eating air, breathing sand, taking up valuable space and contributing nothing to the upkeep of the city. They did not even tell stories, though they sighed, often and loudly. Finally, the princess called a meeting. *A citizen*, she proclaimed, *does not always live within a city's walls, nor in its fields, nor even in the vast sands that flow out from its edges. A citizen is a person who carries the image of a city in her heart, and returns to it when the city has need of her, or when she has need of it. A citizen's heart is filled with longing for its home, but its home is within the citizen, as well as within the city's walls. A True Citizen is free to wander and return for her heart is tethered to her home. Go,'* she said, *'wander with your souls. The city will always be yours, and you will always belong to it.'* And so, my foolish husband's great ancestor took up his body, or was taken up by it, and walked out into the great desert. For a thousand years and more his family have wandered and returned, wandered and returned, and slept content both within the city and in strange places, far from here, knowing they are citizens within whom the city's waters eternally flow.'

The old woman's story has taken us to the edge of the camps that surround the city: a sprawling city of tents and mounts and people. We thank her for the story, paying her in salt and dried fruit. Our guides smile and pat the children's heads before they leave. The children look into their ears to see if their souls have wandered home. The Ramoccan's ancestors, too, were wanderers.

There is some daylight left, and though we are certain we will not gain entrance to the city tonight we need to establish our place in the queue by making conversation with those ahead of and behind us. We join a long, unruly column of new arrivals at the northern gate, which is the closest entrance to the pontoon of the Ramocca, and wait, moving forward a few inches each hour, making conversation, sharing stories and cool glasses of tea.

A handful of women, dressed in white, are scattered through the crowd. Their heads are shorn, their teeth blackened, to commemorate the Miracle of Silence. The season of rain is also the season of silence —it is winter, in the northern continent, and summer at home: the season of floods and damp. The halls of Elm College are no doubt swollen with rot and mould. The glass rattling beneath the onslaught of rain while you lie, watching it fall, perhaps wondering if we, like the wanderers, will ever return.

After two hours of conversation we leave the long queue, certain of our place in its complex, negotiated hierarchy, and approach the camp of the Ramocca. Wandering through the temporary streets I see a woman with her lips sewn shut, the scars of past years' observances visible beneath the stitched wounds of the present. She walks among the long lines of camels and hippogriffs, dragons and horses, stretching out her palm to receive offerings, exchanging them for paper blessings folded in the shapes of apple-blossoms, snowflakes and mice. People take the blessings awkwardly, refusing to look into her face, at her wounded mouth. A young man bends his head and allows her to fix a blossom in the thick, dark curls at his temple. Children peer at her curiously as she walks past on her bare, blue-soled feet. One young child begins to cry when he sees her. 'Who did that to her?' he asks his mother, as though he has just discovered cruelty. She pulls him close and smooths his hair as she shushes him. 'Nobody,' she says.

People lean down from their piled mounds of goods to touch her shorn head, to take the small, shabby blessings from her hands in memory of my years of stillness. The children follow her, walking in the fading stain of her blue footprints. How strange they seem now, these rituals that sacralise and transform the past, that make a public spectacle of what was, at the time, an ordinary and private grief.

The camp of the Ramocca is small: a round of low tents. Our guides usher us into the circle, settle the mounts. The evening song rises—in another camp on the other side of the road—and voices closer by lift to meet it. We are greeted by a young man—the Ramoccan leader, so far as they have one—who nods and waves his hand at us, bidding us to sit, but not speak, as he listens. The evening song is brief, gentling the heat of the day, urging the clouds to open. The man closes his eyes, tilts his head. He does not smile. When the song ends I notice the stillness that has fallen beneath it. The ground is warm, the stars are sparse, I can make out the high, square shadow of the city's walls, the tents, the gates, the guards. People settle in their temporary camps, shut off their mounts, light their fires. The road to the northern gate empties of traffic as a man pulls down the shutter of his gatehouse, turns out the light inside it and locks the door. He stands outside his small cubicle for a moment, surveying the crowds gathered in a ragged circle around the city before sighing, lifting his linen bag over his head and turning in through the gate, waving goodnight to the guards.

On the warm, heavy breeze I smell spices and onions tossed in melted butter, and the rich, dark scent of cooking meat, swelling and thickening to meet the high-pitched hum of insects. The sand beneath our feet cools and night comes in, scattering unfamiliar stars across the enormous flat expanse of the sky. We are eating our meal when we hear the first hum of unexpected excitement. Not a particular word or sound, but a rising, inconstant murmur from the other side of the camp. We stand and look out over the roofs of our tents. All around us, others are doing the same. The men pull their children in closer to the fires, or push them into the tents, sensing trouble, while the women step out into the makeshift streets and peer towards the north-eastern gate, where a light is growing, bending up into the sky to form a pale dome, while a crowd thickens at its edge.

I look towards our guide, seated on the ground eating his meal. All around our small circle the Ramoccans' eyes watch him, affecting disinterest. One of our guides has his hand on his waist, fingers curling around the hilt of his weapon, though it is a casual grip, as if he is only barely aware that it is a weapon in his hand. Two of the women are already bending and rolling up the carpets, kicking sand over the fire, storing the still-warm pots inside the mounts. Kapil steps out onto the path, grabs the arm of a young girl running away from the light, towards her own camp, clearly conveying the urgent news of what it is—that light, that fervent buzz of voices. 'What is happening?' he says, nodding over his shoulder towards the light, the crowd.

'A miracle,' she says.

Kapil hesitates, smiling down at her. 'Is it the rain? Has the season come early?'

The girl shakes her head and pulls her arm from his grasp, already turning away, darting barefoot between the crowds towards her own camp. 'Rupetta,' she cries out, her voice tumbling backwards through the crowd. 'She's going to appear at the gate.'

A bicycle passes between us, light flickering in its spokes, the long unbound hair of its rider blowing like a veil. I step out between the tents, and stand beside him. The path is already crowded with people moving towards the gate. Kapil eyes the guards, who, having locked the northern gates, are moving away from their posts, following the crowd. 'We could go into the city,' he says. 'Take advantage of the distraction.'

We are already walking towards the north-eastern gate. I smile and shake my head. 'I have never seen myself,' I say.

A woman rushes into the path in front of us without looking where she is going, a small child in her arms, pushing me into Kapil. We falter and he almost falls before I catch and steady him. The woman looks up and smiles, a gap-toothed smile.

Our Ramoccan guide joins us. His leader beside him. 'We will walk with you,' he says. 'As far as the gate. That was our promise.'

Kapil nods and we walk on, moving with the crowd, becoming part of its smiling, humming anticipation. Bracelets of pink and orange light circle the arms of the children. Almost immediately, it seems, the camp-city is awash with these cheap children's lights, bobbing on the ends of mounts, on people's umbrellas and bicycles, strung on their belts and circling their brows. The camp looks, suddenly, like the site of a festival. A man stands at the side of the path with his mount's sides opened to form a makeshift stall, selling the light bracelets. Another is selling boxes with mirrors in them, for seeing over the heads of the crowd.

When we reach the north-eastern gate we push to the front—not an easy task, but one we manage with silent, determined roughness. Across from us, two of the silent, white-clothed women stand together at the front edge of the semi-circle. They are aglow with expectation, feverish with it, like saints or madwomen. They peer towards the gate, leaning forward on their blue-painted toes while trying to appear calm and patient. One of them has split open two stitches, one at each corner of her mouth, perhaps from smiling.

The gate is half-closed. Before it stand a half-dozen Penitents. Between the Penitents are their stone-eyed mounts, folded on the ground in a loose semi-circle. Behind them, walking side by side, are the Consort and the False Wynder. It is a shock, after so long, to see their faces. Familiar and foreign. His eyes and stance are the same; the same unruly shock of hair, the same too-big mouth resting like a threat beneath his nose. Beside him she seems small and fragile, though I remember well the force of her temper. He must slow his gait to meet hers as they pass ceremoniously along the edge of the crowd. She accepts the flasks of water, the folded paper packets of tea and spices. She smiles and reaches out her left hand, her Wynder's hand, to pat the heads of the small children pushed forward by their parents as though bestowing a blessing.

One child stands at the barrier holding onto a potted plant, its leaves limp and already turning brown. When the Wynder leans to take it from her, the child tucks the pot behind her back. 'Not for you,' she says, looking towards the gate. 'For the other one. The copper lady.'

Beside us, a man snorts. 'As if she's really here,' he says. 'As if she's real.'

'You think they would travel without her?' Kapil says.

The man peers at Kapil, at our guides, at me, weighing each of us with his gaze. 'Believers?' he says.

The Ramoccans look away, watching the Penitents, watching the gate, forty paces away, assessing the distances, the crowd, the shifting gaps through which we might pass. 'You don't believe in Rupetta?' Kapil says.

'What's to believe? She's a woman, or a doll, or a man in the guise of a woman and doll. Whatever she is, she's an illusion. An elaborate, dangerous hoax. Look at them,' he says, gesturing with his chin towards the crowd who jostle and elbow each other to get a better view, who have paid too much for a cheap periscope so they can see something, anything. They lean forward, peer in through the gap in the open gate. When a light passes by behind it a swell of urgency passes through them, like wind passing across a field of wheat. 'It's a circus,' the man says. 'They're only here to see her fall, to see how false she really is. To know for certain she isn't real.'

'Is that why you're here?' I ask him.

The man leans in close, puts his hand on my elbow and whispers. 'I know the truth,' he says, his breath fragrant with cloves. He doesn't let me go, but waits, his breath warming my own. After a moment, his eyes flicker. He has said too much, and to a stranger. He glances towards Kapil, towards the Ramoccans, who stand watchful as the crowd ripples around them. Someone cries out my name, and I turn towards the cry, foolishly, thinking I have been found out.

Nobody is looking at me.

The crowd pinches closed, pushing forward, collapsing in on itself until it is a single, airless body. Kapil puts his arm around me. We surge sideways, crushed and breathless in the muscled, bony mess of strangers. A woman is pressed against my chest. She smiles and nods, her chin thrusting uncomfortably into my shoulder, her breasts squashed flat against my chest. 'Don't worry about the old man,' she says, before being pulled away, 'he's just a crazy old Oikos.' I grasp Kapil's forearm and drag him with me, through the strong tide, forcing our way towards the wall of the city. When we reach our spot—braced against the wall with the gate only metres away, behind a group of six people who have linked arms to keep the crowd behind them from pushing through—I circle my arms around Kapil, holding him from behind so we are, as much as possible, a single cell in this bruising mass.

Alazaïs stands in the open gap of the gate, waiting as the crowd settles into an urgent, swollen hush. Slowly, from the centre outwards, the crowd grows still. The false Wynder and the Consort are standing either side of the gap in the barely-opened gates. Alazaïs takes four stiff steps and turns in a stiff-kneed circle. She is standing at the edge of the circle, half-turned towards the gate. We are behind and to the left of her. I can see her profile, the etched pattern on her face: a swirling tattoo spreads along her jaw to disappear upwards into the sweep of her hair and downwards into the collar of her shirt. The etchings are a fine-lined mirror image of those on the Wynder's face and arms. Alazaïs's shirt is backless, revealing the abstraction of her spine—its flat, unboned plane. The crowd around us jostle to see around her, to see what is happening, as the Consort and the Wynder push the gate open just a little wider. In the backlit gap a young girl appears, standing stiffly, her skirts an old-fashioned bell. She slides forward between them as though she is on a trolley, gaitless. I hold my breath, watching her face with its chalk-white skin, its glass eyes. A mannequin child with Perdita's face, stiffened into lifelessness.

Beside us, as the crowd surges forward to see the child, to eat her image from the light, to be the first to say, to know, what she means, a young girl stumbles and is spat out of the crowd to sprawl in the dust of the open ground. Alazaïs does not move and the child does not stop her slow forward progress until the Wynder steps forward and clasps her shoulders. The Consort looks towards the nearest Penitent, whose mount is already standing, her pearl-black teeth sliding forward in her mouth.

'Please,' the fallen girl says, holding out her blue-stained hands. Only then do I notice her white pants, her white shirt stained with yellow dust. 'I only fell,' she says, moving slowly to her feet, keeping one eye on the mount as it swells and rises. When the mount takes a step forward the girl jolts upright, puts out a hand as if to stop it. The Penitent looks over his shoulder at the Consort, who shakes his head. The stumbling girl's shoulders slump, she places her hands on her thighs and drops her head, closing her eyes for a brief second as though with relief.

She takes a deep breath, opens her eyes, and lunges forward, past the half-folded mount and the Penitent, still turning away, past the open-mouthed Consort and the Wynder, whose pretty face is pinched with uncertainty as she drags the little doll backwards with her, towards the gate and the Consort. The girl in white flashes towards Alazaïs, grasps her about the waist and throat, swings around behind her and faces the crowd, the Penitents, the unfolded stone-eyed mounts whose teeth snicker in the sudden quiet.

'My name is Sparrow,' she calls out, 'I am the Oikos. And this,' she slices downward with her knife, through the layers of Alazaïs's gown. 'This is nothing. This is illusion. This is falsity. This,' she says, 'is death.' Another woman's voice rises in the anonymous heart of the crowd—a full-throated, warlike ululation that is soon joined by another, and another. Alazaïs's dress falls away. One of the mounts starts forward, its long tongue flickering forward like a whip, lashing at Sparrow's arms, leaving long, white wounds that quickly brighten and bleed.

Sparrow looks up, catches my eye in the crowd and smiles as if she knows who I am. She lifts the knife, holds it at the base of Alazaïs's throat and slices upwards, diagonally, through the middle of her face that is so like and unlike mine, then down again. The mounts slink forward. One of them breaks from the pack, darting forward as Sparrow, her hands wet with her own blood, her face rigid with determination, peels back Alazaïs's face, tears open her chest, drives her blade into the mess of decorative cogs and pipes inside her. Alazaïs stands unaffected as her face falls away, as her gown and skin slip from her like veils.

The mounts converge, drawing themselves over Sparrow like a dark blanket.

The crowd inhales, draws back and forward at the same time, turning in on itself. Someone cries out in pain. Someone else in anger. The Consort, the Wynder and the childlike doll are gathered up in the sudden rush of the Penitents' retreat and disappear through the gates, into the city. Somewhere close by a child is crying. Beside us, a man covers his mouth with both his hands, shaking his head and staring as Alazaïs, left alone with the ruin of her body, tips backwards over the swarming mass of mounts, over the occasional flash of Sparrow's flesh. The mounts do not hesitate. They move silently over Sparrow's body, twisting around and through each other's bodies, doing their work. Every now and then the squirm of their mass butts up against the fallen Alazaïs, making her twitch, pushing her closer to the edge of the crowd. Her metal armature scrapes against the rocky soil.

The crowd begins to fray apart at its edges. The Ramoccan guides press us forward, towards the gate. As the mounts come apart, sliding away through the gate, a woman darts forward and kneels over Alazaïs. She puts her hand inside Alazaïs's belly and begins pulling pieces out: a pipe, a wheel, a copper cylinder with two thin green wires protruding from one end. A young boy comes forward and hunkers down across from her, leaning forward on his haunches to wrestle with some part that will not come out so easily. Soon, there is a small crowd picking over Alazaïs's remains, bickering over the prizes of her eyes, her teeth, her toes. Someone finds a fresh bone in the sand, marked with tiny, sharp teeth-marks—Sparrow's little finger, perhaps. A fight breaks out and, as the light fades and the crowd slithers and shifts again, finding a new, urgent form, our guides press us forward.

We enter the city. Not, as we had planned, under the cover of darkness, nor as part of a tribe of wandering Architects returning home, but in a swirling, violent distraction of greed and fear and confusion.

I have seen myself, and I have seen myself undone.

The City of Bridges: Present Day

Inside the walls of Nepholi it is dark, and quiet. Our guides have left us, pointing us towards the Errakean pontoon and letting us know they will wait two days in their temporary camp. Unless the rains come. The Penitents and their charges have disappeared ahead of us, into the city's unfamiliar interior. The walls throw long shadows over the streets, which are not stones laid down on the earth, but spidery constructions of rope and timber. The streets are strung up like bridges. They pass from the thin stone shelf that circles the inside of the walls, across the internal moat, to the unique structures of the pontoons. They criss-cross the gaps between the pontoons, providing a complex system of connections that creak and sway as the pontoons shift on the desert sand. Within each pontoon lies a small, self-contained village: shops and houses, bathhouses, libraries, streets and gardens. Though not yet afloat they move against each other, sighing and squeaking in response to the constant readjustments of their inhabitants, and to the gentle, counterweighted pull and push of the traffic on the bridges.

A light twitches on a bridge in the distance, flickering as if to announce that someone is passing, and looking further in—along the dark, deep passages between pontoons—I see lights strung up on many of the bridges, both those at our level, at the level of the ground outside the city, and high above us. As the light sinks, as we make our way into the labyrinth of paths and shelves and bridges, the lights seem more and more like stars by which we navigate our path.

The Errakean pontoon is further north. To get there, according to the map the Ramoccan guides sketched in the sand, we must cross through the Elk pontoon. Each pontoon is named for one of the

308

Architects: the Errakean for one of the women, a still woman, and the Elk for one of the men—Erraka's younger brother—a wanderer.

The entrance to the Elk pontoon is on the fifth level, high above us. As befits the pontoon of a wanderer it does not appear at all boatlike, but square and flat-faced. Its timber walls rise up from the desert floor —stark and unpainted—for three sheer storeys. The ceiling of the third storey is the Plimsoll line, above which the pontoon is decorated with images of deserts, horizons, mounts, tents, tall trees and strange creatures, and caravans of people, silhouetted against whitened skies as they walk into the distance.

We bargain for our entrance over thick, black coffee and smoke, paying more than we should for a week's pass to visit, but not to work. We exchange three packets of Buddha's Tears for enough Elk currency to house, feed and entertain four men for a month, slipping a small but necessary gratuity into our gatekeeper's overfull cup. 'Thank you, thank you,' he says, spooning the coins out, sucking them clean and biting them, one by one. 'Highly irregular, of course, and not at all how things are done among the Elk, but you are strangers here and it is just as well, you see, to be generous, to pay a little extra to ensure you know the tide.' Coffee slops into his saucer and he drinks from it noisily. He unfolds a map of the Elk pontoon and points out the places we should visit. First, the usual tourist spots: the market, the rooftop garden, the museum of the drowned, the fishermen's deck. These our ordinary fee has earned us. Then he spreads the coins of our bribe out on the table at his side, counts them with his eyes and smiles. 'Welcome to the Errakean pontoon,' he says. 'You have paid too much, and know it, and therefore must be seeking more than you are able to pay for. Here,' he says, pointing to a place on the map, 'here is my brother's cafe: I assure you safe passage. Good food, good music, terrible conversation. I send you with my bond; my brother will give you the un-poisoned end of the bread.' He leans forward, grasps my hand, 'A fool, my brother, part of the Oikos when he was younger and deter-mined to hold court, today, after the troubles, like an exiled princess who must rail against the honesty of her exile. I was there earlier this

309

evening, at his establishment, and there was much laughter, much debate, two knife-fights in the courtyard. Tonight, the old Elks will debate. More talk!' He laughs. 'My brother and his herd will be there: old men, telling tall tales and true. Highly entertaining. To hear them would send a wiser person mad, but you are fools, are you not? Travellers intent on fool's adventures? Don't believe a word you hear. His revolution was not a revolution, just a café full of conversation, young men with ideas they got from books, opinions they never paid for. They are poets, philosophers, staying up late and drinking cheap wine. All pointless, all foolish. Go there,' he says, leaning back, smiling as he lights his pipe and breathes in the apple-sharp smoke, 'perhaps I will see you there, steal some of your money for myself. Find out what you really came for.'

Suddenly, and with surprising agility for his age, he stands and ushers us up from our seats, gathering our bundles and heaping them in our arms as he urges us out of his small reception room. 'Time to go,' he says, glancing back over his shoulder as he stands in the doorway to the pontoon's interior, pointing along the timber hall to the left, where we can see by the light there must be an open space—a lightwell, perhaps, with a view downwards and upwards through the structure. He pushes us away from his door, as though we are children reluctantly being sent off to school. He smiles and waves while we are still an arm's length away, all pretence at friendship or personal commitment to our pleasure shut, as quickly and resolutely as the door that slams behind us. We hear the lock turn in our wake.

ജ

The Assassin's Café, one of a series of eateries and libraries, is a crowded, half-darkened theatre of a place. Steaming coffee machines line the walls, and trolleys of food are pushed by exhausted waiters through the too-narrow spaces between tables. A wide, high window looks out—or, rather, in—towards the stepped beds of the Elk's interior garden, but nobody is looking at the view. We are shown to a table squashed up against the dark, external wall: a view of the Juttan pontoon's walls can be glimpsed between the glassless, boarded-up window beside us. 'No view, I'm afraid. Last night's customers had deep philosophical differences,' says the waiter, nodding at the window as he swipes at our table with a cloth, plonks down cups of thick, dark coffee and stuffs the bowl of our pipe with a blank, too-dry smoke. 'The materialist won out. Now, can I introduce you to anybody?' he says, offering a menu in which is listed, not food or drink, but topics of conversation, the names of other clients in the café this evening—at least, of those willing to engage a stranger's interest. For a fee.

Kapil flicks through the pages: politics, both sedentary and epis-temological; nephology; aesthetics, especially the aesthetics of travel; heresies, ancient and modern; aquatics. 'I'm not sure,' he says.

'We're visitors,' I say, as if by explanation

'Aah,' says our waiter, waiting for us to make a selection. I look out at the room, at the tables full of people deep in conversation: laughing, smiling, hissing and blowing smoke at each other. Pouring the dregs of their coffee onto the already-sticky floor and holding up their cups to be refilled by the scurrying waiters as they pass. At the centre of the room is a large, round table. At least twelve men sit in conversation. As I watch I see one of them lean back in his chair and hold up his empty cup in a familiar hand, turning his head to see if a waiter is near.

'What are they discussing?' I ask.

The waiter smiles, his lips thinning and widening as his eyes flatten with greed. 'An expensive conversation,' he says. 'By invitation only, of course. Though I can arrange an introduction.'

'We know that gentleman,' Kapil says. 'He invited us to join him here this evening.'

'I see,' says the waiter. 'A moment.' He races off between the tables, dodging coffee and waiters and dogs and children, to lean and whisper in our gatekeeper's ear. Their conversation is brief, businesslike. The gatekeeper looks towards us as though we may have met, once, a long time ago. The waiter leans closer, listening as the gatekeeper tilts his head and speaks in a low, complicit way, with much nodding and

311

frowning. The waiter asks a question and the gatekeeper nods impatiently, already turning back to the table as a new speaker rises from his seat.

Our waiter returns to us, all smiles, and we are ushered to our new table, to more comfortable seats and fresher coffee. A robust cloud of the familiar, apple-scented smoke hovers above us. 'Made it, I see,' says our acquaintance, the gatekeeper, offering his hand. 'Ilima,' he says, 'and this is my brother, Elki.' We nod and offer our hands, keeping our introductions quiet.

'Good grief,' whispers Elki, 'will this idiot go on all night?'

'Perhaps, perhaps,' says Ilima, 'he spoke for five hours, once, without pause.'

'It is,' says the speaker, warming to his subject, 'a mirror held up to our existence. It is an object by which we know ourselves.'

'Oh, for goodness sake,' says Elki, 'somebody shut him up. Anybody! I'll trade six hours of Littoral Aesthetics to see a bit of wit sharpened against his empty rhetoric.'

'I have no use for Littoral Aesthetics,' says Kapil. 'What else would you trade?'

Elki pauses, takes time to study Kapil before raising his eyebrow at his brother. 'What have you brought me this time, eh?' he asks. 'Troublemakers?'

'They're passing through,' Ilima says, 'looking for something in the Errakean pontoon. I thought you might be able to help them, poor fools.'

'Well,' says Elki, 'what would I know about the city of women? I am just a wanderer, a vagrant.'

Ilima nods, sadly, 'A fool,' he says, 'like our father.'

'And his father before him.'

'And fools, as they say, must travel together.' Elki places his fist on the table before me, turns it over. 'It is you, little brother, who seeks entrance to the city of women, isn't it?'

I nod. 'They have something of mine,' I say.

'Something of mine, too,' Elki says, 'my poor besotted heart rests there. My poor wandering soul. Lost he is—such a fool—followed a woman with pretty feet across the bridge and refuses to return to me. All night I sleep at the window, waiting for him to return, listening for her, watching her windows in the moonlight. I hear his footsteps in the women's city; he rambles along her avenues, steering by constellations I have never seen. He seeks her beating centre, her boulevards; he navigates by her honesties while I remain here, at her edge, a hollow and unconstituted man.'

All around the table our companions hiss and blow—a great cloud of blue smoke rises up around us as the speaker's voice rises higher, louder, battling with the rattle of cups and spoons and pipes.

Elki leans closer, slides his closed palm towards the edge of the table. 'I have become a lover, but you are wanderers, like my father, and his father before him. You seek the chambers of the Wynder,' he says, 'true fools, I see, in search of glory, or revolution. I understand revolution, being a revolutionary myself.' He opens his hand like a plump, white flower and we see, in his palm, the flattened, chipped gleam of Alazaïs's broken door, its hinges twisted where they have been torn away. 'I too seek answers to the riddle of the ages. And so I will show you how to enter the city of women,' he says, 'if you can silence this nattering, prattling fool.'

Kapil nods and Elki leans back, smiling across us at his brother, closing his palm around his prize and drawing it back into his pocket. 'No,' he says, leaning back, watching the speaker as he turns and begins, again, to speak. 'Not you,' Elki whispers. 'The young fool.'

'And so,' the speaker says, 'it is true that triumph has a secret pact with death, and that we all wish to be Deathless with Rupetta, but Rupetta knows there are few among us who want to live as object with her objectivity.'

'Is she object, then?' I ask.

'She is made, and therefore a thing and not a creature.'

313

'If she is an object,' I say, 'then she, by definition, is neither truly a *she* nor truly a *creature*. If she is an object, she is as without intention as she is without sex.'

'A child, an innocent, a mute fish have no intentions, and are not objects.'

'A child's intention is to eat, to play, to live. An innocent's to learn, to undo innocence; a fish's to swim. Being unable to discern a creature's intention is no argument against its having one. If she is object, and not creature, she must be, also, without senses. A table is an object because it cannot taste, or touch, or smell, or hear, or see. It cannot weep, it cannot shudder. It cannot love, or fear death. It knows nothing of its own mortality. Knowing no life, it fears no death. Is this the nature of Rupetta? That of a table?'

'This is heresy.'

'It is merely conversation, old man, merely speculation.'

'The Annals record the fourth miracle, in which Rupetta's tears fell and were caught in a vial. I have seen those tears.'

'Tears are not weeping. A table, too, can swell with moisture, can leak sap, though its heart—its heartwood, if you like—is not therefore broken.'

My opponent smiles, tilts his head as though making conversation with a child. And it is true that, by the measure of his education, my arguments are those of an innocent, ill versed in rhetoric. 'The sensory being is bounded by nature, but the essential being of Rupetta, of the deathless and the dead, is not bounded by false sensory reason, but by the reason of the imagination.'

'Rupetta is clothed in flesh, in bones of copper, and a heart of leather, as we are bound in a body of meat and sinew and bone, as we are clad in the cabinet of our object-ness, and yet it is only through the senses that the interior mystery of her consciousness or ours can be discerned. A person is recognised by her face, sees with her eyes, hears with her ears, opens her mouth to speak, and yet I cannot see what you see, nor hear what you hear, nor feel the words flow across your palate, vibrate in your throat. I cannot think your thoughts. But Rupetta can think the thoughts of another: can feel her feet touch the earth and her ears hearing and her eyes seeing. Unlike the table, or the child, she is both and neither—object and creature.'

A cloud of smoke rises, and I feel Kapil shift beside me. Elki is leaning back, smiling, we have nearly won our entrance to the city of women.

'She is,' my opponent says, 'indeed both.'

'And as such she is flawed, as we are flawed. Human, as we are human. She deserves not our adulation but our pity, not our loyalty but the affection, the tenderness, of foxes. We need to bring to our relationship with her—with our Creation, our Machine—the tenderness with which we love a child, and without which there can be no grace, no room for doubt or death, no humanity, and no capacity for change.'

My opponent blanches, feels the laughter rather than hears it as it rises around us, heating the air in his lungs. He charges across the table. I see his knife before I feel it, jutting from the space between two of my ribs. There is no pain, but I see the seep of fluid darkening my shirt as I sink backwards. I see the speed with which Kapil stands and pushes me out of the way, into the lap of our host. Kapil pushes against the table. It is large and heavy and doesn't move far, though cups and pipes and bowls rattle and spill on its surface. 'This is no conversation,' cries my assailant, as he leans to retrieve his blade from my lungs. 'This is heresy.'

'Sit down, old fool,' I hear Ilima say, 'the old doll is dead. We have been at the gate today, as have you; we have seen her disgrace.'

The speaker turns, staring around the table at his companions, his audience, gauging their interest, their allegiance. 'I was there, too, Ilima, I saw the false doll fall. The Consort must have known an attack was planned and sent out a decoy, a doppelgänger, to protect the True Rupetta, to draw out the heretics. I saw the false doll fall, but I also saw the Oikos fall, and I have heard their cries this evening, seen them torn out of their tents and taken into the Haven. There will be an end to heresy. More importantly I saw, as you did, old friend, the child the

315

Wynder protected so avidly: it blanched with fear at its false mother's death. I saw it quiver. It is the eighth miracle, I know it, and so do you.'

'Don't be a fool,' Ilima says, winking at us. 'I have seen no child, no eighth miracle.' He reaches into the folds of his shirt and slides out a knife, holds it with the blade flat against his chest as he smiles and nods goodbye. 'Go now,' he whispers, 'you have paid my brother's fee most generously.'

'He will kill you,' Kapil says, indicating the florid face of my attacker.

'No,' says Ilima, smiling like a boy about to swing out over a waterfall with a sword between his teeth, pushing us towards the door where his brother waits, 'but he will try.'

જી

We enter the city of women through the gates where the lovers enter. Our hearts are examined, and then our hands. We are searched thoroughly and an old Penitent, her round face smooth with exhaustion, listens to our hearts, winds them backward until we have just a little time—five hours at the most—before we must be wound again. The keys to our hearts are taken by the woman at the gate, who attaches a numbered piece of card to each with a rubber band and hangs them on a hook behind her desk. There are many hooks on the wall, and many keys. Some of the cards are curled with age, some of the keys are rusted and old: nobody has returned to collect them. She smiles and gives us our receipts.

There are no maps of the women's city. Elki has given us directions —the directions of a fool and a lover—we are to navigate by scent along the avenue of citrus, towards the roses, until we smell the sea, and then to circle backwards, like the moon, around the edge of the city, following a dark, wooded, earthen smell. Rot at its heart, and new growth. We hear water, the tick of a broken clock, and enter a courtyard as dark and quiet as sleep.

The courtyard is a deep lightwell, its rounded walls thick with ivy. Stairs wind up around its edges, and windows and doors peer out through the thick pattern of leaves, as curious as frogs. We have entered the courtyard through a long, high-ceilinged corridor. Across from us is an arched door, guarded by two Penitents and their mounts.

There is no way, in this closed and limited space, to conceal our approach.

Kapil bows towards the guards. 'We have come to see the Wynder,' he says.

The Penitent smiles and glances at his companion, raising an eyebrow at her. 'Really?' he says.

Kapil nods and holds out his hand, on which there is a small, flat stone. It is a Ramoccan beetle, curled in sleep. 'Yes,' he says. 'We have come to discuss the next leg of the journey.'

The guard gestures towards his companion, who comes forward and takes the beetle from Kapil's palm before disappearing through the gate. He is not gone long. When he returns, the Consort is scurrying along in his wake. He hesitates when he sees me, as though he is not sure what to do.

As the guards stand uneasily close by, watching me as though I will rise up like one of their own mounts, he steps forward and puts his hand against my chest, peering into my eyes. 'So,' he says, 'you've found us, after all.'

'Where is she?' I say.

The Consort smiles and steps to the side, gesturing as though he is a doorman inviting a guest to enter. 'Waiting for you,' he says.

Inside the gates is a hallway, along which we pass quickly until we reach the room where the Wynder—the false Wynder—waits. She is seated at a long table with her back to the doorway. The little doll that looks so oddly like my daughter stands against the wall. She doesn't look up as we enter.

'Who was it?' she says.

When the Consort doesn't answer the Wynder turns, her mouth opening, already preparing to rebuke him for wasting time when there is so much to do. Emina removes the headset she is wearing, placing it gently on the blank, wooden head on the table. It glitters and fusses there, the lights above the eyepieces fading out, the mechanisms whirring into sleep. She picks up a piece of cloth and wipes the glass eyepieces clean before covering it with a cloth and turning towards us.

Margause's aunt, Emina, is smaller than her niece, slimmer. Her hands are not so worn or earthy. Her face has not seen so many days of sunlight. She was prettier, once, and still carries herself like a pretty woman. Her clothes are simple, but expensive. The velvet thick and heavy, the feathered white cuffs stitched with seed-pearls. Her long hair is thick, though it has turned white, and wiry, and looks odd bundled at her nape, like a sleeping animal.

She is old—so old—her skin is like paper. She is curving in on herself. Her eyes are sunk in nests of wrinkled skin. Her hand, resting on the edge of the table, is thin and white. Skin wrapped loosely around the bone. The table before her is scattered with spare parts— Alazaïs's legs, arms, and skirts. Four spare faces, featureless and mute as bowls. On the table before her is the shell of another face, and beside it the instrument she has been using to etch the familiar whorls of vines and insects on its surface.

She glances at and dismisses Kapil—an unknown man without weapons or strength to threaten her. When she looks at me, however, she frowns, as though I am a stranger she has met once, long ago. Soon recognition and vicious wariness spark in her eyes.

She looks down at my legs, at the slim, separated swing of them as I cross the room to meet her. 'Did you do that yourself?' she asks, with a mechanician's envious admiration.

'Where is my daughter?'

Emina glances at the Consort—a look that pushes him from the room. 'She does not want to see you,' she says.

'No more lies, Emina. She's just a child; she's not one of your toys.'

'A child? She's nearly as old as you, old clock! Though not as foolish, or selfish. She knows where her duty lies.'

'And where is that, exactly?'

318

'With the future, with the Fourfold Law, with the promises you made to us: transcendence of the body—a future without death. With her, there is real hope of a meshing of our Meat with your Immortality. If we can understand how she is made, how she works, we can be done with these brutal Organic bodies, with their rot and change.'

'I never promised anything of the sort, you know that. Why would I, when death is so necessary?'

'What would you know of the necessity of death? Have you died?'

'You know I cannot, though I have often longed for such a cease.'

'A clockwork heretic. You dream of death, while we are slaves to its whims. You were made to release us. The fact of your existence gave us hope. The fact of Perdita confirms it. She is the evidence of our immortal future. It is what Eloise intended.'

I laugh. 'You know the True History, almost as well as I do. Eloise wanted nothing of the sort.'

'Madness overtook her in the end; she was a woman of her time, frightened of the future she made, frightened of the God she helped unmake.'

Behind us, the doors open and Perdita and Margause are ushered into the room. Six Penitent guards and their mounts form a crown of bristling thorns around them.

Kapil steps towards them and the guards snicker across the room to block him, lowering their weapons from their shoulders. 'Let them go,' he says.

Emina picks up the half-made face she was working on when we entered. 'All my life I have wondered what it would be like to be the true Wynder. Growing up, I saw my sister groomed for the life I deserved.' Emina smiles at Margause. 'You mother was the one born first, but I was the one who understood the path of the Wynder. I was the one who knew what it required. Judit was repulsed by it all—by the necessity of the Wynding—by giving up some secret self to another. She was a timid, witless child. The night of her first Wynding she ran away, hid in our old schoolroom, in the cupboard with the chalks and dusters and old books. I found her there, cowering in the dark. I traded gowns with her. I went down to the Great Hall and stood in her place. It was I who Wound the great doll on the night of *her* Ascension. For years I was my sister's shadow. Standing in the hall before the Penitents when she could not be found. When she was too weak to face her duty.'

'Judit was never weak,' I say. 'You were faithless.'

'I helped you survive—both of you—when I should have let the Penitents have you. I helped you find your precious island exile. How is that faithless? All these years I have stood in her place, borne her name, performed her duties with an empty tin at my side. I have fought to uphold the Fourfold Rupettan Law.'

'It was never my law.'

'How can you bear to live while we die? How can you watch us rot and not reach out to help? You are a traitor. A vile and cruel thing.'

'Do you think I have some secret I am keeping from you? I think you forget, Emina, that there is a great difference between knowing how not to die, and not knowing how to die.'

'And you forget that your life belongs to the Wynders; that it is given to you at great cost and that you owe us a great deal in return.'

'This is your faith? Your loyalty? Today, at the gate, people saw Rupetta fall; they saw her taken apart. All over the city tonight there are traders selling pieces of her. It is over, Emina. Finally, it is over.'

'We can build another Alazaïs. We can discredit any rumours of your demise.' I shake my head and put my hand out towards Perdita.

'Enough,' she barks, one hand rising to the neck of her heavy gown, fingers curling like claws around the neckline. A glimpse of silver against her skin: pink, scarred tissue: a Penitent's heart. Emina sees my look and stiffens, gestures for her guards.

The mounts slide forward and stand between us and the doorway, their bladed teeth already sliding forward in their mouths. Two of the guards charge at Kapil. I let go of Perdita's hand and push her towards Margause. The guard telescopes forward and Kapil ducks, more strength and agility left in him than I had supposed. As the blade slows he claps it between the palms of his hands and twists, tearing it from the joint. With a quick flick he holds the blunt end in his hand and lunges forward. Another guard draws close, slicing into Kapil's thigh as his mounts rise up and unfold.

Two guards move towards me, their blades drawn, their mounts tall behind them. Emina urges them closer. One of them thrusts his blade at my belly. I feel the jagged tip puncture my skin, pull until my gut tents outward. The mounts are less tentative—less human. The first of them comes forward and wraps its teeth around my throat. I feel them drive inwards, through the copper of a bone, shattering a porcelain joint. Its companion binds itself to my belly, tearing away the skin, and the lining beneath. It moves down my side, breaks open my leg and tears away the long pipes that shunt there, bending them in its mouth.

I grasp the mount at my throat and drive my fingers into its body.

The skin on my fingers peels back, the thick layer of fleshy insulation shredding away as I dig deeper, feeling for something I can break. I snap a hollow pipe. The mount bucks in my arms. I wrench it from me—half of my throat comes away in its teeth—and crash its body down on the other mount, driving them both to the ground. As they writhe on the skewer of my shattered arm I snap off their blades, their heads, and watch them twitch, bloodless and silent, on the polished floor.

One of the guards behind me cries and I spin, bringing the blade around, my bare arm stretched out to strike him. He falls against his fellow guard, pushing him off-balance. As they stumble together, I hammer a mount's black blade into his heart.

I am striding towards Kapil, watching him thrust his blade upwards through another mount's ribs, when I hear Emina say my name. Beside her, a guard holds Perdita.

Emina stands behind her niece, her blade at Margause's throat. 'Enough,' she says. 'Stop now, and leave, and I will spare my niece.'

I glance at Perdita. Her dark hair frames a face that is heartbreakingly small. Perdita tips her head in a gesture faintly reminiscent of Perihan's. The birdlike fineness, the quick shift and sudden stillness. The dark, colourless eyes. 'Go,' she says.

Emina relaxes a little, lets her blade drop down to Margause's breast. 'Unlike you, Perdita is no heretic; she will not deny humanity its future,' she says.

In one movement Perdita steps forward, a short blade in her hand, lunging towards Emina in swift, black-eyed silence. Margause moves at the last moment—a strange, involuntary jerking to block the blade from her aunt's frail body. Borne forward by momentum, Perdita's blade judders along Margause's shoulder, slicing across her throat before sliding home between two of her ribs.

Margause slides onto the floor, her hand rising to her wound as if she cannot quite understand what it is, this blade that has cut her open, that protrudes so rudely from her gut. She is slumped on the floor, sitting with her back resting against her aunt's heavy skirts. She looks up at Perdita's white face, frowning.

Kapil has his hand on my wrist, is pulling me backwards, away from my Wynder, whose blood is pooling in the folds of her own gown. Perdita has knelt on the ground, is putting her hands to the wound in Margause's throat and belly, her face pale. Death hurtles down through the nightblack sky.

'Help me,' she says: a child, after all.

I shake myself loose from Kapil's grip and kneel beside Perdita. I put my hand against Margause's heart and feel its thrum, as swift and strange as a bird's. I can feel Margause's death rising through her and away, pulling her away from the world, and away from me. I am becoming unmoored, as though a thousand tiny threads are snapping between us. A ship at the harbour, pulling away while the passengers and their well-wishers wave to each other, the pretty, bright threads they are holding snapping one by one.

I turn to my daughter, whose hands are red with her playmate's blood. How old she has suddenly become. A thousand deaths flock in her eyes. The world blurs and shifts. Margause's eyes are pin-sharp, peering at us. 'I'm sorry,' she says, reaching out to put her hand on my chest. Our heart beats so slowly. One dull, wet beat. And then another. Each beat drifts us a little further apart, like drumbeats fading into a terrible distance. Slowly, they separate. I feel my own heart, beating faster: a swooping dactylic beat, while Margause's heart stutters into distended spondaic tremors.

'What have I done?' Perdita says.

She is a thousand, a hundred thousand miles away. She bends over us, closes her hands around the blade in her playmate's chest. I smell the wildness in her hair; see the blue block of that other sky swell behind her like a cloud.

Her eyes sharpen as her hands press at the wound in Margause's chest; feeling her heart judder and stop. I see my daughter rise and spin, turning towards Emina in one balletic movement. Her skirts swirl around her knees. I put out my hand to catch her, to say something, but she is already gone. So very far away. She moves towards Emina; tears at the velvet collar of her dress. Feathers and pearls are torn free and spill on the ground, in Margause's blood. Emina smiles as Perdita wrenches the door to her old heart open, as she drives her hand in, deep and true, and tears out the tickering clock of the false Wynder's heart.

The room is quiet. Kapil is kneeling beside me, my head in his lap. I am holding onto Margause's hand as it stiffens and cools in my grasp. I am caught by an image of her hand when it was small—a tiny, plump star—reaching up and curving around Perdita's finger while she sleeps.

Kapil has opened the chamber of my heart and is peering into me. For a moment I wonder if he will find the beetles, the seeds a child planted inside me so long ago. I half expect to see him pull out an apple-seed. A dragonfly. He is tinkering, adjusting the edges of things, while the fine threads that connected me to Margause loop and flail invisibly in the air like exposed nerves.

'Is she gone?' Perdita says, kneeling beside us, setting Emina's silent, silver heart on the ground at her side. 'Is she dying?'

Kapil shakes his head, frowning, his hands working at something within me before he closes the door and buttons up my shirt.

'You'll have to get her out, take her back to the Territory,' Perdita says.

'Henri,' I murmur, my words like bubbles—each one discreet and unfamiliar—floating out of my mouth to haunt the room. The flailing threads are fading, curling backwards into me, like seedlings withdrawing into the earth from which they came.

Perdita shakes her head. 'You will go home, to Henri,' she says. 'But we cannot leave here together. They will be looking for us: a woman and a child.' She smiles, wryly, her eyes shining with unshed tears. 'A goddess and a monster.'

'You could come with us,' Kapil says.

Perdita shakes her head. 'You know I can't.'

I reach into my pocket and take out my old companion, Perihan. Its bright head tips to the side and it chirrups, sadly, as though it knows what all this means, where it might end. I place the bird in Perdita's hand, fold her fingers closed over its tiny breast, and turn away.

Elm College: The Day of Tears

Kapil is sleeping beside me as we come up over the last rise and I see, at last, the city I once called home. I rein the horse in, and he slows as we make our way down through the mountains. The cool air disperses as the city spreads itself out before us, green and lush, the river winding away from me towards the harbour. From the incoming road I can see clear to the river mouth, where several ships are tied to the wooden docks. A winter-blue dirigible floats overhead, casting its shadow onto the dock-workers as they hurry up and down the gangplanks. Kapil wakes at the change in pace, at the new angle of the cart. He gazes tiredly at the scramble of houses scattered on the hills below us, at the already-busy streets rambling towards the harbour. In a familiar bend of the river below us, not far from the darker, more jumbled streets of the market, we can see the Elisabettan Academy, the lawns and paths already filling up with students on bicycles. The domed roof of the Penitent's Haven rises above an open space not far from the familiar huddle of buildings around Elm College. I can almost see the glitter of the glasshouse roof. I imagine you there, Henri, in the morning coolness, tending the orchids, lazily brushing the ferns with your fingertips as you pass. For months now I have dreamed of this moment, dreamed of moving among well-known streets once more, of walking into the glasshouse and seeing you turn towards me, of moving to hold you, of pressing my face into the crook of your shoulder and breathing in, once more, the rich scent of earth and skin that is so definitely, so completely, the scent of home. But now, when only an hour of journeying through familiar streets lies between us, I cannot imagine lifting my face to meet your gaze: I cannot imagine how I will bear the mixture of sorrow, fear, anger, disappointment, pity, hopelessness and,

325

perhaps, love in your eyes. After so long away, such a long journey home, I hesitate, reluctant to go down into the city, reluctant to return to you knowing I have failed.

It has been a long time since I have seen the Haven from such a distance. Up close it is easy to forget the grandeur of its architecture; its unearthly golden sheen awes and repulses me. On the broad green lawn of the common that spreads out in front of the Haven there are small groups of people. From this far away they appear like elongated specks, ants scurrying about on the felted green of the lawn, many of them trailing scraps of blue. Somewhere in the southeast corner of the common someone starts to run and a fluttering blue diamond flies out behind them, slowly rising as they reach the midpoint of the field. 'Kapil,' I say, leaning back to tap his knee, 'it's The Day of Tears.'

Kapil leans forward to peer at the scene below us, easing a blanket around my shoulders as he does so, to hide the open scars I still bear: the bloodless flesh gaping open to reveal damaged metalwork beneath. He has just woken: his hair is wild and his face warmly-crushed with sleep, but he watches the square with sharp, thoughtful concern, scanning the rooftops for people. 'Perhaps we should wait,' he says. 'We can go down later tonight, when it's dark, slip into the College when the others are sleeping and find your Henri.'

He puts a hand against the blanket, against the unrepaired wounds within me, which rattle and creak beneath his touch. 'You will have to let me repair this first, or there is no point. And there are other things, are there not, Volta, which must be returned to their former shape?'

I nod brusquely, refusing to meet his eyes. Though I resent the necessity of the time wasted on repairs, on the return to an old body, and old sex, he is right: after tonight's work I will have to hide who I have been during this year of searching, even from myself, though never again from you, Henri, no matter what the cost.

We pull over beneath a spreading tree and let the horse out of her harness. I feed her an apple and rub her warm neck as Kapil rummages in our packs for something to eat. Our supplies are low, almost gone.

326

I pull our thin mattress from the rear of the cart and lay it out in the shade of a tree, where we can sit and watch the city from a safe distance. Kapil unrolls his toolkit, eager to use the time to effect what repairs he can while we wait. When he moves to fold back the blanket from my shoulder I twitch away from him, impatient and confused. If I come to you damaged, the stains of the journey burned on my skin, I believe you might forgive me for failing. If I come home perfect, untouched, what mark will there be of the pain and terror and struggle of this year? I want to be marked by Perdita's loss, to bear the suffering like an ancient Christian saint: wounds that bleed, tears that burn. I want you to know, to see, that I have done everything I could.

I move away, stand at the edge of the road and look down into the city. Where are you, my love? At home in Whitestone Shute, sitting beside your father, or here somewhere? In the rooms where we met, and loved, and lost each other? In the glasshouse, the garden, the kitchen? At the table where we sat, so many nights, reading and drinking tea. Are you in the orchard, looking up at the stars that burned so white and pure when we lay beneath them? Are you on the common with the others, your hands dug deep in your pockets as you watch the young men boast and jostle on the green, their hands already streaked with blood from the sharp tug of their kite-strings?

From so far away the kites are beautiful, a flood of blue, teardrop-shaped silk, cotton and paper rising and bobbing over the city. Occasionally, there are grey kites. Kites with ribbons trailing behind them, long strands of glittering white or pale, iridescent pink. Soon the sky is crowded with them, jostling for space. Somewhere in the western quarter of the city a single kite is cut free and floats skyward, jerking uneasily. Two kites become tangled together and then there is a shout as a dark, heavy kite cuts a swathe through one of the side streets, its glass-coated string slicing through the competition. A woman wails and soon, I imagine, you will turn away as you always do and return to the safety of the College. Fights will break out on the common, spreading quickly through the streets.

Kites fall and jag across the city, losing their moorings or getting torn apart by the razor-wire of another kite's string. On rooftops all over the city families gather to watch the spectacle from a safe distance as battles begin in earnest and kites tilt and drop from view. Here and there I hear a drumbeat, or someone singing, as the sky empties. Finally, only a handful of kites remain in the sky as, slowly and silently, a train of Penitents emerge from the open doors of the Haven.

They move in single file, each supporting a section of a long bundle of white silk. The last Penitent is dressed in green, and holds in his hands the bundled ends of the threads that spread backwards from the silk. The Penitents form a circle, spreading the silk out until it forms a broad, flat oval. I hear the mournful dirge of the traditional hymn of the Miracle of Tears rise from the common as the last, green-robed Penitent walks beneath the silk to anchor the threads. When he reaches the centre the Penitents at the oval's perimeter lower the silk to the ground and wait. An edge billows, a shadow forms, a pink blush spreads across the silk. Shapes form; first a closed eye, then the bridge of a too-perfect nose, unnaturally-even lips. As the Penitents' song reaches a painful, longing note, the eyes flick open. My face—her face —Rupetta's silk face, begins to rise.

The whole town is silent, watching as the disembodied visage rises, tilting upwards as the wind gathers force behind it. I can see people all over the town, up on their flat roofs and bunched together on balconies, watching my face rise like a hard-edged cloud. Soon, the Tears of the Fourth Miracle begin to fall.

Some of the people hold out their hands, others cups and pans, buckets and dishes, whatever they can find to hold the precious water. Children throw back their heads and open their mouths. As the storm of Tears begins to spread out, reaching the edge of town, Kapil urges me to turn away. He rolls up the mattress, and we climb into our cart, beneath the tarpaulin cover, to wait out the storm. Down in the streets of the city, children will be sent home for dry towels, grown men will drink until they cannot stand up, the women will bake, wrapping tear-shaped Lachrys biscuits in clean, white sheets of paper. By late afternoon a marquee will be raised in the common and trestle tables placed in long rows beneath it. The tables will be heavily laden with food; roast meats and great bowls of freshly-picked produce, pies, cakes, creams and custard. Glowing and chuckling tea urns will dispense fragrant tea flavoured with cinnamon, cardamom, ginger and rose petals. There will be music and laughter and those who were cut by the glass-coated strings of the kites in the morning will brandish their injuries like medals, competing with each other over glasses of warm beer to see who was cut deepest, whose wounds will settle into the most impressive scars. They will joke and laugh, their bare feet sunk in the muddy coolness of the common.

Not all of the wounds are so glorious, however, or so proudly or easily borne.

Somewhere, a mother will wrap her child in the bone-white paper of a Tear-fallen shroud and the Penitents will come to take her daughter away; the blood of her wounds already beginning to seep through onto their palms. For weeks afterwards the mother's neighbours will visit daily, leaving small gifts of food and fragrant, expensive tea, but after a while the stream of consolation, of friendship, will trickle out and die. Sorrow is too dark, too violent a thing to be soothed with easy comforts. She will sit, day after day, at the windows of her home, watching the other women with their children. She will try not to weep anymore. *She died a holy death on a holy day*, she'll tell herself, though her heart will be filled with a broad, black rage.

As darkness settles over the city and the lights go on, one by one, Kapil and I settle our horse into his harness and head home. The roads are wet and slippery, our progress slow, but soon we are moving through the streets of the city. We ride over fallen kites, bruised with mud; their thin spines crackle and snap as we pass. People pass us in happy mobs, laughing, slung around each other. We leave the cart at the stables, say goodbye to our horse and make our way, on foot, towards home. The halls of the Colleges are empty, our footsteps echo in the empty rooms.

329

It is almost morning. A shadow—your shadow—moves across a window of your room and peers out at the orchard. I see your hand held up against the glass and the steam of your breath forming on the glass. Soon, you will come into the kitchen, put on the coffee, open the doors and windows, check the seeds in their warming pots, sweep the leaves from the paths.

You open the doors of the kitchen and sit on the back step to pull on your boots. You are bent over your left boot when I emerge from the orchard and stand in front of you. The sun is rising behind me, over the trees. I can see your worn boots before me; the long feet and the well-worn caps, as if you have stumbled often while I was away. You looked up, shading your eyes, squinting into the sun. 'Can I help you?' you say.

I shift on my feet. As I move I block the light of the sun. A shadow forms between us and I can see, suddenly and all at once, your face. Your familiar face, after all.

When you stand to take me in your arms I am no longer the tiny woman whose head had fitted beneath your chin.

I tilt forward, leaning against you, unable to kiss you—not yet, not yet—and our foreheads touch. Our hands meet, palm to palm. The toes of our boots touch. The bones of our hips, the tips of our breasts, our chins. I put a hand up and touch your cheek, brush away the tears, put my hands into the tangle of your unruly hair.

Later, when we had said what we needed to say, when we had discovered what it was we had lost, and gained, and lost again, we walked away.

We went, perhaps, into the mountains, or to the island, or the cottage in the woods. Each year the seasons turned and we grew a little older, a little more remarkable. And each year, in the winter, Perihan came and sat on the edge of the table in the garden and sang for us. Each year it sang a new song: one we had never heard before, one we remembered. Each year we waited for our child to come home. And each year she came, and each year she was lost to us again, as children are and should be.

We loved each other there, for as long as we were able, perhaps longer.

And then we passed out of narrative time, out of History, into the unrecorded, anonymous throng of the unwritten. There—here—though History had owned us for a time, and though we have said what we must for you, and written what we can, and left behind the traces that, one day, another might uncover and turn into her own story. And though we had been said and been written, and had no sense of where our story might lead us once we passed out of the familiar circumference of its embrace, still, we passed into the present tense.

We move forward, as you must, into the trembling wave-flow of the future, which cannot, with any honesty, be written.